I0647485

The Whiskey Run Chronicles

The Complete Volume 2

(Episodes 8-14)

B.R. Snow

ISBN: 978-1-942691-49-5
Website: www.brsnow.net/
Twitter: @BernSnow
Facebook: facebook.com/bernsnow

Cover Design: Reggie Cullen
Cover Photo: James R. Miller

Other Books by B.R. Snow

The Thousand Islands Doggy Inn Mysteries

- The Case of the Abandoned Aussie
- The Case of the Brokenhearted Bulldog
- The Case of the Caged Cockers
- The Case of the Dapper Dandie Dinmont
- The Case of the Eccentric Elkhound
- The Case of the Faithful Frenchie
- The Case of the Graceful Goldens
- The Case of the Hurricane Hounds
- The Case of the Itinerant Ibizan
- The Case of the Jaded Jack Russell
- The Case of the Klutz King Charles
- The Case of the Lovable Labs
- The Case of the Mellow Maltese
- The Case of the Natty Newfie
- The Case of the Overdue Otterhound
- The Case of the Prescient Poodle
- The Case of the Quizzical Queens Beagle

The Whiskey Run Chronicles

- Episode 1 – The Dry Season Approaches
- Episode 2 – Friends and Enemies
- Episode 3 – Let the Games Begin
- Episode 4 – Enter the Revenuer
- Episode 5 – A Changing Landscape
- Episode 6 – Entrepreneurial Spirits
- Episode 7 – All Hands On Deck
- The Complete Volume 1

The Damaged Posse

- American Midnight
- Larrikin Gene
- Sneaker World
- Summerman
- The Duplicates

Other Books

- Divorce Hotel
- Either Ore

To all the wonderful people

who love the Thousand Islands and the St. Lawrence.

I drink a toast in your honor.

Episode 8

The Sleaze Factor

"Milk might build strong bones and bodies. But I've found that a milk can builds fortunes."

Milo Razner

English Lessons

Melvin English grabbed another of Milo's cigarettes from the pack sitting on the coffee table then lit it and exhaled three smoke rings in rapid succession. Pleased with himself, he grinned at Milo as he sat back on the sofa.

"That's quite a talent, Melvin," Milo said, nodding. "You might be wasting your time running for public office. I think I see a vaudeville career in your future."

"No, that's okay," Melvin said, apparently thinking Milo was serious. "Now that I've entered the race, my juices are really flowing. I don't know why I didn't think of running for mayor earlier. I'm so glad you suggested it."

Milo lit a cigarette of his own and draped a leg over his knee as he remembered the exact moment when the idea had come to him. He'd been eating lunch with the current mayor, a nice enough fellow who ran the local hardware store and regularly took advantage of the horizontal freebies Fannie offered him at her place; a perk of office that more than made up for the minuscule salary.

Milo had almost choked on his sandwich when the guy mentioned it was time for him to take a closer look at the bootlegging activities going on around town. *Tough on Crime*, that's my campaign slogan the guy had said through a mouthful of egg salad. At first, he didn't worry about the mayor's threat, but when the guy started prattling on about working more closely with the state and federal authorities, Milo got twitchy. That was when he got the idea of convincing the man sitting across from him blowing smoke rings up at the ceiling to run. Fortunately, given Melvin English's high opinion of himself, it hadn't taken much to convince him.

"We had over a hundred people at the debate last night," Melvin said, dropping ash all over Milo's couch.

"Yes, I noticed," Milo said, grimacing at Melvin's half-hearted attempt to brush it away.

"You were there?" Melvin said, surprised.

"I was sitting in the back. I wanted to get a good look at how the crowd was responding."

"What did you think?" Melvin said, crushing out his cigarette and immediately reaching for another.

"I thought your counterargument about our God-given rights to individual freedom and the capitalist way of life was well-delivered."

"Thanks," Melvin said, nodding.

"All forty-five minutes of it."

"Too much?" Melvin said, raising an eyebrow.

"Maybe a tad. You might consider dropping the fifteen minutes where you compare yourself to Thomas Jefferson," Milo said, reaching for his glass of whiskey. "But the crowd certainly turned on the mayor when he started talking about cracking down on the bootleggers."

"They sure did," Melvin said. "I almost got a standing ovation when I said, if elected, I would have more important things to worry about than some folks smuggling a few cases of Canadian for their personal consumption."

"I especially liked that part," Milo said, smiling and raising his glass in salute.

"You sure you wouldn't like me to find a couple of cases for you?" Melvin said.

"No, that's quite all right, Melvin," Milo said, refilling their glasses.

"Where do you get your booze from?" Melvin said. "You're always so well stocked."

"I have an arrangement with the speakeasy downstairs," Milo said with a casual shrug. "I'm not sure where they get their inventory, but they certainly do a good job finding it."

"Well, if you do decide to change suppliers, you know where to find me," Melvin said, knocking back a big gulp. "Can I ask you a question, Milo?"

"Of course, Melvin," Milo said, suddenly on guard.

"What do you think I'll actually have to do if I do win?" Melvin said, genuinely puzzled.

"Hopefully, not much," Milo whispered.

"What?"

"I said, just such and such," Milo said. "I wouldn't worry about it, Melvin. You're a smart guy. You'll figure it out."

"You really think I'm going to win?"

"Yes, I do," Milo said, again raising his glass in salute. "And I imagine one of your first orders of business will be to find a new police chief."

"Really?" Melvin said. "It's kinda nice not having one. You know, it gives me lots of room to maneuver."

"I'm sure it does," Milo said with a laugh. "And I doubt if Roland Doyle is much of a bother these days."

"No, Doyle's been pretty quiet since that night he arrested Oscar in the middle of the River," Melvin said, laughing.

"I heard that the coast guard and the other prohibition agents still aren't very happy with Mr. Doyle."

"They're not. The guy who runs the Coast Guard station in Sackets Harbor told Roland the next time he had a brilliant idea to just keep it to himself. Oscar and Roland standing on a shoal in the middle of the River," Melvin said, chuckling. "I wish I could have seen that."

"Yes, I imagine it was quite a sight," Milo said, smiling at the memory. "Did the mysterious thousand cases of whiskey ever turn up?"

"Nah, just the five that Oscar had in his boat," Melvin said. "And I'm not sure how much longer I can stall the judge. He's making noises about letting him out. Says he needs the room for more important criminals."

"But as Oscar's lawyer, you're doing everything you can to prevent it, right?" Milo said, grinning.

"Yeah," Melvin said, returning the grin. "I suppose I should feel bad about that."

"Probably. But wasn't your lack of *moral clarity* one of the reasons you became a lawyer in the first place?"

"Yeah, there is that," Melvin said, giving the idea some serious thought.

"But without a chief of police, you know who's going to get all the calls when something does happen, don't you?"

"Who?"

"You, Melvin," Milo said, shaking his head.

"Of course. Damn. People are gonna want to talk to the man in charge when they have a problem," Melvin said with a frown. "I think you're right, Milo. I am going to have to find a new police chief." Melvin stared off into the distance, then scowled. "How the hell am I supposed to do that?"

"I'm sure someone will turn up," Milo said, extinguishing his cigarette.

"Yeah, you're probably right. You're going to vote, right?"

"I certainly am, Melvin. As many times as possible."

Milo gently tapped the bell at the front counter then turned around and acknowledged the furtive glances and nods he received from several men coming and going. He smiled when he recognized the soon to be ex-mayor slumped down in a chair in a dark corner of the room getting friendly with one of Fannie's girls. Milo didn't know her but was surprised by the resemblance. The mayor couldn't miss the big wave Milo was giving him and finally removed his hand long enough from the woman's leg to return the greeting.

"Well, if it isn't my favorite dairy farmer," Fannie said, poking her head through the curtains behind the reception counter. "How are you doing, Milo?"

"Just wonderful, Fannie," Milo said, unable to miss the enormous amount of cleavage she had on display. "It looks they might be planning an escape."

Fannie glanced down then back at Milo with a grin.

"Oh, I always know where to find them," she said.

"I imagine they are tough to hide," Milo said, laughing.

"So, did you stop by to flirt, or do you need to talk business?" she said.

"I thought we might do a bit of both," Milo said. "Like I always say, there's no reason business can't be fun."

"Come on back," she said, holding the curtain open.

Milo stepped through the curtains and, as always, was transported back in time. Dozens of photos of Fannie, often naked, from her younger days filled the walls, and plush chairs and a couple of couches took up most of the floor space. Fannie pointed at one of the couches, and Milo sat down as she headed to her desk to pour drinks. She handed Milo a glass then sat down next to him. He looked around at the photos then lingered on one.

"Is this the same couch as the one in that photo?" Milo said, taking a sip of whiskey.

"It is," Fannie said. "It's still in good shape. And I can't bear to part with it. Too many good memories."

"For you, or the couch?" Milo said with a grin.

"Good one, Milo," Fannie said, laughing. "Yeah, I suppose I should be glad that this couch can't talk."

"Oh, I don't know, Fannie. I imagine it would pretty much say the same things you do."

"Like what?" she said, frowning.

"You can get off me now," Milo said with a shrug. "Or maybe, try not to spill anything on me."

Fannie roared with laughter and clinked glasses with him.

"You're in a good mood tonight," she said, taking a sip then reaching for her pack of cigarettes.

"Yes, I am, aren't I?" Milo said, lighting her cigarette. "Things are going really good at the moment."

"I can't complain either," she said, exhaling smoke. "But then again, it's pretty hard to lose money selling pussy and booze. So, what brings you by?"

"I just wanted to check in and see if Daisy has settled down," Milo said.

"That girl is gonna drive me crazy," Fannie said with a shake of her head. "You'd think that four months off on full salary would make her happy."

"So, she's still resisting?"

"No, I wouldn't call it that," Fannie said. "It's more constant complaining."

"But she's only complaining to you, right?" Milo said, staring at her.

"Yeah, Daisy's good about that," Fannie said. "Whenever she's with a client or in mixed company, she keeps her mouth shut."

"I'm glad to hear that," Milo said, lighting a cigarette. "I'd hate to have anything happen to her."

"Tell me about it. That girl is sitting on a gold mine. When are you going to need her?"

"The way the weather's been lately, it won't be too long. Definitely before the end of the month."

"I can work with that," Fannie said. "I've got some new girls arriving soon, but I doubt if any of them are going to match Daisy's charms."

"You'll just have to make it up in volume, right?" Milo said with a grin.

"I like the way you think, Mr. Razner."

"Is that a new girl I saw out in the greeting room with our mayor?" Milo said.

"Yeah. Her name's Jessie. I found her working on the street in Watertown," Fannie said. "She's a good kid."

"The mayor certainly seems to like her."

"He pretty much likes anything with a pulse," Fannie said. "I've been seeing a lot of him lately."

"Getting in all the freebies he can before leaving office?" Milo said, shaking his head.

"Exactly. And I suppose Melvin is going to expect the same treatment?"

"I'm surprised you even have to ask," Milo said, laughing. "We are talking about Melvin."

"As long as he doesn't start sticking his nose where it doesn't belong, he can have all the freebies he wants," Fannie said, grabbing both their glasses and heading to the desk to refill them.

Milo glanced around and admired the photos on the wall while he waited.

"You were remarkable back then, Fannie," Milo said.

"If you're trying to flatter me, Milo, you'll have to do better than that," Fannie said, pouring the drinks. "Back then?"

"You know what I mean," he said. "You were simply breathtaking."

"I was twenty," Fannie said with a shrug as she sat back down and handed Milo his drink.

"Are you all set for election day?" Milo said.

"I am," she said, stretching out on the couch and putting her feet in Milo's lap. "All my girls will be voting, and I've been having the bartenders get the word out that the mayor is talking about cracking down on booze and the people who run it across the River."

"Good. And you're still going to be helping count the votes?"

"I wouldn't miss it. I consider it part of my civic duty to do everything I can to ensure good government," Fannie said with a grin. "And I've got a whole box of extra ballots sitting over there on my desk."

"Really?" Milo said, massaging one of her feet. "How the heck did you manage that?"

"I offered to handle the printing of the ballots. I used a guy I know in Watertown," she said, then groaned softly. "Oh, that feels good, Milo. Feel free to go higher."

"Higher? How much higher?" Milo said, raising an eyebrow at her.

"I'll tell you when to stop," she said, grinning at him over the top of her glass. "Maybe."

"And run the risk of ruining a beautiful working relationship?" Milo said.

"Yeah, you're probably right," she said. "Oh, well, a girl can dream, right?"

"You're an amazing woman, Fannie," Milo said, massaging her foot harder. "Just remember to be careful on Tuesday."

"Careful how?"

"Don't stuff too many ballots in the box," Milo said. "We don't want anybody getting suspicious. After all, it is a small town with a lot of non-voters."

A New Day Dawns

Melvin English, as he always did when walking past the cell of the drooling man, veered right and waited for the glob of spittle he was certain was headed in his direction. But nothing came his way, and Melvin stopped and looked at the man who was sitting quietly on the small cot in his cell.

"How ya doin'?" Melvin said, giving the prisoner his standard greeting.

"Good day, sir," the man said, his mouth dry, the wild-eyed stare nowhere in sight. "I assume you're here to visit your friend in the next cell."

Melvin, surprised and curious, removed his fedora and twirled it on his finger as he studied the man sitting with his hands folded in his lap.

"Well, I'm not sure I'd call him a friend," Melvin said with a small shrug. "Actually, I'm his lawyer."

"Yes, I've figured that out over time. You're a brave man, sir," the man said, nodding. "Representing a reprehensible human being like him must test your patience. Perhaps, even make you question your chosen line of work."

"I heard that," Oscar Hyde said from the adjacent cell. "Get your ass over here, Melvin."

"Hold your horses, Oscar. I'll be there in a minute. It's not like you've got a train to catch," Melvin said, continuing to study the man sitting on the cot.

"It's not like he has a train to catch," the man said, chuckling. "Good one, Melvin."

"I'm sorry to be rude," Melvin said to the man. "But I gotta ask. I've been here at least a dozen times, and the only thing I ever got out of you was a glob of spit. When did you start speaking?"

"Well, my mama said I started talking right around the time I started to walk," the man said with a shrug.

"Okay," Melvin said, frowning. "Thanks for clearing that up."

Deciding that dealing with one weirdo in the morning was more than enough, Melvin placed the fedora back on his head then gave the drooling man a small wave and headed for Oscar's cell. He stood near the bars, and Oscar approached scratching a two-day stubble.

"You going for that sexy cowboy look, Oscar?" Melvin said with a grin. "I'm sure the other inmates love it."

"I didn't feel like shaving," Oscar said, then gestured at Melvin. "Okay, hand it over."

Melvin shook his head as he looked around to make sure the guards weren't watching. Then he reached into his coat pocket and passed a quart of whiskey through the bars. Oscar grabbed the bottle and poured a quarter of it down his throat. He burped, wiped his mouth with the back of his hand, then took another long pull.

"Charming," Melvin said, studying Oscar's performance.

"That's better," Oscar said, taking a small sip. Then he focused on Melvin. "It sure took you long enough to get here."

"It's raining, Oscar. And the wind is up. It was a rather slow and uncomfortable drive," Melvin said, removing his raincoat and draping it over an arm.

"I'd be happy to switch places with you," Oscar said.

"No, I think I'll pass. Cold and wet is much better than confined and nervous."

"You got an update for me about when the hell I'm getting out of here?" Oscar said, taking another long swig.

"You might want to pace yourself, Oscar. That bottle is supposed to last you a couple of days until I get back."

"I don't like its chances," Oscar said, again sipping before sliding the cork into the bottle and tossing it onto his cot. "Update, Melvin. Give me some good news."

"I wish I had some, Oscar," Melvin said, again removing his fedora and twirling it around his finger. "I spoke with the judge earlier, and he's in no hurry to get your trial on the docket."

"Why the hell not?" Oscar said, grabbing the bars with both hands.

"He doesn't like you," Melvin said with a shrug.

"The bastard," Oscar snapped, expelling small globs of spittle that went through the bars and landed on Melvin's jacket.

Melvin glanced down and brushed it off with the back of his hands. But he remained calm as looked at Oscar and shrugged.

"And since you're a two-time offender, I think he wants to make an example of you. You know, just to get the attention of other people who might be considering a career smuggling booze."

"Maybe if I agreed to cooperate, the judge might decide to go easy on me," Oscar said, giving Melvin a small smile.

"Cooperate how?"

"Oh, I don't know. Maybe give him the name of my partner in crime," Oscar said, his grin growing bigger. "A certain lawyer I've been known to associate with."

"Go right ahead, Oscar," Melvin said, glaring through the bars. "Who do you think the judge is going to believe? An upstanding member of the legal profession or a corrupt ex-cop who's been caught smuggling illegal hooch twice?"

"I got set up both times, and you know it," Oscar said.

"Be that as it may, Oscar. Drop my name with the judge, and you'll find yourself without representation. And since your ability to pay for a lawyer is rather limited these days, do you really think you'll find someone else who's willing to work for free?"

Melvin let his comment sink in for a few moments before continuing.

"But you go right ahead, Oscar. Do whatever you feel is best."

"You gotta get me out of here, Melvin."

"I'm doing everything I can," Melvin said with a shrug. "But the judge still isn't willing to grant bail."

"For getting caught with five lousy cases of Canadian?"

"The word on the street is that you were trying to smuggle a thousand cases," Melvin said.

"Where the hell would I get my hands on a thousand cases?" Oscar said, gripping the bars tighter.

"That seems to be the question everyone wants answered," Melvin said. "And as your partner, I must say I'm interested in finding out as well. You been setting up your own side deals behind my back, Oscar?"

"For the tenth time, no, Melvin," Oscar snapped. "I had five cases in the boat. And that was all of it. I have no idea where the thousand cases nonsense came from."

"So, these thousand cases aren't going to show up at some point?" Melvin said. "I know that Roland Doyle has been looking hard for them."

"Roland Doyle," Oscar said with a guttural growl. "Somebody needs to do something about that revenuer."

"And if he does find them-"

"He's not going to find them, Melvin. Because they don't exist."

"Then you shouldn't have a problem, Oscar," Melvin said with a grin. "Eventually, Doyle will quit looking for them. And then you'll be charged for the five cases. At that point, I'm sure I can convince the judge to let you out on probation and time served."

"When?"

"Eventually. Be patient, Oscar," Melvin said. "You're a former lawman. I'm sure I don't have to explain how slowly the *wheels of justice* turn.

"They better start turning soon, Melvin. Or you and I are gonna have a big problem when I do get out."

"You see, Oscar. That's what I'm talking about," Melvin said, taking a step back from the bars. "That's exactly the sort of talk that puts people off. You really need to work on your people skills."

"Yeah, I'll do that," Oscar said, grabbing the bottle off the cot.

Melvin watched as Oscar turned the bottle upside down and chugged half of what was left. He shook his head again then glanced at the next cell where the drooling man was still sitting quietly on his cot with his hands folded in his lap.

"What's up with Quasimodo in the next cell?" Melvin whispered through the bars. "He almost seems normal today."

"He's getting out," Oscar said, sliding the cork back into the bottle. "As soon as he heard that, he started talking. And he's barely shut up since."

"What's he been in for?" Melvin said, sneaking another look at the man.

"Bank robbery," Oscar said. "But they don't have enough to hold him. No witnesses. And they can't find the money."

"That should give you some hope, Oscar," Melvin said with a big grin. "No evidence, no crime, right?"

"Yeah, I'm on the edge of my seat with anticipation," Oscar said, glaring at Melvin.

"Hang in there, Oscar," Melvin said as he slipped into his raincoat. "Well, I need to run. But I'll be back as soon as I get some news about your case."

"When will that be?"

"Eventually," Melvin said, giving Oscar a mock salute.

Melvin strolled off and paused outside the drooling man's cell.

"I understand you're getting released today," Melvin said.

"I am," the man said with a grin and a nod.

"Congratulations. I imagine you're anxious to get home."

"Not really," the man said.

"Where exactly do you call home?" Melvin said.

"Actually, I consider myself a citizen of the world."

"That must make it easier for you when you have house guests," Melvin said, laughing. "You know, lots of room for everyone."

"Indeed. A lawyer with a sense of humor. Wonders never cease."

"I'll take that as a compliment," Melvin said, touching the brim of his fedora. "Enjoy your day, sir."

"You too, Mr. English."

"You know my last name?"

"Yes, I've heard it mentioned a few times," the man said, giving Melvin a look that made him feel uneasy. "Your friend in the next cell is downright chatty at times. Especially when he's been drinking."

Melvin frowned as he headed for the exit. Oscar did tend to run his mouth, and the longer he was locked up, the greater the chances he would be blabbing to other people. And not just people in general: He'd be running his mouth to criminals who just might be interested in taking a closer look at Melvin and his operation. Maybe, he decided as he stepped outside into a cold rain, the time had come to put Oscar back on the street where he could keep a close eye on him.

Melvin climbed into his car and sat for a few moments with the engine running as he remembered the strange look the man had given him. The look left Melvin with the distinct impression that the man was potentially dangerous and had a mean streak that ran deep and wide. It was also a look that left no doubt that he'd be seeing him again. Melvin shook it off then headed for a nearby diner to grab lunch before heading for home. As he slowly drove through the hard rain that continued to pound down, his thoughts again returned to the look on the man's face.

"I think I liked him better when he was a drooler."

Picking A Daisy

Milo rolled over and slowly opened his eyes. Then he beamed when he got a good look at Annabelle just before she slipped into her robe.

"You are truly remarkable, Miss Caffey," Milo said, propping himself up on his elbows. "You're up early."

"I still have some papers to grade," she said, leaning over to give him a kiss. "And you should head out before the sun comes up."

"What sort of papers do fourth-graders write?" Milo said, frowning.

"Usually, really bad ones," she said, laughing. "But I do have a couple of kids who are quite good at organizing their thoughts and getting them down on paper."

"A most useful skill," Milo said, climbing out of bed.

"Yes, I thought the same thing. And it's also one of your better qualities," Annabelle said, glancing around then spotting her hairbrush. "It's right up there with your nocturnal skills."

"You're so sweet," Milo said, sidling up close to her.

"You should get going. We don't need the neighbors seeing you leave my place."

"I'd be more worried about them seeing what we were doing last night," Milo said as he began to get dressed.

"You're bad," Annabelle said, playfully swatting Milo with the brush. "What's on your schedule today?"

"I have to pay Ruby a visit," Milo said, shaking his head at the prospect.

"You're having a *meeting* with Mrs. Crankovitch?"

"No," Milo said, laughing. "I'm afraid the days of Ruby and me having *meetings* are over."

"Good."

"Good? Am I picking up a touch of jealousy, Miss Caffey?"

"Perhaps," she said with a small shrug. "Or maybe I just don't want you getting distracted, Milo."

"Because that's your job, right?"

"Perhaps," Annabelle said with a grin as she ran the brush through her hair. "What do you need to talk with Ruby about?"

"I have a few things to discuss with her about the farm. Then I'm sure she'll want to talk about how miserable she is."

"Is she still harping about you finding her something else to do?"

"Constantly," Milo said. "But since she does such a great job running the farm, I've been putting it off. I was hoping she'd eventually come to her senses, but she's made up her mind. And when Ruby makes up her mind, you can forget about trying to change it."

"Do you have any idea what you're going to have her do?" Annabelle said.

"Not exactly," Milo said, already dreading the day. "But it's starting to come together."

"Just don't let her get herself into trouble, Milo. I'd hate it if we had to take drastic measures," Annabelle said. "We've got something special going on here."

"That reminds me," Milo said, reaching into his coat pocket and handing her a thick envelope. "This is for you."

"Nice," Annabelle said, thumbing through the stack of bills. "We had a good month."

"Biggest one yet," Milo said, yawning. "Given the size of your teaching salary, I know you aren't putting all that cash in the bank. Where are hiding all your money?"

"None of your business," she said, laughing. "Now go."

"When can we do this again?"

"Just as soon as possible," Annabelle said, gently shoving him toward the door.

"Tonight?"

"Not a chance."

"Tomorrow?"

"No. We need to keep us under wraps for the time being," Annabelle said.

"Then how about under the covers?"

"Go," she said, giving him a peck on the cheek before opening the door.

Milo stepped outside into the darkness and headed for the path that ran behind her house. He made the short walk back to his suite at the Crossley by cutting through the park that ran along the edge of the downtown area. He climbed the set of steps that led to the hotel entrance and was greeted by the doorman.

"Good morning, Milo," he said, opening the door. "You been out for another morning walk?"

"Hey, Wilbur," Milo said. "Yeah, I headed out early. Must have been before you started your shift."

"Did you get a good workout in?" Wilbur said, gesturing for Milo to step inside.

"Oh, yeah," Milo said, looking at Wilbur but thinking about Annabelle. "One of the best yet."

Milo waved over his shoulder as he entered the lobby and climbed the stairs. He took a hot bath then ate a room service breakfast before changing into fresh clothes. When he was putting the finishing touches on his outfit in front of the mirror, he heard a knock on the door. Expecting to see the waiter returning to retrieve the breakfast dishes, Milo was surprised to see the woman standing at the door.

"Good morning, Daisy."

"Hi, Milo," she said, stepping past him. She sat down on the edge of his bed and kicked her shoes off then stretched out with an exasperated look on her face.

"Make yourself comfortable," Milo said, shaking his head.

"I can't do this, Milo."

"I assume you're not referring to getting horizontal. Because it looks like you've pretty much perfected that."

"Funny, Milo," she said, pouting. "You know exactly what I'm talking about."

"Daisy, we've been through this a million times. What now?"

"It's the same problem, Milo," Daisy said, cocking her head at him. "There's no way I'm going to be able to survive a whole winter over there on that island."

"You'll be fine, Daisy," Milo said, sitting down in a chair close to the bed. "You're going to have all the food and drink you can handle. You'll have a complete library of books to read. And I'm going to do everything I can to make sure there's a radio over there that can pick up a signal."

"But no telephone, right?"

"No, absolutely not," Milo said, shaking his head. "There's no way I'm putting a phone in over there."

"But who am I going to talk to?" Daisy said.

"Billy and Tom will be there with you the whole time. And you'll be seeing Birdie and me often."

"My mama is going to worry about me," Daisy said.

"Not if you write her letters," Milo said. "And you'll have lots of time to do that. I'll even mail them for you."

"Tell me again why you need me over there," Daisy said.

Milo took a couple of deep breaths and did his best to remain calm.

"I need you on the island to keep Billy happy," he said.

"You mean to keep him cooking for you, right?" Daisy said, sitting up in bed.

"He does his best work when he's happy, Daisy," Milo said. "And there's nobody who can make him happy like you do, right?"

"Billy's easy to keep happy," she said with a shrug. "I don't even have to work up a sweat."

"And you like him, right?"

"In small doses, sure," she said with a scowl. "But not every day."

"That's where Tom comes in," Milo said. "When you get tired of talking to Billy, spend some time with him."

"I don't know, Milo," Daisy said, shaking her head. "Maybe you should just talk to Fannie and get another girl."

"I don't want another girl, Daisy," Milo said. "I want you."

"Aren't you sweet," she said, turning coy.

"Not as sweet as this," he said, walking to his desk and unlocking a drawer. He returned with an envelope and sat back down in the chair.

"What's that?" she said, nodding at the envelope.

"It's the first month of your winter salary," Milo said, tossing the envelope on the bed.

Daisy grabbed it and fanned out the stack of bills inside.

"This is just the first month?" she said, glancing at him with a surprised look.

"You feeling a bit better about spending the winter on the island?"

"Not really," she said, sliding the envelope into her bag. "But I'm sure I'll figure out a way to deal with it. And what you said still goes, right?"

"About what?" Milo said, frowning.

"About me not having to do *special favors* for either one of them," she said.

"Whatever special favors you decide to do or not do is completely your call, Daisy."

"And they both know that?"

"They do," Milo said, nodding. "But I'm sure you'll remind them."

"No doubt about that," she said, then shrugged. "But I'll probably cave in at some point. Going that long would probably be some kind of world record."

"I'll alert the press," Milo whispered.

"What?"

"Nothing," Milo said, flashing her a smile. "Now, if there's nothing else on your mind, I really need to get going."

"Sure, Milo," she said, hopping off the bed and slipping into her shoes. "When am I going to have to leave for the island?"

"Sometime before the first ice," Milo said. "A couple of weeks, maybe a month."

"Okay," Daisy said, heading for the door. "And thanks for the envelope."

"My pleasure."

"Oh, you have no idea, Milo," she said with a grin and a playful over-the-shoulder finger wave on her way out.

Unfulfilled Requests

Roland Doyle woke early with his head on fire and his hands shaking. Following a routine that had become the norm, Roland put a pot of coffee on, splashed cold water on his face, and washed down a small handful of aspirin with the vestiges of the quart of Canadian he'd fallen asleep next to. He poured half a cup of coffee, added one spoonful of sugar, then topped off his cup with a healthy splash from a fresh bottle. He finished two cups and smoked three cigarettes before finally feeling ready to face the day. Roland was just about to prepare another cup when his phone rang. He took the bottle with him into the living room and set it down on a table before answering.

"Roland," he said, then coughed long and hard. He spat into his handkerchief and wiped his mouth before picking the receiver back up. "Sorry about that. This is Roland Doyle."

"Good morning, Roland," the man on the other end of the line said. "Sounds like you're fighting a cold."

"Who is this?" Roland said, frowning.

"It's Vernon."

"Vernon?"

"Vernon Adams," the man said, annoyed. "Your boss."

"Oh, Mr. Adams. Sure. Sorry about that," Roland said. "I didn't recognize your voice at first. I think my ears must be blocked from this bug I'm dealing with. What's up?"

"I just thought I'd check in," Vernon said. "I haven't heard from you in a couple of weeks."

"Yeah, I've been busy," Roland said, trying to reach the whiskey bottle he'd set down on the table. "You know, tracking down bootleggers who are filling our shores with illegal hooch."

"You catch any lately?" Vernon Adams said.

"Uh, no," Roland said, setting the phone down momentarily then grabbing the bottle from the table. "But I'm hot on the trail of a couple of them at the moment." Roland took a swig of whiskey and wiped his mouth with the back of his hand.

"Did those mysterious thousand cases ever turn up?"

"No, they vanished without a trace," Roland said, frowning at the memory. "And the guy I arrested still isn't talking."

"Oh, well. I'm sure there are lots more where they came from," Vernon said.

"That's what I'm counting on," Roland said. "Hey, since I've got you on the phone, have you given any more thought to my request for some help up here. It's a big area to cover."

"Actually, I'm right in the middle of assigning a new batch of agents," Vernon said. "And I do have a few more covert assignments to finish up."

"Covert?" Roland said. "You mean, like secret?"

"I think I've said enough," Vernon said. "But let me see what I can do."

"That would be great, Mr. Adams," Roland said. "I can use all the help I can get."

"Yes, I'm sure you can," Vernon whispered.

"What?"

"I was simply agreeing with you, Roland."

"So, is that a yes?"

"Let me think about it," Vernon said.

"And then you'll let me know?" Roland said, taking a small sip from the bottle.

"Let's say you'll know if and when she arrives and leave it at that," Vernon said.

"Sure, I get that," Roland said, nodding. "You don't want to be talking about assigning covert agents over the phone, right?"

"Yes, that *was* my intent, Roland," Vernon Adams snapped. "Good day. Happy hunting."

Roland hung up the phone and stood in the middle of the living room pondering all the different ways he might be able to use an undercover agent. He grinned, took a long pull from the bottle, then felt his stomach roil. He set the bottle back down on the table and raced to the bathroom to throw up, thereby completing his new morning ritual.

Milo grabbed his keys and was heading for the door when his phone rang. He walked back to his desk and sat down before answering.

"Milo Razner."

"Hi, Mr. Razner."

"Oh, hi, Violet," Milo said, putting his feet up on the desk. "How are you this fine morning?"

"I'm good, Mr. Razner. But I just heard something that's got me thinking."

"And you felt the need to tell me about it?" Milo said, lowering his feet and paying close attention.

"Yes, I did. Straight away," Violet Hollman said.

"I see. Please, continue."

"Roland Doyle just got a call from his boss in Washington," Violet said.

"Okay," Milo said, frowning. "What did they talk about?"

"I've been telling you about how Roland is always asking his boss for help."

"Yes, I remember," Milo said, rubbing his forehead.

"Well, today was a bit different," Violet said. "And they let something slip I'm pretty sure Roland's boss didn't want to get into."

"Interesting," Milo said, nodding. "And this slip was related to Roland's request for help?"

"It was," Violet said. "Roland's boss said he was currently assigning a new batch of agents. Covert agents."

"I see. And what exactly did he say?"

"Not much after that," she said. "The guy in Washington definitely didn't want to talk about it over the phone."

"I guess your reputation proceeds you, Violet," Milo said with a grin.

"I suppose," she said, nervously. "Have I screwed up, Mr. Razner?"

"Not at all," Milo said. "You're doing a wonderful job. And I plan on putting a little something extra in this month's envelope as a special thank you."

"That would be great, Mr. Razner. Thanks."

"Tell me more about their conversation," Milo said, lighting a cigarette.

"When Roland asked if the guy was going to get back to him with a final decision, he said, you'll know if and when she arrives."

"Interesting. And then they finished the call?"

"Pretty much," Violet said. "I thought you'd want to know about it right away."

"You thought right, Violet," Milo said, getting up out of the chair. "Keep me posted if you hear anything else."

"Will do, Mr. Razner," she said, hanging up.

Milo put the phone back in its cradle and began a slow pace back and forth across the living room. Deep in thought, he slowly worked his way through his cigarette. Then he picked the phone up and waited for Violet to answer.

"Yes, Mr. Razner?"

"Violet, could you please connect me with Birdie?"

"Sure. Do you need some privacy on this call?" she said. "I'm due for my break."

"No, that won't be necessary," Milo said. "It's going to be a short call."

"Okay. Hang on a sec."

"This is Birdie," he said, seconds later.

"Birdie. It's Milo."

"Hey, Milo. What's up?"

"I need you to meet me with the boat at the farm," Milo said.

"I was just about to have some breakfast. When do you need me there?"

"A couple of hours is fine. Take your time. I'll meet you down at the dock."

"We got a problem?" Birdie said.

"No, not yet," Milo said. "This is more of a preemptive strike."

"I'm sure you'll explain everything to me."

"I certainly will," Milo said.

"Be sure to dress warm," Birdie said. "It's gonna be a cold boat ride."

"Will do," Milo said. "I'll see you later."

Milo hung up, grabbed a thick sweater and his winter coat and left the suite. He made the drive to the dairy farm still deep in thought. He parked next to the house and found Ruby in the kitchen stirring a large pot.

"Good morning, Ruby," Milo chirped. "That smells fantastic."

"I'm making a stew for lunch," she said, apparently in a good mood. "I thought I'd surprise all the workers."

"That's very nice of you," Milo said, nodding.

"I am capable of being nice, Milo," Ruby said, gesturing at the kitchen table. "Or have you forgotten that?"

"No, I remember," Milo said with a grin as he sat down. "But I must say that it's a fading memory."

"What do you want, Milo?" Ruby said, sitting down across the table from him.

"I just thought we should catch up," he said. "It's been awhile since we had a chance to talk."

"Whose fault is that?" Ruby said, her good mood rapidly disappearing.

"Fair point," Milo said, helping himself to one of the biscuits on the table. "These are good."

"Thanks," Ruby said, staring at him. "So, what do you want to talk about?"

"Oh, I thought we'd discuss the farm and how things are going."

"Things are going great," she said, shrugging. "The place runs like clockwork."

"Thanks to you."

“Yes. Thanks to me.”

“Have you seen Billy lately?” Milo said, polishing off the last of his biscuit.

“He stopped by a couple of nights ago. He rode along with Birdie when he was making his delivery. Billy wanted to pick up some more winter clothes.”

“I’m sure he’ll need them,” Milo said. “How is he feeling about spending all winter on the island?”

“I imagine he’s delighted about it,” Ruby said, now sullen. “He’ll be spending his days cooking, and his nights with the trollop you hired for him.”

“What makes you think I hired Daisy to do that?” Milo said.

“Don’t start blowing smoke up my skirt, Milo,” Ruby snapped. “I used to be married to him. And there’s no way Fannie’s number one earner is going to take four months off to spend all her time stuck on an island with that blabbering idiot.”

“Perhaps you’re right,” Milo said, treading carefully.

“How much did that cost you?” Ruby said, raising an eyebrow at him.

“Enough,” Milo said with a shrug. “You seem troubled, Ruby.”

“Troubled?” Ruby said, laughing. “That’s the word you want to use?”

“It seems appropriate,” Milo whispered.

"Sure, let's go with troubled," she said. "Wasn't our agreement that you would do everything you could to make me happy, Milo?"

"I'm afraid my memory isn't what it used to be," Milo said, reaching for another biscuit.

"Don't try to get cute with me today, Milo," Ruby said, her eyes flaring wide. "I am not in the mood."

"Yes, I noticed," Milo said. "Maybe we should take a meeting. That always seems to brighten your mood."

"Those days are over, Milo," Ruby said. "But you already knew that, didn't you?"

"Yeah, I already knew that," Milo said, glancing around the kitchen. "So, what do you want to do, Ruby?"

"Something different, Milo. I'm going stir crazy spending all my time around cows."

"Just think about all the money you're making. I know that always puts a smile on my face."

"I could be making both of us a lot more," Ruby said, glaring across the table.

"Doing what?" Milo said, staring back at her.

"Working on the booze side," she said. "What else would I be talking about?"

"I've pretty much got all that covered," Milo said.

"How convenient for you," she said.

"It's not a matter of convenience, Ruby. Things are the way they are out of necessity."

Milo offered his pack of cigarettes to her then lit both. Ruby blew a cloud of smoke up at the ceiling then focused her stare on him.

"So, you're saying you need me here," Ruby said.

"Of course, I need you here," Milo said. "You're an integral part of this thing."

"I could be doing a whole lot more," she said, exhaling another cloud of smoke. "I hate dairy farming."

"Do you need some more workers to help out? I'd be happy to hire them."

"No, I got plenty of people. More than enough," Ruby said. "I'm talking about me, Milo. And if you aren't willing to do something about it, I'm sure I can find someone else who'd be interested in what I have to offer."

"I see," Milo whispered.

"There must be a ton of people running booze these days," she said, casually tossing it out.

"Yes," Milo said, nodding. "But nobody who does it as well as I do, Ruby."

"I could show them how you do it," she said with a shrug.

"No, Ruby," Milo said, giving her a death stare. "That is the one thing you cannot do. Am I making myself clear?"

"Crystal clear, Milo," Ruby said with an evil grin. "Just like Billy's Miracle."

"I'm not joking, Ruby."

"Then we both understand each other, right?"

"Let's try a different tack, shall we?" Milo said, exasperated. "Why don't you try to explain exactly what it is you're looking for?"

"I want a life beyond cows, Milo," Ruby said, softening a bit. "I want a social life, to dance and go to parties wearing pretty dresses. It's all about lifestyle, Milo. I just want to enjoy the same things your customers do."

"Like drinking themselves into a stupor?"

"I said I'm not in the mood for your jokes, Milo," Ruby said, annoyed again. "You know what I'm talking about."

"Yes, I think I do," Milo said, extinguishing his cigarette. "But it would be a shame to waste your talents on a party lifestyle, Ruby. You have a remarkable head for business."

"Oh, I'm going to keep working," Ruby said, frowning at him. "I just want to be around people while I'm doing it. People who can hold up their end of a conversation. You must have something I can do."

"Nothing comes to mind at the moment," Milo said with a shrug.

"Well, you better think of something fast," she said. "I'm on my last legs. I can't stand being here."

"How long would it take you to train someone to run the farm?"

"Johnny is ready to handle it," Ruby said. "But you'd have to bring him into the circle."

"Do you trust him?"

"I trust him with my life," she said. "And as soon as you start paying him what you pay me to run this place, you'll own his ass."

"I'd prefer yours, Ruby," Milo said with a grin.

"I'm sure you would, Milo," she said, reaching for another cigarette and waiting for him to light it. "And if you are able to come up with a suitable arrangement for me, maybe I'll even reconsider *taking a meeting* with you."

"Oh, I do like working toward a goal," he said, laughing.

"Figure something out, Milo. And soon."

"I'll get right on it, Ruby," Milo said, getting to his feet. "I need to run. I'm meeting Birdie down at the dock."

"Aren't you forgetting something?" Ruby said, cocking her head at him.

Milo frowned, then nodded.

"Of course. I almost forgot."

Milo reached into his coat pocket and tossed a thick envelope on the table. Ruby picked it up and casually flipped through the stack of bills.

"Nice. We had a good month," she said, setting the envelope on the table in front of her. "But we could be doing even better, Milo. Just find me the right spot, and I'll prove it to you."

"I'll do my best, Ruby," Milo said. "But in the short-term, maybe all you need is a break."

"A break?"

"Yeah, like a vacation," Milo said, grinning at her. "I'll be in touch."

You Can't Be Too Careful

Melvin exited the diner burping and patting his chest after inhaling a big bowl of chili spicy enough to melt wallpaper. He frowned when he saw the drooling man leaning against his car holding a paper bag in one hand and a small suitcase in the other. Melvin couldn't miss the strange smile on his face and approached the car with caution.

"They let you out," Melvin said. "Good for you."

"Right after you left," the man said. "I thought I saw you go into the diner. I was going to join you for lunch, but I had to pick up a few things."

"Do you have a place here in Watertown?" Melvin said, trying to decide if it would be rude to get in the car. He continued to stand next to the driver side door as he glanced up at the sky that, while still grey, was clearing a bit.

"No," the man said with a small shake of his head.

"So, you had your stuff in storage?" Melvin said.

"In a fashion, yes," the man said, staring at Melvin like he was expecting something.

"Where are you off to?" Melvin said, going for casual and hoping his nervousness wasn't showing.

"Well, I guess that depends, Mr. English," the man said, his strange expression refusing to leave.

"On what?"

"On whether or not you're going to offer me a ride."

"A ride?" Melvin said, surprised. "You need me to drop you off somewhere in town?"

"No, Mr. English. Actually, I'd like a ride to Alex Bay."

"Alex Bay?" Melvin said, fighting the urge to jump in the car and drive off. "That's where I live."

"So, I've surmised," the man, finally breaking into a facial expression that resembled a grin.

"Do you know people there?"

"No," he said, shaking his head. "But based on what I overheard you and your friend in the next cell talking about, it sounds like a beautiful spot."

"Well, it's pretty cold this time of year," Melvin said. "And it's going to be getting a lot colder. Summer is a much better time to visit."

"I don't mind the cold," the man said.

"Tell me that again in February, and I just might believe you."

The man gave him a slit-eyed stare that caused Melvin to flinch and look away.

"And there's really nothing to do this time of year," Melvin said.

"Is that so? From what I heard you two discussing, it sounds like there's a lot going on up there at the moment."

Melvin recoiled but discovered a bit of backbone and returned the man's stare over the hood of the car.

"Is there something on your mind?" Melvin said. "I get the distinct impression there's something you're not telling me."

"Nothing worth discussing at the moment, Mr. English," he said. "But since I find myself so close to such a magical place, it only seems appropriate for me to pay your town a visit."

"Magical is probably a bit of a stretch," Melvin said with a shrug. Then he grimaced and pressed a hand against his chest.

"Are you okay, Mr. English?"

"I'm fine. I just ate that chili too fast," Melvin said, then burped loudly. "Oh, that's better."

"I believe it's starting to snow," the man said, glancing up at the dark sky. Then he focused his stare on Melvin.

"Yeah, I see that," Melvin said, then pursed his lips as he stared off into the distance. Eventually, he nodded. "Sure, I'll be happy to give you a ride. Hop in."

Milo hunkered down low in the front seat as Birdie opened the throttle. The boat sped across the water, and Milo snuck a peek at the speedometer that was holding steady at fifty miles an hour.

"Beautiful day for a boat ride, huh, Milo?"

"Are you out of your frigging mind?" Milo shouted above the roar of the engine. "It's freezing out here."

"Just wait until the snow and ice arrive," Birdie yelled back.

"Yeah, I'm really looking forward to that," Milo shouted, then shook his head in disbelief. "You want to slow down a bit?"

"If I slow down, it's only going to make the trip longer," Birdie shouted.

"Can't argue with your logic, Birdie," Milo said, pointing a finger at the horizon.

Birdie nodded and opened the throttle all the way. When the boat hit sixty miles an hour, Milo hunkered down even further and said a silent prayer to the God of Boating Safety. Five minutes later, Birdie pulled the throttle back as Whisperer Island came into full view, and he slowly drove to the back of the island and entered the long stone boathouse. Milo climbed out and tied the boat off, then helped Birdie make his way onto the dock.

"I still can't believe you own this place, Milo," Birdie said, staring up at the high ceiling.

"It is nice, isn't it?" Milo said, beaming as he looked around. "Let's go see what the guys are up to."

Milo walked slowly so as not to leave the limping Birdie behind, and they made their way up an incline that led to a stone structure halfway up the path and a couple hundred feet below the main house. Milo opened the door and waited for Birdie to enter before following. He beamed again when he saw the immaculate condition of the well-lit room. Four large stills dominated the space, and one side of the room was filled with bags of corn and sugar neatly stacked against a wall. To the immediate left of the stills were two large tanks. Four more sat on the other side of the stills, and dozens of ten-gallon milk cans were lined up on the other side of the room. Milo did a quick silent count of the milk cans then nodded his approval.

"Hey," Tom Collins said, noticing their presence. "I didn't think you were coming over today. Hi, Birdie."

"Hey, Tom," Birdie said, rolling a cigarette with one hand.

"Slight change of plans," Milo said. "How are you doing, Billy?"

Billy Crankovitch, cooker-extraordinaire and inventor of Miracle, looked up from the beaker he was studying and waved without turning around.

"Hey, Mr. Razner," Billy said. "You need to talk with me?"

"Actually, I need a word with Tom," Milo said. "What are you working on over there?"

"Just checking the latest batch of Miracle," Billy said, holding the beaker of clear liquid up to the light. "I've been playing around to see if I can get the proof up without changing the taste. You want to try it?"

"Well, if you insist," Milo said, laughing as he walked across the room. Billy handed him a shot glass, and Milo took a whiff then tossed it back. He immediately felt the surge of warmth the moonshine always produced and beamed at his cooker. "Remarkable. You're a genius, Billy."

"Thanks, Mr. Razner," Billy said, smiling with pride.

"What's the proof of this one?" Milo said, waving off Billy's offer of another shot.

"180."

"You got it up from 160?" Milo said, glancing at Tom Collins who shrugged. "How the heck did you do that?"

"Well, if I told you that, Mr. Razner," Billy said with a grin. "You probably wouldn't need me around, right?"

"I wouldn't worry about not being needed, Billy," Milo said, momentarily caught off guard. Maybe the rube wasn't as dumb as he appeared. "You're my main man."

"The 180 is going to save us a nice chunk of change when I cut it and turn it into Red Deer," Tom said, grabbing a notebook off the table. "I've been playing around with the numbers. You're gonna like it."

Milo studied the page for several moments then tossed the notebook on the table and nodded.

"Impressive," Milo said. "You guys have been busy."

"Well, there ain't a lot to do over here other than cook," Billy said. "Which reminds me, Mr. Razner. Have you had a chance to have another talk with Daisy?"

"I have, Billy. As a matter of fact, I saw her this morning."

"And?"

"Daisy can't wait to spend the winter over here with you," Milo said.

"That's great," Billy said, beaming. "Because I sure do enjoy her company."

"And she says the same thing about you, Billy. Just don't let her distract you too much."

"I was thinking that I'd only let her distract me at night," Billy said. "That would be okay, wouldn't it, Mr. Razner?"

"That's the perfect time to be distracted, Billy," Milo said. "Now if you can spare Tom for a few minutes, I need to have a chat with him."

"Sure," Billy said, already engrossed in his work.

Melvin took his eyes off the snowy road just long enough to glance over at the man who was sitting in the passenger seat and staring contentedly out the window.

"I still don't know your name," Melvin said.

"It's Jimmy," the man said without taking his eyes off the passing countryside. "Jimmy Sleaze."

"Jimmy Sleaze," Melvin said with a shrug. "I bet people like to have some fun with nicknames for you."

"Not for long, they don't," Jimmy Sleaze said, the contented look gone.

"Yeah, I get that," Melvin said, slipping into his habit of talking too much when nervous. "My name is pretty ripe for making fun of. Melvin. Mel-vin. Melly. Melly Belly. That one started when I was young. I was pretty chubby when I started walking, and my grandpa gave me the nickname. Then when it took me forever to get out of diapers, my parents started calling me Smelly Melly Belly. Fortunately, I lost that one by the time I started school."

Melvin glanced over and caught the dark glare Jimmy Sleaze was giving him.

"Yeah, nicknames can be cruel," Melvin said, then bit his lip. He decided a change of topic was called for. "I'm running for mayor. The election is next Tuesday."

"You don't say?" Sleaze said. "So, you're a lawyer and a politician?"

"Quite the combination, huh?" Melvin said, grinning as he glanced over.

"I suppose," Sleaze said, staring out the window. "It would be like killing two birds with one stone."

"Yeah, good one," Melvin said, barely able to get his nervous chuckle past his lips.

Jimmy Sleaze's attention focused on a truck that passed them heading in the other direction. He turned his head and continued to watch it until it disappeared from sight.

"Was that a milk truck?" Sleaze said.

"Yup. Razner's Dairy," Melvin said. "Milo's got a whole bunch of milk trucks. He's doing very well for himself."

"Milo Razner?" Sleaze said, frowning. "That's the guy's name?"

"Yeah, another name you could have some fun with," Melvin said. "*Mi-lo Raz-ner*."

"Where's his dairy farm located?"

"Alex Bay," Melvin said. "Actually, I'm the one who brokered the deal for him."

Melvin frowned as he remembered the money he'd lost on the deal, then shook it off.

"Yes, Milo has become a community pillar," Melvin said. "Do you know that he provides breakfast to all the local schoolkids?"

"How the hell would I know that?" Sleaze growled.

"Of course, how would you?"

"How many milk trucks does the guy have?" Sleaze said.

"Oh, by now, he has to be up to half a dozen," Melvin said. "He delivers all over the area. And I think he's up to two trips a day to Watertown. Which makes sense since it's the largest town around."

"I see," Sleaze said. "That's a lot of milk."

"Indeed. I think he's got close to three hundred cows. Maybe even more."

"So, there's money to be made in milk?" Sleaze said, frowning.

"There has to be," Melvin said. "Like I said, Milo is doing very well."

Milo trailed by Tom and Birdie, headed for the door. They stepped outside and realized it had started snowing. Milo turned his coat collar up and made his way up the path fighting the wind the entire time.

"Winter's on the way," Tom said, hugging himself for warmth. "It's gonna be long and lonely."

"Hang in there, Tom," Milo said, climbing the steps to the enormous verandah that wrapped around the house. "I'll think of something."

They entered the house and stepped directly into the massive living room constructed, like the rest of the eight-bedroom house, of wood, glass, and stone. Milo headed straight for the floor to ceiling fireplace on the far side of the room and stoked the embers. Tom tossed a couple of logs onto the fire, and when they caught, Milo removed his coat and sat down in an overstuffed chair.

"So, what's up?" Tom said, pouring Red Deer and passing the glasses out.

"I got a call from Violet this morning," Milo said, taking a sip. Then he nodded at Tom. "This is a great batch, Tom."

"Thanks, Milo," Tom said. "Billy and I have got the quality control down cold. Who did Violet happen to be eavesdropping on today?"

"Roland Doyle," Milo said.

"What's our favorite revenuer up to these days?" Tom said, laughing. "He didn't happen to run aground again, did he?"

"I don't think he's been out on the water since his last adventure," Milo said, laughing at the memory. "And he's already got his boat stored for the winter at Frank's place. Doyle was on the phone with his boss in D.C."

"Okay," Tom said, frowning.

"His boss let it slip that he was thinking about putting another agent up here," Milo said. "An undercover agent."

"Isn't that Annabelle's job?" Birdie said.

"It is," Milo said. "And I can't imagine she's going to be happy when she hears about it."

"Doyle still doesn't know that Annabelle's working undercover, does he?" Tom said.

"No, he doesn't," Milo said. "But if his boss is willing to put another agent up here who's assigned to Roland, he's up to something."

"Maybe he's getting pressure from his bosses," Tom said. "Roland certainly hasn't set the world on fire since he got here."

"And that's precisely the way we like it," Milo said. "Just when we finally get Roland where we want him, his boss decides to screw up the natural order of things."

"Natural order as in keeping Roland drunk and clueless?" Birdie said with a cackle.

"Exactly," Milo said, raising his glass in salute.

"Did Violet get any details about when this agent might be showing up?" Tom said.

"No, all she really learned was that it's going to be a woman," Milo said.

"Maybe he's thinking about transferring Annabelle," Tom said.

"Yeah, I was thinking the same thing. But I was sure she had the guy wrapped around her finger."

"He works for the government," Tom said with a shrug. "Who knows what's on his mind? I mean, these are the same people who are talking about bringing back Daylight Saving Time."

"Yeah, I heard our friend, Senator Miller, is co-sponsoring the bill," Milo said, shaking his head. "Who else besides the government could cut a foot off the top of a scarf, sew it back on the bottom, then try to convince you that you now had a longer piece of wool to keep your neck warm?"

"Are you going to tell Annabelle?" Tom said.

"Of course," Milo said. "But she'll need to be careful about how she plays her hand."

"Yeah," Tom said, nodding. "I'm sure the guy in D.C. would wonder how she found out."

"I know I would," Milo said, refilling all three glasses.

"You need us to do anything?" Birdie said.

"No, not yet," Milo said, shaking his head. "But keep an eye out for new women arriving in town. Especially at Fannies. And if you find anyone getting overly friendly with you, let me know right away."

Milo stared into the fire for a long time deep in thought.

"It's no big deal, Milo," Tom said. "We'll figure it all out and take care of her when the time is right. What's the matter?"

"It's just a thought I can't shake," Milo said, taking a sip of whiskey.

"You're wondering if this is all some elaborate setup and Annabelle might be part of it?" Tom said.

"You're a wise man, Tom Collins," Milo said, glancing over at him.

"But why would she do that?" Birdie said. "She's on her way to becoming a very rich woman."

"Yes, she is," Milo said. "But you can't be too careful. Stranger things have happened." Milo tossed back the rest of his whiskey then exhaled loudly. "Oh, I sure hope she's not involved in something like that. That would just break my heart."

"And it wouldn't do much for her, either," Birdie said. "I mean, if we caught her trying to set us up like that, I wouldn't like her chances."

"Can't argue with your logic, Birdie," Milo said, shaking his head. "No, I can't believe Annabelle would do that."

"Can't or won't?" Tom said.

"For now, that's a distinction without a difference, Tom."

Melvin pulled over to the side of the street in the middle of downtown and came to a stop. He glanced over at Jimmy Sleaze and gestured with both hands.

"Welcome to Alex Bay," Melvin said.

"It's small," Jimmy Sleaze said, glancing out the window as the snow continued to fall and accumulate. "But it looks nice enough."

"We like it," Melvin said, also glancing out. "And we have a pretty decent train schedule. So, after you take a look around, I'm sure you'll be able to catch a train out to the destination of your choice."

"You trying to get rid of me already, Melvin?" Jimmy Sleaze said with a look that made Melvin's stomach do backflips.

"Oh, no. Of course not," Melvin said, then chuckled nervously. "I was merely pointing it out."

"Can you recommend a place to stay?"

"Stay?" Melvin said with a wide-eyed stare.

"Yeah, you know. A place to sleep and rest my weary bones," Sleaze said.

"Well, the Crossley down the street is nice," Melvin said. "But it's a bit expensive."

"What about a place to get a drink?"

"Drink?"

"What's the matter, Melvin?" Sleaze said, frowning. "That bowl of chili starting to affect your thinking?"

"What? Oh, no, I'm fine," Melvin stammered. "It's just that alcohol is illegal."

"Do I look I just fell off the turnip truck, Melvin?"

"Of course not," Melvin said, shaking his head. "I wouldn't even know what a turnip looks like."

"So, where can I get a drink?" Sleaze said.

"There's a speakeasy at the Crossley," Melvin said. "But you might also consider the blind pig that's located at Fannies."

"Fannies?"

"It's a place where you can find…let's call it, horizontal refreshment," Melvin said with a small shrug. "She also runs a blind pig in her back room. It's a good spot to meet a lot of the locals. The speakeasy at the Crossley usually attracts more travelers and business people."

"That's good to know, Melvin," Jimmy Sleaze said. "You've been very helpful. And I can't thank you enough for the ride."

"Don't mention it," Melvin said, anxious for the strange man to get out of his car.

Jimmy Sleaze peered into the paper bag that had been sitting on his lap the entire trip and removed a ten-dollar bill. He handed it to Melvin. "This is for you."

"Oh, no, you don't need to pay me for the ride," Melvin said, shaking his head.

"Take it," Sleaze commanded.

Melvin accepted the bill and nodded his thanks. Jimmy Sleaze reached into the backseat for his suitcase then opened the door. He climbed out then poked his head back inside the car.

"I'll be seeing you around, Melvin."

He slammed the door shut and Melvin watched as he began strolling down James street.

"That's what I'm afraid of," Melvin said, then turned the car around and headed for home.

Milo watched Tom tend the fire then glanced over at Birdie.

"It's going to be dark soon," Milo said. "You got any plans for tonight?"

"Nah, not really," Birdie said. "I was thinking about maybe swinging by Fannie's place at some point. She's got a new girl that just started. Why do you ask?"

"I thought we might just stay here tonight and get drunk with Tom and Billy," Milo said.

"That's an idea," Birdie said. "Maybe play cards."

"Yeah, I'd like that," Milo said. "What do you say, Tom? You feel like having some company tonight?"

"Gee, I don't know, Milo. Billy's such a brilliant conversationalist, I'm not sure I'm willing to share him," Tom deadpanned. "Yeah, I think I can handle that." He set the fireplace poker down and took his seat. "Did you stop by the farm today?"

"I did," Milo said, then grinned when an idea popped into his head.

"How's Ruby?"

"Grumpy," Milo said, his grin widening.

"Did she hit you up again about doing something different?" Tom said.

"She certainly did. And I'm going to have to do something about it soon. She's starting to lose it and is making threats about running her mouth."

"I hope you reminded her of the implications of doing something that stupid," Tom said, shaking his head.

"I did. And I'm sure she just said it to piss me off. But I do need to figure out a way to make her happy. Ruby is too valuable to lose," Milo said. "You know, maybe she's right. Maybe I have been undervaluing her skill set."

"Do you know what job you're gonna give her?" Birdie said.

"I think I just might," Milo said, again staring into the fire.

"You gonna tell us?" Birdie said.

"No, it's too early to start talking about it," Milo said, focused on one of the burning logs. "I'm gonna need some time to set this one up." Milo looked at Tom. "Are you and Ruby still on good terms?"

"Yeah, not bad," Tom said with a shrug. "She's cooled off a bit, but I think that's because she's distracted by being so pissed off at you. Why do you ask?"

"I think Ruby needs a vacation," Milo said.

"And you want me to take her?" Tom said, frowning.

"No, you're not going anywhere, Tom. But Ruby might be."

"On vacation?"

"Yes."

"Where is she going to go?" Tom said, thoroughly confused.

"Why here, of course," Milo said.

"Here? All winter?"

"I'm not sure, but she'd definitely be here awhile."

"Ruby's probably not going to like that idea, Milo," Tom said.

"At first, I'm sure she won't," Milo said. "I just need to convince her to take the long view."

"You're gonna put her and Billy on an island together?" Birdie said. "In the same house with Daisy?"

"Sure, why not?" Milo said.

"Oh, where do I start?" Birdie said, shaking his head. "You sure do work in mysterious ways, Milo."

"Thanks, Birdie," Milo said, raising his glass in salute.

"Is what you're thinking of giving Ruby going to be enough to calm her down?" Tom said.

"If it isn't, then I don't have a clue what to do with her," Milo said.

"Except maybe put her at the bottom of the River?" Birdie said.

"Oh, let's hope it doesn't come to that."

Sleaze Happens

Apart from too little sleep and a hangover that could kill a horse, Milo entered his suite at the Crossley in a great mood. He went straight to the bathroom and began drawing a bath then headed for his desk and began making a list of some of the things that would need to be taken care of before he could put his burgeoning plan about what to do with Ruby in place. He dozed off in the tub but woke with a start when the water turned cold. He toweled off, slipped into his robe then ordered room service for lunch with an eye toward an extended afternoon nap on a full belly. Milo's hangover seemed to worsen as he waited for his food to arrive, and he forced himself to remain patient.

When Milo heard the knock, he quickly crossed the room and opened the door. Stunned by what he saw, his stomach dropped, and a sense of dread washed over him that was both unexpected and unwieldy.

"Jimmy Sleaze," Milo said with a cold stare at the man standing in the doorway. "Sonofabitch."

Jimmy grinned at Milo and shrugged as he worked his way past him into the suite.

"I've been called worse. How are you doing, Milo?"

"I've been better."

Jimmy Sleaze glanced around the suite nodding his head in approval.

"You're moving up the world."

"I thought you were still in prison."

"No, actually the Commonwealth of Pennsylvania, bless their heart, decided six months ago that I had paid my debt to society," Sleaze said, helping himself to one of Milo's cigarettes.

"Why the hell did they do that?" Milo said, baffled. "You were supposed to get six years."

"I decided to help them out with a predicament they were having in the City of Brotherly Love," Sleaze said, casually. "They were most grateful for my assistance."

"You ratted somebody out?" Milo said, raising an eyebrow. "I'm surprised, Jimmy. Whatever happened to your philosophy of honor among thieves?"

"Survival trumps philosophy, Milo," he said. "You should know that better than anybody."

"Who did you give up?"

"Oh, I'd rather not say," Jimmy Sleaze said. "I'm afraid word getting out about that might put me in a rather uncomfortable position."

"A position like being stuffed into a barrel and cemented in?" Milo said, lighting a cigarette.

"I knew you'd understand," Sleaze said, laughing. "I hear you've gotten into the milk business."

"Where the hell did you hear that?" Milo said, frowning.

"Oh, I've heard all sort of things, Milo. This truly is a remarkable suite. You live here full-time?"

"I do," Milo said, sitting down on the couch. "Who have you been talking to?"

"I've spent the past several weeks next door to an absolutely delightful human being," he said, laughing.

"I'm not following, Jimmy," Milo said, then called out loudly when he heard another knock on the door. "Just leave it outside the door." Milo glanced at Jimmy Sleaze. "Room service."

"By all means, don't let me keep you from having lunch."

"That's okay. I've lost my appetite," Milo said, trying to get control of his thoughts. "Who have you been talking to?"

"Actually, I've mostly been listening, Milo."

"Okay, now I get it," Milo said, nodding. "The only time you do a lot of listening is when you're behind bars. Are you still doing that drooling imbecile routine?"

"Why change now?" Jimmy Sleaze said with a grin then headed to the desk after spotting a whiskey bottle. He poured himself a generous shot, tossed it back, then poured another. "Good whiskey. Why on earth would anyone want to ban something this delicious?" He pointed the bottle in Milo's direction.

"I'm sure they had their reasons," Milo said, waving off Sleaze's offer. But he did light a cigarette, his mind racing. "Where were you locked up?" he said, frowning.

"A lovely little town not far from here," Sleaze said, remaining coy.

Milo's frown deepened as he tried to put some things together. Then a possibility emerged, and he stared across the coffee table at his former partner in crime.

"Watertown?"

"You're still sharp as a tack, Milo," Sleaze said with a grin.

"That's right," Milo said after a long pause. "First National got knocked off last month. That was you?"

"That's what the police seem to believe," Jimmy Sleaze said, his grin widening. "Unfortunately for them, they can't quite figure out how to prove it."

"How much did you get?" Milo said without emotion.

"Thirty thousand and change."

"Nice. And you don't have to split it," Milo said, nodding. "So, where are you headed next?"

"You know, Milo. After taking a good look around town, I thought I might just stay here for a while. It's a beautiful spot."

"I hate to tell you this, Jimmy, but there's only one bank in town. And with your ability, you'd be in and out before breakfast. You'd be bored here."

"Actually, I've been thinking about getting away from banks," he said.

"To do what?"

"Smuggling booze looks quite promising," Sleaze said. "And if done well, I imagine it's very profitable."

"You were in the cell next to Oscar Hyde, weren't you?" Milo said, stunned by his bad luck.

"Despicable man," he said, shaking his head. "But most chatty at times."

"And I assume you also met a man by the name of Melvin English?" Milo said.

"I did," Jimmy Sleaze said, nodding. "Actually, Melvin was kind enough to give me a ride yesterday."

"Then you know that the two of them are running booze from Canada," Milo said. "Neither one of them can keep their mouths shut."

"Yes, I did hear that," he said. "But it doesn't sound like their enterprise is going well."

Milo hid his smile when an idea emerged.

"From what I understand, they're a bit undercapitalized at the moment," Milo said. "You know how hard it is to get something off the ground without adequate funds."

"That's never really been a problem for me," Jimmy Sleaze said, shrugging.

"Because if you need money, you just steal it," Milo said as a simple statement of fact.

"It does come in handy," Sleaze said, grinning at Milo. "But I understand their problem. And it's made worse by the fact that one of the major players is currently in jail." The Sleaze rubbed his chin as he stared off deep in thought. "And Oscar's partner is a lawyer who seems to be dragging his feet when it comes to getting his colleague released. Either Mr. English is an incompetent fool, or he has a good reason for trying to keep that disgusting creature in jail. I haven't quite figured that one out yet."

"But you will," Milo said.

"Of course," he said with a small shrug. "So, what's your deal, Milo? You really expect me to believe you've gone straight?"

"Believe what you want, Jimmy," Milo said, giving him a cold stare. "But I finally figured out that life is a whole lot easier when you don't have to worry about being locked up in a cage or getting shot in the back."

"I see," Jimmy Sleaze said, studying Milo's expression closely. "Milk, huh?"

"Yes. And cheese."

"And cheese," he said, laughing. "Nice touch, Milo. You were always good with the details."

"What do you want, Jimmy?" Milo said, his patience beginning to fade.

"Did I hear Oscar correctly when he mentioned that our old friend Roland Doyle was working as a revenuer in town?"

"You did," Milo said, nodding.

"That's wonderful news. I can't wait to catch up with Mr. Doyle again," Jimmy Sleaze said. "We have some unfinished business that needs to be cleaned up." Then he drifted off for a moment before looking at Milo. "Have you heard from her?"

"No. Not a word since she left," Milo said, shaking his head. "Have you?"

"No. Just the letter," he said, again staring off. "It's probably better if I don't see her."

"For you, or for her?"

"Yeah, there is that," he said, grinning. "I'm not sure I'd be able to control myself if I did happen to run into her."

"You should probably move on and let it go, Jimmy."

"Yes, I'm sure you're right, Milo. Sage counsel, as always. Perhaps I'll take a trip to California after I deal with Roland Doyle."

"No," Milo said, his voice rising a notch. "Doyle's ancient history. Let it go, Jimmy."

"Oh, my. I just touched a nerve," Sleaze said, reaching for another of Milo's cigarettes and lighting it. He leaned back in his chair and studied Milo's expression closely. "Unless I'm missing something, which is highly unlikely, it sounds like you're happy that someone as incompetent as Doyle is assigned up here."

"It makes no difference to me who the Feds assign," Milo said, forcing himself to remain calm. "As far as I know, selling milk is still legal."

"For now," Jimmy Sleaze said, laughing. "I'm sure the government will eventually find something wrong with it." He exhaled smoke, watched it dissipate, then focused on Milo. "Is Doyle still drinking?"

"He is," Milo whispered.

"Even better," Jimmy Sleaze said with a grin. "I bet you could have a field day crossing back and forth across the border."

"For the second time, what do you want, Jimmy?" Milo said, then grimaced when his hangover made its presence known again. "Don't make me ask you a third."

"I just wanted to catch up with my old pal," he said.

"And?"

"And maybe get a name from you. Someone I can trust who might have some ideas about how to get into the bootlegging business," Jimmy Sleaze said.

"Well, if I were you, I'd talk to Melvin," Milo said, shrugging.

"I doubt very much if Mr. English is any sort of mastermind," Jimmy Sleaze said. "Despite his rather high opinion of himself, it's obvious that Melvin is a follower."

"I don't know what to tell you, Jimmy," Milo said. "Melvin's the only one I can think of who might be able to help you."

"There has to be someone else who's running things around here."

"Maybe Melvin will be able to tell you who else you can talk to," Milo said.

"But not you, right?"

"Jimmy, the only thing I can tell you about booze these days is what kind I like to drink," Milo said, crushing out his cigarette. "But if you want to talk cows, I can go all day."

"Can you now?" he said, laughing.

"Absolutely. For example, did you know that cows have to be milked twice a day?"

"Really?" Jimmy Sleaze said with a frown. "I did not know that."

"Yeah, it kinda caught me by surprise, too."

Episode 9

Casting A Wide Net

"I love prohibition. Nothing makes people want something more than telling them they shouldn't want it, can't have it, or don't do it. Just ask the kid with the burnt hand."

Milo Razner

The Best Laid Plans

Milo smiled as he glanced around the living room at the expectant looks he was receiving then lit a cigarette and took a sip of whiskey. Then he turned serious and started talking.

"Gentlemen, we have a problem. Potentially a very big problem."

"What's up, Milo?" Birdie said, glancing up briefly from the cigarette he was rolling with one hand.

"Jimmy Sleaze," Milo said, carefully enunciating both names.

The others in the room looked around at each other and shrugged or shook their heads.

"Is that name supposed to mean something to us, Milo?" Tom Collins said.

"Not at the moment," Milo said. "But it will soon."

"Who is he?" Frank Slack said.

"He used to be one of my business partners," Milo said.

"What business was that?" Tom said.

"Let's call it finance and leave it at that."

The others again glanced around at each other. This time they had grins on their faces.

"Okay, Milo," Tom said, nodding. "I think we get it. What's he doing in town?"

"He's thinking about getting into the booze business," Milo said, making eye contact with each of them individually to reinforce his point.

"And you want us to help you come up with a way to stop him from doing that, right?" Birdie said, lighting a match with a flick of his thumbnail.

"Not at all, Birdie," Milo said. "In fact, we're going to do just the opposite. We're going to give him all the help he needs."

"As usual, Milo, you lost me," Birdie said, blowing smoke up at the ceiling.

"You'll understand soon. Jimmy Sleaze is a dangerous man, Birdie," Milo said. "And he is also smart. Some might say, he's too smart for his own good."

"As smart as you, Milo?" Tom said, raising an eyebrow.

"No, fortunately, he's not," Milo said with a grin. "But he's close enough to worry about. The real problem with Jimmy is that he's like a dog on a bone when he gets his sights set on something he wants. So, we're going to help him get set up in business."

"And then set him up, right, Milo?" Birdie said.

"There you go. I told you you'd catch on," Milo said, raising his glass in salute. "That's what we're going to do. And I have a pretty good idea about how we're going to do it."

"You gonna tell us?" Birdie said.

"Eventually," Milo said. "But it's part of something bigger I'm working on that I'm not ready to discuss yet. I'll tell you as soon as I can."

"Wouldn't it be easier to just shoot the guy?" Birdie said. "Or toss him in the River?"

"Normally, I'd agree with you, Birdie," Milo said. "And that was my first thought. But when I realized just how helpful The Sleaze could be to us, I decided to go the other way."

"I don't know, Milo," Birdie said. "I'm not getting a good feeling about this."

"You will," Milo said. "The Sleaze also has a history with Roland Doyle. Bad history."

"The plot thickens," Tom said, shaking his head. "And you're worried that this Sleaze guy might do something stupid like take Doyle out?"

"Since getting rid of Roland could ruin everything, I was at first."

"Yeah, we might end up with a revenuer who actually had a clue about how to do his job," Birdie said, laughing.

Everyone laughed along, and Milo waited until he again had their undivided attention.

"We need to do everything in our power to make sure Mr. Doyle stays safe and sound."

"By helping Sleaze get into the business and telling him how incompetent Doyle is?" Frank said.

"Jimmy already knows he's an idiot," Milo said. "And it won't take him long to figure out that Roland has the potential to be a *useful idiot* who couldn't catch a bootlegger if he fell over him in the boat."

"You really want the guy sniffing around, Milo?" Tom said. "It sounds like he could make a lot of trouble for us."

"Oh, he could. There's no doubt about that. But the trick to handling The Sleaze is to keep his mind occupied," Milo said. "And as soon as he gets his own operation off the ground and starts making some money, he's going to spend all his time focused on growing the business and making even more."

"And the more he's focused on his stuff, the less time he has to start sticking his nose into ours," Frank said. "I like it, Milo. Just how dangerous is this guy?"

"I once watched him pull a guy's fingernails out one at a time with a pair of pliers."

"Was he trying to get the guy to talk?" Birdie said.

"No, Jimmy was just bored," Milo said, shaking his head.

"He sounds like a psychopath," Frank said.

"Calling him that gives psychopaths a bad name," Milo said.

"Okay, you officially have my attention," Frank said, taking a sip of whiskey.

"I'd be disappointed if I didn't, Frank. So, for now, we're going to focus on helping my dear friend, The Sleaze, get started in the business we all love so much."

Milo raised his glass in toast, and the others followed suit.

"To The Sleaze," Milo said.

"To The Sleaze," the others called out.

They drank, then Milo got up from his chair and began pacing the room.

"Okay, here's what we're going to do. Jimmy has been in jail the past several weeks in Watertown," Milo said.

"What did he get arrested for?" Frank Slack said.

"He's the one who knocked over First National," Milo said.

"Really?" Tom Collins said with a frown. "And they let him go?"

"The cops can't prove he did it," Milo said. "And they never will. Jimmy's very good at robbing banks."

"Which is something you know from first-hand experience, right?" Birdie said, laughing.

"Vicious and unfounded rumors, Birdie," Milo said, grinning at him. "He got caught once when he got a little too smart for his own good. But I'm sure he learned his lesson and will be extremely careful in the future. But he got thirty grand from the bank, so he's got lots of working capital."

"And we're going to help him spend some of it, right?" Birdie said.

"We are," Milo said. "Actually, Willy will be doing most of the work on that side."

"Me?" Willy said, staring at Milo.

"Oh, good," Milo said, laughing. "You are paying attention. I was starting to worry. You usually aren't this quiet, Willy."

"I'm just trying to process what you're saying, Milo," Willy Lawless said. "You want me to help this guy get started?"

"I thought it might be more fun if we added you into the mix via an introduction from one of our mutual friends," Milo said.

"Which one?" Willy said, frowning.

"Our soon-to-be mayor, of course," Milo said.

"You want to bring Melvin into this?" Frank said. "Geez, Milo. I was right with you up to that point."

"No, relax, Frank," Milo said. "We won't be telling Melvin anything about our operation. As far as Melvin is concerned, I'm just the milkman. But The Sleaze already knows that Melvin and Oscar are running booze."

"How the hell does he know that?" Willy said.

"He was in the cell next to Oscar's the whole time he was locked up," Milo said, shaking his head, still having a hard time believing it had happened.

"Wow, what are the odds of that?" Tom said. "And he overheard Oscar and Melvin talking?"

"He did," Milo said. "And I'm sure he heard a lot. Fortunately, neither one of them have a clue what we're doing, or they would have been blabbing about that as well. If and when we decide to let The Sleaze in on our little secret, it'll be my call. And my call alone. Got it?"

Milo paused and waited until he got nods from everyone in the room.

"I'm going to talk with Melvin about The Sleaze and let him know who he's dealing with. You know, a little friend to friend chat."

"To what end?" Tom said.

"To encourage Melvin to take on a new partner," Milo said, starting to pace the room again.

"Why would Melvin agree to do something like that?" Frank said.

"Money. What else?"

"What do you need from me, Milo?" Willy said.

"Just make yourself available when The Sleaze comes calling," Milo said. "Jimmy is going to want to personally meet everyone he could end up working with. You need to be helpful, but vague. Under no circumstances can you reveal the name of your supplier on the Canadian side. If Jimmy ever found that out, he'd cut you out of the loop faster than it takes to knock back a shot of Miracle."

"And then cut out Willy's heart?" Birdie said.

"At a minimum," Milo said. "As long as Jimmy starts getting all the booze he wants, we'll be fine. The Sleaze can actually be pretty entertaining when he's in a good mood. But don't ever try to get cute with him by lying about price or shorting him."

Milo stared at Willy a long time until he was sure his message was received.

"How do you want to handle Oscar?" Tom said.

"As long as he's still in jail, we don't have to worry about him," Frank said with a shrug.

"Oh, Oscar will be getting out soon," Milo said.

"He will?"

"Absolutely. He needs to get back to work."

"Running booze?" Tom said, frowning.

"No, as chief of police," Milo said with a huge grin.

"You're joking, right?" Frank said.

"I'd never joke about something like that, Frank," Milo said. "And Oscar is going to be an important part of our plans."

"If you say so, Milo," Birdie said, shaking his head. "Oscar back as police chief? I wouldn't have guessed that in a month."

"Me either," Tom said, then looked at Milo. "How does Melvin feel about that?"

"Oh, Melvin doesn't know yet," Milo said, topping off everyone's glass. "But I plan on telling him tomorrow."

"You want some company?" Tom said, laughing. "I'd love to see the look on his face."

"No, but I'll be happy to share the details," Milo said, grinning. "Okay, gentlemen, that's it for now. I'll be in touch soon."

Everyone finished their drinks, bundled up, then headed for the door.

"Hey, Willy," Milo said.

"Yeah?"

"Stick around for a few minutes," Milo said.

"Sure," Willy said, removing his coat and sitting back down. "What's up?"

"I just wanted to go over some things with you alone," Milo said, pouring fresh drinks then lighting a cigarette. "Who knows about your little side business with Green?"

"Just you, Milo. I figure it's nobody's business, right? I mean, except for you."

"Good. But maybe it's time to start thinking about adding a couple of partners."

"You're not talking about Sleaze, are you?"

"No, absolutely not," Milo said. "At least, not directly."

"Some extra help would be good. It's not so little anymore," Willy said, adding ice to his whiskey. "Green's talking about going to two hundred cases a week."

"You're still at a hundred, right?"

"Yeah. And given the winter, I told Green that I couldn't get to two hundred. I agreed to go to a hundred and fifty for now and then bump it up in the spring."

"You got enough inventory to last you through the winter?" Milo said, stifling a yawn.

"I should. I've been stocking up. Unless we get a really bad one," Willy said. "As long as the ice is out by early March, I'll be fine. Why do you ask?"

"Well, The Sleaze has arrived at a bad time to get his hands on any product," Milo said. "Once that ice sets in, only an idiot would try to get back and forth across the River."

"You mean, apart from an idiot like you, right?" Willy said, laughing.

"Yeah, there is that," Milo said, laughing along. "But I need to buy some time and also keep The Sleaze busy while I'm doing it. Are you still using the same guy as Oscar for your buys?"

"Occasionally," Willy said, taking a sip. "But he could never get past fifty cases a week, and when Oscar got locked up for the second time, he started to get really nervous. Now, I only use him when my regular guy is running a bit short. And both of them are going to be shutting down soon for the winter."

"Yeah, that's a problem," Milo said. "If Jimmy can't start making some real money until the spring, he's gonna have way too much idle time on his hands."

"I still think it would just be easier to toss the guy in the River," Willy said, lighting a cigarette.

"Yeah, it would," Milo said. "But The Sleaze is going to help me solve a couple of big problems."

"But he doesn't know that, right?"

"I knew you were a sharp guy as soon as I met you, Willy," Milo said raising his glass in salute. "Now, how the hell am I gonna do this?" Milo crushed out his cigarette and sat quietly for a few minutes. When an idea popped, he looked at Willy. "Can I ask you what you're paying for a case?"

"I get it for thirty bucks a case from both guys," Willy said. "Melvin told me he pays forty for it. He thinks he's so clever."

"You're okay with that?" Milo said.

"Yeah, it's only five cases at a time. It's not enough money to worry about," Willy said, then laughed. "And Melvin thinks I'm selling it for sixty."

"But you're getting seventy-five, right?" Milo said with a grin.

"Yeah, I am," Willy said, his eyes dancing. "Are you sure you don't want in on it, Milo? I feel bad about you not making anything off my deal. Especially since you were the one who helped me get started."

"I'm sure you'll learn to live with it, Willy," Milo said, then shook his head. "No, I don't want any part of it. I just want you to keep Ben Green happy and supplied with top-shelf product until I tell you to stop."

"Okay, Milo. Whatever you say. I'm sure you got your reasons. So, what can I do to help?"

"Swing by Frank's place the day after tomorrow around noon."

"That's it?"

"No, there's more, Willy. A whole lot more."

"I'm sure you'll explain everything when you're ready," Willy said, downing the last of his drink.

"You can count on it."

Melvin's Minor Meltdown

Milo fought a stiff wind as he made the short walk from the Crossley to Melvin's office. He stepped inside and found him in his office making notes in a journal. Apparently stuck for the moment, Melvin frowned as he chewed on the end of his pen then noticed Milo and waved him in.

"Hey, Milo. Glad you stopped by. I could use a little help with my acceptance speech."

Milo removed his coat and hat and tossed them on a table then sat down.

"Feeling confident, huh? That's what we like to see," Milo said, draping a leg over his knee.

"I think it's gonna happen, Milo," Melvin said, nodding his head vigorously. "Mayor English." He nodded some more. "It's got a nice ring to it."

"Music to my ears, Melvin," Milo said. "What are you stuck on?"

"I'm running out of ideas to add to the list of things I'm going to do as mayor," Melvin said.

He began reading the list, and Milo listened closely then held up his hand.

"What's the matter?" Melvin said. "It's a good list, right?"

"It's a great list, Melvin. But if I were to offer a suggestion, it would be for you to remember rule number two."

"Rule number two. Got it," Melvin said, starting to write it down.

"No, Melvin. I said to remember it, not write it down."

"Oh, okay," Melvin said, then stared at Milo. "Just one question."

"Sure. What is it?"

"What is rule number two?"

Milo took a couple of deep breaths then forced a small smile.

"You're gonna make a great mayor, Melvin."

"Thanks, Milo."

"Rule number two is to always under promise and over deliver. And not the other way around."

Melvin thought about it then nodded again.

"Oh, that's good, Milo. I should probably write that down."

"I'm sure it couldn't hurt," Milo said, reaching for his cigarettes.

"By the way, what's rule number one?"

"Don't scratch the boat," Milo said.

"Oh, yeah. That's right. Could I bum one of those?" Melvin said, eyeing the pack.

Milo held the pack out then lit both cigarettes and settled back into his chair.

"I heard you gave somebody a ride to town yesterday," Milo said, staying casual.

"I did," Melvin said, scowling as he shook his head. "Horrible man. Scared the crap out of me. And I sure hope he doesn't decide to stick around for long." Melvin paused and stared across the desk. "How did you know I gave him a ride?"

Melvin took a long drag on his cigarette as he replayed the delicate conversation he was about to have.

"He told me," Milo said eventually with a casual shrug.

"Where did you run into him? Fannie's place?"

"No, he stopped by my suite at the Crossley."

"Why the hell did he do that?" Melvin said, confused.

"He stopped by to say hello."

"You know this guy?" Melvin said, his eyes widening.

"Unfortunately, yes, I do," Milo said, crushing out his cigarette. "I once sort of testified against him. In Philadelphia."

"You testified against that guy, and you're still walking around?" Melvin said.

"Well, it wasn't really formal testimony in court," he said. "It was more like a friendly chat with the cops."

"You're a brave man. I was worried he was going to cut my throat just for talking too much."

"I'm sure the thought crossed his mind," Milo said.

"What did he do?"

"He robbed a bunch of banks," Milo said.

"So, he was the one who knocked off First National?"

"I'm sure he was," Milo said.

"How the hell did you get mixed up with that guy, Milo?"

"It's complicated," Milo said. "I did some dumb things in my younger days."

"Tell me about it," Melvin said, shrugging. "I'm still doing stupid shit. What happened to him after you sold him out?"

"He got six years," Milo said.

"Ouch. So, he's come all the way up here to pay you back?" Melvin said.

"No, we came to an understanding before he went inside," Milo said. "I agreed to do a few favors for him while he was a guest of the Commonwealth."

"Such as?" Melvin said, dropping his elbows on the desk and leaning forward.

"I made a…personal visit to a guy who had some damaging information about Jimmy and was threatening to go public with it," Milo said.

"More damaging than six years?" Melvin said with a frown.

"Oh, yeah," Milo said. "If it had leaked out, Jimmy never would have seen the light of day again."

"You had to kill a guy for him?" Melvin said, sitting back in his chair.

"No, it was nothing like that, Melvin," Milo said, laughing. "I merely convinced him that an extended vacation overseas was his best option. I even paid for it."

"Really?" Melvin said, staring at Milo in disbelief. "Why would you do that?"

"It was a complicated situation. But that wasn't all of it."

"What else did you have to do?" Melvin said.

"I promised to take care of Jimmy's wife," Milo said, shrugging.

"His wife? A woman actually agreed to marry that guy?"

"Yeah. Not one of her smarter decisions."

"Is she still around?"

"No," Milo said. "She's not."

"You *took care* of her?"

"No, Melvin," Milo said, laughing again. "What kind of guy do you think I am? I looked after her for about a year, then she finally worked up the courage to write Jimmy a letter in prison. She said she couldn't wait around for him, but if he wanted to reconnect after he got out, she'd be in California."

"Did she go?"

"I imagine so," Milo said, holding the pack of smokes out. He took one for himself, lit both, and they smoked in silence for a few minutes.

"Do you think this guy Sleaze is gonna stick around awhile?" Melvin said.

"I'm sure of it," Milo said. "That's the reason I stopped by."

"Okay," Melvin said, giving Milo a confused frown.

"Jimmy Sleaze wants to get into the booze business," Milo said.

"Great," Melvin said, shaking his head. "You're full of good news today, Milo."

"And he asked me who he should talk to about getting started."

"But you don't know anything about running booze," Melvin said, still confused.

"That's what I told him," Milo said, relaxing a bit. "The Sleaze was just fishing around to see if I might know somebody who was."

"The Sleaze. I like that," Melvin said with a grin.

"Word of advice, don't ever call him that to his face," Milo said.

"Got it. So, what did you tell *The Sleaze*?" Melvin said, chuckling.

"Well, since he already knows that you and Oscar are smuggling booze-"

"That damn Oscar just can't keep his mouth shut," Melvin snapped.

"Yes, I'm very aware of that," Milo said. "And since The Sleaze wants to get into the business and is already aware of your involvement…I told Jimmy he should talk to you."

Milo sat back and waited. He didn't have to wait long. Melvin's eyes went wide, and he gave Milo an open-mouthed stare.

"Are you out of your goddamn mind?"

"Relax, Melvin," Milo said, heading for the cabinet where Melvin kept his whiskey. "Trust me, I don't want the guy sticking around either."

"You told him to talk to me?" Melvin said, his voice loud and whiny. "Jesus, Milo. I thought we were friends."

"We are, Melvin. That's why I told him to talk to you," Milo said as he poured the drinks. He handed one to Melvin who tossed it back. Milo refilled the glass then sat back down and took a sip of his. "Relax, everything is going to be fine."

"Start talking," Melvin said, glaring at Milo. "This I gotta hear."

"Okay, here's the deal," Milo said, leaning forward and placing his arms on the desk. "I know how this guy operates. And once he's made his mind up about something, you can forget about changing it. The Sleaze is going to get into the booze business whether you like it or not."

"Let him," Melvin said. "There's plenty to go around."

"Yes, I'm sure there is," Milo said. "And as soon as The Sleaze figures that out, he's gonna want it all."

"Keep talking, Milo," Melvin said, downing half of his drink. "I'm still half a step behind."

"And if his goal is to get it all, the only way he can do that is by eliminating all the competition."

Melvin scratched his stubble as he thought about it.

"Shit," Melvin said with a sad shake of his head.

"Exactly. So, since The Sleaze is undoubtedly going to start eliminating his competitors, don't you think it would be better, and a whole lot safer, for you to be working with him instead of trying to compete?"

"That still wouldn't keep him from turning me into fish food."

"No, you're probably right. But it will keep him from doing it for the time being."

"I'm not following, Milo," Melvin said, topping off his drink.

"He needs your help, Melvin. And as long as he does, The Sleaze would never do anything to hurt you. In fact, as long as he considers you a valuable member of his operation, he's going to do everything he can to protect you."

"I don't know, Milo. Maybe I should just get out of the business altogether."

"Now, there's a thought," Milo said, nodding. "I'm sure you'll be able to manage on what you make as a lawyer and the tiny salary you'll get for being mayor."

"Yeah, maybe," Melvin said, frowning. "I will be saving a lot of money at Fannie's."

"It is a nice perk," Milo said, nodding. "Much better than a car allowance."

"I can't wait to get a shot at Daisy," Melvin said. "I've never been able to afford her."

Milo made a mental note to move up Daisy's departure to the island before Melvin officially took office. It was the least he could do for her.

"But if you do decide to walk away from the business, how much money will you be leaving on the table?" Milo said, taking a sip of whiskey.

"Probably a lot," Melvin said, reaching for another cigarette. Then he paused and looked at Milo. "You don't mind, do you?"

"Not at all," Milo deadpanned. "You're actually helping me cut down."

"What to do? What to do?" Melvin said, scratching his stubble hard like a dog going after a flea.

"Perhaps there's an alternative, Melvin."

"Like what?"

"Maybe you could work with The Sleaze for a while," Milo said. "And as soon as you start to get uncomfortable-"

"Oh, I'm sure I'd be uncomfortable right from the jump."

"Yes, you're right. It pretty much goes with the territory when it comes to The Sleaze. Then let's say, as soon as you start to get concerned for your safety, you could get out. You know, make your money and take off."

"And go where?" Melvin said.

"I'd recommend someplace where he'd never find you."

"Yeah, thanks for the tip," Melvin said with a frown. "I don't know, Milo. I'd hate to have to deal with him on a regular basis."

"I wouldn't worry about having to do that, Melvin."

"I guess we're different that way, Milo," Melvin said, exhaling smoke.

"Just assign the task of dealing with The Sleaze to someone else," Milo said.

"Like who?"

"Oscar."

Melvin blinked several times then shook his head.

"If I did that, then I'd have two people to worry about. Not to mention the fact that I wouldn't have any control over Oscar."

"Of course, you would, Melvin," Milo said with a grin.

"How do you figure that?"

"Because as mayor, he'd be working for you."

"Doing what?"

"Police Chief, what else?"

Melvin took a long drag from his cigarette as he stared off into the distance then looked across the desk at Milo. A small grin eventually emerged.

"Sonofabitch. That's brilliant, Milo."

"Yes, I thought so too."

Miss Peppin's Problem

Milo parked in the alley behind the cheese shop and walked up the driveway. Inside, he spotted one of his milk trucks making their morning delivery and checked his watch. Right on schedule, he noted, pleased with the two new drivers Ruby had hired. Beulah Peppin was talking with one of her workers but cut her conversation short as soon as she spotted Milo. She approached with a confused smile on her face.

"What are you doing here?" she said, giving him a kiss on the cheek. "I didn't think you were coming down this week."

"Slight change of plans," Milo said. "We need to talk."

"Okay," she said, frowning. "Let's go to my office."

Milo followed her and waved to several people on the way. Inside the office, she closed the door behind them then gave Milo what he considered a more appropriate greeting. Eventually, she broke the kiss and sat down on the couch.

"Whew," Milo said. "How I've missed those kisses."

"Oh, I'm sure Miss Caffey is making you forget all about my kisses," Beulah said.

"As Mr. Green is making you forget about mine?" Milo said.

"Touché, Milo," she said, laughing. "But they're just temporary distractions, right?"

"Absolutely. Just part of the cost of doing business," Milo said, then turned serious. "We've got a problem, Beulah."

"We do?" she said. "But things are going so well. What's going on?"

"You'll never guess who dropped by my suite at the Crossley," Milo said.

"Another one of your admirers, I'm sure," she said. "Who was it?"

"Jimmy."

Beulah's face fell, and she lowered her head and stared down at the floor. Then she slowly got to her feet and began walking around the office in small circles. Milo sat quietly and waited until she composed herself.

"I can't believe it," she said, tearing up.

"Yeah, I was a little surprised myself," Milo said.

"How did he get out? He had another three years to go."

"He ratted somebody out, and they let him go as a thank you," Milo said.

"Who was it?" Beulah said.

"He wouldn't say. But my guess is that it was one of Balducci's gang," Milo said, helping himself to a piece of cheese.

"Maybe it was Balducci himself," she said.

"No, it couldn't have been the old man. That would have been all over the news," Milo said, reaching for another piece. "This is good cheese."

"Yes, it is," she said. "Remind me to give you some to take home." She sat back down on the couch and exhaled loudly. "Did he ask about me?"

"He did," Milo said, nodding. "I told him I haven't heard a word from you since you wrote him the letter."

"Did he buy it?" Beulah said.

"Yes, I'm sure he did."

"Then we'll be fine," she said. "I'll just keep a low profile until he leaves."

"That's the problem," Milo said. "Jimmy's talking about getting into the booze business."

"Sonofabitch," she snapped. "You didn't tell him about our thing, did you?"

"Really? You're really going to ask me that question?"

"I'm sorry, Milo," she said, placing a hand on his arm. "Then you'll just have to stop him. Take him out on the boat and throw him in the River. Jimmy's not a swimmer."

"You know, I'd completely forgotten about that," Milo said, nodding. "That could come in handy."

"You've still got time before the ice sets in," Beulah said, squeezing his hand. "Take him out for an early-winter tour of the islands. Problem solved."

"Normally, I would agree with you," Milo said. "But I have bigger plans for The Sleaze."

"Such as?" Beulah said, cocking her head at him.

"I'll tell you as soon as the time is right."

"And when's that going to be?"

"When the time is right."

"Milo, don't try to get too cute with Jimmy," she said, her voice rising. "You know better than that."

"I do," Milo said. "But I need The Sleaze's skill set for something I'm working on."

"Please don't tell me you're planning on robbing a bank."

"Absolutely not. I'm talking about Jimmy's skills in the areas of duplicity and greed."

"He certainly is a master at those," Beulah said. "How are you going to use them?"

"By very carefully threading a couple of needles," Milo said. "Don't worry, Beulah. If I'm able to pull this off, it'll be a story will be telling our kids for years."

"And if you don't?"

"If I don't, we won't have to worry about kids," Milo whispered.

"Oh, that makes me feel so much better," Beulah said, managing a small laugh. "Do you think he bought the story about you just being a dairy farmer?"

"I doubt it," Milo said, shaking his head. "But try not to worry too much. I've hooked him up with Melvin English.

Between him and Oscar, The Sleaze is going to have his hands full until he gets up to speed."

"Oscar? Isn't he still in jail?"

"We're going to get him out so he can get back to work," Milo said with an evil grin.

"Back to work? Doing what?"

"The chief of police."

Beulah stared at him with a cocked head and bemused expression.

"What are you up to, Milo?"

"You'll see."

Jimmy Sleaze stepped inside the office and glanced around. Seeing no one in sight, he walked down a short hallway and peered into an office. Melvin English seemed to bounce in his chair when he saw him.

"Oh, Mr. Sleaze," Melvin said. "You startled me."

"And I wasn't even trying," Jimmy Sleaze said, sitting down without waiting to be asked.

"How can I help you?" Melvin said. "Don't tell me you need legal representation already."

Jimmy didn't find the joke funny, and he gave Melvin a cold stare.

"Actually, Milo Razner suggested that I speak with you."

"Really? About what?"

"About you helping me get started in the booze business," Sleaze said, watching Melvin's reaction closely.

"I see," Melvin said. "I wish he hadn't done that, but I'm sure Milo had his reasons. It's certainly no secret that I dabble in that venture from time to time."

"At first, I thought Milo might be the guy I should be talking to," Sleaze said.

"Milo?" Melvin said, laughing. "No, I'm afraid not. While Milo is very good at drinking it, he knows nothing about how to smuggle it."

"I see," Sleaze said, still studying Melvin's face. "But you do, right?"

"Yes, I do."

"And you're going to be mayor soon," he said, nodding. "I assume that the chief of police will be reporting to you?"

"You assume correctly," Melvin said.

"That should come in very handy," Sleaze said. "For both of us."

"Both? I beg your pardon."

"I thought you might be interested in expanding your operation," Sleaze said, glancing around the office. "From the looks of things, it appears that you could use some help."

"Oh, I'm just a man who likes to live modestly," Melvin said with a nervous chuckle. "You know what they say, don't flaunt your good fortune in the face of others."

"The only people I've ever heard say that are the ones who don't have any money," Jimmy Sleaze said, again giving Melvin a cold stare.

"Yes, of course," Melvin said, tittering again. Then he exhaled and leaned forward. "What sort of role would you be expecting to play, Mr. Sleaze? Assuming that I might be interested in using your services."

"*Role*?" Jimmy Sleaze said, grinning. "Sure, why don't we talk about my role?"

Melvin chewed his bottom lip like it was a piece of gum and fought a nervous tic in his eye.

"How many cases are you running a week?" The Sleaze said, lighting a cigar.

"Would you mind if I had one of those?" Melvin said, sniffing in the air.

He tossed a cigar to Melvin who fumbled it, and it rolled across the desktop onto the floor. In his attempt to grab it, Melvin's forehead bounced off the edge of the desk. He retrieved the cigar, got it lit with shaking hands, then sat back in his chair smoking as he massaged the bruise.

"Are you okay?" The Sleaze said, laughing.

"Yeah, I'm fine," Melvin said, blowing smoke up at the ceiling as he continued to rub his forehead. "What was your question again?"

"How many cases are you running a week?"

"Oh, right," Melvin said, blowing several smoke rings in succession. "Five."

"Hundred or thousand?" The Sleaze said, perking up.

"No, five," Melvin said with a shrug.

"Five? You're kidding, right?"

"Actually, for the moment, it's none. Given Oscar's situation, we've been forced into what you might call a temporary holding pattern."

"Five cases? Jesus, Melvin, that's not worth walking across the street for. How much do you make on a case?"

"Twenty bucks."

"A hundred a week?" Sleaze said. "And you have to split it? Man, you need to lift your game."

"I beg your pardon?" Melvin said, annoyed. Then he remembered who he was talking to and smiled across the desk. "Yes, lift my game. I'm sure you're right."

"Who's your supplier on the Canadian side?" Sleaze said, casually.

"Oh, I don't know," Melvin said, shaking his head. "Oscar handles that side of the partnership."

"Don't start lying to me, Melvin," Jimmy Sleaze said with a dark stare. "If you do, it's gonna be a short partnership."

"No, honest, Mr. Sleaze," Melvin said, fighting back the urge to pee. "Oscar handles that side of things. I take care of the sale on this side of the border."

"So, you haven't been selling the five cases since Oscar got locked up?"

"No, I'm afraid not," Melvin said. "And our buyer isn't very happy about it."

"Who's your buyer? I'd like to meet him."

"Well, I suppose that could be arranged," Melvin whispered after a long pause.

"What are your buy-sell prices?" Sleaze said.

"Oscar gets it for…forty a case. I sell it for sixty," Melvin said.

"And you're happy with that?" Sleaze said, frowning. "The margins should be better, shouldn't they?"

"No, I'm quite comfortable with them."

"Okay, if you say so. I guess I can live with that. For now," Sleaze said, still frowning.

"Uh, what sort of percentage would you be looking at, Mr. Sleaze?" Melvin said.

"Half."

"Half?" Melvin said.

"Well, if I'm going to invest twenty-five grand of my hard-earned money in something, it has to be worth my while, right?"

"I'm sorry. Did you say twenty-five thousand?" Melvin said, leaning forward in his chair.

"It's nice to see I've finally got your attention, Melvin.

"Oh, I've been listening. You don't have to worry about that, Mr. Sleaze. That's a lot of money."

"It's a start," Jimmy Sleaze said. "Where would I find your buyer?"

"I'll get something set up for you," Melvin said.

"When?"

"Very soon."

"Good," Jimmy Sleaze said, extending his hand across the desk. "This is gonna be fun."

"Yes, I'm sure it will be quite the adventure," Melvin said, returning the handshake.

"I was wondering if you could help me out with something else," Sleaze said.

"There's more?" Melvin said, raising an eyebrow.

"I need to find a place to live," Sleaze said. "I've never been a big fan of hotels. And I like my privacy."

"Normally, I'd say yes, Mr. Sleaze," Melvin said. "I do also dabble in real estate, but I'm afraid I'm out of inventory at the moment."

"That's too bad," he said. "I was hoping you might have something."

"I'm truly sorry," Melvin said, then beamed. "Hang on. Actually, I do have a vacant house to rent. And it would perfect for you."

"That's great," Sleaze said, nodding. "You wouldn't have time to show it to me now, would you?"

"Yes, I believe I do," Melvin said, getting up from his chair. "Let me grab my coat."

“What’s the place like?”

“Oh, it’s quite nice,” Melvin said, bundling up. “But I imagine you’ll need to air it out for a couple of days.”

“Were there animals in the house?”

Melvin thought about the question for a few moments then shrugged as he opened the office door.

“In a fashion, yes.”

On The Rocks

Milo returned from Watertown just after noon and drove straight to Frank Slack's marina. He parked in front then walked down the long dock with his head down, shivering from the tunnel of frigid air whipping through the structure that was open on both ends. He found everyone waiting for him in Frank's office drinking coffee and eating sandwiches.

"Sorry, I'm late," Milo said, helping himself to a sandwich. "Beulah says hi."

"How's she doing?" Birdie said.

"I think she's had better days," Milo said, taking a big bite. "But she'll be fine." Then he reached into his pocket and removed a wrapped package. "I almost forgot. She gave me a sample of one of her new cheeses."

"Great. I love her stuff," Willy said, opening the package and taking several pieces. "I usually stop by when I'm…in Watertown." He gave Milo a sheepish grin.

"What did you need to talk about, Milo?" Frank said.

"I was thinking the other night that what we really need in town is a new school," Milo said, beaming and glancing back and forth at them.

"A new school?" Frank said, bewildered by Milo's statement.

"Yes, the kids deserve something better than the current one," Milo said.

"And you're gonna build it?" Birdie said.

"Well, it's not like I'm going to build it with my own hands," Milo said. "But, yeah, that's my plan."

"Shouldn't you be talking to the principal and the school board?" Frank said, frowning.

"Oh, I will. In due time," Milo said. "But first, I needed to speak with you."

"This oughta be good," Birdie said with a cackle.

"Oh, it's good," Milo said, grinning. "Gentlemen, I believe I've solved the problem of providing product to The Sleaze during the winter months."

"By building a school?" Willy said.

"Yes. But not just any school. A stone school. I'm thinking granite. *Canadian* granite."

Small grins appeared on all their faces.

"What are you up to, Milo?" Frank said.

"Well, since we have a very limited window of time before the ice arrives, I thought we might want to, let's say, stock up for the winter. And the best way to do that would be to use your barge to make one big delivery before Old Man Winter finally arrives and decides to stick around."

"And then start bringing in Canadian granite to build the school, right?" Frank said.

"Very good," Milo said, nodding at him. "You're on your game today, Frank."

"What can I tell you, Milo? You do keep me on my toes," he said, laughing. "Of course, during the construction of the school, we'd occasionally be using the barge to bring in another Canadian product of the liquid variety?"

"Yes, I imagine you might be doing that," Milo said.

"When did you decide to get into bottled product, Milo?" Birdie said.

"Oh, I won't be involved in this," Milo said, waving it off. "Apart from making sure the school gets built. No, this deal will be between the three of you. And how you decide to handle it is your call. Willy, the floor is all yours."

Birdie and Frank looked at Milo, then stared at Willy and waited for him to speak.

"Uh, I've been doing a thing on the side running top-shelf product," Willy said. "But it's grown to the point where I could use some help."

"Okay," Frank said, confused. "Sure, you can use my barge all you want." He glanced back at Milo. "But what was all that about a big delivery before the ice arrives?"

"That's the problem with The Sleaze I was talking about," Milo said. "How long do you figure we'll need to keep the boat out of the water because of the ice?"

"I usually plan on four months," Frank said with a shrug. "Give or take a couple of weeks on either end of the season."

"Sixteen weeks. Fifty a week," Milo said, staring off for a few seconds. "Eight hundred." He glanced at Frank. "Your barge could handle eight hundred cases, right?"

"Easily," Frank said. "But where are you gonna keep eight hundred cases of booze, Milo?"

"You got any room at your storage place?" Milo said, glancing at Willy.

"No, mine's full," Willy said. "Like I told you, I've been stocking up for the winter."

"Maybe you could store them here," Milo said, glancing around.

Frank thought about it, then nodded.

"Yeah, I suppose that would work," he said. "I've got a couple areas I usually close up in the winter."

"Perfect," Milo said.

"There's only one problem, Milo," Willy said.

"What's that?"

"You're talking about twenty-four grand," Willy said. "I'm doing good, but a lot of my money is tied up in inventory, and I just bought an island. My cash is low at the moment."

"I'll lend it to you," Milo said, now on a roll. "Swing by the Crossley tonight. I'll leave it at the front desk for you. It won't take you long to pay me back."

"And you want us to sell it to The Sleaze?" Birdie said.

"No, I want you to sell it to Melvin," Milo said. "If you start selling directly to The Sleaze, Melvin could find himself in some serious trouble."

"You want us to walk up to Melvin and ask him if he wants to buy eight hundred cases of booze?" Frank said.

"Absolutely not. You're going to sell Melvin fifty cases a week for the next four months without him knowing who he's buying it from," Milo said.

"And I assume you're going to explain how we're going to pull that off?" Frank said.

"Of course," Milo said, his eyes dancing. "This is going to be so much fun."

"Fun?" Willy said.

"What's the point of going into business if you can't have some fun doing it. Right, Birdie?"

"Absolutely," Birdie said, nodding.

"I don't know if my suppliers can handle that sort of volume this late in the season," Willy said.

"There's only one way to find out," Milo said.

"Yeah, I'll ask them," Willy said.

Milo stared at him until Willy made eye contact.

"What is it, Milo?"

"What are you waiting for?"

"You want me to go now?" Willy said, frowning.

"Can you think of a better time?"

"No, I guess I can't," Willy said, shrugging.

"Take my boat," Milo said, then glanced at Birdie. "But you need to stay with the boat while Willy handles business. The last thing we want is anybody seeing you making a booze buy."

"Got it, Milo," Birdie said, nodding for Willy to follow him as he limped off.

"And don't scratch the boat."

Melvin parked on the street since the driveway hadn't been shoveled and he and Jimmy Sleaze trudged their way through half a foot of snow that seemed determined to stick around. Sleaze paused halfway up the driveway and lifted his foot and tried to shake the snow off it. Eventually, he placed a hand on Melvin's shoulder for support then removed the shoe and dumped the snow out of it.

"This is a lot of snow," Sleaze said. "You always get this much?"

"I take it you've never spent a winter in the North Country," Melvin said, chuckling.

"No, what's so funny?"

"You'll see," Melvin said, heading for the snow-covered sidewalk that led to the house.

Melvin climbed the steps and stamped his feet on the small wooden porch then unlocked the door and waved Jimmy Sleaze in. He glanced around the living room, and after they had toured the house, they found themselves right back where they had started. Sleaze sat down a couch and bounced up and down a few times to test it out. He took another look around the room then nodded at Melvin.

"This will work," Sleaze said.

"Great. I'm glad you like it," Melvin said.

"I wouldn't go that far," Sleaze said, glaring at Melvin. "How much is the rent?"

"I could probably let you have it for twenty-five bucks a month," Melvin said, then caught the look Sleaze was giving him. "But I'm feeling generous today. Let's say twenty a month."

Jimmy Sleaze dropped his glare long enough to reach into his pocket. He counted out twelve twenties and handed them to Melvin.

"That's for the first year," Sleaze said, getting up off the couch.

"You are planning on sticking around awhile," Milo whispered.

"What?"

"Oh, I said I'm glad you're sticking around awhile," Melvin said, forcing a smile.

"If you are, you'd be the first," Sleaze said, then scowled. "Who used to live here? The place smells like a barn."

"Oscar Hyde," Melvin said, unable to contain his grin.

"This is his house?" Sleaze said, laughing for the first time since Melvin had met him. "He's not gonna like that."

"Probably not," Melvin said, pocketing the twenties. "But life goes on, right?"

"If you get lucky."

Milo made the drive back to Watertown and headed straight for the Woodruff. The hotel sat in the center of town and right behind it was the train station. He parked in front and checked in then headed upstairs to his room. Exhausted, he stretched out on the bed and dozed off until he was woken by a knock on the door. Milo opened the door and grinned.

"I was just dreaming about you," he said, pulling her inside and closing the door behind them.

"Yeah, I bet," Annabelle said, giving him a long, hard kiss. "Did you bring a bottle?"

"I brought two," Milo said.

"Then why don't you grab one, and we'll take a hot bath while we catch up," she said, heading for the bathroom.

Ten minutes later, they were in the tub with Annabelle's back pressed up against Milo's chest. They clinked glasses and sipped. Milo closed his eyes, completely at peace for the first time since The Sleaze had shown up.

"You sure you want to help this guy get started running booze?" Annabelle said.

"It's more out of necessity," Milo said, setting his glass on the side of the tub. "Don't worry, he won't be around long."

"Let me guess, you're going to make him an offer he can't refuse," she said.

"No, I'm gonna kill the sonofabitch," Milo said with a shrug. "But I need him to take care of a few things for me first."

"Like what?"

"Let's not ruin the moment by talking about The Sleaze," Milo said, running the back of his hand across her neck. "What time does our train leave in the morning?"

"Eight-fifteen," she said, snuggling closer. "Are you sure we'll be back Sunday night? I have school on Monday."

"Yeah, we got plenty of time," Milo said, stifling a yawn. "What did Mr. Adams say when you told him you were coming to town?"

"Vernon was pleasantly surprised," Annabelle said. "The bastard. I can't believe he's putting another agent up here without telling me."

"I'm sure you'll get it out of him," Milo said, gently scratching the side of her breasts.

"I just can't figure out what he's up to," she said. "Don't stop."

"The thought never crossed my mind," Milo said, closing his eyes.

"Are you meeting Senator Miller at his office?"

"I am," Milo said. "What time is it?"

"It's a little after six," Annabelle said. "When's dinner?"

"Eight. I'm going to meet them across the street at some Italian joint," Milo said. "Well, since it's already after six, we should get started."

"What?" Annabelle said, glancing at him over her shoulder.

"Take me to bed, Miss Caffey."

Milo studied the menu, decided on ravioli then slid it to one side. He took a sip of wine, then examined the label on the bottle and nodded.

"This is good," he said, taking another sip before glancing around the restaurant. "How do they get away with serving wine?"

"I believe they have an understanding with the local authorities," Ben Green said without looking up from his menu.

"Pretty brazen," Milo said, shrugging. "They paying off the cops?"

"I think they eat for free," Ben Green said, closing the menu. Then he used his head to point out various customers. "That's the chief of police over there in the corner. At that table, are two judges. And that's the local congressman with them."

"They're having a pretty intense conversation," Beulah said. "I wonder what they're talking about."

"Undoubtedly something stupid," Ben Green said, swirling his wine.

"Let's hope they're not talking about something *really* stupid," Milo said, grinning.

"Like repealing prohibition?" Beulah said, laughing.

"Exactly," Milo said. Then he focused on Ben Green. "Are you getting enough product from me?"

"Yes, we're good at the moment," he said. "But I will definitely be increasing the size of my order at some point during the winter."

"Yeah, winter can be a tough time to get booze across the border," Milo said. "That's why I've been building my inventory of Red Deer all fall."

"Are you going to have enough?" Ben Green said, studying Milo's reaction.

"Plenty," Milo said, nodding.

"I still can't believe you get all that product shipped from the Canadian prairies," he said, his tone a mix of disdain and disbelief. "Your transportation costs must be enormous."

"Don't worry about it," Milo said, remembering just how much he disliked the man.

"I won't," Ben Green said with a shrug. "I don't give a shit where you get it. My only concern is that it keeps coming."

"Oh, it's gonna keep coming," Milo said, sipping his wine.

"But I must say that you're a man of your word, Razner. I haven't seen a drop of Red Deer anywhere except my speakeasies."

"And you won't," Milo said. "You're moving a ton of product for us, and there's no need for me to sell to anybody else. You must also be doing great with top-shelf stuff."

“I can’t keep enough of either one of them around,” Ben Green said.

“Thirsty populace,” Milo said, lighting a cigarette.

“Indeed,” Ben Green said. “I just wish we didn’t have to deal with these damn winters.”

“You having any problems getting top-shelf product?”

“An emerging one,” Ben Green said. “And I hate leaving money on the table.”

“How short are you? Maybe I can make it up in Red Deer,” Milo said, leaning forward.

“It may come to that,” he said. “I could use another fifty cases a week.”

“Ouch,” Milo said. “You are leaving money on the table. Just let me know.”

“I’ll do that,” Ben Green said, getting up from the table. “Now, if you’ll excuse me for a moment, I need to hit the john.” He leaned over and gave Beulah a kiss on the cheek. “If our waiter ever shows up, order me the lasagna.”

Milo watched him walk away then reached into his pocket and slid an envelope across the table to Beulah.

“What’s this?” she said, frowning. “You already gave me my cut for the month.”

“It’s traveling money,” Milo said.

“Traveling?” Beulah said, staring across the table. “What’s going on, Milo?”

"Okay, here's the deal," he said. "But put the envelope in your purse before he gets back. I've figured out a way to handle Jimmy, but you're going to need to leave town for a while."

"How long?"

"Two or three months," Milo said, glancing at the men's room door.

"What?"

"There's a couple grand in that envelope. Take a nice vacation to someplace warm. Just tell Green that your mama or somebody in the family is sick and get out of town as quick as you can."

"You're scaring me, Milo," she said.

"You're going to be fine, Beulah. Just do what I ask."

"You're worried Jimmy is going to find me?" she said.

"If you stick around here, I have no doubt about it," Milo said.

"Why?"

"Because Jimmy is about to start selling booze to Green," Milo said.

"He is? That was fast," she said, cocking her head at him.

"Yeah, thanks. Sometimes, I even surprise myself."

"How much booze are you talking about?"

"Fifty cases a week," Milo said, grinning.

With Birdie behind the wheel, they headed out of Frank's marina for the Lake of the Isles. It was dark and snowing, and a stiff breeze was blowing out of the north. In short, it was a shitty night to be out on the River as far as Willy and Frank were concerned.

"Beautiful night for a boat ride, huh?" Birdie said, rolling a cigarette with one hand.

"What are you, part polar bear?" Willy said, above the sound of the engine.

"On my mama's side," Birdie said, then cackled. "Are you sure your guy over there is right about the ice?"

"He swears it's only skim ice," Willy said. "But he did say that this is definitely his last run of the year. He's heading to Florida tomorrow."

"Smart man," Frank said, hugging himself for warmth. "I've never seen eight hundred cases of booze before."

"He's been unloading all day," Willy said. "I told him there was an extra grand in it if he got done today."

"And it's all going to be stacked on shore?" Frank said.

"Yeah, he said we'll be able to pull right in and start loading," Willy said.

"We're gonna be here all night," Frank said.

"It won't be too bad," Willy said. "I just wish it was a little warmer. I'm freezing my ass off."

"Stop whining and just enjoy the ride," Birdie said, glancing back. "Did Milo take care of the note?"

"Yeah, he said he was going to drop it in the mail when he got to Watertown," Willy said. "He wants Melvin scratching his head about who the hell in Watertown is selling him booze."

"Smart," Frank said, nodding.

"It's more than smart," Willy said. "Milo's a frigging genius."

"Attention to detail," Birdie said.

"I never could have come up with this in a thousand years," Willy said. "But it's a good one."

Deciding he should spend the day campaigning, Melvin got up early and headed to the diner to eat breakfast. He lingered after he ate and drank four cups of coffee while greeting and chatting with a couple dozen potential voters. Then he walked the street for a couple of hours looking for other locals who might be out and about. But since the temperature was low and dropping, the streets were pretty much empty except for some kids playing in the snow. Since they weren't of voting age, Melvin turned around and headed to the post office to get his mail.

"Good morning, Sally," he said to the woman working the counter.

"Hey, Melvin. Are you all set for Tuesday?"

"I am indeed," Melvin said. "Can I ask who you're going to be voting for?"

"You got the twenty bucks you owe me?" she said, staring at him.

"As a matter of fact, I do," Melvin said as he retrieved one of the twenties The Sleaze had given him and slid it across the counter.

"You now officially have my vote," she said, stuffing the twenty into her pocket. "Let me get your mail."

Melvin waited for her to return with a small stack, and he casually flipped through it. One of the envelopes caught his eye, and he made the short walk to his office and sat down at his desk. He opened the envelope and read the typewritten note. He blinked several times, got up to pour himself a drink, then sat back down and read it again. Nonplussed, he eventually picked up the phone and waited.

"Hello, Melvin."

"Hi, Violet. Could you please connect me with Oscar's place?"

"When did he get out?"

"Oh, he's still in," Melvin said. "But someone is staying there at the moment."

"Okay," she said, confused.

Moments later, Jimmy Sleaze answered.

"What?"

"Hi, Mr. Sleaze," Melvin said. "It's Melvin."

"What do you want?"

"I was wondering if you could stop by my office," Melvin said.

"For what?"

"I have something to show you."

"Can't you just tell me over the phone? I was about to have an early lunch."

"No, you should see this. In fact, you're gonna *want* to see it."

The Sleaze hung up without answering, and Melvin shook his head as he continued to hold the receiver in his hand.

"What a prick," Melvin said.

"Yes, he was very rude."

"Violet?"

"Yes, Melvin?"

"I really wish you'd stop doing that."

"I don't know why Melvin," Violet said. "Since you're about to become mayor, I would have thought you'd find me to be very useful."

Melvin thought about it then shrugged and decided she was probably right.

"Good point," he said. "Forget I even mentioned it."

Milo stared up at the ceiling of the sleeping car and felt the rumble of the train as it headed south.

"I've never done it on a train before," Milo said, fully enjoying the ride Annabelle was taking.

"It's good, isn't it?" she said, glancing down at him without slowing.

"Most pleasurable," Milo said. "We should take the train more often. Maybe we'll take a trip through Canada at some point in the future. Or maybe down the coast."

"Focus, Milo," she said, as a drop of sweat dripped onto his chest.

"You need a break?"

"Don't you dare move."

"Whatever you say, Miss Caffey."

Jimmy Sleaze read the note a second time then lit a cigarette and sat back in his chair deep in thought.

"Mind if I bum one of those?" Melvin said, eyeing the pack of smokes.

"Go ahead," Sleaze said, glaring at him. "It wouldn't kill you to buy a pack of your own once in a while."

"Yeah, probably not," Melvin said, lighting one for himself.

"You say this just came in the mail?"

"Yeah. Watertown postmark," Melvin said, topping off their glasses.

"Feels like a setup," Sleaze said.

"At the risk of personal injury, I'm going to have to disagree with you."

"Why's that?" Sleaze said, glaring at Melvin.

"I think it's just someone who knows I'm in the business and understands how hard it is to get product in the winter,"

Melvin said. "Perhaps, it's someone who wants to curry favor with the new mayor."

"Nah, it doesn't seem plausible," Sleaze said, swirling the whiskey in his glass. "I don't like it."

"Fifty cases a week for four months, Mr. Sleaze," Melvin said. "That's a lot of booze."

"Do you think the guy you're selling to would want another fifty cases?"

"Can't hurt to ask, right?"

"I suppose. But what's this anonymous shit?" Sleaze said. "I don't like doing business with people I don't know."

"Me either," Melvin said. "But I'm willing to make an exception for this. The money is simply too good to pass up."

Jimmy Sleaze picked the note up again and reread it.

"They're gonna mail us the location of where the booze is every week?"

"Yes, and I imagine they'll be using a different spot every week," Melvin said.

"That's actually pretty smart on their part," Sleaze said. "And we're just supposed to leave the money after we pick up the fifty cases. That means they'll be watching us the whole time. I don't know. It makes me nervous."

"Thirty bucks a case is a great price, Mr. Sleaze. We'll be doubling our money." Melvin caught the look Sleaze was giving him. "I mean, doubling your money."

"Nah, I don't like it," Sleaze said. "Getting caught with fifty cases of illegal hooch I bought from an unknown source is not something I want to deal with."

"You don't have to worry about getting caught, Mr. Sleaze," Melvin said with a huge grin.

"You want to explain why?"

"Because I thought we'd just send Oscar to pick it up."

Jimmy Sleaze stared at Melvin for several seconds then slowly nodded his head.

"You know, Melvin. I'm beginning to think that I may have underestimated you."

Annabelle took a taxi to the restaurant where she agreed to meet her boss after politely refusing his offer over the phone to meet at a hotel. She entered and spotted him sitting at a table near the back.

"Hello, Vernon," she said, bussing his cheek as she managed to avoid his standard greeting, a lower-back clench he was well-known for that would leave fingerprints on her ass if she wasn't careful. "It's so good to see you."

"Same here, Annabelle," Vernon Adams said, giving her the once-over. "You look fabulous. And I must say that you're positively glowing."

"Train rides always get my juices flowing," she said, studying the menu. "What's good here?"

"Pretty much everything," he said. "So, you're in town to see an old friend?"

"Yes, she's in D.C. for a few days, and we haven't seen each other in years," Annabelle said, trying to decide what to have.

"Where does she live?"

"Paris."

"Interesting. Is she French?"

"She is," Annabelle said.

"Single?"

"Married with six kids," Annabelle said, giving him a sad smile. "Sorry, Vernon."

"Well, it couldn't hurt to ask," he said, shrugging. "So, how's work?"

"Actually, it's starting to slow down quite a bit," she said. "It's almost impossible for the bootleggers to get back and forth across the River in the winter."

"I guess that makes sense," he said. "So, how are you going to stay busy until spring?"

"I'm working a couple of angles. There are a few people at my church I think are running booze. And I'm almost positive that one of my teaching colleagues is involved. So, I thought I'd spend the winter throwing some dinner parties and participating in some of the winter activities. You know, have some fun while keeping my ears open."

"Smart," he said, taking a sip of water. "How's Roland doing?"

"He's drunk most of the time," Annabelle said with a shrug.

"He still doesn't know you're a lot more than just a teacher, right?"

"No, he's clueless."

"Good. But keep an eye on him if you can. Ever since that fiasco with the alleged thousand case delivery, he's been a bit of an embarrassment."

"I'm sure he has," Annabelle said, laughing. "And since he's afraid to get back in his boat, maybe you should give him some help. You know, someone to drive him around."

"I'm sure Roland will settle down soon," Vernon Adams said, unable to make eye contact.

"Yeah, you're probably right, Vernon."

"You staying overnight?"

"No, I'm catching a late train out tonight. Back to school on Monday."

"Then perhaps an afternoon session?"

"It's a wonderful offer, Vernon," Annabelle said. "But I am completely worn out. I just want to say hello to Monique then get back on the train and stretch out."

"Okay," he said, disappointed. "But the next time you're in town, make sure you stay over. I'll show you the town."

"It's a deal, Vernon," Annabelle said.

"I'm going to hold you to that."

"You'll have to catch me first," she whispered into her menu then looked up and smiled at the waiter.

Milo studied the photographs on the office walls then sat down on a couch and lit a cigarette. He smoked in silence and smiled at the memory of the train ride, very much looking forward to the trip home. Eventually, the Senator entered and crossed the room with his hand extended.

"So sorry to keep you waiting, Milo," Senator Miller said, grasping his hand and giving it a firm shake.

"Not a problem, Senator," Milo said, sitting down. "I imagine you're a very busy man."

"Not really," Senator Miller said, laughing. "How was your ride down?"

"Memorable," Milo said.

"Yes, there's quite a bit to see."

"Oh, the sights were amazing," Milo said, smiling.

"So, what brings you to town?" Senator Miller said, draping a leg over his knee. "Oh, I'm sorry. You feel like a splash of something? I've got a nice bottle of scotch Ben recently sent my way."

"No, I'm good, thanks," Milo said. "I just thought it was time we had a little chat about the future."

"The future? Yours or mine?" the Senator said, cocking his head.

"Both."

"The future of the business? From what Ben tells me, everything is going great."

"Oh, it is," Milo said. "But I think it could be even better."

"Well, I'm always on the lookout for improvements and opportunities to expand," he said. "What are you thinking about?"

"Top of mind at the moment is your political career," Milo said, offering him a cigarette. He waved it off and stared at Milo, thoroughly confused.

"You want to talk about the future of my political career?" Senator Miller said, now on guard. "Who have you been talking to, Milo?"

"Relax, Senator," Milo said, laughing. "I come bearing good news."

"Good. You had me worried there for a second. Go ahead. Enlighten me."

"I believe your talents are being wasted here in Washington," Milo said.

"Wasted? Milo, I'm a goddamn United States Senator. How can that possibly be a waste?"

"No, the job is fine and all that. In fact, it's an amazing accomplishment," Milo said.

"Thank you," Senator Miller said, casually brushing lint off a pant leg. "Not everybody gets elected to the Senate. It is a rather select group."

"I'm sorry I hurt your feelings, Senator," Milo said, laughing. "My point was that I see an even better job in your future."

"Are you talking about me running for President?" he said, frowning.

"No, that would be a total waste of your talents," Milo said. "I'm talking about you running for Governor of the great state of New York."

The Senator stared off into the distance then refocused on Milo.

"I have always wanted to be Governor."

"I know you have," Milo said. "You've told me that several times over the years."

"You're talking about the distant future, right? The current guy is very popular with the voters. And he's easily going to win another term. Nobody's going to beat him this year."

"Oh, I doubt if he's even going to run this year," Milo said.

"Why on earth would you think that? Senator Miller said.

Milo reached into his briefcase and tossed a thick file on the Senator's lap.

"Because of that," Milo said.

The Senator picked up the file and slowly began working his way through it.

"Maybe I will have that drink," Milo said, getting up.

"Pour me one," Senator Miller said, his eyes wide as he flipped through the pages. "Where the hell did you get all this, Milo?"

"I've had most of it for a while," Milo said, grabbing two glasses. "But I recently did a few updates. You want it with ice?"

"Yes, please. I can't believe you have this, Milo," Senator Miller said. "Where on earth did you get it?"

"I have my sources," Milo said, handing him his drink.

"Please tell me you don't have a file like this on me," he said, staring at Milo.

"Not at all, Senator," Milo said. "Yours is much smaller."

"What?"

"Just kidding, Senator. Relax."

"Remind me never to mess with you, Milo," Senator Miller said.

"Oh, I'm sure you'll remember."

"Yes, I'm sure I will," he said, then nodded at Milo's glass. "I thought you always drank your whiskey straight up."

"Oh, I occasionally like it with ice," Milo said. "And on the rocks seemed appropriate today."

"On the rocks? Like the Governor's career, right?"

"I knew you'd understand."

Milo finished his drink then crushed out his cigarette. Annabelle did the same, and they stretched on the bed in the sleeping car. The gentle rumble of the train as it rolled across the tracks was threatening to put him to sleep. He stifled a yawn as he drew back the sheet and studied her from head to toe.

"Remarkable," he whispered.

"Why thank you, Mr. Razner," she said, opening her eyes. "Is that your way of telling me you'd like to go another round?"

"I wouldn't mind," Milo said, glancing down as he gently stroked one of her thighs. "I can't wait for spring. We both need to get some sun."

"Are you telling me you don't like my winter tan, Mr. Razner?" she said with mock indignation.

"I love it, Miss Caffey. Your legs are like an untouched blanket of snow. I've never seen such purity in my life."

"Okay, Milo," she said, laughing. "You've officially crossed into the bullshit zone. Enough."

"Sorry. Your legs will be our little secret. So, your boss didn't take the bait when you floated the idea of giving Roland some help?"

"No, he didn't," she said, sitting up on her elbows. "The bastard is up to something."

"You'll figure it out."

"Yes, but probably not before you," she said.

"You're so sweet," Milo said.

"How did Senator Miller react when you showed him the file?" Annabelle said.

"Like a three-year-old on Christmas morning," Milo said, laughing.

"You do make a great Santa."

"Ho, ho, ho," Milo said, sliding down and lowering his head.

"Oh, my. I see that our next ride is about to start," Annabelle whispered.

"Yes, it is, Miss Caffey. And it's my turn to drive."

Episode 10

Freezing In A Winter Wonderland

You know what I like best about the winters around here?

Nothing.

Milo Razner

Ruby Heats Up

Milo kept a close eye on the large knife Ruby was holding as she chopped vegetables with a dark, walleyed stare seemingly etched on her face. Milo stirred his coffee, and since his attempts at making small talk had failed miserably, he sipped in silence as he waited for her to finish.

And put the knife down.

Ruby dumped the vegetables into a large pot of soup on the stove then wiped her hands with a dishtowel and brushed the hair back from her face. Milo admired her face and figure, then Ruby caught him staring at her.

"What is it?" she said, making eye contact.

"Remarkable," Milo said.

"What are you mumbling about?"

"I was just sitting here watching you, and it's impossible to miss just how beautiful you are," Milo said.

"What do you want, Milo?" she said, raising an eyebrow at him.

"Nothing. I was merely making an observation."

"Yeah, I'm sure that's all you were doing," she said, glaring at him. "Take the marbles out of your mouth."

Ruby sat down across the table from him and waited for him to continue.

"Can't I even pay you a simple compliment these days?"

"Actually, no, you can't," Ruby said, reaching for his pack of cigarettes. She waited for Milo to light it then exhaled smoke up at the ceiling. "You got an update on what we've been talking about?"

"As a matter of fact, I do," Milo said, grinning at her.

"Finally, something useful comes out of your mouth," Ruby said, taking another puff. "What do you have for me?"

"Well, I really can't go into any details yet," Milo said, treading carefully.

"Bullshit. You're either bluffing or stalling. Which one is it?"

"I can assure you I'm not bluffing, Ruby," Milo said, lighting a cigarette of his own. "And I'm not purposefully stalling. It's merely a matter of timing."

"Timing, huh? How long am I going to have to wait?" she said, glaring at him.

"Probably until sometime in the spring," Milo said, then waited for her reaction.

"Spring? You expect me to spend another winter stuck here with these cows? That's not gonna happen, Milo."

"Yes, I'm very aware of that, Ruby. And that's why my plan is to send you on a nice long vacation. On full pay."

"A vacation?" she said, her mood brightening. "Oh, I'd love a vacation, Milo. I could spend all winter in a nice warm place on the beach with my toes in the water."

"Yeah, well, here's the thing, Ruby," Milo said, glancing over at the stove to make sure the knife was out of reach. "I doubt if you'll be wanting to stick your feet in the water. Or any other part of your body for that matter."

Her eyes narrowed as she glared across the table at him.

"Quit dancing and start talking, Milo."

"I wish I could say that you could start your new adventure right away, but I'm afraid my larger plan is going to take some time to…unfold." He took a sip of coffee and shrugged at her. "But I'm certain you are going to love what I have planned for you. And your income is going to skyrocket."

"But not until the spring?"

"No, I'm afraid not."

"So, where's this big vacation spot you've got planned for me?" Ruby said, placing her elbows on the table and leaning forward.

"Whisperer Island," Milo said as he sat back in his chair.

Her eyes widened, and she stared at Milo dumbfounded.

"You want me to spend all winter on that island? With my ex-husband?"

"And Tom and Daisy," Milo said with a shrug.

"Are you out of your goddamn mind, Milo?" she said, slamming the table with both hands. "No. Not a chance. I won't do it."

"I'm sorry to hear that, Ruby," Milo said, casually smoking his cigarette. "Just when I'm about to offer you an amazing opportunity that will have you traveling in some very interesting circles. Frankly, I have to say that I'm disappointed by your inability to take the long view."

"Kiss my ass, Milo."

"Can I have soup first?"

Milo's comment, combined with a big smirk, brought Ruby out of her seat and throwing a punch he managed to catch just before it landed. He gave her hand a firm squeeze as he lowered it onto the tabletop. Then Milo let go, his expression softening as he placed a hand over hers.

"Please, Ruby. Stop. Just settle down and let me explain."

Ruby slumped back in the chair and folded her arms across her chest.

"You can be a real son of a bitch when you want to, Milo."

"Be that as it may," he said, extinguishing his cigarette. "But I would like to remind you, if it weren't for me, you would still be trying to eke out a living with Billy on that sorry-ass excuse for a dairy farm."

"Maybe," Ruby said, pouting.

"Take the long view, Ruby. Look at what you've been able to accomplish already. And the sky will be the limit once you start your new venture."

"This venture you can't tell me about yet?" she said, calming down a bit.

"Exactly. But I'll explain it all just as soon as I can," Milo said. "But for now, I'm doing everything I can to get you off the farm immediately. You do want to get off the farm, right?"

"Of course, I do."

"Then just agree to do me this one small favor," Milo said.

"Oh, it's a lot more than a small favor, Milo, and you know it."

"I suppose we can agree to disagree about that," he said, getting out of his chair and heading for the stove. He gave the pot of soup a quick stir, then washed and put the knife away before grabbing a bottle of whiskey and two glasses. "The soup smells fantastic."

"Good for the soup," Ruby said, accepting her glass from Milo. She reluctantly touched glasses with him, then took a sip and rubbed her forehead. "Four months stranded on that island?"

"Four at most," Milo said. "Just pray for an early spring. You'll certainly have lots of time to talk to God."

"Don't start with me, Milo. I am not in the mood," she said, her anger again heating up. "I don't know if I can handle that."

"Really? I'm actually rather envious of you," Milo said, taking a long swallow. "I'd love to have four months on that island to sit back and relax with you and Daisy."

"Yeah, I bet you would," Ruby said, nodding at him.

"You've seen the place, Ruby. It's magnificent. And once you get to know Daisy, I'm sure you two will become thick as thieves."

"Yeah, right. Me and my new buddy, the working girl who's getting horizontal with my ex," she said, shaking her head again. Then she fixed a hard stare on him. "What do you expect me to do while I'm there?"

"Not a thing," Milo said. "Like I told Daisy, whatever you choose to do or not do is completely your call."

"Four months being stuck on an island with Billy," she said, exhaling loudly. "Well, at least I'll know what to expect when I get to hell."

"Perish the thought," Milo said. "And by the time you do get to heaven, you'll have more than enough to buy your way in."

"How much money are we talking about, Milo?"

"It's hard to say at the moment. But I wouldn't be surprised if it approaches half a million a year. Possibly even more."

"A half-million?" she said in a low whisper.

"Yes. Now, isn't that worth waiting a few months for?"

Ruby stared off for several moments as she thought about it. Then she looked back at Milo and nodded.

"Yes, it is. But if it turns out that you're blowing smoke up my skirt, we're gonna have a big problem, Milo."

"I'd expect nothing less, Ruby," Milo said, extending his hand across the table. She returned the handshake then sat back in her chair. "You're sure Johnny is ready to handle things around here?"

"Yeah, he's more than ready. But if he does have any problems, just let me know. You'll know where to find me. I'll get a message back to him through Birdie. I assume you're still planning on making winter deliveries from the island to the farm."

"Absolutely."

"I think that's about the stupidest thing I've ever heard," Ruby said.

"Yes, I imagine that is the prevailing opinion," Milo said with a grin. "You better start packing. Birdie and I will pick you up Thursday morning."

Milo climbed the steps and stepped inside. He was immediately hit with the familiar scent of cigarette and cigar smoke tinged with lavender. He glanced around, smiled and waved to several patrons and working girls he recognized, then headed for the counter and tapped the bell. Seconds later, Fannie poked her head through the curtains and beamed at him.

"Milo," she said. "We were just talking about you. Come on back."

Milo worked his way around the counter then through the curtains. He saw Daisy half-dressed and sprawled out on one of the couches and returned her wave. She lifted her legs to give him room, and he sat down. She plopped her feet on his lap and grinned at him as she raised her glass in salute.

"How you doing, Milo?" she said, slightly slurring her words.

"Getting an early start this evening?" Milo said, accepting the glass Fannie was holding out. "Thanks, Fannie. What are you guys up to?"

"We've just been going through the list of Daisy's regulars," Fannie said, sitting down across from them. "They aren't very happy that she's going on an extended vacation, and I want to make sure my other girls are aware of their…proclivities."

"Good word," Milo said, taking a sip. "I just stopped by to let you know I've moved the departure date up to Thursday."

"But the weather is supposed to be decent for the next several days," Daisy said, frowning at him. "What's your hurry, Milo?"

"Well, since Melvin is going to get elected tonight, his first order of business is to start taking advantage of the freebies Fannie will be offering him. And guess who's number one on his list?"

"And you want to get Daisy out of town before he stops by?" Fannie said, laughing.

"I thought I owed her that much," Milo said, laughing along.

"Thank you, Milo," she said, again raising her glass at him. "Talk about dodging a bullet."

"Have you seen any of the early election results?" Milo said, grinning at Fannie.

"Well, I did manage to see a hundred votes go into one of the ballot boxes this afternoon," she said.

"That's my girl," Milo said, then turned serious. "Look, I need to talk to you about a man named Jimmy Sleaze."

"Doesn't ring a bell, Milo," Fannie said, glancing at Daisy who shook her head.

"It will," Milo said. "He's been busy since he hit town, but he'll be dropping by soon enough."

"Who is he?"

"He's a despicable creature I know from a prior life," Milo said. "And I'm afraid he's going to be around awhile."

"What's he doing here?" Fannie said.

"He's planning on getting into the booze business."

"And you're going to stop him, right?" Fannie said.

"No, quite the opposite," Milo said, smiling at her. "I'll tell you all about it at some point. But for now, I'd like to discuss how you might be able to help me out."

"Sure, Milo," Fannie said. "Anything you need."

"That new girl I saw here during my last visit," Milo said.

"Jessie," Fannie said, listening closely. "What about her?"

"She is exactly Mr. Sleaze's type," Milo said. "And I know he's going to want her as soon as he lays eyes on her."

"He wouldn't be the first," Fannie said. "She's off to a great start."

"I was wondering if you think you can trust her," Milo said.

"As much as I trust anybody else around here," Fannie said, then glanced at Daisy. "No offense, Sweetie."

"None taken," Daisy said, downing her drink then holding out her glass for a refill.

"What do you need, Milo?" Fannie said.

"I was wondering if she might be willing to plant a few seeds and keep her ears open about some of the things that Mr. Sleaze is up to," Milo said, picking four fifty-dollar bills from a thick stack and handing them to Fannie.

"I'm sure that can be arranged," she said, sliding the money into her cleavage. "You want me to drop her rate a bit to keep him coming back on a regular basis?"

"No. Actually, I want you to raise it," Milo said. "The Sleaze is an incredibly suspicious man and getting a cut rate for a girl like Jessie might make him start questioning his good fortune. Fortunately, he enjoys what he considers the finer things in life. And the more he has to pay for something, the more valuable it becomes."

"Is this guy dangerous?" Fannie said.

"Very," Milo said. "And he also has a reputation for being a bit demanding when it comes to some of his *proclivities*."

"He's into the rough stuff?"

"Yes, at times I'm sure he is. But only if he thinks he can get away with it," Milo said. "Given what he's doing up here, he's not going to want to attract any negative attention. Just gently let him know when he does show up that roughing up your girls is out of the question. He'll get the message."

"Geez, Milo," Fannie said. "Jessie's pretty green around the gills at this stuff. Are you sure this guy wouldn't prefer someone else?"

"I'm positive. He's going to go crazy over her."

"How can you be so sure?"

"Because she looks an awful lot like his ex-wife."

"Jessie can handle herself," Daisy said, getting up off the couch.

She set her glass down on the table and staggered a bit as she slid onto Fannie's lap. Fannie draped an arm over Daisy's shoulders and beamed at her. Milo was caught off guard and watched in silence as Daisy raised her head and gave Fannie a deep kiss that lingered a lot longer than he expected. He shook his head and took a sip of whiskey.

"I'm sure gonna miss you," Daisy said.

"The feeling is mutual, Sweetie," Fannie said, then grinned at Milo. "Don't read too much into it, Milo."

"I won't," he said. "I'll just wait for the pictures."

They both laughed, and Daisy climbed off Fannie's lap and stretched back out on the couch.

"Rub my feet, Milo," Daisy said, wiggling her toes in his lap. "Oh, that feels good. Yeah, you don't have to worry about Jessie. A big part of that little girl thing she does is just an act. She's smart. And plenty tough."

Fannie stared at Daisy then nodded.

"Okay, I'll have a quiet word with her. But if anything happens to her, it's on you, Milo."

"I understand completely," Milo said. "Don't worry, Fannie. As soon as The Sleaze sees her, she's going to be the safest person in town. But I can't say the same for any of her potential suitors."

"So, he's gonna want her all to himself?" Fannie said.

"I'd be shocked if he didn't."

Out Of Sorts

Oscar stood outside the car and took another deep breath of frigid air. Then he seemed to exhale smoke as he beamed at Melvin who was struggling to get the driver side door open.

"Do you smell that, Melvin?"

"Not since we stepped outside. You need a bath, Oscar."

"Not that. Don't you smell something else?"

"Fortunately, no," Melvin said, sniffing the air. "And try to get it all out of your system before you get in the car."

"I ain't talking about that, either," Oscar said, opening his door. "I'm talking about the smell of freedom."

"Yeah," Melvin said, starting the car and cracking the window a couple of inches. "What can I tell you, Oscar? It's a great country."

"So, how did you get me out?" Oscar said as he turned around and rummaged in the back seat until he found the bottle.

"I finally convinced the judge to grant bail," Melvin said, pulling into traffic. "It wasn't easy. You know, what with you being a two-time offender and all that."

"How much was it?" Oscar said, taking a long swallow from the bottle of Canadian whiskey.

"A simple thank you might be in order, Oscar," Melvin said, glancing over at him.

"Yeah. Thanks, Melvin."

"Don't mention it."

"Make up your mind," Oscar said, taking another long pull from the bottle then burping loudly. "How much?"

"A thousand dollars," Melvin said, lying through his teeth.

"You paid a grand to get me out?" Oscar said, staring at him in disbelief.

"Yes, I did."

Melvin smiled as he remembered his conversation with the judge over the phone who, based on the recommendation of the jail warden, had agreed to drop all the charges for fifty bucks and time served. The judge had also said through a loud laugh that the warden had offered to lend Melvin the fifty bucks if he was having a hard time coming up with it.

"Oh, I forgot to tell you, Oscar," Melvin said, grinning. "You're looking at the new mayor of Alex Bay."

"What are you talking about? Since when?" Oscar said, stunned.

"Since last night," Melvin said, running his fingers over the steering wheel. "I won in a landslide."

"You never mentioned you were running for mayor."

"It must have slipped my mind. Yes, indeed. Mayor Melvin English." He glanced over at Oscar. "It kind of rolls off the tongue, doesn't it?"

"You're the new mayor?"

"Impressive, huh?" Melvin said, beaming out at the road.

"I guess," Oscar said with a shrug before refocusing on the whiskey bottle.

"And just so we're clear, I'd prefer it if you would address me as Mayor Melvin when you're on the clock. Other times, Melvin will be just fine."

"Okay, Mayor Melvin," Oscar said, chuckling. Then he frowned and glanced over at Melvin. "On the clock?"

"Yes."

"Doing what?"

"While serving in your capacity as police chief, what else?"

"What?" Oscar said. "I'm getting my old job back?"

"Yes, of course," Melvin said, glancing over. "Did I forget to mention that?"

"Yeah, it must have slipped your mind," Oscar said, then stared out at a herd of cows huddled in a snow-covered field. "I can't believe it. Is everybody in town okay with it?"

"They seem to be," Melvin said, shrugging. "But it doesn't really matter, does it? I'm the mayor."

"I can't believe it," Oscar said. "Thank you, Melvin."

It sounded like this time he meant it, and Melvin looked over again and nodded.

"You're welcome, Oscar," he said. "Oh, I have a few things to go over with you. Swing by my office later on. But not too late. I've got an early evening appointment at Fannie's."

"Sure. I'll swing by after I get settled back into the house and get cleaned up."

"Oh, yeah," Melvin said, scowling. "The house."

"What about it?"

"Nothing. It can wait."

Roland Doyle stood at the edge of the town dock and stared out at the massive expanse of frigid water and the steam rising off it that reminded him of white cotton candy. Ice was starting to take root along the shoreline and making its way out into the shallow bay. A gust of wind tried to rip his hat off, and he stumbled backward as he reached for it then pulled it down tight over his forehead. He grabbed a pint bottle from his coat and took several small sips as he continued to stare out at the River wondering what the hell he was going to do to keep himself busy all winter.

"You do know that's illegal, right?"

Roland slowly turned to the familiar voice from the past and stared in disbelief at the guy standing a few feet behind him. He shook his head to clear it and blinked several times, at first, wondering if he was experiencing the onset of the DTs and having delusions. But the man was real and giving him a goofy look that Roland had seen many times in the past. As always, Roland immediately wanted to knock the cocky grin off the man's face.

"Sleaze?" Roland said.

"It's nice to see you again, Mr. Doyle," Jimmy Sleaze said, unable to wipe the grin off his face.

"Sorry, Sleaze, but I can't say the same thing. I thought you had another three years to go. Did you bust out?"

"Not at all," Sleaze said, shaking his head. "Fortunately, it didn't come to that. The Commonwealth simply decided that I had paid my debt to society."

"Bullshit," Roland said, sliding the pint back into his pocket. "You gave somebody up, didn't you?"

"Let's say that I did them a small favor and leave it at that," Sleaze said, his expression turning dark. "So, you got tossed off the force in Philly and made your way over to the Feds as a revenuer?"

"Let's say the force and I came to a mutual agreement and leave it at that," Roland said, returning the stare.

"Fair enough."

"What are you doing in town?"

"I happened to be in the area and heard about what a magical place this is," Sleaze said, glancing out at the River. "But I imagine I'm going to have to wait until spring to be convinced of that."

"You reconnecting with Razner?"

"No, I'm afraid not," Sleaze said, laughing. "Milo can keep his cows all to himself. Dairy farming? Not a chance. I don't even *drink* milk."

"Maybe you should take a page from his book," Roland said. "Going straight was the best decision he's ever made. From what I can tell, he's doing very well for himself."

"Well, Milo always did have a good head for business," Sleaze said.

"So, what *are* you doing here?"

"Vacation," Sleaze said with a shrug.

"Vacation?" Roland said, laughing. "Yeah, and I'm the ghost of Christmas past."

"You know me, Mr. Doyle. I like to swim against the current," Sleaze said. "Most people tend to vacation in warmer locales. I prefer to head north."

"Okay, Sleaze," Roland said, laughing. "Whatever you say. I guess I'll be seeing you around."

"Oh, there's no doubt about that, Mr. Doyle," Sleaze said. "Now, you have a wonderful day."

Roland watched the man wheel around and head back down the dock hunkered low to block the wind the best he could. Then Roland smiled and grabbed the pint from his pocket, the problem of how he was going to keep himself busy during the long, cold winter officially solved.

Oscar stared at Melvin in disbelief as he continued to rapidly work his way through the bottle of whiskey.

"You rented the guy my frigging house?"

"I was out of options, Oscar," Melvin said, casually as he made the left turn into town.

"You rented him *my house*?"

"There's no need to repeat yourself, Oscar."

"Why would you do that?"

"Because our new business partner needed a place to stay," Melvin said with a small shrug.

"Business partner? You better start explaining yourself, or I swear I'm going to bust your head open like a melon."

"Relax, Oscar," Melvin said, glancing over at him. "Everything is going to be fine. And quite profitable."

"Start talking, Melvin."

He did.

After he finished bringing Oscar up to speed, he glanced over again and waited for questions.

"How much did you rent the place for?"

"Twenty bucks a month," Melvin said.

"Hand it over."

"You already owe me a thousand, Oscar."

"Shit."

"Yeah, I can understand your frustration."

"Fifty cases a week?"

"Yup."

"But you don't know who's selling it to us?"

"Nope."

"It sounds like a setup," Oscar said.

"The Sleaze said the same thing," Melvin said. "Great minds think alike, huh? I knew you two were gonna hit it off."

"How can you be sure we won't be walking into a trap?"

"That's an easy one, Oscar," Melvin said, grinning at him. "Because you're going to be the one doing the pickups."

"Why me?"

"Because if you did happen to get caught, which is highly unlikely, you simply tell Roland Doyle that you got tipped off and were in the process of getting rid of fifty cases of illegal hooch that was about to hit the street. It's really very simple. And quite brilliant if I say so myself."

"Actually, it kinda is," Oscar said, frowning. "I'm surprised you thought of it."

"You know, at first, I was too," Melvin said, smiling out at the road. "But ever since I decided to get into politics, my thinking seems to be getting sharper."

"Yeah, I'm sure that's it," Oscar said, laughing.

"I thought we'd swing by my office," Melvin said.

"What for?"

"I want to take another look at my property inventory to see if I missed something," Melvin said, waving to someone on the street. "We need to find you a place to live."

"No need to do that, Melvin," Oscar said, taking a long swig.

"Why on earth not?"

"Because I'm going to stay at your house," Oscar said, giving Melvin a glare that let him know the matter wasn't open for debate.

Melvin gripped the steering wheel tight and stared out the windshield with a blank stare.

"Shit."

Cold Heart, Warm Hands

Ruby held out her hand, and Birdie helped her climb down into the boat. The wind whipped the thin, cotton dress she was wearing, and she pulled her coat tight and hugged herself as she bounced up and down on her toes. Birdie shook his head at her.

"You're really underdressed for this, Ruby," he said. "What on earth were you thinking when you got dressed this morning?"

"Obviously, I wasn't thinking at all, Birdie," she snapped, trying to fight off her hangover. "I had a little too much to drink last night while I was getting ready to leave, and I packed all my warm clothes in my suitcase. And since it took me almost half an hour to get the damn thing closed, I couldn't bear the thought of opening it back up."

"You'll be okay," he said, heading for the bow. "I've got a couple of blankets for you and Daisy to use on the ride over."

She watched as Birdie grabbed her suitcase off the dock and struggled to get it in the boat. Then he grabbed the blankets off the front seat and handed them to her. She sat down on the seat that ran across the stern then unfolded the blankets, laid one on top of the other, and pulled them up to her neck. Immediately, she began feeling a bit better. Then she glanced up when he saw Milo and Daisy heading down the dock.

"Good morning, Milo," Birdie said, then tipped his hat to the sullen woman standing next to Milo. "How are you this fine morning, Daisy?"

"Cut the crap, Birdie. Just help me into the boat. Let's get this over with."

"Goddamn it, Daisy. Be careful with those shoes. You're gonna scratch the boat." Milo said, glaring at her. Then he looked at the woman hunched down underneath the blankets. "Good morning, Ruby."

"Hey, Milo," she said, making room for Daisy to sit down next to her.

"Hi, Ruby," Daisy said, tentatively sitting down and keeping a close eye on Ruby's reaction.

"Daisy," Ruby said with a small nod.

Then Ruby draped the thick blankets over both of them until they were both covered from the neck down.

"Are you ready for this?" Ruby said.

"As ready as I'm gonna get," Daisy said. "Are you getting paid to do this?"

"You bet your ass I'm getting paid," Ruby said, glaring at Milo who was untying the lines. "Full salary. You?"

"The same," Daisy said. "I fought it as long as I could, but Milo can be pretty convincing when he wants to be."

"Yeah, he can be a real prick at times."

They both were momentarily caught off guard by the boat's rapid acceleration, and Ruby felt the blast of Arctic air hit her face. Both women hunched down even further as the boat continued to race across the water.

"It's gonna be a long winter," Ruby said.

"What?" Daisy shouted above the roar of the engine.

"I said it's gonna be a long winter," Ruby said, leaning close to Daisy's ear.

"Yes, it is," Daisy said, also leaning in to be heard. "At least, we'll be able to have an intelligent conversation with Tom."

"Yeah, don't expect to get much out of Billy," Ruby said, laughing.

"I don't."

"Are you two still getting horizontal?" Ruby said.

"Occasionally," Daisy said. "But I can see why you decided to divorce him."

"I'd be surprised if you didn't."

"What about you and Tom?" Daisy said.

"He's kind of fun," Ruby said. "But I'm not sure I want a steady dose of him."

"Yeah, I get that," Daisy said. "But Tom's a nice guy."

"Yes, he is. But it doesn't matter. I doubt if I'm going to be in the mood much this winter."

"Oh, I don't know," Daisy said, her lips almost pressed against Ruby's ear.

Then Ruby flinched when she felt the hand on her leg. She remained dead still, her face frozen from both the cold and the gentle squeeze Daisy was giving her upper thigh.

"Are you sure about that?" Daisy said, giving Ruby a look that couldn't be missed.

Ruby stared out at the blurred pines as the boat sped past a long stretch of shoreline, then sidled a bit closer to Daisy and made eye contact.

"Well, I guess we'll just have to wait and see."

"Oh, I doubt if we'll be waiting long, Ruby."

Birdie pulled the throttle back as they approached the island and the boat slowed then planed over. He rolled a cigarette with one hand and handed it to Milo then rolled a second one for himself. Milo lit both, and Birdie tucked the cigarette in the corner of his mouth as he steered toward the boathouse on the back side of the island.

"How are those two doing back there?" Birdie said. "Any fireworks or fistfights yet?"

"No," Milo said, glancing over his shoulder. "They seem to be getting along okay." He returned the smile Daisy was giving him then faced the front. "And as strange as it sounds, Ruby actually seems quite content."

"Billy's ex-wife and the current love of his life stuck on the same island for four months," Birdie said, shaking his head and cackling. "I sure hope you know what you're doing, Milo."

"They'll be fine," Milo said. "After we drop them off, we need to stop by Frank's and make sure he's got the ice boat ready to go. I thought we'd do our first run tomorrow night."

"Are you sure you don't want to get somebody else to help me, Milo? There's no reason for you to be spending your winter nights out here."

"No, I need to see how it's working," Milo said. "But once I'm satisfied, I'll probably find somebody to go with you."

"I suppose I could handle it by myself," Birdie said with a shrug.

"Absolutely not, Birdie. There's no way you're going to be doing winter booze runs by yourself," Milo said, staring hard to reinforce his point.

"Got it," Birdie said, pulling into the boathouse.

Milo hopped out of the boat, tied it off, then grabbed the suitcases from Birdie. Then he helped both women out of the boat. Ruby looked at him with glazed eyes.

"Are you okay?" Milo said. "Did you get seasick on the way over?"

"No, I'm fine, Milo," she said, snapping out of whatever mood she'd been in.

"It's so beautiful," Daisy said, staring up at the high wooden ceiling.

"Wait till you see the house," Birdie said, limping down the dock and wheeling back one of the dollies they used to transport product from the cooking room.

Milo set both suitcases on the dolly and wheeled it down the dock, pleased by how smoothly the device rolled. He whistled as he pushed the dolly up the incline toward the house, taking his time so Birdie could keep up. The two women led the way, and Milo continued to be pleasantly surprised by how well they seemed to be getting along. Tom and Billy stepped out onto the verandah to greet them then each grabbed a suitcase and carried them inside. Milo left the dolly near the front steps and followed everyone into the house. As he always did, he beamed as he looked around the massive living room and the floor to ceiling fireplace that dominated the room. A fire was roaring, and Milo removed his coat and hung it up. He helped Daisy out of hers as she continued to be overwhelmed by her surroundings.

"What do you think?" Milo said with a grin.

"It's unbelievable, Milo," Daisy said. "You really own this place?"

"Yup. The whole island," Milo said. "And everything on it."

"Maybe I should just forget about everything else and marry you, huh?" she said with a grin.

"I'll add you to the list," Milo said, grinning back. "Right on top."

"Top. Bottom. Makes no difference to me, Milo," she said, giving him a peck on the cheek.

"Okay," Tom said. "We've got some food ready. You want a tour of the house now, or do you want to wait until we eat?"

"I wouldn't mind seeing the rest of the house," Daisy said. "Especially the bedrooms."

Willy and Frank admired the fifty cases neatly stacked in the middle of the small garage. Willy removed a pint of brandy from his pocket and offered it to Frank who took a sip then passed it back. Willy took a long swallow then stuffed the bottle back in his pocket.

"You ready to get going?" Frank said.

"Just as soon as I find a good place to put next week's note," Willy said, removing an envelope from a different pocket.

"Aren't you going to mail it?"

"I thought we'd let them think we'll be using the same pickup spot next week," Willy said, slipping the envelope into a crack between two cases. "And then we'll change it before we make the next delivery."

"I'm not following," Frank said, trailing Willy out of the garage.

"None of those three are going to trust each other," Willy said, gently closing the garage door. "So, I thought we might sow a few seeds of discontent right out of the gate."

"You been hanging around Milo so much you're starting to talk like him," Frank said, laughing.

"He does kinda rub off on you, huh?" Willy said with a chuckle as he pointed at the trail that would lead them back to where they'd parked the truck. "In a couple of days, we're gonna mail them another note letting them know that we're not very happy about them staking the place out. And tell them if it happens again, they can forget about getting their fifty cases a week."

"What if they don't stake the place out?" Frank said as he trudged through the deep snow.

"It doesn't matter," Willy said, shaking his head. "As soon as they read the note, they're gonna start wondering right away which one of their so-called partners might be trying to screw them on the deal. Or trying to set them up."

"That's good, Willy. Gotta keep them on their toes, right?"

"We do," Willy said, taking a sip of brandy and passing the bottle to Frank without breaking stride. "At least for the next sixteen weeks."

Jimmy Sleaze stepped inside Fannie's for the first time, studied the large sitting area, then nodded his approval. Compared to some of the other houses he'd visited, this one was smaller, but it was well-kept, and most of the working girls he saw scattered around the room were young and pretty. He walked to the counter then banged the bell hard. Moments later, a woman poked her head through the curtains and stared at him.

"Do I know you?" the woman said, the rest of her still hidden behind the curtains.

"No, we've never met," he said, removing his hat and giving her a small bow. "Allow me to introduce myself. My name is Jimmy Sleaze."

"Oh, Mr. Sleaze, of course," the woman said, emerging through the curtains with a smile.

She propped her elbows on the counter and leaned forward. The Sleaze forced himself to maintain eye contact.

"Melvin mentioned that you would probably be stopping by at some point. "I'm Fannie. It's nice to meet you."

"The same here," Sleaze said, glancing around the room. "Melvin told you I'd be dropping by?"

"Yes, he did. Melvin is a bit of a chatterbox. Can I interest you in some second-floor entertainment?"

"No, not tonight, thank you," Sleaze said, continuing to look around. "But I wouldn't mind quenching my thirst while I'm here."

"Of course," Fannie said, nodding at a hallway to her left. "It's the last door on the right. Tonight's password is iceberg."

"You have a password? Interesting," Sleaze said, again forcing himself to maintain eye contact.

"Well, you can't be too careful," Fannie said. "I change it all the time since I like to know who's drinking here."

"A wise policy in these troubled times," Sleaze said, looking around the room again. Then his casual glances turned into a hard stare, and he pointed at a woman sitting in the corner of the room laughing and chatting with two men he didn't recognize. "Oh, my. Who is that?"

"Oh, that's Jessie," Fannie said. "She's one of my new girls. And very pretty, don't you think?"

"Indeed."

"You sure you don't want to change your mind about the second-floor?" Fannie said, cocking her head and grinning at him.

"No, I'm afraid that won't be possible tonight," Sleaze said. "But I'll be back soon."

"Well, you know where to find us," Fannie said. "Enjoy yourself tonight. And it was nice meeting you, Mr. Sleaze."

"The pleasure is all mine," he said, tipping his hat and taking a final look at the young woman who bore a striking resemblance to Beulah before heading down the hall.

Sleaze reached the door of the blind pig and muttered the password to the man standing guard outside. He stepped inside the bar that was packed with patrons and filled with laughter and a thick cloud of smoke. He worked his way through the crowd, giving a man who stepped on his foot a glare and a hard shove before coming to a stop in front of the bartender. Sleaze tossed his money on the bar and ordered a shot and a beer. He downed the shot, nodded for another, then stood with his back to the bar sipping beer while surveying the crowd. When he spotted a man fitting the description Melvin had given him, he downed his second shot and elbowed his way to the table doing everything he could to not spill his beer.

"Are you Mr. Lawless?" Sleaze said, staring down at the man who was sitting by himself at a small table.

"Who wants to know?"

"I do," Sleaze said with a cold stare.

"And you are?"

"My name is Jimmy Sleaze."

"Never heard of you. What do you want?"

"I'd like to discuss a mutually beneficial business opportunity," Sleaze said.

The man stared up at him, then eventually nodded and shoved the empty chair back from the table with his foot. Sleaze sat down, lit a cigarette and sipped his beer taking all the time he wanted to size the guy up. But the guy didn't seem to mind, and he waited patiently for Sleaze to collect his thoughts.

"The reason I stopped by, Mr. Lawless, is that Melvin said you might be interested in getting your hands on some quality product," Sleaze said.

"It sounds like our new mayor is downright chatty these days. Melvin must be having a hard time getting out of campaign mode," the man said. "And call me Willy."

"Melvin certainly does like to run his mouth," Sleaze said. "But in this case, I'm willing to overlook it. You know, since he was kind enough to arrange an introduction."

Willy studied The Sleaze's face for several moments, then shrugged and lit a cigarette. He exhaled a cloud of smoke then leaned forward in his chair.

"Okay. How much product are we talking about?" Willy Lawless said.

"Fifty cases a week," Sleaze said without emotion.

"Fifty a week?" Willy said, laughing loudly. "Oh, that Melvin is something else." He shook his head in amazement. "Fifty cases a week. That's a good one, Mr. Sleaze."

"I'm afraid I don't see the humor," Sleaze said, glaring across the table.

"No offense, Mr. Sleaze," Willy said. "I hate to tell you, but I ain't the guy you should be talking to. You're looking at somebody who's at the bottom of the booze-running food chain. I'm lucky if I can unload the four or five measly cases I get my hands on. My customers are more of the household variety if you catch my drift. You know, a bottle or two every couple of weeks to an overworked farmer or lonely widow." Then he laughed again and shook his head in amazement. "Fifty cases a week. That Melvin is too much."

"I see," Sleaze said, pissed off but trying not to show it. "Then perhaps you might be able to point me in the direction of someone who might be able to handle a quantity like that."

"I doubt if there's anyone local who could," Willy said, frowning. "I'm sure Fannie doesn't move anywhere near that much product. And I think the speakeasy up at the Crossley has an arrangement with the company that owns the place. From what I understand, they own a bunch of hotels and buy in bulk from a distillery across the border." Willy leaned forward and whispered to Sleaze. "I heard they get their booze for twenty bucks a case."

"Twenty bucks a case?" Sleaze said, surprised by the number.

"They buy a ton of booze for their hotels," Willy said. "I imagine they get a nice volume discount."

"So, where should I be looking for a potential buyer?" Sleaze said, finishing the last of his beer.

"Gee, let me think on that for a sec," Willy said, sipping his drink. "You'd probably need a bigger town that has a lot of speakeasies. Yeah, that's probably where I'd be looking."

"A place like Watertown?" Sleaze said.

"Yeah, I suppose that might work," Willy said. "I'm sure they've got lots of speakeasies down there."

"You got anybody specific in mind?"

"Nah, I don't," Willy said, shaking his head. "I get down there from time to time, but I don't drink when I'm in town. I don't like boozing it up around that many strangers. It makes me nervous these days."

"Sure, I get that. Do you know anybody who might be able to give me a name?" Sleaze said, already tired of talking to the bumpkin.

"Gee, let me think on that for a sec," Willy said, lighting a fresh cigarette. "Sorry, but I can't, Mr. Sleaze. No, hang on."

"Did you come up with a name?" Sleaze said.

"I think George might be able to help you out."

"Who's George?"

"He's a salesman who travels around the area. And he loves to drink," Willy said. "No, that won't work. George just got transferred to Chicago. Let me think on it for a sec." Then he cocked his head and snapped his fingers. "Hang on, I just might have an idea for you."

"That's great," Sleaze said, leaning forward.

"Fannie's got a new girl I enjoyed the company of the other night," Willy said. "And I think her last stop before she got here was Watertown. I imagine a working girl like her might know a bit about how things work down there."

"What's this girl's name?" Sleaze said, keeping his fingers crossed.

"Jessie," Willy said, then nodded. "A little expensive for my budget, but she was worth every penny."

"I wouldn't get used to it if I were you," Sleaze said, his cold stare returning. Then he relaxed and forced a smile. "I must be going. Thank you, Willy. You've been very helpful."

"It was nice meeting you, Mr. Sleaze," Willy said. "And if you ever find yourself needing a bottle or two on short notice, you just let me know."

"Yeah, I'll keep that in mind."

A Question Of Sanity

Milo stood between Frank and Birdie on the dock at the dairy farm and stared down at the strange contraption Frank Slack had piloted into the boathouse just before sunset. It was a little over twenty feet long and wider than Milo remembered. Two large metal runners were attached to the bow, but it was the large propeller inside a metal cage in the stern that got most of Milo's attention. Behind the propeller was a large metal fin used to steer and turn the boat. In front of the propeller was a gasoline engine secured to the deck, and in the center of the boat, circular slots were recessed into a wooden platform. The slots, each sized to accommodate a ten-gallon milk can, would be used to secure the fifteen containers they'd be transporting back and forth between the island and the farm. Inside the small cabin designed to minimize the cold as much as possible was a wooden bench and a steering wheel on the starboard side.

"How was the trip over?" Milo said to Frank.

"It was okay," Frank said with a shrug.

"Just okay?" Milo said, now on edge.

"I opened it up on the thick ice near shore just to see how it handles speed," Frank said.

"And?" Milo said.

"And it's fine as long as you don't try to make any sudden turns," Frank said with another shrug. "I almost flipped it when I turned the wheel a bit too fast."

"How fast were you going?" Birdie said, rolling a cigarette with one hand.

"A little over forty."

"You were going forty miles an hour in that thing?" Milo said, scowling. "Are you out of your mind, Frank?"

"I needed to see what it will do," Frank said. "And over ice going downwind, I gotta say it's pretty quick. But changing directions is tricky."

"That fin in the back is what makes it turn, right?" Milo said, again studying the boat.

"Yeah, it works like a rudder on a regular boat," Frank said. "You're basically forcing air against the tail to turn it."

"So, it kinda works like a sailboat," Birdie said, nodding.

"Assuming you've got a really fast sailboat," Frank said. "I scared the crap out of myself."

"It's wider in the bow," Milo said.

"Yeah, I made a small design change. I figured that having it a bit narrower in the stern would help shorten the turning radius," Frank said.

"Smart," Birdie said as he studied the propeller and fin.

"Thanks, Birdie," Frank said. "Just remember that, while this baby can really motor over the ice, it's gonna slow down in a hurry as soon as you hit open water. Give yourself lots of time and don't get cocky with this thing. I'd hate to be trying to fish your bodies out of the River in the middle of February."

"Excellent safety tip, Frank," Milo said, gently punching Birdie on the shoulder. "Slow and steady, got it?"

"Got it, Milo," Birdie said. "I think we should use a ninety-degree course back and forth."

"You lost me, Birdie," Milo said, frowning.

"Gee, there's a first," Birdie said with a cackle. "Instead of using the angled route we usually take from the farm to the island, we can hug the shoreline going downriver for a couple miles. Then we'll head straight across the open water. If we stay upriver from the island, the current will do a lot of the work for us. Then when we reach solid ice on the other side, we'll hug the shore again until we get close to the island. The good news is that the current running behind the island is strong enough to keep the boathouse area from ever freezing over. It's a longer route, but I think it might end up being a bit faster."

"How long do you think the trip to the island is going to take?" Milo said, staring out at the descending darkness.

"My best guess is that it's gonna be about an hour. Maybe forty-five minutes when we aren't fighting the wind," Birdie said.

"Since Tom and Billy are going to have the product down at the dock, it shouldn't take more than a couple of minutes to load," Milo said. "Around two hours for the round trip. We should be able to make two trips a night and still get home in time for a nightcap."

"Yeah, but as soon as the ice starts breaking up when it gets warm, you should plan on only one trip a night," Frank said. "Going in and out of that pack ice is going to be slow going. And those trips are definitely going to be the most dangerous."

"How thick does the ice need to be to support this thing?" Milo said.

"Three inches should be plenty," Frank said. "But four would be better. Especially when you're carrying a full load."

"Suddenly, I find myself praying for cold weather," Milo said, laughing. Then he looked back and forth at them. "Anything else we need to talk about?"

"No, I think we're good," Frank said. "Swing by the marina tomorrow and let me know how it went."

"Will do," Milo said. "Thanks, Frank. You need Johnny to give you a ride home?"

"No, it's not far. I'll just walk back," Frank said, bundling up.

"Why on earth would you do something crazy like that?" Milo said.

"Says the man who's about to cross the St. Lawrence in an ice boat," Frank said.

Milo grinned at him then turned to Birdie.

"Are you ready, my good man?"

"Let's do this," Birdie said, climbing in behind the wheel. "It's a beautiful night for a boat ride."

"That guy is frigging nuts," Frank said, laughing as he watched Birdie start the engine.

Milo stared at his friend with the permanent limp and grinned.

"Well, he did fall off a roof when he was a kid."

Jimmy Sleaze climbed the stairs to the second floor and knocked on the third door on the right. A young woman opened the door and beamed as she waved him in. She was wearing a red nightie with black stockings, and her hair was long and thick. Sleaze picked up the scent of roses and jasmine, but nothing dominated the overall fragrance. Surprised, he reached out and held a strand of her hair to his nose. Then he leaned in and smelled her neck.

"It's nice, isn't it?" the woman said.

"It's wonderful," Sleaze said, giving her the once-over. "What is it?"

"It's called Chanel Number 5," she said, with a coy smile. "It's a new perfume from France. I love it."

"I can see why," he said, still awestruck by how much she looked like Beulah.

"I'm Jessie," she said, leading him by the hand to the bed. "Make yourself comfortable. What's your name?"

"Jimmy. Jimmy Sleaze," he said, removing his coat and tossing it on a chair before sitting down on the edge of the bed.

“It’s so nice to meet you, Jimmy,” she said, pouring two whiskeys and handing him one. “You would like a drink, right?”

“Yes, I would,” Sleaze said, feeling nervous around a woman for the first time in ages. He touched her glass with his and took a sip without breaking eye contact.

“You feel like chatting, or would you like to get straight to business?” she said, sitting in the middle of the bed and crossing her legs underneath her.

“Oh, let’s talk first,” he said, stretching his legs out and leaning back against one of the supports on the four-poster bed. “We got plenty of time. I paid for all night.”

“All night?” she said, sounding pleasantly surprised. “That must have cost you.”

“I’m quite sure you’re gonna be worth it,” Sleaze said, again admiring her from head to toe. “Tell me a bit about yourself.”

“There’s not much to tell,” she said, taking a small sip. “I grew up across the River on the Canadian side, then moved around a bit. Eventually, I landed here.”

“I see. How long have you been…?”

“Selling my ass for money?” she said with a grin.

“I guess that’s one way to put it,” Sleaze said with a frown, not pleased with her blunt turn of phrase.

“Not long,” Jessie said. “I bounced around different jobs for about a year. Sold women’s clothing. Hated it. Worked in a grocery store. Hated that even more. Then I ended up waitressing for six months until I met a woman who suggested I might be happier working at her place in Syracuse."

"A place like this?" Sleaze said.

"Yeah, but not as nice as this one," she said, topping off their drinks. "And Fannie takes care of her girls a lot better. She's much better to work for than Shirley. After I had a big fight with *The Bitch*, that's what all the girls called her, I left and ended up in Watertown working the streets until Fannie found me. You might say that she rescued me."

"Fascinating story," Sleaze said, torn between wanting to know a lot more about the woman and his need for information. "Working the street must be hard."

"Yeah, it can be. Especially this time of year," she said, shrugging. "You're lucky if you can even make eye contact with a guy given the way everybody is always walking around with their head down fighting the wind. I eventually figured out a way to start working inside where it was warm after that stupid law got passed."

"Prohibition?"

"That's the one," she said, raising her glass in toast.

Jimmy raised his glass and smiled back.

"So, you figured out a way to do business inside joints selling illegal booze. Speakeasies, right?"

"That's them," she said, lighting a cigarette. "I had a favorite joint I did pretty good business at. But I eventually had to get out of there."

"Why's that?"

"Over time, I ended up sleeping with different guys who drank there and were friends with each other. They eventually decided they didn't like sharing me," she said, shrugging. "And after a fight one night when one of the guys got cut up pretty bad with a knife, I was told to hit the bricks. The bastard who ran the place told me in no uncertain terms to get lost."

"And this guy had some serious juice, right?" Sleaze said. "I mean, he must be someone not to be trifled with."

"Nah, he's a total lackey for the guy who runs all the speakeasies in the area," Jessie said, crushing out her cigarette and finishing her drink.

"Who would that be?" Sleaze said, doing his best to control his excitement.

"I don't know the guy," she said, shaking her head. "I never met him. Some guy named Ben." She frowned as she tried to remember it. "Ben…Green," she said, eventually. "Yeah, that's it. Ben Green."

"Ben Green," Sleaze said, committing the name to memory.

"Yeah," she said, stretching out on the bed. "So, Jimmy, are we going do this or not?"

Milo cringed when the latest blast of wind hit him, and he felt a bone-chilling cold that reached the tips of his toes. Even crouched down in the small cabin and protected by the windshield, the frigid air seemed impossible to control, and his eyes watered until his face resembled someone mourning the passing of a loved one.

"You know, it's not so bad out here," Birdie said, rolling a cigarette with one hand as they neared the back of the island. "Are you okay, Milo? You look like your dog just died."

"They're tears of joy, Birdie," Milo said, wiping his eyes with his handkerchief.

"Yeah, that makes sense. If I were you, I'd be downright ecstatic most of the time," he said, cackling. "Hang on. I'm gonna leave the ice and get back in open water."

Birdie slowed down, and Milo felt the bow dip about a foot when it reached the water. But the runners on the front provided more than enough support, and Birdie slowly maneuvered the iceboat forward until the stern landed in the water with a gentle splash. Birdie headed for the boathouse that sat about a hundred yards away. He rolled a cigarette for Milo as the iceboat was pulled downriver by the current.

"All things considered," Birdie said, lighting both cigarettes. "This contraption works great."

"Apart from the weather, I agree," Milo said. "I've never been this cold before in my life."

"I imagine you'll be saying that a lot, Milo," he said, laughing as he turned the strange looking craft into the boathouse.

Tom and Billy were standing on the dock next to thirty milk cans lined up in a long row. Birdie turned the engine off, and

Billy caught the bow and turned the boat around until it was facing out then tied it to the dock. Milo climbed out and checked his watch.

"Forty-seven minutes," he said to Birdie. "Hey, guys. How's it going? Billy, do you mind helping Birdie load?"

"You got it, Milo," Billy said with a sad frown then got to work.

"How was the trip over?" Tom said, glancing at Milo.

"Actually, not bad at all," Milo said. "But I've got the best driver on the planet, right?"

"How cold was it?"

Milo gave him a look that told Tom everything he needed to know and accepted the bottle of brandy he was holding out.

"How's it going so far?" Milo said, nodding up at the house.

"It was a bit strange at first," Tom said. "But we've settled into something I guess you could call a routine."

"Then why is he so goddamn grumpy?" Milo said, watching Billy's sullen movements. "Is he fighting with Ruby already?"

"No, they pretty much ignore each other most of the time," Tom said.

"Don't tell me Daisy is withholding favors from him," Milo said, taking another sip from the pint of brandy.

"I'm afraid Daisy is taking her favors elsewhere at the moment," Tom said with a grin.

"Geez, Tom," Milo snapped. "What the hell is the matter with you? I brought Daisy over here to keep Billy happy."

"No, Milo," Tom said, shaking his head but unable to shake the grin. "Daisy's not doing any favors for me."

Milo thought about Tom's comment then stared at him in disbelief.

"Really?" Milo whispered. "Daisy and Ruby?"

"Yeah, I think so," he said.

"Man, I can't catch a break," Milo said, glancing at Billy who was helping Birdie secure the fifteen milk cans then covering them with a tarp. "From the look on his face, I'm gonna guess he has the same suspicions as you."

"Yeah, I'm sure he does. He hasn't said anything about it yet, but it's definitely weighing on his mind."

"I can't believe it," Milo said. "Daisy and Ruby. How about that?"

"Best laid plans, right?" Tom said, laughing. "Do you want me to say something to them?"

"Absolutely not," Milo said. "They're grown women, and it's their call about who they want to lie down with." Milo frowned and scratched the stubble on his chin. "Wow. I did not see that one coming."

"This could send Billy over the cliff, Milo," Tom said, turning serious. "The new love of his life dumps him for his ex-wife. And while they're living in the same house with no way for him to get away from it."

"Yeah, I know. It could be a big problem," Milo said. "Are you sure you'll have his recipe down by spring?"

"No doubt about it. I'm getting close to figuring out how he finishes the process," Tom said. "How do you want me to handle him for now?"

"Encourage him to focus on his work," Milo said, giving Tom a crooked grin. "You know, to take his mind off his troubles."

"You mean, keep him cooking like there's no tomorrow?" Tom said, laughing.

"Exactly," Milo said. "And keep an eye on Daisy and Ruby and let me know what you find out."

"You think they'll let me watch?"

"Hope springs eternal, Tom."

Breaking Balls And Curves

Oscar Hyde stared out the window at the falling snow that seemed to be coming down harder by the minute. Wondering what was keeping Melvin, Oscar decided to pass the time by raiding the liquor cabinet. Then he grumbled and cursed his new boss when he saw the lock Melvin had recently installed. Oscar was just about to try and pick it when Melvin strolled in, surprised to see him there.

"Aren't you supposed to be out fighting crime?" Melvin said, sitting down at his desk.

"In this weather?"

"Whatever happened to all that rain, sleet, and snow crap?" Melvin said, glancing around for something on top of the desk but not finding it.

"I don't work for the post office, Melvin," Oscar said.

"Oh, that's right," Melvin said. "That's their thing, isn't it?" Then he made eye contact with his chief of police. "And it's Mayor Melvin."

"Yeah, I got it, Melvin."

"Where the hell is it?"

"What are you looking for?"

“The letter about where to do tonight’s pick up,” Melvin said.

“It’s right here,” Oscar said, removing the note from his shirt pocket.

“Don’t touch the stuff on my desk, Oscar,” Melvin snapped.

“Well, I figured that since I’m the one picking the booze up, I kinda needed to know where to go.”

“Try not to think too much, Oscar. It always gets you into trouble.”

“Geez, you’re in a good mood. Why don’t you head over to Fannie’s for a freebie and take the edge off?”

“I just came from there,” Melvin said, getting up from his desk to unlock his liquor cabinet. He poured two drinks and handed one to Oscar who downed it and held his glass out for another. “One more. You gotta be sober tonight when you do your pick up.”

“I gotta say, Melvin. For-”

“Mayor Melvin,” he said, downing his drink and pouring another.

“Yeah, sure. Like I was trying to say, Melvin,” Oscar said, taking a sip. “For a guy who just got his ashes hauled, you sure seem to be a bit testy.”

“That’s the problem. I didn’t,” he said. “First, Daisy decides to take a long vacation.” Melvin shook his head. “I still can’t believe I missed my shot at her by *one day*. And now Fannie tells me that The Sleaze has exclusive rights to that new girl, Jessie.”

"Exclusive? How much is that costing him?" Oscar said.

"I'm sure it's a lot," Melvin said.

"She is a pretty young thing. You know who she reminds me of?"

"Who?" Melvin said, topping off his drink.

"That woman who used to run the Temperance Society," Oscar said. "The one who's now running that cheese shop in Watertown. What was her name again?"

"Beulah Peppin," Melvin said. "You're right, Oscar. They do look a lot alike. Damn it. I can't believe I missed my shot with her too. Fannie said that The Sleaze definitely wants her all to himself."

"So, he hasn't gone exclusive with her yet?" Oscar said, eyeing the bottle sitting on the cabinet.

"No, The Sleaze and Fannie are still negotiating," Melvin said.

"Then what's stopping you? Just set something up with her before The Sleaze closes the deal."

"I don't think that would be a smart thing to do, Oscar," Melvin said, shaking his head.

"Then find another girl. Fannie's got a bunch of them working for her," Oscar said.

"I know," he said. "But I was looking forward to having somebody new. Especially Daisy."

"Where did she go on vacation?" Oscar said.

"Some island somewhere," he said, shrugging. "Fannie didn't say. Look, you should get going. It's getting dark."

"Yeah, I'll get going soon," Oscar said, reaching for the bottle and pouring himself another drink.

"That has to be the last one until you're done with the job, Oscar," Melvin said, giving him a hard stare.

"Relax, Melvin," Oscar said. "I know exactly what to do. You know, since The Sleaze told me to just put all fifty cases in *my garage*. You know, the garage at *my house*."

"Let it go, Oscar," Melvin said, exasperated.

"And I'm not happy with my share," he said, downing his drink.

"It's the best I can do, Oscar," Melvin said. "Since The Sleaze is putting up all the money, I really couldn't argue with him about the split."

"I can't believe you agreed to him getting sixty percent."

"Yeah, well, believe what you want. And try to be happy with half of forty." Melvin glanced over at the chief of police. "That's twenty percent in case you were having trouble with the math."

"Yeah, thanks for helping me out with that. What's this anonymous seller charging you per case?"

"Uh…forty bucks," Melvin said, glancing out the window. "We'll be selling it for sixty."

"So, we're making twenty bucks a case?" Oscar said, turning his glass upside down to get any last drops. Then he licked the inside of the glass.

"Yes. For the tenth time, Oscar, Sleaze is making twelve bucks a case, and we're getting four each."

"That don't seem fair," Oscar said.

"Oscar, you're going to make two hundred dollars tonight just for picking up and dropping off fifty cases of booze," Melvin snapped. "And if it wasn't for me, your ass would still be sitting in jail. You're back as police chief and making some good money on the side. Don't be an ingrate."

"Yeah, I'll see what I can do about that," Oscar growled.

"And don't forget," Melvin said. "Until I get the thousand back you owe me, I'm gonna to have to ask for half of your two hundred each week."

"You know something, Mayor Melvin?"

"What's that, Oscar?"

"I really don't enjoy people breaking my balls."

"Don't worry, Oscar. You'll get used to it."

Oscar was still pissed off when he arrived to pick up the fifty cases. And maybe, he decided, his mood had gotten even worse. It was bitter cold and still snowing, he hadn't eaten dinner and was sober, and by the time he was halfway through the loading process, his back was killing him. Oscar almost missed the envelope that was slid between a couple of cases, but he picked it up off the dirt floor and stuck it in his pocket. When all fifty cases were secured on the truck, he drove to his house – the one that had been rented right out from underneath him by his new boss - and noticed that The Sleaze wasn't home. Deciding that one little case wouldn't be missed, Oscar unloaded and stacked forty-nine cases in the garage then headed to Melvin's place to get good and drunk. And maybe read the letter if he had time.

Jimmy Sleaze cursed the wind and snow as he made the drive in the truck he'd picked up cheap from a guy selling everything he owned before moving to Florida. The heater didn't work, and the hole in the floorboard under his feet only added to the cold, but the engine ran great, and the tires were new. Sleaze slowed when he hit Watertown and started checking the names of the streets. He grinned when he drove past the jail, then made a right turn and slowed to a crawl when he realized the side streets hadn't been plowed. But the truck, despite the fact that it was as cold inside as out, churned through the thick blanket of snow.

He managed to find a place to park in a nearby lot, then trudged his way through the snow to the house. Despite the miserable weather, Sleaze grinned and congratulated himself as he made the short walk. As soon as he'd gotten the guy's name out of his new girl and spent the next day checking a few things out, Ben Green hadn't been hard to track down.

Sleaze knocked and waited for the door to open. When it did, a scowling face appeared and gave him the quick once-over.

"Can I help you?"

"Are you, Mr. Green?"

"Who wants to know?" Ben Green said, watching him closely.

"Allow me to introduce myself. My name is Jimmy Sleaze."

"So?"

"So, nothing," Sleaze said, taking an instant dislike to the man. "I'd like to discuss a business proposition with you."

"You selling door to door? In this weather?" Ben Green said, laughing. "You must be the Fuller Brush guy. Or maybe you're pushing bibles."

Jimmy Sleaze bit his bottom lip hard to control the urge to deck the guy right on his front porch.

"No, Mr. Green," Sleaze said. "I can assure you that what I'm selling is a lot more interesting than a toilet brush."

"And just what might that be?" Ben Green said, still studying his face.

"Booze. What else?"

Ben Green flinched and continued to stare at him.

"Booze? No, I'm not interested," he said. "You're talking to the wrong guy."

"Oh, I'm pretty sure I'm talking to the right guy, Mr. Green," Sleaze said. "Now, are you gonna keep breaking my balls, or are you gonna let me in so I can at least explain what I have to offer?"

Ben Green maintained his hard stare then gave Sleaze a small nod and opened the door. Sleaze stepped inside the warm house and smiled.

"That's much better," Sleaze said. "I can't believe this winter weather."

"Don't worry. It's gonna get a whole lot worse," Green said. "What makes you think I might be interested in buying booze? I run a produce market."

"Somebody I trust gave me your name," Sleaze said, sitting down near the fireplace.

"I really don't care who you can trust, Mr. Sleaze," Green said. "What matters is who I can trust."

"Of course, that's completely understandable. Two-way trust is essential in any business venture."

"So, who is this mysterious individual who felt compelled to share my name with you?" Green said, leaning against the mantel.

"I believe she used to work in one of your establishments," Sleaze said. "At least, in a fashion."

"What's her name?" Green said, glaring at him.

"Her name's not important. Let's just say she's a working girl and leave it at that."

"Working girls are all over this town," Green said. "I have no idea who you're talking about."

"Apparently, some of your patrons weren't comfortable sharing this girl's...*affections*."

"That's what happens when you buy pussy on a short-term basis," Green said with a shrug.

"Indeed. The transactional approach is fraught with problems," Sleaze said. "I much prefer pussy as part of an ongoing process."

"Do you now?" Green said. "Can I assume you use the same approach when it comes to selling booze?"

"Of course," Sleaze said. "I've found that using a consistent, ongoing process is truly the only way to build and maintain a lasting relationship."

"I see. And what exactly does your ongoing process look like?" Green said.

"Fifty cases a week guaranteed for the next four months," Sleaze said. "And as soon as we make it through this dreadful winter, I'll be more than happy to discuss raising that number.

"That's a lot of process," Green said, nodding. "How do I know you aren't working for the Feds?"

"Oh, I imagine you might have a few doubts at the beginning," Sleaze said. "But I'm sure I'll be able to convince you otherwise."

"How do you plan on doing that?" Green said.

"By shooting one of them the first chance I get," Sleaze said without emotion.

"That would do it," Green said, nodding. "So, if I were somehow interested in your offer, how much do you want per case?"

“Seventy bucks,” Sleaze said, making eye contact.

“I see. And when would you be able to deliver the first fifty cases?”

“They’re right outside parked just down the street. I’ll even throw in the truck.”

Milo finished the last of his stew then dredged a piece of bread through the remains of the gravy. He stared across the table at Annabelle as he savored the last bite. She caught the look he was giving her and smiled back at him.

“What is it?” she said, cocking her head.

“Remarkable is the word that comes to mind,” Milo said, topping off her wine glass.

“The stew?”

“That too. Dinner was delicious,” Milo said, leaning back in his chair. “So, dear, how was your day?” he deadpanned.

“Don’t start with that shit, Milo,” she said, laughing as she lit a cigarette. “Tell me about the trips to the island.”

“Frank’s a genius,” Milo said. “It’s the goofiest looking thing I’ve ever seen in my life, but it works like a charm.”

“As long as Birdie is driving it, right?”

“Of course,” Milo said, also lighting a post-meal cigarette. “I’m never getting behind the wheel of that thing.”

“Are you still making two trips a night?” Annabelle said.

“Yeah, we are,” Milo said, nodding. “Three hundred gallons a night.”

"And Billy's able to keep that volume up?"

"So far. He's got a ton of cooking capacity to work with. And he's been working a lot lately," Milo said, tapping the ash off his smoke. "It's about the only thing Billy has to do at the moment."

"That's odd. I would have thought that Daisy would be more than enough to take his mind off work," Annabelle said.

"That was my original thinking as well," Milo said. "But it appears that Daisy has other ideas."

"Tom?" Annabelle said, frowning.

"No," Milo said, grinning as he shook his head. "Ruby."

"Really? Now, that's interesting," Annabelle said, exhaling smoke. "I take it Billy isn't pleased with that recent development."

"No," Milo said, laughing. Then he frowned. "I still can't believe I didn't see that one coming."

"Well, given Daisy's line of work, it shouldn't shock you," Annabelle said. "But I am a bit surprised about Ruby."

"Daisy can be very persuasive," he said. "Tom's getting worried that Billy is going to do something stupid."

"Gee, what are the odds of that?" Annabelle deadpanned. "Has Tom got Billy's process figured out yet?"

"No, not yet. Billy is a bit reluctant to let anybody know how the whole cooking process works."

"Maybe he's not as dumb as he comes across," Annabelle said, taking a sip of wine. "So, what's your plan?"

"Tom's keeping an eye on things and trying to keep Billy as calm as possible. But I may need to do something at some point."

"You're still not ready to get Ruby's new venture going?"

"No. It's gonna be awhile before I can do that," Milo said. "But at least she's calmed down for the moment. Tom says the ladies are really enjoying their new routine."

Annabelle raised an eyebrow and waited for him to continue.

"Champagne and hot baths."

"They could be doing a lot worse," Annabelle said, then noticed the look on Milo's face. "What's the matter?"

"I don't know," Milo said. "It's just that every time I figure out a way to solve a problem, another one seems to pop up."

"Oh, you poor baby," Annabelle said, laughing.

"Yeah, you're right. Okay, I'll stop pouting now," he said, sipping his wine. "What's the latest from D.C.? How's your buddy Vernon Adams doing?"

"Actually, I just sent him my monthly report today," Annabelle said.

"And?"

"Like I wrote in the report, things are all quiet on the northern front," she said, grinning.

"You don't mail your reports directly to him, do you?" Milo said, frowning as a potential loose end emerged.

"No, Vernon has all his undercover agents send their reports to a post office box in Arlington."

"Smart," Milo said, nodding.

"And he makes us use his alias," she said, crushing out her cigarette. "Adam Wonders. Vernon thinks he's so clever."

"So, no news about another agent being assigned up here?"

"Not a word," Annabelle said. "What's going on with The Sleaze?"

"I am on my way to Fannie's soon to get that very question answered," Milo said.

"You're going over there tonight?"

"Not a chance," Milo said, getting up to stack the dinner dishes in the sink. "Unlike Billy, I have someone very special to take my mind off of work."

"Yes, you do, Milo. Try not to forget it."

"All you need to do is just keep reminding me, Miss Caffey."

Milo accepted the glass Fannie was holding out and admired the photos on the wall while she got settled into the chair across from him.

"So, Daisy got her hooks into Ruby, huh?" Fannie said, chuckling. "That didn't take long."

"Daisy can be very persuasive," Milo said, taking a sip of his whiskey.

"She certainly can," Fannie said. "And yet she's never been able to persuade you, Milo."

"No, my relationship with Daisy has to remain professional," Milo said. "At least for the foreseeable future."

"You don't know what you're missing, Milo," Fannie said, laughing.

"I'm sure I get the general drift," he said, raising his glass in salute. "How are things going with Jessie and The Sleaze?"

"You were right about him," she said, reaching for a cigarette. "He's talking about her going exclusive with him."

"Good. Remember to charge him a small fortune," Milo said. "Was she able to work Ben Green's name into their conversation?"

"She was," Fannie said. "That girl has a bright future in front of her. Role-playing seems to come natural to her."

"The Sleaze hasn't tried to get rough with her, has he?"

"No, just the opposite. Jessie says he's very protective. Overly protective, in fact."

"Okay, then I suppose she'll be all right for the moment," Milo said. "But keep a close eye on things. And when she does go exclusive, tell her in no uncertain terms that she can't flirt or barely even talk to any of the other customers. The Sleaze can turn into a jackal at the drop of a hat."

Jimmy Sleaze listened closely as Melvin prattled on about his plans for the town as soon as spring arrived. But when Melvin started talking about gardens and asking him what sort of flowers he should plant to brighten up James street, Sleaze held up a hand and shook his head at the mayor.

"Melvin, please," Sleaze said. "Enough. I'd rather be buried in a box than listen to any more of this. Plant whatever kind of flowers you want. I really don't give a shit."

"Sorry."

"Where is he?" Sleaze said.

"We're talking about Oscar," Melvin said with a shrug. "Who the hell knows where he is?"

"Doesn't he work for you?"

"Yeah, well, I'm not sure I'd actually call it working," Melvin said. "Oscar's more of an occupational hazard."

"If he pulls that shit again," Sleaze said. "Oscar's going to experience first-hand just how cold the water around here is in January."

"I understand completely, Mr. Sleaze," Melvin said, his hands shaking slightly as he poured two drinks. "But while we wait, perhaps we can settle up."

Sleaze glared at Melvin, then took a sip of whiskey and tossed an envelope on the desk. Melvin took a few moments to count the money.

"Uh, perhaps my math skills are slipping a bit," Melvin said, tentatively. "But I think the envelope is a little short."

"Do you now?" Sleaze said, glaring at Melvin over the top of his glass. "Enlighten me, Melvin."

"Fifty cases bought at thirty, sold for sixty. That's a profit of fifteen hundred. Fifty percent of that is seven-fifty. From what I see, and, again, I may have miscounted, but it looks like there's only six hundred and ninety here."

"Your math is fine, Melvin," Sleaze said, lighting a cigarette. "But it was only forty-nine cases."

"Yes, but I just assumed that…"

"That it would come out of my end?" Sleaze said, laughing at the idea. "Bad assumption, Melvin."

"Yes, I suppose you're right," Melvin said, scowling. "But we only paid thirty for the missing case. I don't see why you expect me to pay the full sales price for it."

"I see. Then go right ahead, Melvin," Sleaze said, a cold stare fixed on his face.

"Go ahead with what?"

"You're a lawyer. Make your best case. Try to argue the point," Sleaze said, rubbing his fingers with his thumbs on each hand. "I'd love to debate it with you."

"No, that's okay," Melvin said, swallowing hard. "I'll just take it out of Oscar's cut."

"I'd expect nothing less, Melvin."

They both looked at the door when it opened, and a disheveled Oscar shuffled into the office and plopped down in the chair next to Jimmy Sleaze.

"Sorry I'm late," Oscar managed to get out. "I overslept. What did I miss?" He rubbed his eyes then his eyes caught sight of the bottle on the desk. He reached for it, but Melvin pulled it back out of reach. “Hey, what’s your problem?”

“I think you need to stay sober for a while, Oscar,” Melvin said. “We’d like to have a word with you.”

“About what?” Oscar said, glancing back and forth at them.

“About a missing case of whiskey,” Sleaze said.

“I don’t know nothing about that,” Oscar said, trying to sound casual as he glanced around the office.

“I see,” Sleaze said, nodding. “Okay, Mr. Hyde. I suggest you listen closely to what I’m about to tell you. Because I’m only going to tell you once. If you ever try to steal from me again, the consequences to you will be dire.”

“Dire?” Oscar said with a confused frown.

“It’s mean disastrous, Oscar,” Melvin said. “You know, really bad.”

“Okay, I get it. But accidents happen,” Oscar said, shrugging. “A case must have fallen off the back of the truck when I was driving home.”

“And maybe I’ll just slit your goddamn throat,” Sleaze said as he tossed back his drink then stood up. “Let me know as soon as you receive the location of this week’s delivery.” Sleaze pulled his coat on and placed the fedora on his head. “Good day, gentlemen.”

“Asshole,” Oscar said after The Sleaze had left the office. He reached for the bottle and poured himself a drink.

"Are you out of your mind?" Melvin said, shaking his head at the chief of police.

"It was one lousy case," Oscar said, tossing his drink back then wiping his mouth the back of his hand. "Man, I got a wicked hangover."

"It's coming out of your end," Melvin said.

"What?"

"I'm certainly not going to pay for your stupidity," Melvin said, removing two twenties from the envelope Sleaze had given him and sliding them across the desk.

"What's that?" Oscar said, nodding at the money.

"Your cut. What else would it be?"

"Forty bucks? You're joking, right?" Oscar said, helping himself to another drink.

"Two hundred minus a hundred of what you owe me," Melvin said. "And minus sixty for the case you stole."

"You trying to screw me over, Melvin?" Oscar growled as he pocketed the twenties.

"Not at all, Oscar," Melvin said with a sad shake of his head. "You don't need any help from me."

Vernon Adams read the report again and was finally satisfied with the checkmark in the box next to the Nothing of Significance to Report category. The winters up there must be brutal he decided, and that had to put a serious crimp in the bootleggers' ability to get product across the river given the snow and ice and brutal cold. He wondered about how Annabelle was spending her days and nights then smiled when he replayed their one and only night together. Then Vernon glanced down at the reports from the rest of his undercover agents and tossed them on the stack with the others.

"I probably should have just waited until spring," he said out loud to himself.

Vernon glanced up at the clock on the wall and smiled again when he realized it was quitting time and remembered he had an early dinner scheduled with someone who'd contacted him about a possible job with the Unit. He packed up and was just about to slip into his coat when his intercom buzzed.

"Yes, Jamie," he said. "I was just getting ready to head out. What is it?"

"Roland Doyle is on the phone," she said, laughing. "Nice way to end your day, huh?"

"Yeah, great," Vernon Adams said, sitting back down. "Put him through."

"Mr. Adams?"

"Hi, Roland. How are things going up there?"

"Okay, I guess," Roland said. "But it's been real quiet. It's too damn cold to go outside much less try to smuggle booze."

"Yes, I'm sure you're right," Vernon said.

"But I am keeping a close eye on a guy I've crossed swords with in the past," Roland said.

"Really?" Vernon Adams said, perking up. "Someone with a history of bootlegging?"

"No, he's a bank robber," Roland said. "But I'm sure he's thinking about making a career change if you catch my drift."

"Yes, I'm sure I do. Good for you, Roland. Be sure to keep me posted," Vernon said, glancing up at the clock again. "So, what can I do for you?"

"I was just wondering if you've made a decision about that thing we talked about?"

"Actually, I have, Roland," Vernon said, glancing at the stack of reports. "And I'm afraid I have some bad news on that front. I simply wasn't able to make that particular resource available."

"I see," Roland said, disappointed. "Have you given any more thought to my request for a transfer?"

"I certainly have, Roland. But at the moment, you're simply too valuable in your current position. Perhaps we can revisit the issue sometime in the spring."

"Yeah, okay. I guess that's it, huh?"

"Yes, for now," Vernon said. "But you stay in touch and let me know if you need anything."

"Yeah, I'll do that. Goodbye, Mr. Adams."

"Goodbye, Roland. Stay safe and warm."

Vernon Adams hung up and congratulated himself again for keeping the alcoholic agent out of the loop. Then he slipped into his coat and headed out of the office to do a little nighttime recruiting of a pretty young thing with curves exactly where he liked them and who was just dying to help him keep America safe and dry.

Episode 11

Wild Rides

Now that I think about it, I've never really appreciated the arrival of spring. After this winter, I won't be making that mistake again.

Milo Razner

Rising Temperatures And Boiling Points

Milo fought the urge to scream when the ice boat began to tip. But it landed back on both runners and continued its deliberate forward progress. He glanced over at Birdie who had his eyes fixed on a spot directly in front of them. Birdie had a one-hand death grip on the steering wheel, and he worked the throttle back and forth as he inched the ice boat forward until it cleared the last of the pack ice. When the stern landed in open water with a soft splash, Birdie put the boat in neutral and shut the engine down and let the current do its thing while he rolled cigarettes for both of them. Milo lit both and took a long drag on his to help him relax.

"That was the worst yet," Milo said, waiting for his heart rate to return to normal. He glanced back over his shoulder into the darkness. "I thought we were gonna go ass-up for a second there."

"No, we were fine, Milo," Birdie said, his cigarette tucked securely in the corner of his mouth. "I had it under control the whole time."

"I wish this weather would make up its mind," Milo said.

"It happens, Milo. And anytime it gets above freezing during the day, then dips back down at night, the ice starts to get confused."

"I guess that's one way to describe it," Milo said, shaking his head.

Birdie started the engine and accelerated across the open stretch of water until they reached a smaller section of pack ice on the other side. Birdie, who seemed to be getting better each day dealing with the constantly changing conditions, worked the boat onto a large, bobbing chunk of ice, crossed it, inched the boat across two more of the unsteady blocks, then accelerated after he was sure the ice was holding. Milo finally relaxed when Birdie made a right turn, zipped along the thick ice near the shoreline, and eased the ice boat into the stretch of open water that ran off the back of the island.

"See," Birdie said, grinning at Milo. "Nothing to it."

"Remind me to give you a raise," Milo said, patting him on the shoulder.

"I can't spend what you're paying me now, Milo," Birdie said, gently turning into the boathouse. Then he cackled and grinned at him again. "But if you insist."

Tom greeted them at the dock with the milk cans lined up in three rows of ten. Milo tossed him a line, and Tom tied the boat off then helped Milo and Birdie out of the boat.

"Let's take a little break, Birdie. I need to have a word with Tom."

"I'll start loading," Birdie said, limping down the dock to grab one of the milk cans.

Milo stared after him with an admiring look.

"I wish I could bottle that sort of work ethic," he said, then focused on Tom. "How's it going?"

"It's been a tough day," Tom said, frowning. "Billy headed up to the house for an early lunch and caught them going at it in front of the fireplace."

"Shit," Milo said. "I take it he didn't handle it well."

"He headed straight back to the cooking room and hasn't left since," Tom said. "He's threatening to leave. Says he's got more money than he knows what to do with and wants to get as far away from this place as he can."

"Goddamn it," Milo snapped. "How much more time do you need?"

"At least through the rest of winter," Tom said. "He's getting a bit better about trusting me hanging around during the finishing process, but I still don't have it."

"Okay," Milo said, nodding. "Tell you what, you take this run with Birdie, and I'll go have a little chat with him. Then I'll have a word with the lovebirds."

"You got it, Milo," Tom said. "Let me run up to the house and throw some more clothes on."

"Word of advice. When you get to the point where you think you've got enough on, add another layer."

Tom laughed and jogged down the dock then disappeared from sight.

"He thinks I'm joking. Birdie, I said take a break," Milo said, shaking his head as he watched the limping man struggle with getting the first can onto the boat. "Let me give you a hand with that."

"Maybe I will take a break," Birdie said, wiping his brow. "The last thing I want to be doing is working up a sweat in this cold."

"Look, Tom is gonna take the first run with you. I need to have a word with our cooker."

"Is there a problem?"

"There's always a problem," Milo said, then started down the dock. Then he stopped and turned around. "Slow and steady, right?"

"I got it, Milo. Slow and steady."

Jimmy Sleaze read the note a second time then glared across the desk at Melvin who was doing his best to avoid eye contact.

"You mind explaining what the hell is going on?" Sleaze said.

"I swear, Jimmy," Melvin said with a shrug. "I don't have a clue what they're talking about."

"Since you've been staking out the place, we might need to reconsider our arrangement," Sleaze said, reading from the note. Then he fixed another hard glare on the mayor. "What have you been up to, Melvin?"

"Honest, Jimmy. I swear I don't know what the hell they're referring to," Melvin said, managing to pour drinks without spilling.

"Oscar," Sleaze said, almost spitting the name out. "Where is he?"

"I imagine he's still in his office sleeping it off," Melvin said.

"Get his ass over here."

Melvin nodded and picked up the phone. He waited until Violet came on the line then asked her to summon the police chief to his office. He hung up and sipped his whiskey, again doing his best to avoid the death stare The Sleaze was giving him.

Milo entered the cooking room and spotted Billy standing in front of a long table. He whistled softly, and Billy turned and gave him a small wave. Milo crossed the room and was surprised to see the large number of milk cans neatly arranged along one wall. He was tempted to do the math, but he focused on the immediate problem of how to handle his increasingly incalcitrant Miracle worker.

"Hey, Billy."

"Hi, Mr. Razner," Billy said, turning around and leaning against the table with his arms folded across his chest.

"Working late, huh?"

"I suppose."

"You seem upset, Billy. What's the matter?"

"It's those two up at the house, Mr. Razner," Billy said. "I really don't care what they do with each other, but they don't need to rub my nose in it."

Milo let the image that flashed in his head pass without comment, then nodded sympathetically.

"Yes, Tom mentioned that you happened to walk in on them today," Milo said.

"Yeah," he whispered as he stared down at the floor.

"I'm sorry, Billy," Milo said. "It certainly wasn't part of my plan. I was sure that you and Daisy had a chance to build a future together."

"It don't matter," he said, staring at Milo. "I'm getting out of here just as soon as I can."

"I see. Where are you thinking about going?"

"I don't know yet," Billy said. "Somewhere far from here, that's for sure. And definitely somewhere warmer."

"Sure, I get that," Milo said, nodding. "And I can't say that I blame you, Billy. No man should have to see his ex-wife and his girlfriend doing that. Especially in the living room."

"I knew they'd been keeping company pretty much since the day they got here," he said, exhaling audibly. "But that was too much for me to handle."

"The last straw, you might say?"

"Exactly," Billy said with a defiant nod of his head. "That's exactly what it was, Mr. Razner."

"I understand completely, Billy."

"Really?"

"I do. In fact, I understand it so well that I'm going to help you get set up in a new place."

"You don't need to do that, Mr. Razner," Billy said. "You've already done way too much for me."

"No, I insist," Milo said. "In fact, I have some property out in California that is just sitting idle at the moment."

"California?"

"Yes. Up north above San Francisco. And I'd be happy to let you stay there as long as you want."

"You would? Why would you do that?"

"Because the property needs someone to take care of it," Milo said. "And you're looking for a place to go."

"Geez, California," Billy said, scratching the stubble on his cheek. "I have always wanted to go there."

"It's beautiful out there. And far away from your current problems," Milo said.

"Wow. I gotta say that sounds pretty good at the moment. Can I think on it for a spell?"

"Take all the time you need, Billy," Milo said. "You've got all winter."

"Yeah, I suppose I do," he said, shrugging.

"But if you do decide to leave the area, can I ask you to do one small favor for me?"

"Sure, Mr. Razner," Billy said.

"I need your help solving a problem I'm going to have," Milo said.

"I'll try. What problem are you talking about?"

"Your departure will create a major void in my operation," Milo said, choosing his words carefully.

"Void?"

"An empty space," Milo said. "Like a giant black hole."

"You mean, sort of like what you see when you look out at the River at night?"

"Yes, that's exactly what I mean," Milo said. "And since I plan to continue my operation after you're gone, I'm going to be in a world of hurt without the skills of my Miracle worker. Do you understand what I'm saying, Billy?"

"It's a little hard to miss that one, Mr. Razner."

"Good. I'm glad we're on the same page," Milo said as he began pacing back and forth. "What am I gonna do without you, Billy?"

"I think I've got an idea."

"Really? Do tell," Milo said, coming to a stop directly in front of his cooker.

"How about I just show Tom how the whole process works? He's smart as all get out. And the quality of his Red Deer is off the charts good."

"You'd be willing to do that?"

"Sure, Mr. Razner," Billy said. "I'm always pretty protective about my cooking, but since I won't be around, that's the least I can do."

"That's a mighty generous offer, Billy," Milo said. "Tell you what, I'll swap you straight up. The deed to my property in California for your recipes and cooking process."

"You got a deal, Mr. Razner," Billy said, extending his hand.

Milo returned the handshake and beamed at his cooker.

"See, Billy," Milo said. "Like I always say, there's always a solution to every problem as long as you're willing to keep looking."

"I need to remember that one," Billy said.

"You might want to write it down," Milo said. "Now, if you'll excuse me, I'm going to head up to the house and enjoy a sandwich."

"With those two?" Billy said, frowning.

"No, Billy. A real sandwich. I missed dinner," Milo said, shaking his head. "I'll see you soon."

"Hey, Mr. Razner."

"Yeah?"

"You might want to make some noise going in the house. You know, just in case."

"Yeah, thanks, Billy. I'll do that."

Milo gave him a small wave and headed for the door. He walked up the inclined path that led to the house hunched down to block the wind that had picked up.

"You're slipping, Milo," he said to himself, laughing as he tiptoed his way through a deep patch of snow. "You should have thought of that a long time ago."

Oscar read the note through bloodshot eyes then coughed and hacked up a mouthful of phlegm. He glanced around the office, thought about just swallowing it then noticed the handkerchief Melvin was holding out. He spit into it, wiped his mouth, then blew his nose. When he was finished, he tried to hand it back to the mayor.

"Keep it," Melvin said, glancing at The Sleaze who was sitting next to Oscar.

"You want to explain yourself, Oscar?" Sleaze said.

"Explain what?" Oscar said, glancing back and forth at them thoroughly confused.

"The reference to someone staking out the location of the drop-off," Sleaze said, slowly enunciating each word.

"I ain't been staking anything out," Oscar said. "I've been drunk all week. I can barely make it to my office."

"Well, obviously somebody has," Sleaze said. "And if it wasn't you, who was it?" He looked at Melvin and fixed a cold stare on him.

"Don't look at me," Melvin said. "I've been at Fannie's every night this week. And she can verify that."

"Yeah, you ain't got the balls to try and screw me over," Sleaze said, rubbing his chin.

"Gee, thanks for noticing, Jimmy," Melvin said.

"Maybe it was you," Oscar said to The Sleaze.

"I beg your pardon?"

"You're the only one left," Oscar said. "Yeah, I bet it was you. Trying to set us up."

"Easy there, Oscar," Melvin said, his voice rising in warning. "He doesn't mean that, Jimmy."

Sleaze continued to glare at Oscar until the police chief looked away.

"Be very careful, Oscar," Sleaze growled. Then he turned to Melvin. "But what I don't understand is the reference to changing the delivery location. How would we even know about another location?"

"Oh, yeah," Oscar said, cocking her head. "I completely forgot."

"Forgot about what?" Melvin said.

"The letter," he said, fumbling for his pocket. "Hang on. I think I've got it here somewhere."

Milo found the first-floor empty then heard laughter coming from upstairs. He started toward the stairs then stopped and headed back to the kitchen. He grabbed a champagne glass from a cabinet then climbed the long, curved stairway and knocked on the door of the master bedroom.

"What do you want?" Ruby snapped.

"I need a word with you two," Milo said, opening the door a crack.

"Milo?" Ruby said.

"Yeah, it's me. Where are you?" he said, stepping inside the massive bedroom with a king-sized bed that had recently been used.

"We're in here," Daisy said.

Milo headed for the bathroom and stood in the doorway. They were in the tub with Ruby stretched out with her back pressed up against Daisy. They both gave him sleepy-eyed grins, and he grabbed a chair from the bedroom and sat down next to the tub. He grabbed the champagne bottle from an ice bucket and poured himself a glass.

"How are you doing, Milo?" Daisy said, holding her glass out for a refill.

Milo topped off both their glasses then slid the bottle back into the bucket and took a sip. He lit a cigarette and smoked in silence as he continued to glare at them.

"I think we're in trouble," Ruby said with a giggle.

"Maybe we should ask him to join us. That'll cheer him up," Daisy said, laughing. "What do you say, Milo? There's plenty of room."

"Perhaps another time," Milo said, exhaling smoke. "I must say that things have taken an interesting turn."

"Definitely a turn for the better," Daisy said, running a hand up and down Ruby's arm.

"I'm happy for you," Milo said.

"You don't look very happy, Milo," Ruby said. "You did say that we were free to do whatever we wanted over here, remember?"

"I remember, Ruby," Milo said, nodding at her. "So, I take it you're now quite content spending the winter over here?"

"I'm delighted, Milo," Ruby said. "Thanks for asking. And thanks for sending this beautiful creature my way."

"Aren't you sweet," Daisy said, nuzzling her neck.

"What are you doing here, Milo?" Ruby said.

"At the moment, I'm trying to clean up your mess," he said, taking another sip of champagne.

"Billy?" Daisy said.

"No, I'm talking about the dirty dishes in the sink," Milo snapped. "Of course, I'm talking about Billy."

"Yeah, we're sorry about that one, Milo," Ruby said. "But that roaring fire this morning was too good to pass up."

"Well, the next time you two feel like stretching out in front of the fire, how about you just use the fireplace in the bedroom?"

Milo said, glancing back and forth at them. "Just how good a look did he get?"

"Oh, it was pretty up close and personal," Daisy said, then they both burst into laughter.

"Look, I really don't care what you do," he said evenly. "In fact, if this is what makes you both happy, knock yourself out. It'll be two fewer things I have to worry about. But Billy is very fragile at the moment, and I need to get him settled down and keep him that way until he leaves."

"Leaves?" Ruby said. "Where's he going?"

"I'm sure he'll tell you all about it," Milo said. "But until he goes, I expect you two to try to keep your hands off each other when he's around." He paused and waited until he was sure they were paying close attention. "Am I making myself clear?"

"Yes, we got it, Milo," Ruby said.

"Yeah," Daisy said. "You think we should apologize to him?"

"At a minimum," Milo said. "I expect you to make it right and put at least a semblance of a smile back on his face. Do we have an understanding?"

"We do," Ruby said, nodding. "Sorry, Milo. We'll try to do better."

"You're going to do more than try, Ruby," Milo said. "And if you don't figure out a way to cool things down over here for the rest of the winter, I may have to reconsider my offer."

"What?" Ruby said, giving him a wide-eyed stare.

"Oh, good. I finally have your attention," Milo said, crushing out his cigarette.

"You can't do that, Milo," Ruby said, sitting up quickly and splashing water onto the tile floor.

"Watch me."

"What would I do for work?" Ruby said with a sullen frown.

"Talk to Fannie," Milo said, heading for the door. "I'm sure Daisy will give you a great recommendation."

Milo headed outside and carefully made his way down the slippery incline until he reached the boathouse. He stood on the dock and smoked two more cigarettes before he spotted the lights of the ice boat. Moments later, Birdie eased the boat into the slip and shut the engine down.

"Any problems?" Milo said to Birdie.

"No, it was fine. Tom was a bit of a baby, but he eventually settled down," Birdie said with a cackle.

"That scared the shit out of me," Tom said, shaking his head. "You guys are nuts. How about next year we just build inventory for the winter and store it at the farm?"

"Not a chance," Milo said, shaking his head. "Never mess with something that's working for you."

"We must have a different definition of working," Tom said, shaking his head. "How did it go with Billy?"

"Quite well, actually," Milo said with a grin. "We came to an agreement. I'm giving him a property in California in return for him teaching you all his recipes and overall cooking process."

"You're joking, right?" Tom said, stunned.

"I'd never joke about something like that," Milo said, unable to shake the grin. "He'll be leaving in the spring as soon as we get the boat back in the water. So, put your learning hat on and pay attention in class."

"Wow, great job, Milo," Tom said. "Did you talk to Daisy and Ruby?"

"I did," Milo said, nodding.

"Were they taking their champagne bath?" Tom said, laughing.

"They were."

"That must have been a sight to behold," Birdie said.

"It's the Eighth Wonder of the World, Birdie," Milo said. "I gave them a friendly reminder about the need to take the long view, and I expect things to settle down around here. But if it doesn't, you let me know straight away."

"Will do, Milo," Tom said. "Billy's moving to California, huh?"

"He is."

"I didn't know you owned property in California," Tom said.

"I don't," Milo said with a shrug. "But I'm definitely gonna be buying some."

"And then just give it to him?"

"Why not?" Milo said, shrugging.

"You sure do work in mysterious ways, Milo," Birdie said.

"Yeah, well, I just couldn't bring myself to putting the kid at the bottom of the River."

Higher Aspirations

Ben Green crossed the living room of his suite and opened the door. He waved the Senator in then took his hat and coat and hung them up.

"How have you been, Senator?" Ben Green said, pouring drinks.

"Just great, Ben," Senator Miller said, taking in the suite and nodding his approval. "This is nice. I think I'll stay here the next time I'm in town."

"I must say I was surprised when you said you wanted to meet in Syracuse," Green said, handing the Senator his drink.

"Well, since I needed to be here to meet with someone who's going to be helping out on my campaign, I thought I'd kill two birds with one stone."

"Campaign? What are you talking about? You've got four years left on your current term," Green said, handing him a thick envelope.

Senator Miller set his drink down and examined the stack of cash inside.

"Well done, Ben. I'm impressed. We had a good month," he said, sliding the envelope into the pocket of his suit jacket.

"Biggest one yet," Green said, taking a sip. "What campaign are you talking about?"

"My campaign for governor," Senator Miller said with a grin.

"You're running for governor? Why on earth would you do that? Nobody's going to beat that priss."

"He's not going to run," the Senator said. "He's going to announce it in a couple of days."

"Why the hell wouldn't he run?" Green said, sitting down on a couch.

"Because of Milo Razner," the Senator said, also sitting down and draping a leg over his knee.

"Razner? What's he been up to?"

"All sorts of things," the Senator said. "He gave me a file on the guy thick enough to choke a horse. I took a few snapshots of some of the more lurid items and mailed them off. Mr. Razner is quite remarkable. And if he wasn't so valuable to our operation, I'd be doing everything I could to get him to work for me."

"I don't trust the guy," Ben Green said with a shake of his head.

"Be that as it may, Ben," the Senator said. "But Milo is definitely someone we need to keep on our good side." He glanced around the suite then back at Green. "Where's Beulah?"

"She had to head home for a while," Green said. "Her mama's sick."

"I'm sorry to hear that," the Senator said. "Send her my best. So, where do we stand at the moment?"

"I'm opening two new speakeasies next week. That will bring us to a hundred and five. And I'm up to two hundred cases of the top-shelf stuff. I'm getting fifty of them from a new guy I don't like. But I don't have much choice of suppliers this time of year."

"What's the matter with him?" the Senator said.

"You ever meet anybody and develop an intense hatred for them on the spot?" Ben Green said.

"I'm a U.S. Senator, Ben," he said, laughing. "What do you think?"

"Yeah, I suppose you get that all the time," Green said, nodding.

"How's Milo doing with his deliveries?"

"Razner keeps coming up with more product. Every time I bump my order, it shows up right on time. I have no idea how he's moving that much booze across the Canadian plains, especially in winter."

"Don't worry about it, Ben. As long as it keeps coming, I don't care if he's bringing it in by dogsled."

"Yeah, but still," Green said, shaking his head. "Something ain't right about it."

Birdie studied the menu and finally decided to go with the special. He slid the menu to one side, noticed Roland Doyle sitting by himself at the counter reading a newspaper, then stared out the window at the snowfall that was starting to accumulate on top of the two feet they already had. He glanced at the door when it opened, and a pretty woman stepped inside and glanced around the crowded diner. Then her eyes landed on his, and she tentatively approached the booth.

"I'm sorry to be so forward," she said, smiling down at him. "But this place is packed at the moment. Would you mind if I shared your booth with you?"

"No, not at all," Birdie said, momentarily caught off guard. "Please, have a seat."

"Thank you so much," she said, removing her coat and sliding into the booth. "You're very kind. I'm Sally Anderson."

"Nice to meet you, Sally. I'm Birdie."

"Birdie? Just the one name?"

"I only ever needed one," he said with a shrug. "I don't think I've ever seen you before. Are you new in town?"

"As a matter of fact, I am," she said with a smile he could look at all day. "I'm a nurse working for Doc Early. Doc's getting up in years and decided he needed some help."

"Sure, I know Doc," Birdie said. "Everybody does."

"He's a wonderful man," Sally said, studying the menu. "What's good here?"

"Not much," Birdie said with a grin. "I usually go with the special."

"Then the special it is," she said, flashing him the grin again as she slid the menu to one side. "Now, why don't you tell me all about yourself?"

Milo looked across the coffee table and shook his head repeatedly. When The Sleaze finally shrugged that he'd gotten the message, Milo topped off their drinks then sat back to light a cigarette.

"What happened to you, Milo?" The Sleaze said, reaching for Milo's pack. "You gone soft in your old age?"

"Let's say I've matured. Like I told you, Jimmy, I enjoy life a whole lot better when I don't have to be looking over my shoulder all the time."

"Who's gonna catch you?" The Sleaze said with a laugh. "Roland Doyle?"

"You do have a point," Milo said, laughing along. "I imagine it's fertile ground around here for the bootleggers."

"Don't you miss the excitement?" The Sleaze said.

"Not really," Milo said. "And I sure don't miss the gunfire."

"You could get rich," The Sleaze said, cocking his head.

"I'm already getting rich," Milo said, shrugging it off. "Milk and cheese are quite profitable."

"And very boring."

"At my age, I don't mind being bored one bit," Milo said. "I take it you found a supplier."

"Yeah, for now," The Sleaze said. "It's only fifty cases a week, but as soon as it warms up, I'll be ramping up."

"Fifty?" Milo said, surprised. "That sounds like a lot. Who the hell is drinking that much around here?"

"No, I'm unloading it in Watertown," The Sleaze said, exhaling smoke. "Some guy runs a bunch of speakeasies with a lot of thirsty customers."

"I suppose if you bought off the right cops and judges, speakeasies wouldn't be a bad way to go," Milo said, tapping ash off his smoke. "The bar business is probably where most of the money is being made. You know, on the retail side."

"Hmmm. You're probably right about that. Interesting. I need to think on that."

"I'd be surprised if you didn't, Jimmy," Milo said, grinning at him. "You always did have higher aspirations."

"Yeah, that's a very interesting idea," The Sleaze said, nodding. "And why should that son of a bitch be getting rich off me?" The Sleaze said, nodding. "You see, that's what I'm talking about, Milo. With your brain and my muscle, we could be cleaning up. Just like the old days."

"No way, Jimmy," Milo said, shaking his head again. "But thanks for the offer."

"You're gonna end up regretting it, Milo," The Sleaze said, tossing back his drink and refilling his glass.

"I'm sure I will. Remember to send me a postcard after you buy Miami," Milo said, reaching for his glass. "Fannie tells me you went exclusive with one of her girls."

"Yeah, I did. Jessie," The Sleaze said, grinning. "I can't believe how much she looks like Beulah."

"I thought the same thing the first time I saw her," Milo said. "Is she worth the money?"

"She's getting there," The Sleaze said. "I just need to teach her a few of the finer points."

"Don't start roughing her up, Jimmy," Milo said, scowling. "Fannie's place is like a historical landmark around here, and word travels fast. And given your new profession, you don't need that sort of negative attention."

"Yeah, you're probably right," he said, grinning as he reached for another cigarette. "I'll try to control myself."

"Good," Milo said, nodding. Then he chuckled and took a sip. "Melvin rented you Oscar's house, huh?"

"Yeah," The Sleaze said, laughing. "I have to give Melvin credit for that one. Oscar is still pissed off about that."

"How can you tell? The last few times I saw him, he could barely stand up."

"He is pretty much useless," The Sleaze said. "I'm gonna need to do something about him."

"Don't start killing cops, Jimmy," Milo said. "That would attract even more attention."

"I suppose," he said. "But maybe I can come up with a way to take him out without anybody knowing who did it."

"And run the risk of ending up with a police chief who actually knows what he's doing?"

"Yeah, you're right, Milo," The Sleaze said. "But it's so damn tempting."

Oscar glanced over at The Sleaze sitting in the passenger seat and scowled. Then he stared back out the windshield and followed the set of tire tracks on the small trail that wound through a stand of pines. When he caught a glimpse of a small log cabin tucked between several more snow-covered trees, he stopped the truck and again scowled at his traveling companion.

"I still don't know why you insisted on coming along," Oscar said.

"It's simple, Oscar," The Sleaze said, yawning. "I don't trust you as far as I can throw you."

They both hopped out of the truck and trudged through the snow until they reached the front porch. Sleaze turned his flashlight on and glanced around as he pulled a pistol from his pocket.

"What do you think you're doing with that?" Oscar said, nodding at the gun. "There ain't nobody here."

"Let's call it an insurance policy," Sleaze said, shining the light through a window. "There they are. Sitting right inside the door just like they said they would."

"I wonder whose cabin this is," Oscar said, slowly opening the door.

"Obviously someone who values their privacy," Sleaze said, stepping inside. He shined the light around the space then focused on the stacks of whiskey cases. "Okay, all fifty are here." He glanced at Oscar. "Let's make sure that number doesn't change."

"It won't," Oscar mumbled. "As long as one doesn't fall off the truck."

Milo heard the knock and headed for the door, hoping that Annabelle had decided to surprise him with a late-night visit. But when he opened it, he saw Birdie standing in the doorway.

"Hey, come on it," Milo said, ushering him inside.

"Sorry to drop in on you unannounced, Milo," Birdie said, sitting down on the couch.

"Don't worry about it," Milo said, pouring him a drink then sitting down across from him. "What's the matter? Did you have a problem making your runs tonight?"

"No, they went fine," Birdie said. "And Johnny's working out great."

"Good. So, what's up?"

"I ate lunch with somebody today," Birdie said.

"It's been known to happen."

"Not like this, Milo," he said, rolling a cigarette with one hand. "I was sitting in a booth at the diner when this pretty young thing walks up and asks if she could join me."

"Okay," Milo said, suddenly on edge. "Just like that?"

"Yeah. The diner was packed, and she said she only had a half-hour to eat lunch. I didn't even give it a second thought. You know, since she was so pretty."

"Then what happened?"

"She started asking me a whole bunch of questions," Birdie said. "Stuff like did I grow up around here, what did I do for work, did I have any hobbies. The questions just kept coming all through lunch."

"You think she was just being friendly?" Milo said, frowning.

"Maybe," Birdie said. "But I thought I should let you know."

"Yeah, good call, Birdie," Milo said, rubbing his forehead. "Did she say what she does for work?"

"She's a nurse. She just started working for Doc Early."

"Okay, then that's what I'll do," Milo said.

"What's that?"

"I'm overdue for my annual checkup," Milo said with a grin. "And I have been getting heartburn a lot lately."

"Yeah, you definitely want to get that checked out," Birdie said, grinning back at him. "What should I do if I see her again?"

"Be real nice to her. And keep your ears open and your mouth shut."

Milo entered the doctor's office and waved to the elderly woman sitting behind a desk. She waved back with a big smile and got up to shake his hand.

"Hi, Milo. It's nice to see you."

"How are you, Mrs. Early?"

"Oh, I'm getting by," she said, laughing. "Doc's finishing up with someone at the moment. Just head on back to the exam room on the left, and I'll send Sally back."

"Sally?"

"She just started. I finally convinced the old coot he needed some help."

"Another doctor?"

"No, she's a nurse. You gonna like her. She's really pretty," she said, then cocked her head at him. "Now, you behave yourself, Milo."

"Perish the thought," Milo said with a wave and a grin as he headed down the hall.

Milo hopped up on the padded exam table and kicked his legs back and forth as he glanced around the small room. Moments later, a nurse wearing white entered, and Milo flinched when he got a good look at her. Pretty had been an understatement.

"Let's see," she said, reading from a clipboard. "Mr. Razner?"

"Milo," he said, beaming at her.

"Milo, it is," she said, flashing him a smile he found irresistible. "I'm Sally Anderson."

"Should I call you Nurse Sally?" he said, overtly flirting with her.

"Well, I suppose you can call me anything you like, Milo," she said. "As long as it isn't mean."

"Mean is the last thing that comes to mind, Nurse Sally."

"Aren't you sweet," she said. "Now, if you wouldn't mind rolling up your shirtsleeve, let's get a look at that blood pressure."

Milo complied and picked up the scent of jasmine when she got close. He closed his eyes and let her scent envelop him. He snapped out of it when he felt the band around his arm get tighter. She focused on the instrument, then released the pressure gradually and removed the band.

"One-twenty over eighty," she said, nodding. "Perfect. You must lead a stress-free life, Milo."

"It has its moments," Milo said.

"What do you do for work?" she said, making eye contact.

"I'm a dairy farmer," Milo said, rolling his sleeve down.

"Really?" she said. "I never would have guessed that. Interesting work?"

"Oh, cows are fascinating creatures. Did you know they have to be milked twice a day?"

"As a matter of fact, I did know that," she said, again flashing him that smile. "Open your mouth."

"If you insist, Nurse Sally."

"You're bad," she said, flirting back. "Let's check your temperature."

"I'm sure its gone up since I arrived," he said, then let her slide the thermometer under his tongue.

"Are you always this forward?" she said, putting her hands on her hips.

"Umtimes," Milo managed to mumble.

"I'll try to remember that."

Milo stared at her until she removed and checked the thermometer.

"Ninety-eight point six," she said, nodding. "You obviously lead a clean life, Milo."

"Occasionally. How long have you been in town?"

"Only a few days," she said. "And I must say, I'm looking forward to spring already."

"Have you had a chance to meet many of the locals?" Milo said, staying casual.

"A few," she said. "And I love the Earlys. They've been married fifty-five years. Can you believe that?"

"That's a long time…to do anything," he said.

"Indeed," she said, laughing. "Now, if you don't mind, please step on the scale, and we'll get your weight."

Milo hopped off the table and did what he was told.

"One-seventy," she said. "You do take good care of yourself."

"It's all that milk. You know, it builds strong bones and body."

"So, I've heard."

"And I try to eat sensibly."

"That's good to know."

"Do you enjoy good food, Nurse Sally?"

"Is that your way of asking me out to dinner, Milo?" she said, flashing the smile.

"Now, there's an idea," he said. "Since you don't know many people around here."

"Well, let's see," she said, giving it some thought. "Yes, I suppose we could start with dinner."

The door opened, and an elderly man with a full head of white hair entered the exam room smoking a cigarette.

"Milo," Doc Early said. "How the hell are you?"

"I'm great, Doc," Milo said, returning the energetic handshake.

"I see you've met, Sally," he said, beaming at his new nurse. "Is she taking good care of you?"

"I've got no complaints so far," he said, glancing at her.

"Well, you're in good hands with her," Doc Early said.

"I'm sure of that," Milo said.

"I'll leave you two alone," Sally said, flashing a smile at Milo. "It was nice meeting you, Milo."

Then she turned and left the office. Both men watched her walk away.

"She's something special, isn't she?" Doc Early said.

"Remarkable. Where did you find her?"

"She answered an ad my wife placed in the paper."

"Good hire, Doc. She's got a ton of personality."

"She does," Doc Early said, taking a final drag before crushing out his cigarette. "And from what I've seen and heard, she's *real friendly*, Milo."

"You don't say?" Milo said, raising an eyebrow at the doctor.

"Oh, yeah," Doc Early said with a wink. "I don't think her expertise with the human body is confined just to work. If you catch my drift. Now, let's talk about this heartburn problem you're dealing with."

Horizontal Chats

Jimmy Sleaze took a sip of the whiskey the bartender had poured then stared at the shot glass before tossing back the rest. Then he motioned for another.

"What is this stuff?" Sleaze said to the bartender.

"Red Deer," the bartender said. "It's good, huh?"

"It certainly is," Sleaze said, tossing back the second shot. "Where do you get it?"

"That's not a question we like customers asking around here," the bartender said. "And I wouldn't have a clue where he gets it."

"He being Mr. Green, right?" Sleaze said.

"You seem to know a lot what with you being a stranger and all," he said. "With all due respect, who he is really ain't none of your business."

"Fair enough," Sleaze said. "Let me take a look at that bottle."

The bartender set the bottle in front of him, and Sleaze tossed a five on the bar. The bartender grabbed the bill then wandered off.

"From the plains of Alberta," Sleaze said, reading the label. "That's a long way for booze to be traveling."

Then he shrugged and poured himself another shot.

Annabelle paced back and forth across her living room, paused to toss another log on the fire, then resumed her stroll, deep in thought. Milo watched her with a contented smile until she caught him staring at her.

"Penny for your thoughts, Milo."

"Are you sure you really want to hear them?"

"Yeah, on second thought, maybe you better save them for later," she said, stopping in front of his chair and leaning down to give him a kiss. "A nurse," she said, nodding. "I have to give Vernon credit for that one. What better way to meet a lot of people in a hurry, right?"

"Yeah, that was pretty smart," Milo said. "If she is actually working for the Feds."

"It has to be her, right?" Annabelle said, leaning against the mantel. "I don't see anybody else just happening to show up in town in the dead of winter."

"No, me either. And it is the perfect cover. I wonder how he even knew Doc Early was looking to hire somebody," Milo said.

"Vernon must have a subscription to the Watertown paper," Annabelle said.

"Or he's got somebody else working down there," Milo said. "I got a bad feeling about this one."

"Me too. Vernon is definitely up to something," she said, finally sitting down. "I think it might be time for me to have another chat with him."

"A chat, huh?"

"Yes, unfortunately, it might come to that," she said, shaking her head. "Geez, the things I do for this job." She got up and draped herself across his lap. "Do you ever think about getting out, Milo?"

"No, never," he said, shaking his head. "And we made a pact that we were gonna let this thing run its course until they eventually get around to repealing that stupid law."

"I know," she said, gently stroking the side of his face. "But we're making a fortune, Milo. How much money do we need?"

"How long is a piece of string?"

"Oh, so you're gonna go philosophical on me tonight, huh?"

"I doubt if you'll be thinking about philosophy later on," Milo said with a grin. "But if you start quoting Karl Marx, I'll know I'm in big trouble." He shook his head. "Yeah, I hate to say it. But maybe you should have a little chat with your boss."

"Are you going to handle the nurse?"

"Yeah."

"By taking a *meeting* with her?" Annabelle said, giving him a coy smile.

"Maybe. But I thought I'd start with dinner."

"Don't do anything stupid, Milo."

"Like what?"

"Like starting to like her, what else?"

"I wouldn't worry about that, Annabelle."

"Why not?"

"One undercover Fed in the house is more than enough."

Jimmy Sleaze rolled off the woman and sat on the edge of the bed. He poured a couple of drinks, handed one to her then lit a cigarette.

"That was amazing," Jessie said, covering herself with the sheet as she sat up in bed.

"It was," Sleaze said, staring off at the far wall.

"What's the matter, Jimmy?"

"Oh, I'm just thinking about work," he said, taking a swallow of whiskey.

"Your mysterious moving business, right?" she said, laughing.

"Yeah, my moving business," Sleaze said. "I'm starting to get some customers in Watertown. That's where I was today."

"Moving furniture?" Jessie said, reaching for a pack of cigarettes.

"Some furniture," he said, still staring off. "And I had to move a stove today. Almost broke my back trying to get the damn thing in the truck."

"Maybe you should try moving lighter stuff," Jessie said, exhaling smoke. "Like plants and flowers."

"Yeah, I'll keep that in mind."

"You don't have another girl down there, do you, Jimmy?"

"What?" Sleaze said, turning around to look at her. "No way. I don't need or want another girl, Jessie."

"Good. Because that would break my heart," Jessie said, reaching out to stroke his arm.

"I'd never do that to you," Sleaze said, going in for a kiss.

"You're the perfect guy for me, Jimmy," she said, giving him a loving stare. "And I want us to be even closer. You know, maybe even go the distance."

"That thought has crossed my mind," Sleaze said.

"And since I'm pretty much out of the life for the moment, I need to find something to do to stay busy. I'm bored out of my mind most days. You know, now that I'm not selling my ass by the hour."

"Yeah, I get that," Sleaze said, cringing at her bluntness. "What do you want to do?"

"I don't know," she said. "Anything, really. Even moving furniture would be better than sitting around all day."

"You know, maybe you would be able to help me out from time to time," he said, nodding.

"Just let me know," she said. "Now, come back to bed. I'm getting cold."

Milo topped off both wine glasses, then sat back and stared at the woman who was delicately sliding a small piece of fish into her mouth. Then she swallowed and set her knife and fork down and took a sip of wine.

"Whew, I'm stuffed," Sally said, pushing her plate away. "That was delicious, Milo."

"I'm glad you enjoyed it," he said. "I hope you saved room for dessert."

"I'm afraid I'll have to wait awhile for that," Sally said, accepting the cigarette he was offering. She leaned forward as he lit it for her then sat back in her chair and smiled at him.

"There's no hurry," Milo said. "We got all night."

She stared at him, then slowly nodded.

"Yes, I suppose we do," she said, flashing that smile again. "Tomorrow's my day off. Do you have to work in the morning?"

"No, I'm gonna take it easy tomorrow."

"But the cows never take a day off," she said.

"That's what I pay other people to worry about," Milo said. "Why don't we go sit on the couch and have an after-dinner drink? I've got a bottle of something really special I think you're going to like."

"Don't you worry about having illegal booze here?" she said with a coy smile.

"Hey, I'm just drinking it, not selling it," Milo said, heading for the liquor cabinet behind his desk. He grabbed a clear bottle filled with a yellow liquid and sat down next to her on the couch.

"There's no label on it," she said, examining the bottle.

"There's a local guy who makes it," Milo said. "It's from an old recipe his grandmother gave him."

"What is it?" she said, sitting back to give him room to pour.

"It's called Limoncello. It's made by mixing lemons and some other stuff with vodka."

"Limoncello," she said, enunciating the word carefully. "It sounds Italian."

"It is," Milo said, raising his glass in toast.

"So, this man who makes it is Italian?" she said, cocking her head at him.

"You'd think that, but no," Milo said.

They both took a sip, and Sally grinned.

"It's delicious," she said.

"Yeah, I like it after dinner. It settles the stomach," Milo said, taking another sip. "But be careful," he said, laughing. "The guy who makes it is always saying that after three of them nothing gets two people out of their clothes faster than this stuff."

"Well, then," she said, tossing back her drink. "By all means, let's have another."

"And then a third?"

"If you insist, Mr. Razner."

"No, Nurse Sally, I won't be doing that," Milo said, shaking his head.

"Why not?"

"Because you look like a woman who doesn't like to be told what to do."

"You're a quick study, Milo."

Spits And Spats

Milo waited patiently for Birdie to bring the ice boat to a stop inside the boathouse then hopped up onto the dock and tied the boat off. He extended a hand to help Birdie up then glanced down the dock when he heard the sound of the dolly rolling over wood planks.

"You got here early," Tom said, stopping the dolly next to the fifteen milk cans that were already sitting on the dock.

"We got lucky with the ice tonight," Birdie said, rolling a cigarette. "If the weather stays warm, this week's run are gonna be smooth sailing." Then he grinned at Tom. "What do you say, Tom? You want to make a run tonight? It's a beautiful night for a boat ride."

"Thanks, but I think I'll pass," Tom said, frowning at the ice boat. "Unless you need me to go, Milo."

"No, I'm fine," Milo said. "Hey, Billy."

"Hi, Mr. Razner," the cooker said, grinning at him. "I gotta tell you, Tom is a real quick study."

"I'm glad to hear that," Milo said, glancing at Tom who confirmed it with a small nod.

“If you’ve got a few minutes, I do need to talk to you, Milo,” Tom said. “Up at the house if it’s okay with you. Don’t worry, it won’t take long.”

“Sure,” Milo said, checking his watch. “We’re way ahead of schedule. Birdie, why don’t you and Billy get loaded then just relax until I get back?”

“I was actually going to wait to get loaded until after we finished tonight’s runs,” Birdie deadpanned, then cackled loudly.

“Yeah, that’s a good one, Birdie,” Milo said, waving for Tom to follow him down the dock. “What’s up?”

“I hate to have to tell you this, Milo, but we might have another problem.”

“Goddamn it. Now what? Did Billy catch them going at it on the kitchen table?”

“No, it’s nothing like that,” Tom said as they reached the long incline that led up to the house. “They’re fighting.”

“What the hell happened?”

“I don’t have a clue. Neither one of them will talk about it,” Tom said. “At first, I didn’t worry about it. You know, I figured it was just a lover’s tiff of some sort. But it’s still going on.”

“I’m sure they’ll settle down soon,” Milo said.

“I don’t know, Milo.”

“Why do you say that?” Milo said, sliding on a patch of ice and almost falling. Tom grabbed his arm, and Milo steadied himself. “Thanks for catching me. I am so ready for some warm weather.”

"No problem," Tom said. "Things took a turn for the worse last night."

Milo came to a stop and looked at Tom and waited.

"Daisy stormed downstairs while Billy and I were playing cards in front of the fire," Tom said.

"And?"

"Daisy grabbed Billy by the hand and pretty much dragged him upstairs to the bedroom right next to the master suite."

"Let me guess," Milo said, shaking his head. "Daisy was in particularly good voice last evening."

"I've never heard anything that loud before," Tom said. "You know, that loud between two people getting friendly."

"Shit."

"Yeah, at first, Daisy was just moaning and screaming. Then she started getting personal," Tom said, doing his best not to laugh. "Oh, Billy, this is what I need. How could I have been so stupid? How did Ruby ever let you get away? Ruby just can't make me feel the way you do. A whole bunch of stuff like that. Then Ruby came downstairs and spent the next hour staring into the fire until they finally quieted down."

"Did Ruby do that thing where her eyes get real narrow, and her mood turns dark?"

"Black as night dark," Tom said, nodding. "Then this morning, things took another turn for the worse."

"I can't wait to hear this," Milo said, lighting a cigarette.

"Billy did something stupid."

"Gee, what are the odds of that? What did he do?"

"He invited Daisy to go to California with him."

"Sonofabitch," Milo snapped. "What did she say?"

"What do you think she said? He's offering her a chance to get out of the business and move to California. Billy told her she'll never have to work another day in her life what with the money he's got saved up."

"I'm sure he's right about that. Do you think she agreed to go just to piss Ruby off?" Milo said, glancing up at the house.

"Maybe," Tom said. "But I got the distinct impression today that she is definitely giving it some serious thought."

"So, that's why Billy is in such a good mood tonight," Milo said, rubbing the ember on his cigarette out with the tips of his fingers then sliding the butt into his pocket.

"Yeah," Tom said. "But if it turns out that Daisy is playing him just to get back at Ruby, who knows what he might do? He's got a mean streak a mile deep when he gets riled up,"

"You don't think he'd do something really stupid and try to hurt them, do you?"

"I hate to say this, Milo, but if he gets his heart broken again and slips back into the mood he was in a couple of weeks ago, I wouldn't put anything past him."

"You're full of good news tonight, Tom," Milo said, rocking back and forth on his heels. "Okay, this could take awhile. On second thought, I am gonna need you to take the first run. Sorry."

"Shit. Okay, you got it, Milo," Tom said, heading down the incline before turning around. "I suppose it could be worse. I could have your job tonight."

Then Milo heard Tom's laughter as he continued down the incline to the boathouse. Milo headed for the house and stepped into the empty living room. Milo hung up his coat, tossed another log on the fire, then climbed the stairs. He knocked on the door of the master bedroom and waited.

"Who is it?" Ruby snapped.

"It's me."

"Milo? Come on in."

Milo opened the door and saw Ruby in bed wearing flannels pajamas and reading a book. She marked the page and tossed it aside then pointed at a chair near the bed.

"What are you doing here?" she said.

"In case you've forgotten, I own the frigging place," Milo said, glaring at her.

"That's not what I meant, and you know it," Ruby said, giving it right back to him.

"I'm sorry to say that I'm really beginning to question your ability to manage even the simplest of problems, Ruby."

"What are you talking about?" she said, reaching for her cigarettes.

"Daisy and Billy going to California together?" Milo said, raising an eyebrow at her.

"She's bluffing," Ruby said, lighting the cigarette then exhaling up at the ceiling.

"You sure about that?" Milo said, helping himself to a glass of wine.

"Why would she do something like that?" Ruby said, holding her glass out for a refill.

"Oh, I don't know," Milo said without emotion. "Not having to work while living on the coast of California and being able to spend all her time upright. I can see why a girl like Daisy might be interested in an opportunity like that."

"Nah, she's bluffing," Ruby said. "She'll come to her senses soon enough."

"Will she now?"

"Yeah, she ain't ever gonna leave here."

"For your sake, I hope not, Ruby," Milo said, taking a sip of wine.

"What's that supposed to mean?" she said, glaring at him. "Are you threatening me, Milo?"

"Not at all," he said. "It just looks like I may have to find someone else to handle the opportunity we discussed. You know, given your inability to manage even the simplest of problems."

Ruby took a long drag on her cigarette, then exhaled a cloud of smoke as she processed his comment.

"She's smothering me, Milo," Ruby said after a long pause.

"I see," Milo said with a grin.

"What are you smiling about?"

"I'm just sitting here thinking that it's nice to know that your inability to commit extends beyond the male species."

"Don't start with that crap about my so-called intimacy issues, Milo," Ruby said.

"One can't help but wonder," Milo said, grinning at her. "So, what are you two fighting about?"

"We were talking the other night about the future when I sort of let it slip that you had something big planned for me in the spring."

"Sort of let it slip?" Milo said. "You see, Ruby, that's the perfect example of why I'm starting to have my doubts about you."

"I didn't tell her anything about it, Milo."

"Only because you don't know anything about it," Milo said. "Right?"

"Maybe," Ruby said, exhaling loudly. "I was in a compromising position at the time, and we'd had a lot of champagne."

"So, what happened?"

"As soon as I let it slip that there might be something big happening for me, she started talking about tagging along to wherever you're sending me. You know, *we'll* be able to do this and that. I can't wait until *we're* able to get our own place. Sounding like we were gonna be this long-term couple and live happily ever after."

"You could do a lot worse, Ruby," Milo said with a shrug.

"I'm not doing that, Milo," she said. "At least, not for the time being. Who knows what sort of people I'm gonna meet and the opportunities that might open up for me?"

"Well, Ruby, if there's one thing I have to say, it's that you're remarkably consistent in your ability to focus on what is truly important."

"Thank you," she said, nodding.

"Which in your case is yourself."

"Screw you, Milo," she said, extinguishing her cigarette. "Where are you going?"

"To get Daisy in here, what else?"

Melvin glared at Oscar who continued to hack and cough then spit into a handkerchief that had seen better days. Then Melvin resumed studying this week's note he'd received in the mail today.

"Do you know where Bailey Square road is?" Melvin said, then stared at Oscar who was drinking straight from the bottle of whiskey Melvin had opened a few minutes earlier. "For chrissakes, Oscar. I'm drinking from that bottle, too. Use a glass."

"Sorry. Yeah, I know where it is," Oscar said, pouring himself a drink. "It's not far. Twenty minutes max in good weather."

“Good. That’s not bad. From what The Sleaze told me about last week’s run, it was way out of town,” Melvin said, rubbing the side of his face.

“It was,” Oscar said. “Count your blessings, Melvin. You weren’t the one who was stuck in that truck with him. There’s definitely something wrong with that guy. You know, it’s like some of his wires get crossed from time to time.”

“Yeah, I know. But we need The Sleaze’s money for now. And we’re gonna have to figure out a way to keep this thing going after spring gets here.”

“How are we going to do that?” Oscar said, burping loudly.

“Well, for starters, we need to figure out who our mysterious supplier is,” Melvin said.

“Maybe they’ll eventually let us know,” Oscar said.

“Yeah, maybe. And we need to figure out who The Sleaze is selling it to,” Melvin said.

“That shouldn’t be too hard,” Oscar said with a shrug.

“How’s that?”

“I’ll just follow him,” Oscar said.

“Sure,” Melvin said, shaking his head. “What could possibly go wrong with that?”

Milo gently pulled Daisy along by the arm down the hall until they reached the master bedroom. Then he opened the door and pointed.

"No, Milo," Daisy said. "I told you I don't want to talk to her."

"Get your ass in there," Milo snapped, then closed the door behind them. "Have a seat."

Daisy and Ruby glared at each other, then Daisy sat down in the chair he'd been in earlier. Milo grabbed another and slid it next to her then sat down.

"Okay, start talking," Milo said to Daisy.

"About what?" she said, frowning at him.

"About how you think the Yankees are gonna do this year," Milo said, shaking his head. "What did you tell Billy?"

"I told him I'd love to go to California with him," Daisy said, glaring at Ruby.

"And you were serious when you said that?" Milo said.

"Maybe," she said with a shrug.

"I told you she was bluffing," Ruby said, laughing.

"Nobody's talking to you, Ruby," Milo said. "Why would you tell him something like that, Daisy? You know what Billy is like."

"At the time, I just felt like it," Daisy said. "I don't see what the problem is, Milo. Besides, he'll be gone soon. And he'll get over it. I was just trying to make him feel better."

"And then break his heart all over again?" Milo said, glaring at her.

"It was a stupid thing to do," Ruby said.

"Yeah, well at least I'm not someone who cuts something off just when it's starting to get good," Daisy said.

"I wasn't cutting you off, Daisy. I was merely saying that I was going to need some time before we could take things any further. I'm sure we'll be able to get together from time to time."

"Yeah, I know what that means. Whenever you get twitchy, you'll expect me to come running. You're no different from most of the johns I've met. Well, you can just kiss my ass, Ruby. I don't appreciate being treated like a piece of meat that's passed back and forth."

"I would have thought you'd be used to it by now," Ruby whispered just loud enough to be heard.

Milo restrained Daisy as she lunged toward the bed and eventually got her settled back in her chair.

"Maybe I should just take you two out for a late night swim and start over fresh," he said, glaring back and forth at them. "Don't you understand what lies ahead for both of you? I'm offering you a chance to set yourselves up for the rest of your goddamned lives, and this is what I get? What the hell is the matter with you?"

Both women settled down but continued to glare at each other.

"So, what do you want us to do, Milo?" Ruby said, lighting a fresh cigarette.

"First, for the moment, Daisy is going to keep her promise about going with Billy to California."

"For how long?" Daisy said.

"Until I can come up with something better," Milo snapped, glaring at her. "And you're going to be sweet to him and tell him how much you're looking forward to it."

"Actually, it doesn't sound too bad," Daisy said, shrugging. "At least, the part about moving to California."

"Then, by all means, go," Milo said. "You have my blessing. I'm sure I can find another working girl who might be interested in what I have to offer."

"What are you offering, Milo?" Daisy said.

"I'm sorry, Daisy," Milo said, his voice rising. "But until I'm convinced you're committed to this thing we're doing and can trust you, I'm not telling you a goddamn thing. But feel free to go to California with Billy. Set up house and knock out a bunch of kids. Maybe plant yourself a flower garden."

"Okay, Milo," Daisy said, tearing up. "You've made your point."

"What do you need from me, Milo?" Ruby said.

"I expect you to help Daisy out keeping Billy grounded until I can get him the hell off this island."

"I can do that," Ruby said, nodding.

"And while you're at it, see if you can figure out if it's possible for you to ever even think about someone other than yourself."

Ruby glared at him as she chewed her bottom lip but let it pass without comment.

Stirred And Shaken

Fannie stretched out on the couch and placed her feet on Milo's lap then wiggled her toes.

"Give me one of your special foot rubs, Milo."

Milo complied but used one hand to take a sip of whiskey.

"That feels nice," Fannie said. "So, what did you need to see me about?"

"I'd like to borrow one of your girls," Milo said.

"I see," she said, closing her eyes. "I assume you're using the term *borrow* in the general sense?"

Milo laughed and got to work on Fannie's feet with both hands.

"Yes, I am. Don't worry, Fannie. You'll be more than adequately compensated."

"I'd expect nothing less, Milo," she said, opening her eyes to wink at him. "Feel free to go higher."

"I'd expect nothing less, Fannie."

She laughed then closed her eyes again.

"Do you have someone specific in mind?" she said, then groaned softly. "You got magic hands, Milo."

"Thank you. As a matter of fact, I do have someone in mind."

"Who?"

"Jessie," Milo whispered.

Fannie pulled her legs back and sat up on the couch. She studied Milo's expression closely then gestured for him to keep talking.

"I have a small problem at the island," Milo said. "And I think she might be able to help me out."

"I gotta say, Milo," Fannie said. "Helping you out with that small problem might just create a real big one for me. The Sleaze is gonna be extremely pissed off if I do anything that changes his current arrangement with that girl."

"Oh, I'm sure he's gonna be furious," Milo said. "And that's just the mood I'm going to need him in."

"I don't like this one, Milo," she said, shaking her head as she lit a cigarette.

"You'll be fine, Fannie," he said. "What does his regular schedule look like?"

"He's around here most nights," Fannie said. "Except for Thursdays. Jessie says he always has to work late that day."

"Is she getting close to him?" Milo said.

"Very. She's already talking long-term with him. Why do you ask?"

"I just want to make sure she's doing okay," Milo said. "The Sleaze has a habit of shifting his affections on a dime. And when he does, it usually means bad news for the folks who are close to him when it happens."

"What do I tell the guy?" Fannie said.

"Sick mother always works pretty well," Milo said, making a mental note to drop Beulah a note in the mail. "So, Jessie is already thinking about getting out of the business?"

"There's no doubt about it," Fannie said. "Personally, I think it would be a total waste of her talents, but I bet she'd take off at the drop of a hat for the right offer."

"Interesting. So, her heart really isn't into it?"

"No, it's not. And she's very happy about being exclusive with Sleaze," Fannie said. "And like I say, the two of them are thick as thieves."

"Don't worry about that," Milo said. "One conversation with me about him will be enough for her to put a whole bunch of distance between her and The Sleaze."

"Why do you need Jessie over there?"

"Because I need to find a good woman to get my cooker settled down."

"Crankovitch?" Fannie said, topping off their drinks then stretching back out and wiggling her toes at him.

"Yeah," Milo said, rubbing her feet as he stared off at the wall. "My winter plan blew up in my face, and it's the least I can do for the kid."

"I'm not following you, Milo. I think you've done more than enough for that bumpkin."

"Yeah, as far as money goes," he said. "But I've been manipulating the kid since I first laid eyes on him. It's just not sitting well with me at the moment."

"Well, what do you know?" Fannie said, laughing. "Milo Razner develops a conscience."

"Yeah, I know," Milo said, raising his glass in salute. "Don't tell anybody."

"Your secret's safe with me," she said, shaking her head. "How long are you gonna need her?"

"Probably about a month. You think you can talk her into it?"

"For the right price, Milo, I'm pretty sure I can talk anybody into anything."

"Good, that's my girl," Milo said, giving her feet a hard squeeze. "Just don't forget to give The Sleaze a full refund."

Annabelle leaned over Milo's shoulder and glanced down at the letter he was working on.

"How much longer are you going to be?" she said, nuzzling his neck. "I thought we might hit the hay early."

"What time does your train leave in the morning?"

"Around nine," she said. "What are you telling Beulah?"

"I'm just bringing her up to speed about what's going on."

"I sure hope you know what you're doing, Milo," she said, sitting down across from him.

"Yeah, me too," he said, flashing a grin at her. "You got your strategy worked out for how you're going to handle Vernon?"

"It's really not that hard of a strategy," she said, laughing. "Get him drunk, get him naked, then get him talking."

"Ah, an oldie but a goodie," he said, laughing along as he tossed the pen aside then folded and slid the letter into an envelope.

"Where are you at with the nurse?" Annabelle said.

"I'm still working on her," Milo said as he licked and sealed the envelope.

"I bet you are," she said, laughing. "What does she have to say for herself?"

"She asks a ton of questions, but she's good at making them sound casual. You know, just being friendly while she's busy being nosy."

"She's been trained well," Annabelle said.

"Yeah, she definitely paid attention in class," Milo said.

"So, what's her story?"

"What do you mean?"

"How did she explain her willingness to hop right into the sack with you?"

"Oh, that. She chalks that up to her being a nurse," Milo said. "You know, just being comfortable with the human body and understanding her own needs and desires. And then she lays it on thick about how all she really wants to do is settle down and have a family. She says she wants to have at least half a dozen kids."

"I take it she's a lot of fun," Annabelle said, studying him closely.

"You really want to know?" Milo said, raising an eyebrow at her.

"No, not really," she said.

Jessie stared in disbelief at Fannie and gulped audibly. Fannie held out a pack of cigarettes and Jessie took one with shaking hands. She managed to hold it still long enough for Fannie to get it lit, then sat back on the couch and tucked her legs underneath her. Fannie took her time getting settled in her chair, then fixed a smile at the nervous young woman.

"You want me to leave?" Jessie said. "Did I do something wrong, Fannie?"

"Of course not, Sweetie," Fannie said, exhaling smoke. "You're doing great. I just need you to do me this small favor."

"I'd do pretty much anything for you, Fannie," Jessie said, tearing up. "But going away for a month? I can't do that. And Jimmy will kill me when he hears I'm leaving."

"Don't worry, Jessie," Fannie said, reaching out to pat her hand. "He's not going to know anything. As far as Jimmy knows, you've gone home to take care of your sick mama."

"But, Fannie," she said, pleading. "I'm getting so close to Jimmy. And now just isn't a good time."

"Doesn't it always seem to go like that?" Fannie said, beaming at her. "Just as soon as you think you've got life figured out, it jumps up and bites you in the ass."

"Please, Fannie," Jessie said. "I'm begging you. I'm just about to start helping Jimmy out with his business. He needs me."

"Geez, just listen to you fighting me on this. After everything I've done for you. It's only for a month, girl," Fannie said, firmly. "I'm sure an industrious man like Jimmy will be able to figure out a way to get around his temporary workforce problem. And like they say, absence makes the heart grow fonder," Fannie said, as she began counting out a stack of fifties.

Milo greeted the young woman on the dock inside Frank Slack's marina and took the suitcase she was holding. He beamed at her and tried to ignore the scowl she was giving him.

"Hi, Jessie," Milo said.

"Hey, Milo," she said, glancing around the large, dark space. "I gotta tell you, I'm still not happy about having to do this."

"Yes, I know. Fannie has made that perfectly clear to me," Milo said, gesturing for her to head down the dock to where Birdie was waiting with the ice boat. "But I'm sure you are the perfect person to cheer my friend up. Billy is a wonderful young man, but he's going through a bit of a rough patch with women."

"Well, cheering men up is what I do for a living," Jessie said. "But still, a month stuck out there on an island? It doesn't sound very appealing."

"Just wait until you see the place before you jump to any conclusions," Milo said, coming to a stop next to the boat. "Do you know Birdie?"

"Yeah, I've seen him around Fannie's place. How are you doing?"

"I'm good. You ready to get going? It's a beautiful night for a boat ride," Birdie said.

"I'll take your word for it," she said, holding her coat tight as they helped her into the boat. "This is a weird looking contraption."

"Indeed. No arguments from me," Milo said, laughing. "Well, you have a nice trip."

"Aren't you coming?" Jessie said, frowning at Milo.

"No, I'm afraid not," Milo said, shaking his head. "That would require me to sit in the back in the open air, and that is simply beyond the pale of my tolerance for the cold. But I will be stopping by the island soon to make sure you're all settled in."

"Okay," Jessie said with a shrug, then paused. "Oh, I almost forgot. I didn't have time to get to the post office today. Would you mind dropping this off in the mail for me?"

"Not at all. I'll be happy to do that for you," Milo said, accepting the envelope she was holding out. "Have a safe trip. Slow and steady, right, Birdie?"

"Yeah, I got it, Milo," Birdie said, starting the engine.

Milo watched them until they disappeared from sight, then turned and whistled as he strolled back down the dock. Then he glanced at the envelope she had given him, stared at the name, then staggered backward like he'd been punched and almost fell off the dock.

Annabelle rolled off her boss onto her back and pulled the sheet up to her neck. She stared up at the ceiling wondering about life choices and just how far she seemed willing to go to get what she thought she needed. Then she shook her head to clear it and took a sip of wine.

"That was wonderful," Vernon Adams said, rolling onto his side to gaze at her.

"Yeah, you're something else, Vernon," Annabelle said, continuing to stare up at the ceiling.

"You need to get down here more often," he said. "How did you manage to get away from your teaching duties?"

"We're off this week," she said. "Mid-winter break."

"Really?" Vernon said, frowning. "Why on earth do they do that?"

"Primarily to save some money not having to heat the place for a week," Annabelle said, sitting up and holding her wine glass in her lap.

"I guess that makes sense," Vernon said. "The winters are really that bad, huh?"

"They're brutal," she said.

"Well, if you're interested, I'd be more than happy to arrange a transfer for you. I'd love to have you back in town."

"I don't know, Vernon," Annabelle said, finally making eye contact. "If you did that, all you'd have up there would be Roland Doyle."

"Oh, I don't know about that," Vernon said with a coy smile.

Annabelle stared at him then snuggled close.

"What are you blabbering about, Vernon?" she said, laughing.

"Well, let's say I've been working a little magic of my own the past few months," he said, puffing up with pride.

"Magic, huh? Like a card trick?"

"Well, tricks are definitely part of the equation," he said, chuckling.

"I'm not following, Vernon," she said, nuzzling his neck.

"A couple of months ago, I got the idea to backtrack," he said, propping himself up on an elbow. "Since we've been having trouble identifying booze at the source, you know, when it hits the ground from Canada, I thought a more useful approach might be to work from where it's sold and follow the thread backward."

"You've got somebody working in a local speakeasy?"

"Not per se," he said, shaking his head. "But I imagine she does frequent them from time to time. You know, to enjoy a cocktail with some of the patrons and then throw a few favors their way."

"You've got a working girl set up as an undercover agent?"

"Well, technically she's not a working girl, but I'm quite sure her act is most convincing," he said, laughing. "You know, speaking from experience."

"Yeah, I got it, Vernon," Annabelle said, her mind racing. "Where is she located?"

"Well, I originally had her in Syracuse, but she's slowly been working her way north. I believe she's currently in Watertown, but I can't be sure. She hasn't checked in lately. But in her initial report, she said she thought she might be onto something big."

"So, you've only got one field report from her so far?" Annabelle said, running her nails across his chest.

"Yes. But there wasn't anything useful in it. It arrived soon after she got started. But the girl is very ambitious. And I'm sure she's trying to impress me by connecting a lot of the dots before sending me her next report. You know, she wants to make a big splash."

"Oh, I'm sure she's going to make a big splash."

"What?"

"Nothing. Does Roland know she's around?" Annabelle said, going for casual.

"Absolutely not," Vernon said, shaking his head. "That's the last thing I want."

"Good call, Vernon," Annabelle said, tucking her head against his neck. "I wonder if she's made her way to Alex Bay."

"Anything is possible," he said, yawning. "She seems to have a real knack for this sort of work."

"What's her name?" Annabelle said. "You know, just in case I happen to cross paths with her."

"Barbara Holiday," Vernon said, starting to drift off to sleep. "But I'm sure she's using an alias."

"You're falling asleep, Vernon," Annabelle said, sitting up.

"Yes, I'm afraid you wore me out."

"Then I think I'll head back to my room and let you get your rest," she said, sliding out of bed.

"Okay," he said, yawning. "Thanks for a wonderful evening, Annabelle. Give me a call at the office before you leave tomorrow."

"A call. Right. That's a good idea," she said, throwing her clothes on as fast as she could.

Milo had his feet up on the desk as he smoked and drank and reread the report for the fourth time trying to get a feel for just how much trouble he might be in. He was startled when the phone rang, and he answered it on the second ring.

"Milo Razner."

"Hi, Mr. Razner," said a muffled voice.

Despite the disguise to her voice, he knew who the caller was immediately, and Milo sat upright in his chair and slipped into character.

"Who am I speaking with?"

"This is Geraldine Walk. My husband owns the construction company you hired to design the new school up there."

"Oh, of course. Your husband has told me a lot about you. Why are you calling so late?" Milo said, putting the letter down.

"Yes, I'm sorry about calling you at this hour. But I thought we should talk."

"Okay. You sound troubled, Mrs. Walk."

"That's a word for it," Annabelle said.

"Hang on a second," Milo said. "Violet?"

Milo was greeted with silence.

"Violet," he said, firmly.

"Yes, Mr. Razner," Violet Holman said.

"I think you're about due for a break, right?" Milo said.

"If you say so, Mr. Razner," Violet said, obviously disappointed.

"Thank you, Violet. I appreciate your understanding," Milo said, shaking his head.

"You think she's really gone?" Annabelle said.

"If she knows what's good for her, she is," Milo said. "Right, Violet? Okay, go ahead, Mrs. Walk."

"I'm afraid we may have a big problem, Mr. Razner."

"Some sort of construction problem with the new school?" Milo said, casually.

"Yes, a problem with the new school."

"If it's the same problem I'm thinking about at the moment, I agree."

"Why would you be thinking about the same problem? I haven't even told you what it is yet."

"Unless I'm missing something, there's no need for you to explain it," Milo said. "I just happened to come into possession of a very interesting piece of information this evening. It's a status report on how the construction is going."

"Really?" Annabelle said, stunned. "Does this status report happen to have a number on it?"

"As a matter of fact, it does," Milo said. "And that number is two."

"Two? Oh, that's wonderful news, Mr. Razner," she said, exhaling loudly into the phone. "There really wasn't much information in the first one. Perhaps the second report indicates that my concern has been rectified."

"So, you're familiar with the information contained in the initial status report?"

"Familiar enough to say that it sounds like my concern has been addressed," she said. "Assuming, of course, that you have identified the source of the problem and resolved it."

"Your assumption is correct."

"And?"

"It appeared to be a problem with the foundation. Some of the initial assumptions were incorrect. But they've been fixed. The site is safe and sound," Milo said.

"And it's going to stay that way?"

"Of course. I believe it's now safe to say that the situation has been stabilized."

"I'm so glad I called. Good night, Mr. Razner. I hope you sleep well."

Milo hung up and reached for the report.

"I don't like my chances."

Episode 12

A Little Sunshine

I ran into a guy recently who told me he was thinking about giving up drinking. When he asked me what I thought about his idea, I told him he might consider sticking with the booze but to cut down on his thinking.

Milo Razner

First Light

Birdie kept glancing back and forth at Milo as he steered the ice boat next to the dock and shut the engine down. Milo hopped out and tied the boat off then extended a hand to help Birdie out of the boat.

"She's a Fed?" Birdie said, still stunned by the news.

"Yeah."

"The woman I drove over here last night?"

"Yup."

"You knew she was a Fed and you brought her *here*?" Birdie said. "I know you work in mysterious ways, Milo, but that's frigging nuts."

"I didn't figure it out until after you'd left the dock," Milo said, glancing around the boathouse. Then he spotted a canoe hanging on the back wall. "Is that canoe the only one we have around here?"

"Yeah," Birdie said. "At least I think so."

"I need you to walk the entire island. Cover every inch of ground twice and make sure there's nothing she can use to get away. And grab that canoe and anything else you find and get it the hell off this island."

"You got it, Milo," Birdie said. "Why go to all that bother? Just toss her in the River."

"I'm sure it'll come to that at some point," Milo said, heading down the dock. "When you're done, just head on up to the house. We'll have some breakfast."

"You got it, Milo."

"And not a word to anybody about this, Birdie."

Milo headed up the incline in record time. He stepped inside the house and removed his coat then heard voices coming from the kitchen. He forced himself to go slow and found the entire group sitting around the kitchen table eating breakfast. Jessie was chatting with Daisy and laughing. She smiled up at him when she spotted him standing in the doorway.

"Good morning, Milo," she said. "I have to say you were right. This is a beautiful island."

"Good morning, Jessie," Milo said, beaming at her. "I knew you were going to like it."

"What are you doing here?" Ruby said. "It's barely first light."

"I own the place, remember?"

"We told you we'd handle things, Milo," Ruby said, glaring at him.

Jessie stopped her conversation with Daisy and glanced back and forth at them listening closely.

"No, that's not why I'm here," Milo said. "I need a word with Tom and Billy." He glanced at Tom. "I've got a problem at the farm I might need their help with."

"What's the matter?" Ruby said.

"It's a muscle problem," Milo said. "Johnny is thinking about putting up a new storage shed, and he needs a couple of extra guys to help him get the framing up."

"He never said anything about a new storage shed," Ruby said, frowning.

"I guess he didn't feel the need to tell you, Ruby," Milo said, glaring at her. Then he nodded for Tom and Billy to follow him out of the kitchen.

"Oh, Milo?" Jessie said.

"Yes," Milo said, pausing in the doorway.

"Could I trouble you to mail another letter for me?"

"Of course, Jessie. I'd be happy to do that. Another letter so soon?"

"They're for my uncle," she said with a sad smile. "He's been sick lately, and I like to make sure he knows I'm thinking about him.

"That's very sweet of you," Milo said, flashing her a big smile. "Don't worry, I'll make sure I get it before I leave."

Milo led the way to the door and slipped into his coat. Tom and Billy both gave him odd looks.

"Cooking room," Milo said, heading out the door.

He walked down the incline until he reached the stone structure then held the door open for both men. Milo closed the door behind them and removed his coat.

“Grab a seat. This is gonna take some time.”

“Geez, Milo,” Tom said. “What’s going on? You seem upset.”

“He sure does,” Billy said. “But I gotta thank you for sending Jessie over. She’s something else.”

“Funny you should mention that,” Milo said, lighting a cigarette. “She certainly is something else.”

“And she’s already mentioned the possibility about the two of us spending some time together and getting a little closer,” Billy said, grinning. “She’s no Daisy, but she sure is pretty.”

“Knock yourself out,” Milo said, shrugging. “It probably couldn’t hurt.”

“What’s going on, Milo?” Tom said.

“Jessie’s an undercover Fed,” Milo said. “With the Prohibition Unit.”

“What? That woman is a Fed?” Tom said, stunned. He looked at Billy who was also wearing an open-mouthed stare. “Are you sure?”

“Yeah, I am,” Milo said. “And now that I’ve gone and ruined your day, I suggest we sit here for a while and discuss how we’re gonna fix it.”

Jimmy Sleaze banged the bell on the counter then looked around the empty greeting area. Fannie poked her head through the curtains rubbing her eyes. She approached the counter and continued to frown at him.

"Hey, Mr. Sleaze," she said, stifling a yawn. "You're here early. What can I do for you?"

"Where's Jessie?"

"Jessie? She left," Fannie said, shrugging. "I thought you knew all about it."

"Left? Where the hell did she go?"

"She said she got a phone call yesterday about her mama being sick and told me she needed to head home," Fannie said. "I guess she couldn't find you last night before she left. It was pretty short notice. I suppose I might be able to find you another girl while she's gone."

"I don't want another girl," Sleaze snapped. "Where did she go?"

"Now, where did she say she was going?" Fannie said, frowning. "Mississippi? No, Missouri. Yeah, that's it."

"Why the hell would she be heading to Missouri? Jessie's from Canada," Sleaze said as little bubbles of spit began forming in the corner of his mouth.

"If I remember correctly, Jessie mentioned that her family was thinking about moving there," Fannie said. "Maybe the stress of moving was too much for her mama."

"How the hell is she getting there?" Sleaze said, his face red with rage.

"Train, I reckon," Fannie said with a shrug. "She got a ride to Watertown last night, and I imagine she'll be catching the train out of there."

"Who the hell gave her the ride?" Sleaze said with a wide, wild-eyed glare.

"I don't know, Mr. Sleaze," Fannie said, shaking her head. "She didn't say. She just popped her head in last night to tell me her ride was here. Then she headed off."

"Goddamn it," Sleaze screamed then slammed the counter with his hand.

"Be careful you don't hurt yourself, Mr. Sleaze," Fannie said with a blank expression.

"Goddamn it!"

Jimmy Sleaze wheeled around and stormed out the front door.

Milo glanced around the cooking room and did a silent count of the dozens of milk cans lined up in rows against a wall. He did the math to help him relax then lit yet another cigarette.

"You're sure you want to do that, Milo?" Tom said.

"Why not?" Milo said, glancing over at him.

"Well, let's see. Where do I even start?" Tom said, scowling. "We're living under the same roof with an undercover agent from the Prohibition Unit who could put all of us away for the next fifty years, and you want us to open up to her? You want us to give her a goddamn tour of the cooking room and explain how we make booze?"

"Who's she gonna tell?" Milo whispered.

Tom thought about Milo's comment then glanced at Billy. He scratched his head then shook it as if to clear the cobwebs.

"You do have a point, Milo," Tom said, shrugging. "Who's she gonna tell?"

"Exactly. And she's not getting off this island until I'm good and ready," Milo said. "But if she thinks she can swim a couple of miles in that freezing water, I'm willing to take that chance."

"But why don't we just take care of her now, Milo?" Billy said.

"Excellent question, Billy," Tom said.

"Thanks," Billy said with a goofy grin.

"Because I'd like to make sure we get every possible piece of information she might know out of her before we do that. Those letters she's mailing off are the status reports she sends to her boss in Washington. And since she already wrote another one last night, my guess is that she's already suspicious about what we're doing over here."

"And you want us to help her know even more?" Tom said, shaking his head.

"Yes," Milo said. "But don't say anything about the farm. Let's see just how smart she is at putting all the pieces together."

Milo fell silent for several moments and drummed his fingers on his knee.

"What is it, Milo?" Tom said.

"I'm just wondering if Fannie has broken the news to The Sleaze that Jessie's gone," Milo said, scratching his two-day stubble.

"Why would Fannie be telling him that?" Tom said.

"Because Jessie is The Sleaze's girlfriend," Milo said with a grin.

"Now, that's interesting," Tom said, laughing.

"Yeah, I thought you'd enjoy that. My original plan was to bring her over here just to keep her safe and piss The Sleaze off at the same time. But now, I sense an opportunity."

"Are you gonna tell The Sleaze that he's been getting horizontal with a Fed?" Tom said.

"No, for the moment, I don't believe I will," Milo said, slowly shaking his head. "But I do need to tread cautiously. I almost outsmarted myself on this one."

"I'm not following, Milo," Tom said.

"I'm the one who had Fannie plant Ben Green's name with Jessie," Milo said. "And if he ever happened to find that out, I'd be a dead man."

"From what you've told me about the guy, I'm sure you're right," Tom said. "And if he finds out that The Sleaze has brought an undercover agent into his operation, I reckon he'd be even more pissed off."

"That's what I'm counting on," Milo said with a grin as he got to his feet. "Okay, gentlemen. You know what to do. Feel free to talk but keep a very close eye on her."

"What about Ruby and Daisy?" Tom said.

"What about them?"

"You gonna tell them what Jessie's up to?"

"No, I'm not. I'm going to see if they're up to the task," Milo said.

"What task is that?" Tom said.

"The task of proving they're worthy of further employment," Milo said, then caught the odd look Billy was giving him. "What's the matter?"

"You sure it's okay if I agree to get horizontal with her? You know, just in case she does happen to make the offer."

"Oh, I'm sure she'll be offering," Milo said. "Probably both of you."

"Gee, I don't know if I could do that, Milo," Tom said.

"Why not?"

"She's a Fed," Tom said, shrugging.

"Look at this way, Tom. You'd be getting a chance to do to someone from the government the same thing they've been doing to you for years."

"I do like the way you think, Milo," Tom said, laughing.

"And if it were me," Milo said. "I'd be making her work extra hard for every bit of information she wants."

"I suppose it couldn't hurt," Tom said. "What do you say, Billy?"

"It has been a long winter," Billy said with a shrug.

"There you go," Milo said, starting to head for the door. Then he stopped and fixed a stare on his cooker. "Just one more thing, Billy."

"What's that, Mr. Razner?"

"Do not invite her to go to California with you."

Bad Reports And Grades

Milo nodded as the foreman outlined the progress they were making then glanced out at the foundation that was already beginning to take shape. Milo watched a crew pour cement while other workers were hauling and organizing blocks of granite.

"You guys are doing great, Walt," Milo said as he continued to study the workers.

"Well, we've been able to pick up the pace now that the weather is improving," the foreman said.

"I suppose you could call this an improvement," Milo said, shivering from the north wind as he looked up at the threatening clouds. "Are you able to work the Canadian granite in with the local stones?"

"Yeah, but I still don't know why it's so important," he said. "As far as I'm concerned, a rock is a rock."

"I like the color of the Canadian granite," Milo said. "It's a subtle highlight."

"Whatever you say, Milo," he said with a chuckle then waved as he headed off.

Milo spotted Annabelle slowly walking in his direction. She smiled at him when she got close and extended her hand.

"It's nice to see you, Mr. Razner."

"You're looking well, Miss Caffey," Milo said, giving her a quick once-over. "How did you manage to escape the rug-rats?"

"They're having lunch," she said. "Thanks to you."

"Hey, a kid can't learn on an empty stomach," Milo said. "I thought I'd swing by your place tonight after it gets dark."

"Perfect," she said, cocking her head at him. "We do need to catch up."

"Definitely. And you should know that I'm shooting for straight A's tonight."

"I'm sure you'll do very well, Milo," she said, grinning at him. "Just as long as you don't get an incomplete. What would you like for dinner?"

"You."

"I'm not talking about dessert, Milo," she said, laughing. "How does roast chicken with vegetables sound?"

"Almost as good as dessert."

"Okay, Milo," she said, shaking her head. "I get the point. Enjoy the rest of your day."

Milo watched her walk away then focused on the work crew feeling good about what he was doing for the kids. But what really put a smile on his face were the things she'd be doing for him tonight.

Melvin tapped a pen on his desk, scribbled on a blank piece of paper, then scratched it out and started tapping again. He jumped in his chair, startled when Jimmy Sleaze stormed into his office and helped himself to a glass of whiskey. Sleaze wiped his mouth, then poured another drink and plopped down in the chair on the other side of the desk.

"Make yourself comfortable," Melvin said with a blank stare.

"Didn't I just do that?" Sleaze snapped, taking a sip then removing a pack of cigarettes from his pocket. "I suppose you want one of these?"

"Well, since you're drinking all my good whiskey, it only seems fair," Melvin said, reaching for a cigarette. "What sort of bug crawled up your ass and died?"

"None of your goddamn business."

"Okay," Melvin whispered as he tossed the pen aside. "What can I do for you?"

"We need to get the name of the guy who's selling us the booze," Sleaze said. "We only got a couple weeks left, and I have no intention of stopping. Am I making myself clear, Melvin?"

"Yeah, I get it. Oscar and I have been discussing the same thing."

"A little late-night pillow talk with your roomie, Melvin?" Sleaze said, laughing and slapping his thigh.

"Yeah, good one, Jimmy," Melvin said, getting up to pour himself a drink.

"Bring the bottle," Sleaze snapped.

"Of course," Melvin said, then sat back down and slid the bottle forward. "So, do you have any ideas about how we're going to figure out who they are?"

"Once we get this week's note, I was thinking about just staking the place out," Sleaze said, pouring what was left into his glass and tossing the bottle on the floor. "And I'm gonna need your help."

"I doubt if it's going to be worth the effort, Jimmy," Melvin said, taking a sip.

"Why the hell not?" Sleaze growled.

"Because I imagine they're delivering the booze to the pickup spot before they mail us the note," Melvin said.

"Goddamn it," Sleaze said, slamming the desk with his hand.

"Did I say something to upset you?" Melvin deadpanned.

"Don't start, Melvin. Today is not the day for you to be giving me shit," Sleaze said, glaring across the desk.

"I wouldn't think of it, Jimmy," Melvin said. "Say, why don't you head over to Fannies and take the edge off? I'm sure Jessie can help you out with that. Isn't that what you pay her for?"

"Sonofabitch," Sleaze roared as he lifted Melvin's desk and flipped it over, pinning Melvin against the wall.

"Okay, bad suggestion on my part," Melvin said, making enough room for him to slide his chair out. Then he leaned against the liquor cabinet out of reach of the enraged creature who was rapidly making his way through his drink. "But now that I think about it, perhaps your idea of a stakeout might work."

"How so?"

"Since staking out the pickup location isn't likely to bear fruit, we might consider keeping an eye on a different location."

"Like where?"

"Maybe the post office in Watertown," Melvin said, shrugging.

The Sleaze thought about Melvin's suggestion for several moments, then nodded and stormed out of the office.

"That oughta keep him busy awhile."

Annabelle read the status report Milo had gotten from Jessie before she got into the boat while he read the latest one he'd picked up earlier today before he left the island.

"You better hope Ben Green never finds out you're the one who leaked his name," Annabelle said. "His name is all over this report."

"Yeah, I know. And I doubt if Jimmy would be pleased to hear the news," Milo said, munching on a chicken leg and getting grease all over the report. "I thought I'd help Mr. Green figure out at some point it was Jimmy who was behind that." Milo flashed her a big grin. "After all, The Sleaze is the one who's working with the Feds, right?"

"How are you gonna do that?" she said, laughing.

"I'm still working on that," Milo said. "Suddenly, I find myself having to adjust my plans on the fly."

"You'll figure it out," Annabelle said, squeezing his hand before focusing on the report again. "Did you know Green was using a produce company as his front?"

"I did," Milo said.

"He told you that?" Annabelle said, surprised.

"Yeah," Milo said, nodding without looking up from the report. "Green hates my guts with a passion. And he doesn't trust me one bit. But he does open up occasionally."

"Probably only because he doesn't have a choice," she said.

"I'm sure you're right about that," Milo said. "But he's going to be trusting me a whole lot more soon." Milo stared down at the page and frowned. "Sonofabitch."

"What is it?"

"This girl is way too smart for her own good. Listen to this. I'm currently on an island where I was transported earlier this evening in a boat specially made for winter travel across the St. Lawrence. Built into the boat deck are fifteen recessed circles. I'm quite sure these are used to secure illegal liquor that is being transported in bulk quantity. My thinking at this point is that the liquor is being cooked on this island and then transported to Razner's dairy farm where it is probably being shipped to another location using his milk trucks. Sonofabitch."

"She figured all that out in one night?" Annabelle said. "Just by looking at the boat?"

"I can't believe it. How the hell did she do that? She hasn't even seen the cooking room yet."

"Vernon said that she was extremely smart and really ambitious. According to him, she has a very bright future ahead of her."

"Is that so? Well, I don't like her chances. I'm sure it's pretty dark at the bottom of the River," Milo said, then slid the report to one side. "You're sure she didn't have a chance to tell your boss anything?"

"I'm positive," Annabelle said. "Ever since I told him about how much Violet loves to eavesdrop, Vernon has forbidden everybody from talking about anything important over the phone. And it's either a face to face meeting or a written report mailed to that post office box."

"Well, there's no way she managed to have a face to face with him. She hasn't left town since she got here, and The Sleaze was definitely keeping a close eye on her. So, I think we're gonna be okay."

"You sure about that?" Annabelle said.

"Yeah, we're gonna be just fine. She's not going anywhere, and I've got Tom keeping a close eye on things while she's there."

"Including her, right?" she said, grinning at him.

"Yeah, I did sort of encourage both of them to get friendly with her," Milo said. "You know, to go the extra mile just to make sure she feels welcome."

"Sort of like doing a special project for extra credit?"

"There you go," Milo said with a grin. "Yeah, let's call it a homework assignment."

"I'm sure Tom will pass with flying colors," she said, then turned serious. "Are you sure about this, Milo? Just say the word. We can walk anytime you want."

"Why would you want to stop now?" Milo said with another big grin. "It's just starting to get interesting."

Tom Collins looked up from the book he was reading in bed when he heard the knock.

"Yeah?" he called out.

The door opened partway, and Jessie poked her head in.

"Hey, Jessie. What's up?"

"Oh, I was just having trouble sleeping and saw your light on," she said, closing the door behind her. "You wouldn't feel like chatting for a while, would you?"

"Sure," he said, sitting up and tossing the book on the mattress. "You want a drink? I've got a bottle over there on the dresser."

"That sounds wonderful," she said. "No, you stay right there. I'll get the drinks."

Tom studied the thin robe she was wearing from behind, then flinched when she turned around and noticed it was open. She walked across the room holding two glasses, handed him one, then climbed onto the bed and sat facing him with her legs tucked underneath her. She made no attempt to close the robe then smiled when she caught him staring at her.

"Nice robe, huh?" she said, raising her glass in toast. "I borrowed it from Daisy."

"Yeah, Daisy's got some great robes," Tom said, taking a sip. "Did she also teach you how to wear it?"

"I beg your pardon," she said, confused.

"I was just wondering since that's generally the way Daisy wears them. You know, untied."

"Would you like me to tie it?" Jessie said.

"No, I like it just fine the way it is," Tom said, smiling as he touched glasses with her.

"Do you like me too?" she whispered, sliding closer to him.

"What's not to like? You're a beautiful woman, Jessie."

"Oh, now you've done it," she said, turning coy. "You're making me blush."

"It's the truth," Tom said, sipping his whiskey. "So, what would you like to talk about?"

"Oh, nothing specific," she said, glancing around the room. "This is very nice. Do all the bedrooms have fireplaces?"

"Yes, I believe they do," he said, nodding.

"I love fireplaces. This is such an amazing house," she said. "Mr. Razner must be doing very well with his milk business."

"I suppose he is," Tom said, shrugging. "But I don't know much about it."

"Really? I thought you said you worked for him," Jessie said.

"Oh, I do. Just not on the milk side."

"I see. So, what do you do for Mr. Razner?"

"I make booze," Tom Collins said with a smile then downed what was left of his drink.

"Fascinating," she said, cocking her head. "I'd love to hear all about that."

"Well, I don't know how fascinating it is. But sure, I don't mind explaining how I do it. You want to talk about it now?"

"Why not?" Jessie said. "In fact, why don't we stretch out in front of the fire and get comfortable? Then you can tell me all about it."

Gearing Up

Milo stepped inside and waved to one of Fannie's girls who was trudging up the stairs leading an obviously nervous client by the hand. Milo spotted Fannie behind the counter reviewing a stack of receipts, and she waved him over then went back to work.

"Hey, Milo," she said, not looking up. "Hang on. I'll just be a sec." She scribbled in a notebook then stuffed it along with the receipts into a metal tackle box and slid it into a drawer and locked it. She grabbed the stack of cash off the counter, quickly counted it, then slid it into her cleavage. "Busy night," she said, looking up with a grin. "Come on back."

She held the curtains open for him then followed him into the office. He glanced around admiring his favorite photos on the wall while she poured drinks. They both sat down, took a sip of whiskey and lit cigarettes. Then they each draped a leg over a knee.

"Look at us," Fannie said, laughing.

"I'm not following," Milo said.

"We got our routine all worked out. Just like an old married couple. Hey, I haven't seen you since you took Jessie to the island. How's that working out?"

"Initially, not as well as I had hoped. But it's getting better," Milo said. "How did The Sleaze take the news?"

"How do you think he took it?" she said, shaking her head. "I thought he was gonna blow a gasket."

"Has he been back in since then?"

"No, I offered to find him another girl, but he turned me down flat."

"I have to tell you something, Fannie. Something that's definitely going to twist your knickers. But I think I've already got the problem fixed, so try not to panic."

She stared at him with a confused look and waited.

"It's about Jessie," Milo said.

"What about her?"

"She's an undercover agent with the Prohibition Unit," Milo said as a simple statement of fact.

That got a wide-eyed stare out of his good friend.

"What?"

"Yeah, it kinda caught me by surprise, too."

"Goddamn," she said, tossing back her drink. "That's some real bad news, Milo."

"We're going to be okay," he said. "But it was definitely a very close call. And I think that both of us should probably tighten up our hiring practices."

"What did you do with her?" Fannie said, topping off their drinks. "Bottom of the river?"

"No," he said, shrugging. "She's still at the island."

"Doing what?" she said, baffled.

"For now, learning the ins and outs of my business," he said, grinning.

"What are you up to, Milo?"

"A whole bunch of stuff, Fannie. But don't worry. You're gonna like it."

Roland Doyle glanced around the empty police station and was about to leave when he heard snoring coming from one of the cells off to his left. He found the chief of police on his back with a stream of drool leaking out of one side of his mouth. Roland cleared his throat, got no response from the snoring man, then grabbed a broom that was leaning against a nearby wall and dragged the handle back and forth across the bars of the cell.

"Goddamn it. Quit making all that racket," Oscar said, opening one eye. "Knock it off."

Oscar slowly came to and almost fell off his cot before working himself into an upright position. He held his head with both hands and finally managed to make eye contact.

"Doyle?" Oscar said, then coughed long and hard. He got to his feet and headed for a small sink to cough and spit and splash water on his face. "What the hell are you doing here?"

"I wanted to have a word with you," Roland Doyle said. "But perhaps it might be better to wait until you're sober."

"I'm sober," Oscar said. "And I've got the hangover to prove it. What do you want?"

"Well, since the weather has turned, I thought I'd make my offer again," Doyle said, spotting a half-filled whiskey bottle sitting on a nearby cabinet.

"You mean all that crap about us working together to catch bootleggers?" Oscar said, also spying the bottle. "Hand me that."

Doyle grabbed the bottle and held it out. Oscar took a long swallow then exhaled loudly. He held the bottle out to Roland.

"You want some?"

"No, thanks," Doyle said, lying through his teeth. "So, what do you say?"

"Catching people running booze is your job, Doyle."

"I'm very aware of what my job is, Oscar. I just thought that combining our forces would double our chances of catching criminals in the act," Doyle said.

"Well, you thought wrong," Oscar said, climbing to his feet and taking another long swallow. "If you're so interested in catching bootleggers, why don't you just ask for some more help?"

"I'm afraid there are budgetary concerns in Washington that are preventing that from happening," Doyle said.

"So, the government passes a law making booze illegal then doesn't put up the money to catch the people breaking it?" Oscar said, laughing. "Good plan you guys came up with. Real smart." Oscar took another pull from the bottle then made his way to his desk. "Sorry, Doyle. But I'm busy doing other things."

"Okay," Doyle said. "But just so you know, Oscar. The next time I do catch someone, I'll make sure you don't get any of the credit."

"Oh, no. Not that," Oscar said, laughing. "You're breaking my heart."

Milo watched Birdie roll a cigarette with one hand, as always amazed by his proficiency. Willy and Frank were also watching closely then Birdie flipped the cigarette into his mouth and lit it in one motion. When he noticed all three men staring at him, he glanced around, exhaling smoke.

"What are you guys looking at?" Birdie said.

"How do you do that?" Frank said.

"It's just something my mama taught me," Birdie said, leaning back on the couch and relaxing.

"To good parenting," Milo said, shaking his head as he raised his glass in toast. Then he glanced down at his list. "Okay, let's get started. First up is the boat. When can we get it back in the water?"

"I'm dropping her in first thing in the morning," Frank said. "There's just a little bit of skim ice left in the bay at the marina. And that's always the last ice to leave."

"That's great news," Birdie said, then glanced at Milo. "Let's take her out for a spin. It's gonna be a beautiful day for a boat ride."

"How the hell do you know that?" Willy said, frowning at him.

"Let's call it a hunch," Birdie said, shrugging.

Milo and Frank laughed then Milo checked his list again. He looked at Willy.

"Has your major supplier got back from Florida yet?"

"Yeah, he has," Willy said. "He gave me a call yesterday and said he'll be ready to go by the weekend."

"You're not talking specifics over the phone, are you?" Milo said.

"No, we cover our tracks good, Milo," Willy said. "We work the details in when we're talking about hockey."

"Good," Milo said, reviewing the list.

"Are you sure you got Violet under control, Milo?" Willy said. "I can always hear her breathing on the line. I know you got her on the payroll, but she makes me nervous."

"Yeah, me too," Milo said, nodding. "But don't worry, I'm going to be dealing with Violet soon enough."

"Aren't you gonna put her on the list, Milo?" Birdie deadpanned.

"She's already on the list," Milo said, grinning. "And don't be such a smartass."

"Sorry, Milo. It just seems to come natural," Birdie said, rolling another cigarette.

"Yeah, I've noticed. Roll me one of those," Milo said. "Willy, I'm going to need you to increase the size of your order."

"By how much?"

"Fifty cases a week," Milo said, glancing over at him.

"I'm already planning on doing that," Willy said. "I gotta keep Ben Green happy, right?"

"No, I want you to sell the extra fifty cases to Melvin and The Sleaze," Milo said.

Willy shook his head and crushed his cigarette out in the ashtray. Milo cocked his head at him.

"What's the matter?"

"No offense, Milo. But you're starting to put a serious crimp in my plans for expansion. That'll make a hundred cases a week I'm not making a nickel on."

"Yeah, I know, Willy," Milo said, nodding sympathetically. "But for the time being, I need you to tell Ben Green that you're stuck at a hundred and fifty cases."

"Geez, Milo," Willy said with a scowl. "Really?"

"Just try to be patient," Milo said, then thought for a few moments. "Tell you what, go ahead and increase the price per case to forty bucks. They're making enough now to afford it."

"Thanks, Milo," Willy said. "I appreciate it."

"Just hang in there with me, Willy. When this situation finally plays itself out, I'm going to more than make it up to you."

"Okay, Milo," Willy said. "But I hate helping The Sleaze out. It really sticks in my craw."

"Yeah, I get that," Milo said. "Try not to think of it as helping him. Think of it as leading him right down the path we want him to take."

"So, I take it we're going to keep selling to them anonymously?" Frank said.

"We are," Milo said. "And since it worked so well the first time, I think another big run using your barge is the way to go. You know, fewer runs, fewer problems."

"Sure, Milo," Frank said. "But with the season coming up, I'm gonna have way too many people around to be storing all that booze at the marina. And I'm gonna need that space for other things during the summer."

"Yeah, I've been thinking about that as well," Milo said. "And I have the perfect solution."

"I can't wait to hear this," Birdie said, blowing smoke up at the ceiling.

"Willy, how would you like to get into the furniture business?" Milo said, grinning.

"The place in Rockport that Tom was running for a while?" Willy said.

"That's the one," Milo said. "It's been closed all winter since Tom's been over at Whisperer. I think it's time we reopened."

"Milo, I won't be able to run a furniture store and make all the deliveries by myself," Willy said.

"No, you're definitely gonna need some help," Milo said.

"Judging by the look on your face," Willy said. "I'm gonna guess you already have somebody in mind."

"Yeah, I do," Milo said, grinning as he studied the list. "Birdie, do you think Frank's barge will fit into the boat slip behind the furniture store?"

"It might be a tight fit, but I'm pretty sure it will, Milo."

"Perfect," Milo said, crossing the item off.

"I gotta say, Milo, you're surprising me tonight," Willy said.

"How's that?"

"You've always kept yourself a mile away from bottled product," Willy said. "And while I'm glad you're taking an interest in it since you're a goddamn genius, but I gotta ask, what's changed your thinking?"

"I'm going to start taking much more of an active role, Willy. At least until we get our current situation worked out with The Sleaze and our friend on the island."

"I still think you should just throw her in the River," Birdie said.

"Try to be patient, Birdie," Milo said, taking a sip of whiskey.

"Take the long view, right?"

"Don't worry. It won't be long."

Melvin decided that a quick drink was in order before he headed upstairs for another session with the pretty redhead who seemed to like him. Or, at a minimum, tolerate him. At least she didn't start complaining right in the middle of his freebies which was something a lot of the other girls did that ruined his concentration and really put him off his game. The man working the door outside the blind pig didn't even bother asking him for the password, and he opened the door and waved the mayor in. Melvin glanced around the half-filled room then headed straight for the bartender and ordered a shot and a beer. He stood with his back to the bar and surveyed the crowd waving to several locals. Then he spotted a man sitting at a table by himself and quickly walked toward him shaking his head the whole way.

"Goddamn it, Oscar. What are you doing here?"

"What does it look like I'm doing?" Oscar said, pouring himself another shot.

"You're the police chief, Oscar," Melvin said, glaring down at him.

"I know that," Oscar growled. "And so does everybody else in here. What difference does it make if I drink here or not?"

"I can't believe I even need to have this conversation with you," Melvin said, his voice rising. "You're the chief of police, Oscar."

"And you're the mayor," Oscar said, returning the glare. "What's your point?"

"That's different," Melvin said, puffing up. "As the mayor, I need to be out among my constituency to stay on top of things and make sure I'm addressing their problems in a timely fashion."

"Good one, Melvin," Oscar said, laughing. "How long did it take you to come up with that?"

"About an hour," Melvin said, taking a sip of beer. "I go where my constituents take me. And if they lead me here, so be it."

"Okay, Mayor Melvin. Whatever you say?" Oscar said. "Oh, Roland Doyle stopped by my office earlier."

"He's finally come out of hibernation?" Melvin said, waving to someone.

"It looks that way," Oscar said. "He asked me again to partner up with him to catch bootleggers. I told him to pound sand."

"Good. At least you got that much right."

Milo stood next to Birdie on the dock watching Frank Slack use a hand crank to lift the ice boat out of the water. The boat, supported underneath by a set of canvas straps, slowly rose then Frank and one of his workers wheeled it away.

"I can't say I'm sorry we're done with that thing until next winter," Milo said.

"Yeah, me either," Birdie said. "But it sure did the trick, huh?"

"It certainly did. And more important, we somehow managed to survive."

A few minutes later, they heard the familiar roar of the engine, and they both beamed.

"Here she comes," Birdie said, giving the boat a loving stare as Frank slowly drove it out of the marina and came to a stop right next to them.

"Gentlemen," Frank said, hopping out of the boat. "Your chariot awaits."

"Thanks, Frank. I'd almost forgotten how beautiful she is," Milo said, giving the boat a loving stare before climbing in. "Let me know what Willy has to say about the barge run."

"Will do," he said, then headed back down the dock.

Birdie continued to beam as he slowly headed out of the bay then accelerated. Milo felt a blast of cold air and draped an arm on the side rail.

"It's really not so bad out today," Milo shouted over the roar of the engine.

"Like I've been telling you, Milo. Cold is a relative term," Birdie said, rolling a cigarette.

"Remember to remind me of that next February."

Ten minutes later, they pulled into the boathouse at the island, tied the boat off then headed up the incline that led to the house. Halfway up, Milo stopped and looked at Birdie.

"You go ahead and head up to the house," Milo said. "I need to have a quick word with Billy."

Birdie nodded, and Milo watched him limp his way toward the house. Then he headed for the cooking room and found Billy standing in front of a large batch of mash. Milo frowned when he caught a strong whiff of the concoction.

"Hey, Mr. Razner," Billy said, then closed the cover of the vat. "This stuff really stinks, huh?"

"It certainly does. How you turn it from that into Miracle truly is one," Milo said, studying him closely. "So, how's it going over here?"

"It's okay, I guess," he said, shrugging. "The two of them are still fighting, but at least not in front of the rest of us. We occasionally hear them from downstairs."

"What's Jessie been up to?"

"The last couple of days she's been pumping Tom pretty hard for information," he said, shrugging.

"Good for Tom," Milo said. "How about you?"

"Nothing, yet. She hasn't come near me."

"Man, you can't catch a break, can you?"

"Yeah, I think I'm in one of those slumps ballplayers are always talking about," he said. "But Tom is gonna drop a couple of hints about Miracle. That should make her come running, huh?"

"I imagine that just might do the trick," Milo said, laughing.

"So, when can I get off the island, Mr. Razner?"

"Soon, Billy," Milo said, reaching into his coat pocket and removing a large envelope. "In fact, this is for you."

Billy opened the envelope and removed a set of photographs and a folded document. He studied the photos one at a time, then stared at Milo.

"This is the place?"

"That's it," Milo said, grinning. "The document is the deed to the property. I've already signed it over to you. Keep that someplace safe. It's nice, huh?"

"It overlooks the beach?"

"It sure does. Twenty acres and a house big enough for a dozen kids," Milo said, grimacing slightly when he remembered the size of the check he'd written. "I think you're gonna like it out there."

"It'd be hard not to, right?"

"Yeah, it probably would, Billy," Milo said as he glanced at one of the photos. "So, what do you think you're gonna do once you get settled in?"

"I'm not sure yet," he said, shrugging. "I reckon pretty much whatever I want."

"Maybe set up shop and do some cooking?" Milo said with a grin.

"Nah," Billy said, shaking his head. "Apart from a batch of Miracle every now and then just for home consumption, my cooking days are over. At least they will be as soon as I get out of here."

"Quit while you're ahead, right?"

"Exactly. Maybe you should do the same thing, Mr. Razner," Billy said. "I worry about you sometimes."

"You worry about me?"

"Yeah, I do. This thing has gotten real big in a hurry. When things get big, things tend to start going wrong, and people start paying attention," Billy said. "And that pretty young thing up at the house is probably only the first one who's gonna show up and want to get a good look at what you're doing."

Milo listened closely then took a deep breath and exhaled loudly. Then he nodded and smiled at his cooker.

"You're wise beyond your years, Billy."

"Can't say I've ever heard anybody tell me that before, Mr. Razner."

Melvin entered his office and was immediately pissed off when he saw The Sleaze sitting behind his desk rummaging through the drawers.

"What the hell do you think you're doing?"

"Looking for this week's pickup note," Sleaze said. "What does it look like I'm doing?"

"Going through my desk drawers? I'm sorry, Jimmy, but that's crossing the line," Melvin said, motioning for him to get out of his chair.

"What are you gonna do, Melvin," Sleaze said with a low growl. "Have Oscar arrest me?"

"Forget it," Melvin said, backing down as he sat down. "Just try to show some respect for the office."

"Yeah, respect for the office," Sleaze said, laughing. "That's what we need more of around here. Is that the mail?"

"It is," Melvin said, opening the envelope he'd been waiting for. "Well, how about that?"

"What?"

"Our prayers have been answered," Melvin said. "They want to sell us another fifty cases a week."

Melvin slid the note across the desk and watched The Sleaze read it.

"Damn it," Sleaze snapped.

"What's the matter?" Melvin said.

"Read the rest of the note," Sleaze said, sliding it back.

"Sonofabitch. They're raising the price to forty bucks a case. Do you think we should pay it?"

"We don't really have a choice, Melvin," Sleaze said, rubbing his chin. "Maybe I can raise the sales price."

"That would be good," Melvin said. "Because losing ten bucks of profit on every case is really gonna hurt our margin."

"It sure will," Sleaze said. "And until I'm able to sell it for more, I'm afraid it's gonna have to come out of your end."

Milo entered the house and found Ruby sitting by herself in the living room, deep in thought. She was sipping coffee and staring into the fire, and Milo stood back to admire her profile.

"Remarkable," he whispered.

"Oh, hi, Milo," Ruby said, glancing over her shoulder at him. "I thought I heard the boat. When did you get it back in the water?"

"Just this morning," he said, sitting down in the chair next to her. "What's wrong, Ruby? You seem…subdued."

"Yeah, I got some stuff on my mind I can't shake," she said.

"Daisy stuff?"

"Nah," Ruby said with a laugh. "I don't give the crap she's been tossing around a second thought."

"Where is she?"

"I think she's still sleeping."

"So, what's bothering you?" Milo said. "If it's about your new venture, just hang in there. It won't be long."

"No, that's not it," Ruby said. "I know you'll tell me as soon as you're ready. It's Jessie."

"What about her?" Milo said, leaning forward.

"There's something not right about her," she said, lowering her voice. "She's been asking a whole bunch of questions and dropping serious hints about wanting to visit the farm. She says she loves being around cows." Ruby stared at Milo. "Which is a total line of shit. I can't be sure, Milo, but I think she might be working for the Feds."

Milo sat back in his chair and stared at her.

"Well, butter my buns and call me a biscuit," he said, stunned. "How the hell did you figure that out?"

"You mean, I'm right?" she whispered.

"Yes, you certainly are," Milo said, nodding and unable to shake his grin. "I knew you were the right woman for the job."

"You knew she was a Fed and didn't tell me?" Ruby said, suddenly cranky.

"I wanted to see if you could figure it out for yourself," Milo said, glancing around. "Where is she?"

"Upstairs banging Tom's brains out," she said. "Can I ask you why the hell you brought her over here if you knew what she was up to?"

"At first, I wanted her here to keep Billy settled down until he left," Milo said. "But when I figured out what she was up to, I decided to keep her here until it was safe."

"Safe for her?" Ruby said, frowning.

"No, I think we can rule out any concerns about her personal safety, Ruby," Milo said. "But I'm getting close to making a move, and the last thing I need is a Fed sticking her nose into things."

"Do you think she's already been talking?" she said.

"No, I got to her just in time," Milo said. "And those letters she's sending to her sick uncle are actually status reports she's sending to her boss in Washington. As you can imagine, I've refrained from dropping them in the mail."

"Good call on not putting a phone in over here."

"Thanks," Milo said, still impressed by her powers of deduction.

"So, that's why Tom has been downright chatty with her?" Ruby said, lighting a cigarette.

"Yes, I encouraged him and Billy to open up to her."

"You want to keep getting a good look at those letters and see how much she's been able to piece together," Ruby said.

"Exactly," he said. "And I'm hoping she has another one ready for me today. I'm sure her uncle is dying to hear from her."

"Smart. That's a really good plan, Milo," Ruby said. "Look, I need to apologize. I'm sorry I've been giving you such a hard time."

"Don't worry about it. I'm sure it won't be the last," Milo said, laughing.

"Yeah, it probably won't," Ruby said, laughing along. "Well, I don't know when she would have had time to write her report. They've been going at it non-stop."

"Well, I did suggest that Tom make her work hard for the information." Then a thought popped into his head. "But please promise me you won't use the same approach with her. The last thing we need is Daisy going into another tailspin."

"That won't be a problem, Milo," Ruby said, shaking her head. "If I decide to hit from that side of the plate again, Daisy will be doing the pitching."

"I'm sure that's a wise choice," he said, grinning and just dying to know. "Good, huh?"

"I've had worse winters," she said, laughing. "Should I tell Daisy what's going on?"

"I don't think so," Milo said. "Daisy has a tendency to get chatty at the wrong time."

"Who's she gonna tell?"

"I'm thinking about after she leaves the island," Milo said. "There are definitely going to be people showing up looking for Jessie at some point, and we don't need Daisy helping them out."

"Good thinking," Ruby said. "The long view, right?"

"I knew you'd get there, Ruby," he said, reaching out to stroke the side of her face. "I sure do miss our meetings."

"Like I said, Milo. If this new venture turns out to be as good as you say, I just might have to revisit that decision," she said, flashing him a coy smile. "So, how do you want me to play it with Jessie?"

"That's completely your call," Milo said, getting up. "Now, if you'll excuse me. I need to go wake Daisy up."

Melvin, still grumpy about The Sleaze's decision to cut his profits, thought about broaching the subject again, then decided against it given Sleaze's reaction to Melvin's second protest. The door opened, and Oscar stumbled into the office and collapsed into a chair.

"A simple knock on the door would be nice, Oscar," Melvin said, glaring at the disheveled police chief. "Are you hammered already?"

"No, but don't worry, Melvin. The day is young," Oscar said, glancing back and forth at them. "What's so important that you had to drag me over here?"

"Well, Jimmy and I need to have a chat with you about a change we plan to make when we're doing our weekly pickup," Melvin said, choosing his words carefully.

"What sort of change?" Oscar said.

"Spring has arrived, and Roland Doyle has come out of his burrow," Sleaze said. "So, we thought it might be a good idea for you to take him up on his offer to partner up."

"Why the hell would I do that?" Oscar said, scowling as he again glanced back and forth at them.

"As a diversion, Oscar," Melvin said. "You're going to come up with weekly tips for Mr. Doyle. And then accompany him on his attempts to catch those dastardly bootleggers."

"And I'll be doing that at the same time you two will be doing the pickup?"

"You catch on quick, Oscar," Sleaze said.

"Why are you all of a sudden worried about Doyle? He's a drunken sot."

"Even a drunken sot can get lucky. Just look at you," Sleaze said. "And it only takes one. Getting caught with fifty cases would be extremely bad for all of us."

"Yeah," Melvin said, winking at Sleaze. "We sure don't want to get caught with fifty cases."

Milo knocked softly on the door then knocked louder when he didn't get a response.

"Who is it?" Daisy said, still half-asleep.

"It's me," Milo said, walking into the bedroom. "Late night?"

"Not really," she said, sitting up in bed. "What's going on?"

"Not much," he said, sitting down in a chair next to the bed. "I just happened to be here and thought it would be nice to catch up."

"Yeah, right. And I'm a Catholic nun," Daisy said, hopping out of bed as naked as the day she was born. "Hold that thought. I need to pee."

Milo flinched when he got a look at her then sat quietly until she returned from the bathroom and climbed back into bed. She lit a cigarette and gave him a blank stare.

"The ice is pretty much gone, Milo," she said, exhaling smoke. "Are you here to make good on your promise to get me off this chunk of rock as soon as spring got here?"

"Actually, I am," Milo said. "You should be able to leave in a day or two."

"Great," Daisy said, reaching for her hairbrush. She held up a strand of hair and examined the tangles. "I must look a mess."

"Not the word I would use, Daisy."

"Aren't you sweet," she said, flashing him a smile before getting to work on her hair. "Did you let Fannie know that I'll be back soon?"

"No, not yet," Milo said. "And that's one of the things I wanted to talk to you about. Are you really looking forward to going back to work there and having to deal with men like Melvin every night?"

"It's the only thing I know how to do, Milo," Daisy said. "In case you haven't figured it out yet, I've never been one who's used her brains to get by."

"I've always considered you to be a very bright woman, Daisy."

"Yeah, thanks, Milo. But I'm street smart. Not book smart."

"Don't sell yourself short. Maybe it's just time for a new challenge."

"Is this the new opportunity you were hinting about the other day?" she said, paying close attention.

"That's exactly what I'm talking about," he said.

"Doing what?" she said, tapping ash off her cigarette.

"Working for me."

"I already work for you, Milo," she said, laughing.

"Yes, but this would be different. A completely new position."

"I don't know about that, Milo," she said, grinning at him. "I'm pretty sure I know most all of them."

"Yes, Daisy, I'm sure you do," he said, laughing.

"Will I still be able to at least live at Fannie's? I kinda like it there."

"I'm sure that could be arranged," he said.

"Good," she said, then pursed her lips and frowned. "But Fannie has put Jessie in my old room. I wonder if I'll be able to get it back."

"I don't think that's going to be a problem," Milo said, reaching for his pack of smokes.

"So, what am I going to be doing when I start this new job?"

"Selling furniture."

A Whole Lot Of Booze

Milo looked around the back room of the furniture store where a man named Clint Farwell had once turned Billy's Miracle into Red Deer. And if he hadn't gotten greedy and tried to screw Milo over, he might still be working for him instead of being at the bottom of the River getting up close and personal with the fish. Milo stared at the hundreds of cases of vodka, scotch, and whiskey stacked high and didn't even try to do the math.

"We sure got some good memories of this place, huh?" Birdie said, also glancing around.

"We sure do, Birdie," Milo said, then watched Frank Slack approach.

"Okay, Milo," Frank said. "That's all of it. I'm gonna take off. I need to get the barge back before the sun comes up."

"Sure. Thanks for your help, Frank," Milo said, patting him on the shoulder. "Don't forget to swing by the Crossley tomorrow."

"That's right," he said, grinning and rubbing his hands. "Payday."

"You're gonna like it," Milo said. "We had a good month." Then he took another look around at the stacks of inventory. "Next month might be a bit lighter given the outlay for all this."

"I'm not worried," Frank said. "We'll make it all back and a whole lot more by the time we're done unloading two thousand cases." Frank took another look around the room then shook his head. "Man, that's a whole lot of booze."

"It does get your attention," Birdie said, nodding.

Frank waved and headed out the back into the boathouse just as Willy and Daisy entered from the storeroom in the front half of the building. Daisy was dressed down, dirty and dusty from her day of cleaning. She stopped in the middle of the room and put her hands on her hips as she looked around with an open-mouth stare.

"Geez, somebody's thirsty," she said, shaking her head. "How long will I be in jail if we get caught with all this hooch?"

"Actually, you don't have to worry about going to jail, Daisy," Milo said. "We're in Canada. And while storing two thousand cases of booze might seem odd to most people, there's nothing illegal about it."

"Smart, Milo," Daisy said, nodding as she took another look around.

"But that doesn't mean you need to be telling *anybody anything*, right?"

"I heard you the first ten times, Milo," she said, making a face at him. "I got it."

"As far as the rest of the world is concerned, you're the manager of a furniture store," Milo said. "So, make sure you start brushing up on your expertise about different kinds of wood and dining room tables and such."

"Actually, I've just got a lovely two-seater couch in," she said, effortlessly sliding into her sales pitch. Then she transitioned back into working girl. "Maybe you'd like to go try it out?"

"That's a very generous offer," Milo said with a grin. "Perhaps another time. At the moment, Birdie and I need to get to another appointment."

"When are you gonna be back to pick me up, Birdie?" she said.

"Hour and a half at most," Birdie said. "Is that okay?"

"That's fine," Daisy said. "I need to finish up cleaning the floor. But I sure am working up a thirst."

"Knock yourself out," Milo said, spreading his arms wide. "Remember, Daisy. Lock up tight whenever you leave the building. And keep the door leading out to the showroom locked at all times. And never open the doors that lead to the boathouse during the day."

"Yeah, I got it, Milo."

Milo and Birdie headed down the dock and climbed into the boat.

"You sure you don't mind driving her back and forth?" Milo said. "Roll me one of those."

"Are you kidding?" Birdie said, handing him the freshly rolled cigarette. "I love being around her. Even if it's just a short boat ride."

"She is pretty special," Milo said, nodding. "Did you get a look at the boat Frank built for Willy?"

"I did," he said, backing out of the slip. "It's nice. And real fast. But not as nice or fast as this one."

"Nothing is," Milo said, running his hand over the varnished wood rail. "Did you get all of Billy's stuff into town today?"

"I did. He's all set," Birdie said. "When's he leaving town?"

"I guess that's gonna depend," Milo said, pulling his hat down tight as Birdie accelerated. "Don't forget to tell him I need to have a chat with him."

Milo heard the knock and opened the door to be greeted with the greatest smile on earth. He waved her into the suite and helped her out of her coat.

"Nurse Sally," Milo said, admiring her. "It's so nice to see you."

"How are you doing, Milo?" she said, glancing around. "I'm surprised you called. You know, after our last conversation."

"Yes, I felt bad about how that one ended," he said, gesturing for her to sit down then pouring drinks for them.

"No, limoncello tonight?" she said, raising an eyebrow.

"No, I'm afraid not," he said, laughing. "We drank my last bottle the last time we…well, you know."

"That's too bad," Sally said. "I need to find a way to get my hands on some more. It's quite delicious."

"I'm sure that won't be a problem," Milo said.

"I've been thinking about what you said, Milo," she said, taking a sip of whiskey. "This is good. I like it." She took a bigger sip.

"So, what are your thoughts on the matter we discussed?" Milo said, topping off her drink then lighting a cigarette and draping a leg over his knee.

"You were right," she said. "You and I really don't have a future together. I'm dying to settle down and raise a family, but your thinking runs in a completely different direction. And it's better to call it off now before we do something silly like fall in love with each other."

"Yes, I am getting very fond of you," Milo said. "And I would hate to hurt you."

Milo thought about his comment and shook his head when he remembered just how close she'd come to ending up on the bottom of the River.

"I know you would, Milo," she said, taking another sip of her drink. "But it's definitely for the best. Besides, you're way too old for me."

"Ouch," Milo said, laughing.

"You know what I mean," she said, raising her glass in a toast.

"Yes, I'm afraid I do," he said, exhaling smoke as he touched glasses with her. "How's it working out with Doc Early?"

"That's gonna be a problem," she said.

"What happened?"

"Mrs. Early is worried about him. She's sure Doc's pretty sick and needs to retire. And I think she's just about got him convinced. Which will put me out of a job."

"Maybe the new doctor will hire you. I'm sure Doc would give you a great recommendation. As would I, if you ever needed it."

"Thanks. Yeah, maybe," she said. "I don't know. I'm thinking about just heading out. It's a big world out there, and I might as well see some of it while I'm still young enough to enjoy it, right?"

"I'm so glad to hear you say that, Sally," Milo said. "And I think I might be able to help you out with that."

"Do you now? How are you going to do that, Milo?"

They both turned to the door when they heard the loud knock.

"Hold that thought," Milo said, heading to the door. "Hey, come on in."

Milo ushered the man into the room and beamed back and forth at them.

"Sally Anderson. I'd like you to meet Billy Crankovitch."

What Should I Call You?

Tom Collins poured a shot and held it up to the light. He tossed it back and smiled to himself as he felt the warmth spread through his body.

"How is it?" Milo said, studying his new cooker's expression.

"You tell me," Tom said, handing him a shot glass filled to the brim.

Milo held it up and examined the clear liquid. Then he drank it and beamed.

"Magnificent, Tom. Well done," Milo said, slapping him on the back.

"Billy's a frigging genius," Tom said, refilling their glasses.

"Billy? Who's Billy?" Milo said, laughing.

"Has he left town yet?" Tom said, laughing along.

"No, he's still around," Milo said. "But he'll be heading off as soon as he can convince his new friend to go with him."

"New friend? A woman?"

"Oh, yeah. She's all woman," Milo said.

"What does she do?"

"She's a nurse."

"A nurse, huh?" Tom said, giving it some thought. "Good for him. That could come in handy."

"How's our friend doing?" Milo said, nodding at the house.

"Well, she finally got everything out of me," Tom said. "Toward the end, I was making up all sorts of crazy shit just to keep her interested. She's pretty much cooled off toward me. Now she's driving Ruby nuts with all her questions."

"How's Ruby handling it?"

"She's showing remarkable patience," Tom said. "Which, I have to say, has really surprised me."

"Good," Milo said, nodding. "Did you get a chance to look at the new numbers?"

"I did. And it's way too generous, Milo," Tom said. "You don't need to pay me anywhere near that much."

"Don't be silly," Milo said, shaking his head. "You're my main guy, Tom. And you need to be adequately compensated."

"Oh, it's way more than adequate, Milo. What am I gonna do with all of it?"

"I'm sure you'll come up with something," Milo said. "What do you think about my idea of adding a couple more stills and mixing tanks?"

"I like it. And we've got plenty of room," Tom said. "But I'm gonna need some help at some point."

"Yeah, I'm already working on that," Milo said. "And if Daisy wasn't doing so well at the furniture store, I'd probably try convincing her to come over here."

"Is she selling any furniture?"

"She's selling a lot," Milo said, laughing. "She's got customers coming and going all day."

"Well, I know I wouldn't be able to say no to her," Tom said, shaking his head. "What did Fannie say when you told her she wasn't getting her top earner back?"

"At first, she put up a fuss about it," Milo said. "But she settled down as soon as she heard my offer. I gave her five percent of the business."

"Really? Why would you do that?"

"I like Fannie," Milo said with a shrug. "And there's a chance I'm going to need to use her expertise at some point down the road. Okay, I'm gonna head up to the house to see if there's a letter I need to drop in the mail."

Milo found Jessie in the kitchen putting the finishing touches on a casserole. She glanced up when she heard him enter and gave him a big smile.

"Hi, Milo. You hungry?" she said, opening the oven and sliding the casserole in. She wiped her hands with a dishtowel and brushed the hair back from her face. "It'll be ready in about half an hour."

"No, I don't think I can stay, but thanks," he said, sitting down at the table. "So, how are you enjoying island life?"

"It's been very interesting. I've learned a lot," Jessie said. "And it's a beautiful island. You've done very well for yourself, Milo."

"Yes, I have. Running booze is a very lucrative business to be in," Milo said, staying casual.

"And you use the dairy farm as some sort of front?" Jessie said, sitting down across from him. "You know, as a way to keep prying eyes looking elsewhere."

"Partially, yes," Milo said, nodding. "But the farm is doing very well. I sell a lot of milk and cheese."

"I'd love to get a tour sometime," she said.

"I'm sure that can be arranged."

"Wonderful. And you feed all the local schoolkids breakfast and lunch?"

"Yes, I do," he said, offering her a cigarette then lighting both. "And I'm in the middle of building them a new school."

"Yes, Tom told me. That's incredibly generous of you," she said, placing a hand over his.

"It's the least I can do. The town has been very good to me," he said with a small shrug.

He got to his feet and headed for a cabinet then returned with a jar of Miracle and two glasses. He poured, then clinked glasses with her. They tossed the shots back, and Milo watched her reaction closely.

"Oh, I love this stuff," she said. "The Red Deer is really good, but I like drinking from the source if you know what I mean."

"Billy is very good at what he does," Milo said.

"He's an interesting guy," Jessie said. "Has he left for California yet?"

"No, but it won't be long," he said, pouring two more shots.

"Now that he's gone," she said, tossing her hair back from her face. "I suppose I'll be heading back to Fannie's soon. I really should get back to work."

"Absolutely," Milo said, tossing back his shot and deciding that he'd had enough. "But if you could stay for a few more days and keep Tom company, I'd appreciate it."

"Sure, no problem," she said, downing her drink. "Whew. I need to slow down. This stuff sneaks up on you in a hurry."

"One more can't hurt," Milo said, pouring another one for her. "Do you need me to drop anything in the mail today?"

"Oh, thanks for reminding me," she said, hopping up to grab the letter from a kitchen counter. "Thanks so much for doing that."

"Not a problem," Milo said, glancing down at the familiar address. "You know, I've never seen any letters coming back this way. Doesn't your uncle ever write to you?"

"He's not able to," Jessie said with a sad shake of her head. "The stroke left his whole right side pretty much useless."

"I'm sorry to hear that," Milo said.

"Yeah, it's sad," she said, then brightened. "Say, I've got an idea. Why don't you stay for lunch and then the two of us could head upstairs and spend the rest of the afternoon relaxing?"

"Relaxing?" Milo said, laughing.

"You know what I'm talking about," she said, turning coy. "I'd really like to get to know you better."

"Be careful what you wish for, Jessie," he said, grinning at her.

"I'll take my chances," she said, nodding. "Yeah, I'd like that a lot, Milo."

"It does sound wonderful."

"Good. Then it's settled. It'll give us a chance to work off all the casserole we eat, right?"

"I do like getting some exercise in the afternoon," Milo said. "I just have one question."

"What's that?"

"When we get upstairs, what should I call you?"

"What?" she said, confused.

"Should I call you Jessie?" Milo said with a dead-eyed stare. "Or Barbara?"

Jessie's mouth dropped open, and she stared back at Milo as panic set in. She glanced around looking for an escape route then must have remembered she was stuck on an island. She sat back in her chair and shook her head as she stared down at the floor.

"Sonofabitch," she whispered. "How long have you known?"

"The whole time," Milo said, lighting a fresh cigarette. "And I've really enjoyed your letters. You're a good writer. And very smart."

"How much did I get right?"

"Pretty much all of it," Milo said, shrugging. "As far as you got."

"I got stuck on the part about where you deliver it after you leave the farm," she said, tearing up.

"It goes to a cheese shop in Watertown," he said.

"Beulah's Cheese Emporium?" she said, surprised.

"That's the one," Milo said.

"They make great cheese," she said, tears rolling down her cheeks.

"Yes, they do."

"What are you going to do to me, Milo?"

"Well, I have a lot of options on that front," Milo said. "I could turn you over to Ben Green. And I have to thank you for the part you played on that front, Jessie."

"I'm not following," she said.

"It doesn't matter," he said, shaking his head. "I'm sure Mr. Green would just love to get his hands on you. But not as much as Jimmy Sleaze would."

"Jimmy wouldn't hurt me, would he?"

Milo laughed long and hard.

"Jimmy once carved his name into a woman's back just so she wouldn't forget who owned her."

"What did she do?" Jessie said, her eyes wide and wet.

"She cheated on him," Milo said, extinguishing his cigarette. "What do you think he'd do to you if he found out you were working as an undercover Fed the whole time you were sharing his bed?"

"So, you're not going to turn me over to either one of them?" she said, her hands shaking as she reached for the jar of Miracle and drinking straight from it.

"No, I'm not," Milo whispered.

"You're gonna kill me, aren't you?"

"No, I'm not," Milo said.

"You're not?" she said, cocking her head.

"No," he said. "How well do you swim?"

"Not well."

"Then I gotta say I don't like your chances," he said, giving her a blank stare.

"What?" she said, then teared up again when the penny dropped. "You're gonna toss me in the River, aren't you?"

"Yes, I am," Milo whispered. "Tonight. Just as soon as the sun goes down."

"And not a second too soon," Ruby said, from the doorway.

Milo turned around and saw her and Tom standing behind him.

"How long have you two been standing there?" Milo said, refocusing on Jessie.

"Long enough," Tom said. "It's too bad, Jessie. You're a lot of fun."

"Yeah, such a waste," Ruby said.

"Come on in and have a seat," Milo said. "We're about to eat lunch."

They both sat down and glared at Jessie who was again staring down at the floor. Milo noticed the small pool of tears forming between her feet.

"How did you figure it out, Milo?" she said, looking up at him.

"Let's just say that your boss, Vernon, isn't quite as clever as he thinks he is," Milo said, getting to his feet and grabbing the letter. "Now, if you'll excuse me, I have a little light reading to do before lunch. Keep a close eye on her until I get back."

"Do you mind if I tag along tonight?" Ruby said. "I'd love to see it."

"Not at all," Milo said. "Birdie says it going to going to be a beautiful night for a boat ride."

Tom and Ruby both laughed.

"Hopefully, it won't be a late night. The first thing tomorrow morning, I need to make my way down to Syracuse," Milo said.

"What are you going to be doing down there?" Ruby said.

"Meeting with our soon-to-be governor," he said, flashing her a grin. "Remind me to introduce you to him at some point. You're gonna like him."

"Whatever you say, Milo," Ruby said, laughing.

"That's my girl," Milo said, then grinned at the undercover agent. "So, do you think you're still going to be in the mood after lunch?"

"Screw you, Milo," she said, glaring at him.

"I know it's probably no consolation to you, *Barbara*," Milo said. "But I need to tell you something."

"What's that?"

Milo held his index finger and thumb about half an inch apart up to her face.

"You were this close."

Episode 13

Expansion

I overheard somebody talking to a friend about the problems he was having with his boss, and his friend said something that stuck with me. "If you can't beat them, join them." And I realized that I feel the same way about politicians. I think all politicians should be joined. Joined together. Preferably by the throat.

Milo Razner

Bad Moods And Landslides

Milo gently knocked and twirled his fedora on a finger as he waited. Senator Miller opened the door and waved him in with a big smile.

"Hey, Milo," Senator Miller said, shaking hands. "It's good to see you. Come on in and let me pour you a drink."

"That sounds great, Senator," Milo said, stepping into the suite and taking the place in. "This is nice."

"Yeah, Ben turned me onto it," he said, handing Milo his drink. "Now, it's the only place I stay when I'm in Syracuse."

The Senator raised his glass in toast and grinned.

"To Prohibition."

"To Prohibition. And the politicians who made it possible," Milo said, clinking glasses with him.

"You're welcome, Milo," he said, laughing. "Have a seat."

Milo sat down and got comfortable then took a sip of really good scotch. The Senator held out a box of cigars, and Milo selected one and lit it.

"Cuban," the Senator said, lighting his own and puffing hard until the end was glowing. "Good, huh?"

"You do always manage to get your hands on the finer things life has to offer, Senator," Milo said, raising his glass in salute.

"Yeah, I kinda do, don't I?" he said, laughing as he blew a smoke ring up at the ceiling.

"How's the campaign going?"

"Perfect," the Senator said. "It's gonna be a landslide."

"That's great."

"And the best thing about it is that I didn't even need to cheat to make it happen," he said, laughing. "Thanks to you."

"Then I take it you aren't going to need another campaign contribution," Milo said.

"No, I've got plenty of money," the Senator said, waving him off. "And you've already done way too much for me, Milo. I can't thank you enough. And I won't forget it."

"I hear that our current governor is thinking about taking an extended trip overseas," Milo said, grinning.

"Yeah, he is," the Senator said. "If I were in his shoes, I'd be doing the same thing. You know, just to get away from all those pesky indictments heading his way."

"You sure are in a good mood," Milo said.

"Yes, I am. Life is good."

"Well, then I have to apologize right off the bat for ruining it," Milo said, puffing his cigar.

"Ruining what?" Senator Miller said, suddenly edgy.

"Your good mood," Milo said, reaching into his pocket.

"Shit. What happened?" the Senator said, crestfallen.

Milo tossed one of Jessie's status reports on the coffee table, and the Senator stared at it like it was a rabid dog.

"What is it?"

"Go ahead and read it," Milo said. "It won't bite."

The Senator removed the report from the envelope and studied it for a long time. Then he stared at Milo, put his cigar down, and read it again.

"Where on earth did you get this, Milo?"

"I intercepted it before it was dropped in the mail."

"Can I ask you who you intercepted it from?" the Senator said, wide-eyed.

"You can," Milo said. "I got it from an undercover agent working for Vernon Adams."

"Goddamn it," Senator Miller snapped. "Ben's name is all over this report."

"Yes, I know. I've read it," Milo said, giving the Senator a dark stare.

"How could Ben be that stupid?" he said, downing his drink. "Goddamn it. If this ever gets out, I'll be vacationing overseas with our ex-governor. And Ben, being the prick he is, wouldn't think twice about giving me up if he thought he could save his own ass."

The Senator blew a long series of smoke rings as he thought.

"This is bad, Milo. Really bad."

"It could have been, Senator," Milo said, trying to blow a smoke ring of his own and failing miserably. "I've never been able to figure how to do those."

"You're not holding your mouth right," the Senator said, refilling their glasses.

"I have the same problem when I'm fishing," Milo said.

"I'll take your word for it," Senator Miller said, frowning. "Blowing the perfect smoke ring just takes practice."

"Practice blowing hot air?" Milo said, puffing on his cigar.

"Yeah."

"No wonder you're so good at it," Milo said, laughing.

"Funny, Milo. But I'm suddenly not in the mood for levity. What do you mean it *could* have been bad?"

"I solved the problem for you, Senator," Milo said. "Even before you knew there was one."

"Thanks. How did you do that?"

"By figuring out what she was doing before she had a chance to get her reports in the mail."

"She? The undercover agent is a woman?"

"Yeah, and a very pretty one at that," Milo said. "And you might want to be a bit more careful about who you're getting horizontal with these days. You never know, Governor."

"How the hell do you know who I've been getting horizontal with?"

"You really want to know?" Milo said, taking a sip of scotch.

"No, probably not. What kind of cover story was she using?" the Senator said, leaning forward.

"She was a working girl at a place in Alex Bay," Milo said. "But based on what she put in that report about Green and the speakeasies, she'd obviously spent some time around Watertown."

"You're sure she wasn't able to give that idiot Vernon Adams any information about what we're doing?" he said, studying Milo closely.

"I'm positive," Milo said, with a nod and a grin. "You owe me, Governor. Again."

"No shit," he said, nodding in agreement. "How would you like to be my Chief of Staff? Maybe even Lieutenant Governor?"

"I'd rather run naked through a crowded field of cactus," Milo said, laughing.

"A working girl, huh? That's pretty clever. Maybe Vernon isn't as dumb as he looks," he said, getting back to work on his cigar. "She just happened to hand her reports over to you?"

"Yeah. She wasn't able to make it to the post office," Milo said. "So, she asked me to mail them for her."

"Why couldn't she mail them herself?"

"Because she was stuck on an island," Milo said. "Whisperer Island."

"I knew that place would come in handy," he said, chuckling as he leaned back in his chair.

"You have no idea, Governor."

"Is she still there?"

"No, she decided to go for a late-night swim last night," Milo said, taking a sip.

"Bottom of the river?"

"Eventually," Milo whispered, chasing the memory away as best he could.

"You're sure we aren't going to have a problem with this?" Senator Miller said, pointing at the report.

"No, that problem is fully resolved," Milo said. "But I haven't addressed our other problem yet. I needed to talk to you first."

Senator Miller stared at the wall for several seconds deep in thought.

"The problem of what to do about Ben, right?"

"That is top of mind at the moment," Milo said. "Do you have any suggestions?"

"Sure," he said, shrugging. "I'd probably just shoot the son of a bitch, but that's just me." He looked at Milo and raised his glass in salute. "But that's not your style, is it, Milo?"

"You read me like a book, Governor," Milo said. "Governor Miller. It does have a nice ring to it."

"Yeah, I like it, too. What do you have in mind, Milo?"

"I just can't help but think, as governor of the great state of New York and someone who's up to his neck running a lucrative chain of speakeasies, that you should have a business partner you can trust. Someone who's going to look out for your best interests and not do stupid shit like inviting an undercover Fed inside the tent to have a look around."

"You do have a way of waxing poetic when you want to, Milo."

"Well, my ass is also on the line," Milo said. "And if Ben Green would be willing to give you up to save himself, how long would it take him to sell me down the river?"

"Before you could even get started counting," the Senator said. "He doesn't like you."

"Well, I must say that I've recently taken a rather strong dislike to him as well," Milo said, tapping a long ash off his cigar. "The dumb shit."

"And you'd be willing to take care of this potential problem for me, Milo?"

"I'd be delighted to do that, Governor," Milo said, grinning. "For the right price."

"You want Ben's share of the speakeasies, don't you?"

"I'm so glad that the people of New York are going to have such an amazing brain running things for the next several years," Milo said, exhaling smoke. "What's your current split with Green?"

"70/30. In his favor," the Senator said.

"No, that won't work," Milo said, shaking his head. "I suggest we move it to 60/40."

"You're going to take care of the Ben problem and increase my cut at the same time?" he said, raising an eyebrow at him.

"Yes, that's exactly what I'm going to do," Milo said, tossing back what was left of his drink.

"Why on earth would you do that, Milo?"

"Because you're going to be the next Governor," Milo said with a shrug. "And who knows when I might need your help down the road."

"So, we'll be joined even further at the hip, right?"

"Yes, I'm sure we're going to be getting a lot closer, Governor. And a whole lot richer."

"I do enjoy your company, Milo. And I certainly like money. Okay," he said, extending his hand. "We got a deal."

"I was so hoping you'd say that," Milo said, grinning. "Don't say a word to Mr. Green that you know what he did."

"Okay, Milo. And keep my name out of whatever you decide to do," Senator Miller said, staring hard at Milo.

"You won't hear a word, Governor. Until you read all about it in the papers."

Roland Doyle sat rigid in the front seat of the boat terrorized by the prospect of falling overboard. He glanced at the police chief who was slowly piloting the boat along the shoreline not far from town. Being out on the water was bad enough. Being out here in the dead of night running the boat with no lights and a drunk behind the wheel was something else altogether.

"What's the matter with you?" Oscar said, glancing over at Doyle. "You look like you're about to wet yourself."

"I hate boats. And I hate this River," Roland said.

"Then you might want to start thinking about asking for a transfer," Oscar said, laughing. "You ain't gonna catch many bootleggers around here sitting on dry land."

"Yeah, thanks. I'll try to remember that," Roland said, sitting still as they continued to slowly make their way along the shoreline. "So, tell me more about this tip you got."

"I overheard a couple of guys talking about doing a big run tonight," Oscar said.

"Who were they?"

"I don't know," Oscar said, shaking his head. "I didn't get a good look at them."

"And they're supposed to be making their drop around here?" Roland said.

"Yeah, it's supposed to be around here somewhere," Oscar said. "But there's so much flat shoreline in this stretch of river, I imagine it could be a mile or two in either direction."

"Great tip, Oscar," Roland growled.

"Hey, it's a lot more than you got," Oscar snapped.

"Hang on. Slow down. There they are," Roland said.

"What?"

"Right over there," Roland said, pointing.

"Sonofabitch," Oscar said, confused. "How about that?"

"Hold the boat steady," Roland said, carefully making his way out of his seat. "I'll hit them with the spotlight."

"Okay," Oscar said, still sounding confused. "It's a goddamn miracle."

"What?"

"Nothing," Oscar said. "Get the light on them, and I'll use the bullhorn."

Roland turned on the spotlight and scanned the shoreline until he spotted a small boat with its bow on the rocks.

"This is the police!" Oscar said through the bullhorn. His voice reverberated across the water. "Put your hands up."

"Shit," Roland said. "They're making a run for it. Let's go."

Oscar fumbled for the throttle, missed it completely, then the wheel turned when his momentum carried him forward in his seat, and he lost his balance. The boat made a ninety-degree turn toward shore and almost ran aground before Oscar was able to regain control. He reversed the boat then scanned the shoreline as he searched for the smugglers.

"Damn it, Oscar," Roland said, shining the light into Oscar's eyes. "They got away. Nice job."

"Get that thing away from me," Oscar said, waving the light away as he accelerated toward the spot where the bootleggers had reached shore. "Hey, look at that."

"It looks like they had already started unloading," Roland said.

"Yeah, I see a couple of cases," Oscar said, coming to a stop next to the wooden crates. "The rest of it must still be in the boat."

"You think we should go after them?" Roland said.

"Nah, that would be like looking for a needle in a haystack at this time of night," Oscar said, shaking his head.

"What do you want to do?"

"Well, I really don't feel like doing the damn paperwork for two lousy cases," Oscar said.

"Yeah, that does sound like a waste of time," Roland said.

"Tell you what," Oscar said, glancing over at the Fed.

"What?"

"I'll split it with you."

Roland stared at the two cases then looked back at Oscar and nodded in agreement.

"Okay, just don't tell anybody," Roland said.

"The only person I might tell who would give a shit is you, Roland."

"Yeah, good point."

Cases And Composition

Milo tossed another log on the fire and watched until it began to crackle and burn. Then he sat down across from Annabelle at the dining room table. She had her head down and was writing a letter.

"This might be the last fire you're gonna need," Milo said. "It almost hit seventy today."

"Uh-huh," she said, not looking up as she continued to write.

"What are you doing?"

"My status report," Annabelle said, then glanced at him. "Do you think I should mention anything to Vernon about one of his agents going for a late-night swim?"

"Oh, I'd rather you didn't," he said, lighting a cigarette.

Annabelle put her pen down and frowned.

"How bad was it out there the other night?" she said, reaching for his pack of cigarettes.

"It was tough to watch," Milo said. "Such a waste of a life."

"Did she put up much of a fight?"

"Not until she was in the water," Milo said, shaking his head at the memory. "Up to that point, she'd been pretty calm. Almost resigned to the fact."

"It's so sad," Annabelle said. "But when you boil it all down, better her than us, right?"

"Yeah. Better her than us."

"You still worried that Vernon is going to send some people up here looking for her?" she said, leaning back in her chair and folding her arms across her chest.

"Not since this afternoon," Milo said.

"Why, Mr. Razner," she said, cocking her head at him. "Have you been doing some thinking?"

"I have, Miss Caffey. I think it's time we had a little fun."

"Can I finish writing my report first?"

"I'm not talking about that," Milo said. "At least for the moment. I think it's time we put Vernon Adams on a different path and knock a little varnish off his reputation in the process."

"Ooh, I do like the sound of that," Annabelle said, leaning forward. "How are we going to do that, Milo?"

"By sending him Jessie's final status report," he said. "You still got that typewriter?"

"I do," she said.

"Good. We don't want Vernon recognizing your handwriting. You got more of that official stationery you use for your reports?"

"Yeah, I got plenty," she said, getting up from the table.

Moments later, she returned carrying a typewriter. She set it on the table in front of her and rolled a piece of Prohibition Unit stationery into it.

"Okay," Milo said. "You do the typing."

"And you'll be composing?" she said, glancing at him with a grin.

"Yeah, I've been working on it all afternoon."

"Well, we better start by putting a two in the box in the top corner," Annabelle said, tapping a key. "You know, since this will be Jessie's *second* report."

"All right," Milo said, lighting another cigarette. "Dear, Mr. Adams."

"No, Vernon insists that all the women call him by his first name," she said, shaking her head.

"Good catch," Milo said. "Dear, Vernon. I'm sorry that I haven't sent you a status report recently. I've been very busy, and two things have happened that I'm finally ready to tell you about."

"This oughta be good," Annabelle said, tapping the keys.

"Oh, it's good," Milo said, nodding. "The first item is of a personal nature. I have recently fallen in love with a local man. He's a dairy farmer, and we have decided to get married and move to California."

Annabelle shook her head as she tapped the keys.

"And oldie but a goodie, right?" she said, laughing.

"Yeah, I thought it was a nice touch," Milo said, exhaling smoke. "So, it is with great regret that I need to inform you I am resigning my position with the Unit effective immediately. As such, this is the final status report you will be receiving from me."

"Nice," Annabelle said, typing as fast as she could to keep up. "That should keep the uninvited eyes away."

"Yeah, I thought we needed a little closure on that one," Milo said. "The second item will be of great interest to you and deals with an undercover operation I've been working on for several weeks. I can now confirm that a shipment of a thousand cases of whiskey will be transported across the St. Lawrence three miles upriver from the town of Alexandria Bay on the night of April 13th."

"Ah, those pesky thousand cases," she said, laughing.

"Yeah, nice touch, huh?"

"Why the 13th?" she said, glancing up.

"Butch Cassidy's birthday," he said with a shrug. "He's always been one of my heroes."

"If you say so, Milo," she said, laughing again.

"The shipment will be delivered by barge just after sunset, and you can expect the bootleggers to be heavily armed."

"Barge?"

"Yeah, it's coming by barge," Milo said, nodding.

"Okay. What's next?"

"All we need to do is add a little personal touch at the end to spice things up a bit," he said. "Was she friendly with him?"

"Yeah, Vernon mentioned that they'd gotten horizontal at least once," Annabelle said.

"Perfect," Milo said, then started dictating again. "In closing, Vernon, I just want to say that I will always have fond memories of our time together. And in the late-night darkness, I'm sure I will often harken back to one very special evening when you showed me what it's truly like to be loved and loved well."

"Geez, Milo," Annabelle said, frowning. "You're laying it on pretty thick. The guy is all needlesticks and thumbs in the sack."

"Just type the note," he said, laughing.

She removed the note from the typewriter then typed the address on an envelope. She folded the letter and sealed it then handed it to him.

"I'll drop it in the mail when I'm in Watertown tomorrow. No need to have a local postmark on it, right?"

"Why are you going to Watertown?"

"I need to have a little chat with Ben Green."

Milo passed around the glasses then raised his glass in toast.

"To big money and pretty women."

"To big money and pretty women," the others said, then touched glasses and drank.

"First of all, I'd like to welcome Tom back to the mainland," Milo said, grinning at his cooker. "At least for the night. How does it feel to be able to walk around and not have to worry about falling in the water?"

"I have been going a little stir crazy over there," Tom said. "After the meeting, I think I might head over to Fannie's place."

"Good idea," Milo said. "And tell Fannie to give you one on the house. She owes me." He settled into his chair and glanced around. "Sorry to drag you over here on short notice at this late hour, but I needed to talk to you."

"We got a problem, Milo?" Birdie said, rolling a cigarette.

"No, things are great. And about to get even better," Milo said. "Toss me those rolling papers and tobacco. Watch this. I've been practicing."

Milo fumbled his way through the process of hand rolling a cigarette then held it up.

"What do you think?" he said to Birdie.

"You can't roll a cigarette or blow a smoke ring worth a shit, Milo," he said with a cackle. "You might want to think about giving the habit up."

"Smart ass," he said, then tossed the cigarette on the coffee table. "Roll me one of those." Then he draped a leg over his knee and started talking. "Gentlemen, I think it's time for us to consider increasing the size of our shipment to Melvin and The Sleaze."

"Geez, Milo," Willy said, shaking his head. "You're killing me."

"Relax, Willy," Milo said. "You're gonna like this one. Oh, I almost forgot to tell you. You're about to start a new business venture."

"I am?" Willy said, frowning. "Well, if you keep selling all my booze to Melvin and The Sleaze, I just might have to do that."

"Funny," Milo said, glaring at him. "Since you're about to start delivering a whole lot more booze, we're gonna need some better cover. That truck you're driving at the moment is bound to start attracting attention at some point."

"What's wrong with my truck?" Willy said, offended.

"There's nothing wrong with the truck," Milo said. "It's just not identified with anything. Right now, when people see you making all those trips to Watertown, they might be saying to themselves, gee, I wonder why Willy is making that drive all the time. Plus, it's open in the back, and that tarp you use to cover the product could blow off in a big wind."

"Nah, I got it secured nice and tight, Milo," Willy said, shaking his head.

"It only takes one, Willy," Milo said, staring at him. "No, we need to give you some additional cover."

"So, what's this new business I'm getting into?" Willy said, sipping his whiskey.

"Ice," Milo said with a big grin.

"Ice?" Willy said, stunned.

"You're talking about a seasonal business, right, Milo?" Birdie said, rolling another cigarette. "During the winter."

"No, I'm talking about a year-round operation, Birdie."

"Uh, no offense, Milo," Birdie said. "But I think you might have a hard time getting ice out of the St. Lawrence most of the year."

"Yes, Birdie, I'm very aware of that," Milo said. "That's why we're going to build an ice factory."

"A factory? To make ice?" Willy said, staring at Milo.

"Yeah. We don't have one. And people do love their cold beverages," Milo said.

"You're talking about refrigerated trucks," Frank said.

"Yes, I am," Milo said, beaming at the boatbuilder. "*Enclosed* refrigerated trucks. You think you'd be able to figure out how to do that, Frank?"

"Well, I know the ice cream folks have started using them," Frank said. "It might take me some time, but I'm sure I can figure it out."

"I have no doubt about it, Frank," Milo said, nodding.

"All you'd need to do is put some blocks of ice in the back behind the booze," Frank said. "That's brilliant, Milo."

"Thanks, Frank. I kinda like the idea myself."

"But I don't know anything about making ice," Willy said.

"I think you just need water and some cold weather," Birdie said with a shrug.

"There you go," Milo said, laughing. "Don't worry about it, Willy. Do I look like I know anything about dairy farming? It's not a problem. We'll find somebody who knows how to make ice."

"Okay," Willy said, shrugging. "Ice. I suppose I can handle that."

"I'm sure you can," Milo said. "Now, back to increasing the size of our shipment to Melvin and The Sleaze."

"How much are you thinking, Milo?" Willy said.

"A thousand cases," Milo said as a big grin slowly appeared.

Tom and Birdie glanced at each other then laughed.

"A thousand, huh?" Tom said. "What are you up to, Milo?"

"You'll see. And you're gonna love it."

Green Turns Red

Milo studied Ben Green closely as he peered into the envelope and slowly removed the status report he was featured in. Milo hid his smile as Green's expression gradually shifted from anticipation to wide-eyed panic. Green got up from behind his desk to pour himself a drink then paced back and forth in front of his liquor cabinet while he drank it. Then he poured himself another and brought the bottle with him when he sat back down and read the note again. Milo helped himself to the whiskey and sipped and savored while he waited patiently for Ben Green to find his voice.

"Sonofabitch," Green finally whispered. "This is bad."

He looked up from the note and stared across the desk at Milo.

"This is goddamn bad, Milo."

"We don't agree about much, Ben, but you'll get no argument from me. It's bad."

"Where on earth did you get this?"

"I got it off an undercover agent I happened to cross paths with," Milo said.

"You ran into the Fed who wrote this?" Green said, clasping his hands to keep them from shaking.

"I did," Milo said, nodding.

"Well, I hope you did the right thing and shot the son of a bitch," Green said, again studying the report.

"No, I didn't shoot her. But don't worry, she's been…neutralized."

"Her? A woman?"

"Yes. A lovely working girl who went by the name of Jessie."

"Working girl?" Green said, exhaling loudly. "As much as I hate to give the Feds any credit, that was a pretty smart move on their part. How long had she been at it?"

"My best guess is a couple of months," Milo said, shrugging. "But don't worry, I was able to get to her before she had a chance to update Washington about what she'd figured out."

"Good. Thanks, Milo," Green said, topping off his drink and holding the bottle out to him.

Milo shook his head at the offer and glanced out the window as one of Green's produce trucks pulled into the warehouse and began unloading cases of Red Deer. Milo quickly did the math and smiled.

"Did she manage to figure out anything about your operation?" Green said.

"A little," Milo said. "I think she had put some things together about how I'm bringing in the Red Deer from Alberta, but she didn't get a chance to divulge it. So, we don't have anything to worry about when it comes to her."

Green nodded then his face went white when a thought popped into his head.

"Shit. The Senator. Does he know anything about this?"

"No, and given what's in that report about your operation, I don't imagine you want Senator Miller hearing one word about this most unfortunate situation."

"You got that right," Green said. "Damn. That was way too close, Milo," Green said, beginning to calm down.

"I'm afraid the situation hasn't completely played itself out, Ben."

"It hasn't?" Green said, staring at Milo. "What else is there?"

"Before our working girl Fed was sent to her watery grave, I was able to get the name of who she was working with."

"Damn. There's more?" he said, scowling. "Another working girl?"

"No, this one is a gentleman who goes by the name of Jimmy Sleaze," Milo said, then sat back in his chair to enjoy the show.

Ben Green started with an open-mouthed stare and showed Milo a lot of white in his eyes. Then he started to shake from the shoulders, and the quivers worked their way down his arms and hands. Green held onto the desk with both hands, and his mouth opened and closed like a fish on dry land.

"What?" Green finally managed to squeak.

"What's the matter, Ben? It looks like you might be having a stroke. Are you okay?"

"What did you say this guy's name was?"

"Sleaze," Milo said, cocking his head. "Jimmy Sleaze."

"Sonofabitch."

"What on earth is the matter, Ben? Don't worry about it. All we need to do is track him down and take him out."

"I know the guy," Ben Green whispered, unable to maintain eye contact.

"How the hell do you know the guy?" Milo said, his voice rising a notch.

Green rubbed his head vigorously with both hands and took several deeps breaths before summoning up the strength to answer Milo's question.

"I'm buying a hundred cases from him every week."

Milo bolted upright in his chair and fixed a hard stare on Ben Green.

"You're joking, right? Please, tell me you're joking, Ben."

"I wish I could, Milo," Green said, shaking his head. "A hundred a week."

"How long have you been doing that?"

"I started buying fifty from him right around the start of winter. And I recently increased the order."

"Goddamn it, Ben," Milo said, slamming his hand on the desk and getting to his feet. Deciding it was his turn to pace, he began walking back and forth in front of the desk. "Goddamn, you."

"I'm sorry, Milo," Green said. "But my other supplier wasn't able to keep up with demand."

"Why didn't you just increase your order of Red Deer?"

"I was looking for more top-shelf product," Green said, his voice shaking.

"So, you thought you'd just start buying from the Feds?" Milo said, coming to a stop and glaring across the desk.

"He was real convincing, Milo."

"They're trained to be convincing. You stupid son of a bitch. What the hell were you thinking?"

"Don't worry," Green said, glaring back at him. "I'll fix it."

"You're goddamn right you're gonna fix it," Milo said. "And soon. For your sake, you better hope he hasn't had a chance to start blabbing to his handlers in D.C."

"Are you threatening me, Milo?" Green said, slowly getting up from his chair.

"Yes, Ben. That's exactly what I'm doing," Milo said, standing his ground. "But I am going to give you a chance to make this problem go away. And if it doesn't, my next stop will be the Senator's office to inform him he can forget about being governor, and that he should strongly consider moving to South America."

Green continued to glare at Milo, his nostrils flaring.

"Don't try to give me the tough guy routine, Green," Milo said. "It doesn't work on me. Save it for this guy Sleaze. Remember him? You know, the one you're selling a hundred cases to every week."

"Don't push me, Milo," Green said, his face red with rage.

"Just fix the problem," Milo said, gently placing his fedora on his head. "You dumb fuck."

Milo turned and headed for the door. He heard the loud thump of Green's hands slamming the desk but didn't look back. He grinned and headed for the warehouse where he spied the guy he was looking for talking with a couple of other guys who worked there.

"Hey, Bobby," Milo said, extending his hand.

"Oh, hi, Mr. Razner," he said, returning the handshake. "You're looking well."

"Thanks," Milo said, beaming. "I'm having a really good morning."

"What brings you to town?" Bobby said.

"Just checking in to see how things are going," Milo said, glancing at the stacks of Red Deer. "Are you having any problems on my side?"

"None," he said, shaking his head. "I don't know how you do it, Mr. Razner, but your end runs like clockwork. We sure could use some of that over here."

"I'll see what I can do," Milo said, laughing. "It's good to see you, Bobby."

"You too, Mr. Razner," Bobby said, glancing at Ben Green's office. "I need to have a word with Green. Is he alone in there?"

"He is," Milo said, adjusting his fedora. "But you might want to give him a few minutes."

No Rest For The Weary

Jimmy Sleaze had the same reaction he always did when he got woken up from a nap. Pissed off and expecting to hear Melvin's whiny voice on the other end of the line, he snatched the phone off the hook and barked into it.

"What?"

"Mr. Sleaze?" said the voice on the other end of the line.

"Who is this?" Sleaze said, clearing his throat then lighting a cigarette.

"It's Ben Green."

"Oh, hi, Mr. Green. How can I help you?"

"I'm afraid we have a problem, Mr. Sleaze."

"What sort of problem?" Sleaze said, exhaling smoke.

"A problem with your recent delivery," Ben Green said.

"It's the first I'm hearing of it," Sleaze said. "Why didn't your guys say something about it when I was in town?"

"Because we didn't know about the problem at the time."

"What is it?"

"I'd rather not get into it over the phone," Ben Green said. "But we need to speak. Tonight."

"Tonight? You expect me to drive down there tonight?" Sleaze said, frowning.

"Yes, that would be a bit inconvenient. For both of us," he said. "Tell you what. Let's meet halfway."

"I suppose I could do that," Sleaze said.

"Do you remember seeing a picnic area along the side of the road?"

"Yeah, I drive by it all the time. You want to meet there?"

"Yes, I think that spot will work just fine," Ben Green said, then laughed. "I'll even bring the picnic basket."

"Yeah, you do that," Sleaze said, shaking his head. "What time do you want to meet?"

"How does ten work for you?"

"Ten, it is," Sleaze said, hanging up.

Milo draped a leg over his knee as he watched Daisy get comfortable on the bed. She tucked her legs underneath her and began rolling a cigarette with one hand. Then she held it up and beamed at him.

"I'm impressed," Milo said, lighting the cigarette for her. "Did Birdie teach you how to do that?"

"He did," she said, blowing smoke up at the ceiling. "I love Birdie."

"You *love*, Birdie?" Milo said, frowning.

"No, not like that, Milo," she said, shaking her head. "Birdie's more like my uncle. Or maybe a cousin."

"He's an incredible guy," Milo said.

"Yeah. And he's really good to me. Always looking out for me, buying me little gifts. I've been thinking that maybe I should, you know, thank him in a special way."

"I see," Milo said, frowning.

"Do you think that's a bad idea, Milo?"

"You're a big girl, Daisy. And that decision is completely up to you. But I will say that if you end up breaking Birdie's heart and it starts to affect his work, you and I are going to have a very big problem."

"Yeah, I get it, Milo. And that's what I'm worried about," Daisy said. "He's already pretty attached. Whenever he's around the store, he follows me around like a puppy. I can tell he likes me a lot."

"What's not to like?" Milo said with a shrug.

"You're so sweet," she said, beaming at him as she extinguished her cigarette.

Milo poured drinks and handed her a glass of Limoncello. She took a sip and nodded.

"We were always drinking this at the island," she said.

"You mean when you weren't drinking champagne in the tub with Ruby, right?" he said, grinning at her.

"Yeah," she said, laughing. "We did do that a lot. Until she turned crabby and I had to rename her."

"Rename her?" Milo said, raising an eyebrow at her.

"Ruby Crankybitch," Daisy said, laughing. "You know, a little wordplay with her last name."

"Got it," Milo said, grinning. "That's good. I need to remember that."

"Use it wisely," she said. "Ruby hates being called that."

"So, the two of you are no longer an item?"

"Nah," she said, shaking her head. "We both sort of lost interest in the idea. No biggie."

"Fortunately, Ruby will soon be focused on other things," Milo said. "You know, to take her mind off losing you."

"Yeah, it is her loss, isn't it? Hey, did Billy leave town yet?"

"He and Nurse Sally caught the train out yesterday," Milo said, nodding.

"Maybe I should have gone with him," Daisy said. "California sounds good. And Birdie says the photos of his new place look amazing."

"That would be a giant waste of your talents, Daisy," Milo said, studying her hand movements as she rolled another cigarette. "I have some big plans for you."

"Well, I sure hope they include a lot more than just selling furniture," she said, leaning forward so he could light it. "It's okay for now, and I'm learning a lot about business. But I'm gonna get bored at some point."

Milo topped off both their glasses and took a sip. He sat back in his chair and studied her.

"You got that look, Milo," she said, looking at him over the top of her glass.

"I have no idea what you're talking about, Daisy," he said, flirting back at her.

"Yeah, right," she said, taking a sip. "I do have the day off. And if you want to sit here talking until we finish the bottle, it probably wouldn't take much for you to convince me to spend the night."

"That's an incredibly tempting offer, Daisy," Milo said. "And I imagine at some point in the future, I just might finally succumb to your charms."

"Yeah, don't worry," she said, laughing. "I'll eventually wear you down."

Milo laughed and was about to light a cigarette when the phone rang. He crossed to the desk.

"This is Milo Razner."

"Hi, Milo."

"Oh, hello, Violet. How are you today?"

"I'm good. Thanks for asking. But I just happened to hear something I thought you'd want to know about."

"Okay, go ahead."

"You know that guy, Jimmy Sleaze? The one everybody around town hates."

"Yes, I'm quite familiar with Mr. Sleaze."

"Well, he got a phone call from a guy named Ben Green. And this guy Green was talking about some sort of problem they had. He didn't sound very happy about it. They've agreed to meet up tonight."

"I see," Milo said with a grin. "Did they happen to mention where they're meeting?"

"Halfway to Watertown," Violet said. "You know that picnic area on the side of the road?"

"Yes, I do," Milo said. "What time are they meeting?"

"Ten."

"I see. Thanks for calling, Violet."

"No problem, Milo. Did I do good?"

"Fantastic. And you'll be getting a little extra something in next month's envelope."

Milo hung up and sat back down and noticed Daisy was now stretched out in bed.

"I'm afraid we're going to have to postpone finishing the bottle," he said.

"Is there a problem?" she said, sitting up.

"No, actually things seem to be working out quite well," Milo said. "But there is something I need to take care of this afternoon."

"Okay, Milo," she said, climbing off the bed. "But try to save some Limoncello for me. Now that Billy's gone, I'm not sure we'll be able to find it around here."

"Don't worry about that, Daisy," Milo said, opening the door for her. "I asked Billy to make me a batch before he left."

"Smart, Milo," she said, giving him a kiss on the cheek. "How much?"

"Twenty cases."

"Make sure to put our name on a couple of them," she said, giving him a finger wave as she headed out the door.

Milo poked his head out and admired her stroll down the hall, then exhaled loudly and closed the door. He headed for his desk and picked up the phone. Seconds later, Violet Hollman came on the line.

"Hey, Milo. What do you need?"

"Could you please connect me with Mr. Sleaze?"

"You got it."

Milo lit a cigarette as he waited for The Sleaze to answer.

"What?" Sleaze snapped.

"You might want to work on your phone skills, Jimmy."

"Oh, hey, Milo. What's up?"

"I need to see you right away."

"Right now?"

"Yeah, as soon as you can get over to the Crossley."

"What the hell for?"

"Because I just got a letter from Beulah."

Way Out On A Limb

As expected, Milo didn't have to wait long for The Sleaze to arrive. He brushed past Milo in the doorway then sat down on the couch and helped himself to a drink. He tossed it back, refilled the glass and leaned forward with an expectant look. Milo sat down across from him with a frown etched on his face.

"When did the letter arrive?" Sleaze said.

"I just got it in today's mail," Milo said.

"What did she have to say?"

"Beulah's in trouble, Jimmy."

"What sort of trouble?"

"She's in hiding," Milo said, wringing his hands. "She sounds really scared."

"Hiding? Where's she hiding?"

"Philadelphia," Milo said, pouring himself a small drink.

"What the hell is she doing back in Philly?" Sleaze said.

"I just told you. She's hiding."

"Who's she hiding from?"

"Some guy named Ben Green," Milo said, casually.

Then he waited for The Sleaze's expression to morph. Several seconds later, Milo leaned forward in his chair."

"What's the matter, Jimmy? You look like you've seen a ghost."

"Ben Green?"

"That's what the letter says. What's going on?"

"Where does this guy live?" Sleaze said, his hands shaking as he lit a cigarette.

"Watertown," Milo said. "Somehow Beulah managed to end up there, and then she met this guy, Ben Green."

"Sonofabitch."

"Are you gonna tell me what's going on or not?" Milo snapped.

"You know how I told you I was going to be getting into the booze business?" he said, with a wild-eyed stare.

"Yeah, I remember," Milo said, nodding. "What's that got to do with anything?"

"I sell all my booze to this guy Green," Sleaze said, shaking his head.

"What?"

"Yeah, small world, huh?"

"I guess that's one way to put it," Milo said, biting his lip to keep from grinning. "Are you going to have a chat with this guy about what he's been doing with Beulah?"

"Oh, don't worry. I'll be dealing with Mr. Green in the very near future," Sleaze said. "Why is she hiding from him?"

"Green started roughing her up," Milo said. "And after what she went through with you, she made a promise to herself that it was never gonna happen again."

The Sleaze flinched, then stared at Milo and nodded.

"Yeah, I get that," Sleaze whispered. Then he looked away for several moments as the memory took hold. "Beulah's worried that Green is looking for her?"

"She's positive he's got people all over the place trying to track her down," Milo said. "She said in the letter that she knows way too much about the guy's business. You know, that she's a loose end Green needs to button up. When I read the letter, it didn't make any sense. But now that you're telling me the guy is running booze, it's pretty clear why she's scared."

"How the hell did she end up in Watertown?" Sleaze said.

"I have no idea," Milo said. "She didn't say."

"Hey, hang on a sec," The Sleaze said, scowling at him. "You said before you hadn't talked with Beulah. How did she know how to get in touch with you?"

"She ran into Freddy Four Fingers down in Philly," Milo said. "He and I stay in touch from time to time. Freddy told her I'd settled here."

"So, where's the letter?"

Milo reached into his pocket and tossed it on the coffee table. Milo got up to go to the bathroom while The Sleaze read it. When Milo returned and sat back down, Sleaze was again staring off into the distance.

"She sounds panicked."

"Yeah, she sure does," Milo said. "If you're selling booze to this guy Green, what's he doing with it after he buys it?"

"He's the guy who runs that string of speakeasies around the Watertown area," Sleaze said. "Actually, I've been thinking about making a move on his operation. And this seems like the perfect time. You know, now that he's got my attention."

"Yeah, I imagine he does," Milo said, nodding.

"Nobody gets away with smacking Beulah around," Sleaze said.

"Yeah, because that's your job, right, Jimmy?"

"Ancient history, Milo," he said. "And if I'm able to get her out of the mess she's in, Beulah just might be willing to forgive me once and for all."

"It's certainly worth a shot," Milo said.

"Maybe even two," Sleaze said, removing a revolver from his coat pocket and checking to make sure it was fully loaded. "You know, just in case I don't kill him with the first.

Milo worked his way through the tree line that ran along the back of the property then knocked and opened the back door. Annabelle was standing in front of the stove tending a pot of something that smelled great. He gave her a long kiss and a squeeze on the backside.

"You're not supposed to be here until after dark," she said, playfully swatting his hand with a wooden spoon.

"Slight change of plans," he said. "We're going to need to eat early."

"What's going on, Milo?" she said, wiping her hands with a dish towel as she sat down at the kitchen table.

He spent a few minutes bringing her up to speed about the day's events, and she listened closely.

"So, Green took the bait about The Sleaze being a Fed?"

"Hook, line, and sinker."

"And The Sleaze?"

"It was beautiful," Milo said. "He left my suite like he was on fire."

"How long have you had the letter?" Annabelle said.

"A long time. I had Beulah write it before she left town to take care of her mama," Milo said, grinning. "You know, just in case I needed it."

"One of these days you're going to outthink yourself, Milo," she said, shaking her head.

"Yeah, probably," he said, laughing. "But it won't be today."

"I wish I could see the two of them going at it," Annabelle said. "That would be something."

"Yeah, it's gonna be great," Milo said, his eyes dancing.

"What? You're going to be there?"

"Of course," he said, frowning. "I wouldn't miss it."

"How are you going to pull that one off, Milo?"

"I have a plan."

"Do you now?" she said, laughing. "Why on earth do you need to be there?"

"To make sure the right guy gets shot, what else?"

Birdie slowed the car then pulled off the road and parked in front of the picnic bench. He turned the lights off but kept the engine running. Milo glanced over at his driver.

"Thanks for the ride, Birdie," he said. "Now, just head back toward town a couple of miles and find a good place to stay out of sight. But make sure it's somewhere where you can keep an eye on the road."

"You got it, Milo," Birdie said.

"And as soon as you see The Sleaze driving home, just come back and pick us up. We'll head south from there."

"South?" Birdie said.

"Yeah, I thought we'd spend the night in Watertown," Milo said. "I need to talk to a guy first thing in the morning, so I thought we'd get the jump on it. And then when we get back home tomorrow, you can drop Tom back off at the island."

"Okay, Milo," Birdie said with a shrug.

"And if anybody does happen to ask where we were tonight, just tell them we decided to have a boys night out on the town. Got it?"

"Got it," Birdie said.

"No problem, Milo," Tom said from the backseat. "Actually, a night out does sound good."

"Yeah, we could all use it," Milo said, grinning. "And we're gonna have some things to celebrate. Now, hand me that shotgun, Tom."

"I hope you're not expecting me to shoot anybody, Milo," Tom said, his voice rising.

"Nah, if it comes to that, I'll be the one doing all the shooting."

"Then why did you need me to tag along?" Tom said.

"To do all the talking."

Milo loaded the shotgun then opened the door and climbed out. Tom followed suit and Birdie turned the car around and drove off.

"So, how do you want to do this, Milo?" Tom said, looking around in the darkness as the wind whipped.

"We need to find a spot where we'll be out of sight but still be able to hear everything they're saying."

"Geez, I don't know, Milo. It's still pretty early in the season for there to be much groundcover."

"Yeah, it is sparse at the moment," Milo said, glancing around again. "There we go. The perfect spot."

"Where?" Tom said, again scanning the immediate area.

"Up there," Milo said, pointing at a giant pine tree right behind them.

"You want to climb the tree?" Tom said.

"Why not?" Milo said, handing him the shotgun as he began making his way up the trunk.

Jimmy Sleaze stared out at the road and did his best to control his rage. *Beulah's coming back*, he kept repeating like a mantra to help him maintain his composure. He slowed when he approached the picnic area, then pulled off the road and parked. He climbed out, checked his revolver again, then glanced around the area. Seeing nothing out of the ordinary, he sat down on the bench with his back to the picnic table. Five minutes later, a car heading north slowed then pulled off the road and came to a stop next to his. Sleaze climbed to his feet and walked over to greet Ben Green. They exchanged a perfunctory handshake and stared at each other.

"Mr. Green."

"Mr. Sleaze. Did you come alone?"

"I did. And you?"

"It's just me," Ben Green said. "For issues like the one we're dealing with, I always prefer to handle things on my own."

"I tend to favor the same approach," Sleaze said. "I believe you mentioned something about a problem we have."

"Yes, I did," Green said. "Oh, I almost forgot. I brought along a picnic basket. I missed dinner, and I'm starving. Would you like a sandwich?"

"No, that's okay," Sleaze said, laughing. "But you go right ahead, Mr. Green."

Ben Green grabbed the picnic basket from the car and began rummaging through it.

"Let's see, what have we got?" he said, holding different items up for Sleaze to see. "This looks like ham and cheese. And this one appears to be roast beef. Are you sure you wouldn't like one?"

"No, I'm fine," Sleaze said, shaking his head.

"Oh, here's what I'm looking for," Ben Green said, pointing a pistol at Sleaze's chest and dropping the picnic basket. "On second thought, maybe I'm not so hungry after all. Hands up, Mr. Sleaze."

Jimmy slowly raised his hands in the air and cursed himself under his breath.

"I'm sure there's no need for that, Mr. Green. Why don't you put the gun down, and we'll see if we can talk our way through whatever's bothering you?"

"No, I'm afraid that won't be possible, Mr. Sleaze," Green said with a grin. "Like my papa always used to say right before he started in on me with his belt, you can't talk your way out of a problem you behaved yourself into."

"Okay, fair enough," Sleaze said. "But at least give me the courtesy of telling me what's got your panties in a bunch."

"I'll be happy to do that," Green said, then waved the pistol when Sleaze tried to inch closer. "Take another step, and I'll shoot you in the throat, Mr. Sleaze. You're fine right where you are." Then Green continued, sounding casual. "My current level of…wrath comes from some disturbing news I heard earlier today about a certain working girl."

"A working girl?" Sleaze said, frowning. "If you think I've been stepping out with one of your girls, Mr. Green, you got the wrong guy. I already got a girlfriend I'm getting real close to."

"A working girl by the name of Jessie?"

Sleaze's mouth dropped, and he glared at the man with the pistol.

"How the hell do you know about Jessie?"

"Let's say I have my sources and leave it at that," Green said. "Did you really think you two were going to get away with it?"

"Get away with what?"

"Working undercover for the Feds. What else would I be talking about?"

The Sleaze laughed long and hard.

"Working for the Feds? Are you out of goddamn mind?"

"I happened to read one of her status reports, Mr. Sleaze. In fact, I have it with me. Would you like to take a look at it? I'll even hold the flashlight for you."

"Yeah, sure," Sleaze said, still laughing. "I'll read the report."

Ben Green handed it over then focused the beam of the flashlight on the report. Sleaze began reading, then his eyes grew wide.

"Sonofabitch," Sleaze said, stunned. "Jessie's a Fed? I swear, I had no idea, Mr. Green."

"Nice touch making her a working girl. And setting you up as a guy selling booze was even better. You really had me fooled."

"Honest, Mr. Green," Sleaze said, his voice pleading. "I had no idea what she was up to."

"If that's the case, which I seriously doubt, then you were sharing your bed with a woman who was trying to send me away for a very long time. And that means you are simply too stupid to live."

"Yeah, well, at least I don't go around beating up women," Sleaze snapped.

"What on earth are you talking about?" Green said, frowning.

"I'm talking about Beulah," Sleaze said. "Does it make you feel like a big man smacking her around like that?"

"Beulah? What are you talking about? I'd never hurt her," Green said, confused. "Hey, how the hell do you know about Beulah?"

"She's my ex-wife," Sleaze said. "And nobody lays a hand on my ex-wife without my permission."

"Your ex-wife? No shit. So, you're the scumbag she's always talking about?" Green said, shocked by the news. "Well, then I guess I've really hit the motherlode tonight. I'm so glad you shared that bit of information with me. And I know Beulah will be very happy to hear that she no longer needs to worry about you showing up unannounced. A Fed and a wife beater in one fell swoop. My day has certainly taken a turn for the better."

"I ain't no Fed," Sleaze growled.

"I really don't care, Mr. Sleaze," Ben Green said, pulling the hammer back on the revolver.

Then a loud shotgun blast shattered the cool night air, and Ben Green's expression turned from anticipation into shock as the impact knocked him forward. He stumbled then fell to the ground staring up at Sleaze, then pawed at the dirt in an unsuccessful attempt to reach the gun. He blinked several times with blood oozing from his mouth, then exhaled one final time and his eyes closed for good.

The Sleaze refocused and peered around in the dim light, fully expecting to be the next one shot. But the silence returned, and the only sound Sleaze heard was the sound of the wind whistling through the pines. He continued to look around, stunned by what had just happened.

"Who did that?" Sleaze said after a long pause.

"Toss your gun on the ground."

"What? Where the hell are you?" Sleaze said, again scanning the area. Then he heard the unmistakable sound of another shell being racked, and he slowly reached into his coat pocket and tossed his revolver on the ground. "Okay. You gonna show yourself now?"

"No," the voice said.

"Who the hell are you?"

"I'm the anonymous source of all that booze you've been buying."

"Really?" Sleaze said, still unable to locate the direction the voice was coming from. "No shit?"

"No shit, Mr. Sleaze," the voice said.

"How the hell did you know I was here?"

"I've been following you for days. And it wasn't that hard. You might want to be a bit more careful and start paying attention to who's watching you."

"Why the hell did you follow me?"

"Because I'm about to increase the size of my weekly supply and I needed to make sure you were the right man to sell it to. But given the latest developments, I must say that I'm beginning to have my doubts."

"You don't have to worry about me," Sleaze said.

"I'm a cautious man, Mr. Sleaze."

"Me too."

The voice chortled, and it echoed in the wind. Sleaze scowled at the man's disrespect and clenched his fists.

"I don't like being laughed at," Sleaze said.

"Then stop doing stupid shit."

"I ain't no Fed."

"Yes, I'm very aware of that. But what about your girlfriend?"

"Don't worry. I'm gonna fix that problem," Sleaze growled. "Just wait until I get my hands on her."

"I'm afraid that's not going to be possible. But I do appreciate the offer."

"Okay, I get it. Well, she deserved everything she got," Sleaze said, glancing down at Ben Green who continued to bleed out on the ground. "How much of an increase are we talking about?"

"Just wait for the note," the voice said.

"Am I ever going to get a chance to meet you? Sleaze said, finally giving up on where the voice was coming from. "I don't like this anonymous shit.

"I really don't care what you like," the voice said. "But it's possible that we'll meet at some point. Now, if you would be so kind, get in your car and drive home."

"Just like that?" Sleaze said, his voice rising in pitch.

"Would you like to stand there and chat? Maybe wait for a car to drive by and get a good look at you and the dead guy by the side of the road?"

"No, I don't suppose I do," Sleaze said, reaching down to pick up his gun.

"Leave it right where it is."

Jimmy Sleaze stood tall, raised both hands in the air then quickly walked back to his car and drove off.

Milo emptied the shotgun then handed it to Tom and climbed down out of the tree. Tom tossed the gun to him then made his way down to solid ground. They both took a quick look at Ben

Green then collected both pistols. Milo removed Green's pocket watch and wallet and stuffed them into his coat.

"Good shot, Milo," Tom said, grimacing.

"It was a little hard to miss from there," Milo said. "Great job, Tom."

"Thanks. I had to do a little improvising in a couple of spots."

"No, it was perfect," Milo said. "The Sleaze is gonna be all over the mailman like a rabid dog."

"Yeah, I'm sure he will," Tom said, laughing. "Hey, do you think we'll be able to find a place open when we get to Watertown? I missed dinner."

Milo nodded at the contents of the picnic basket scattered on the ground.

"Have a sandwich."

A Blast From The Past

Milo pulled into Ben Green's warehouse and parked along a far wall to give the delivery trucks enough room to make their way in and out. He hopped out of his car and spotted Bobby chatting with one of the drivers. Milo headed straight for him.

"Good morning, Mr. Razner," Bobby said. "You're up bright and early. Green's not here yet. You want coffee? I just made a fresh pot."

"Coffee sounds good, thanks," Milo said. "Actually, I was wondering if I could have a word with you."

"Sure. What's up?" Bobby said, holding up two fingers to a man who was visible through an office window.

"I'd rather have this conversation in private," Milo said. "We'll use Mr. Green's office."

"Nah, I wouldn't recommend that," Bobby said with a frown. "Green hates it when other people use his office. Especially when he's not around."

"Oh, I don't think he'll mind," Milo said, motioning for the man to follow him.

Milo sat down behind the enormous desk to try it on for size. He glanced around at the well-appointed décor as he waited for Bobby to get settled in on the other side of the desk.

"I thought it was time we had a chat, Bobby," Milo said, glancing at the door when their coffee arrived. "Thanks, George," Milo said, smiling up at the man. Then he took a sip and waited until the door closed with a soft click.

"How long have you worked for Green?"

"Well, I started right around the time that law was passed," he said with a shrug. "What's that been? About a year and a half?"

"That sounds about right," Milo said. "Do you like working for him?"

"Not really," Bobby said, shaking his head. "Green's a total prick. But where else could I come close to making this kind of money?"

"Yeah, I get that," Milo said, taking another sip of coffee. "Can I ask what Green pays you?"

"Sure. I get a quarter on each case of Red Deer. And fifty cents per case on top-shelf product," Bobby said. "It doesn't sound like much, but it definitely adds up."

"Why the difference?" Milo said, leaning forward.

"Green says it's because you do all the work for us," Bobby said. "It's always clean and organized when we pick it up from the cheese store. We never have to do anything with your stuff."

"Isn't the work the same for both?" Milo said, lighting a cigarette and offering the pack to him.

"Yeah, pretty much," Bobby said, leaning forward so Milo could light his. Then he sat back in his chair and exhaled smoke. "As far as all of us who work here are concerned, a case is a case. But since Green moves so much Red Deer, I'm sure he only does it so he can make even more money."

"I see," Milo said, nodding when his initial impressions of the man were confirmed. "Can I ask you a question?"

"Sure, Mr. Razner."

"What sort of career aspirations do you have, Bobby?" Milo said, draping a leg over his knee.

"Career aspirations?" he said, laughing. "Well, let's see. Make some decent money. Be able to keep a good supply of booze around the house. And not end up in jail or get shot in the process. That's about as far as my career aspirations go at the moment."

"Does Green use you to help him collect at the speakeasies?" Milo said.

"No, he doesn't let anybody near the money side of the business. Look, Mr. Razner, are you sure Green isn't going to mind us using his office?" Bobby said, glancing out at the warehouse. "The last time he caught somebody in here, he went off his rocker."

"You can relax, Bobby. Green won't be showing up for work today."

"Oh, I get it," he said, grinning. "That must mean Beulah is finally back in town."

"As a matter of fact, she is," Milo said, nodding. "But that's not the reason he won't be at work today."

"I'm not following you, Mr. Razner," Bobby said, sipping his coffee.

"Ben Green got shot last night," Milo said, trying to blow a smoke ring and failing miserably.

"Green got shot?" Bobby said, surprised by the news. Then he shrugged it off. "Couldn't happen to a nicer guy. Dead?"

"Very much so," Milo said, nodding.

"Who shot him?"

"No one seems to know," Milo said with a shrug. "But my guess is that it was a man by the name of Jimmy Sleaze."

"That guy? He's been selling Green a hundred cases a week," Bobby said.

"Yes, Mr. Green happened to mention that," Milo said, extinguishing his cigarette.

"Why the hell would he do that? Isn't that kinda like biting the hand that feeds you?"

"Yes, any normal person would think that, Bobby. Unfortunately, Mr. Sleaze is far from normal."

"You got that right," Bobby said. "So, what's your take on it?"

"My guess is that Mr. Sleaze is planning to make a move on Green's operation," Milo said. "And the first step toward that end was to remove him. You know, since it's hard to defend your interests when you're stretched out in a pine box."

"Geez, Mr. Razner," Bobby said, scowling. "That's some real bad news. The guy is an even bigger scumbag than Green."

"Yes, that's definitely the word on the street."

"You can't let him do that, Mr. Razner," he said. "A guy like that could ruin everything."

"Unfortunately, Bobby," Milo said, grinning. "I don't have any other choice. At least, for the time being."

"What's going on?" he said, pushing his empty coffee mug to one side. "You're up to something."

"Can I trust you, Bobby?" Milo said, studying him closely.

"If you couldn't, do you think I'd be telling you about what a prick Green was?" he said, reaching for another cigarette.

"Actually, I interpreted your comment to mean that you trusted me," Milo said.

"Trust is a two-way street, Mr. Razner."

"Yes, it certainly is," Milo said, nodding. "How would you like to get a raise, Bobby?"

"I'd never say no to that. I may not have a lot of *career aspirations*, but my mama didn't raise an idiot," he said, then took a long drag on his cigarette and exhaled up at the ceiling. "What do you want me to do? Shoot this guy Sleaze?"

"Absolutely not," Milo said, shaking his head. "I want you to do just the opposite."

"Again, I'm not following you."

"When Mr. Sleaze shows up the next time, make it a point to go out of your way to show him the ins and outs of the business. Make sure he knows that you're his right-hand man. That he can depend on you."

"Why would I want to do that, Mr. Razner?"

"Because it's about the only way to ensure he doesn't kill you," Milo said, holding the man's eyes with his. "But don't worry. As long as The Sleaze needs you around, you'll be safe."

"The Sleaze?" Bobby said, laughing. "That's good."

"Never call him that to his face."

"Got it," Bobby said. "How long is it going to take for this situation to play itself out? I'm not sure I can keep up a front like that, Mr. Razner. The guy gives me the creeps."

"It won't be long," Milo said. "And call me Milo."

"Okay, Milo," Bobby said, nodding. "You've always been a straight shooter with me. Now, about that raise, Milo. Just how much are we talking about?"

"A buck a case. On everything," Milo said.

"Really?" Bobby said, his eyes wide. "And it'll take effect right after the situation with The Sleaze plays itself out?"

"No," Milo said. "It takes effect immediately."

"Are you sure we should do that?" Bobby said.

"Why not?" Milo said. "The Sleaze doesn't know what Green pays you. In fact, I want you to give everybody a raise and tell them to keep their mouths shut if he starts asking questions about it."

"But what if he finds out?" Bobby said.

"How's he going to do that?" Milo said with a big grin. "You gonna tell him?"

Bobby thought about it for a while then nodded.

"Yeah, I suppose that'll work."

"Speaking of money, does Green keep any around here? You know, like a safe or a secret compartment somewhere?"

"Nah," Bobby said, shaking his head. "He never trusted any of the people who worked for him enough to do that. We always assumed he buried it somewhere in his backyard or kept it at his house."

"Okay," Milo said, getting up from his chair.

"Why do you want to know?"

"Because The Sleaze is gonna start looking for it. And we don't want him to have it."

"It just might be enough for him to take off and leave," Bobby said.

"No, that would only make The Sleaze decide to stick around even longer," Milo said. "How much inventory do you have around here at the moment?"

"Probably about a week's worth. Why?"

"Your deliveries are going to be slowing down for the next few days," Milo said.

"Okay. Can you tell me why?"

"Because I want The Sleaze increasingly desperate," Milo said.

"Whatever you say, Milo," Bobby said, laughing. "Green always said you worked in mysterious ways."

"That was probably the nicest thing he ever said about me," Milo said, shaking hands then heading for the door.

"Actually, Milo, one night when we were having a drink in here after work, Green told me how much he respected you," Bobby said. "He thought you were brilliant when it came to business."

"Really?" Milo said, pausing in the doorway. "He never said a word to me."

"Would it have made a difference?"

"Nah, probably not."

Milo climbed the front steps two at a time and knocked on the door. Moments later, it opened, and Beulah Peppin popped her head out partway and beamed at him.

"Get in here," she said, pulling him inside by the arm and kissing him long and hard. "I've missed you, Milo."

"The feeling is mutual, Miss Peppin. You look fantastic. And quite tanned," Milo said, taking a step back to give her the once-over. "How was Florida?"

"Gorgeous," she said, glancing out the window. "Do you know if Ben is in town? He doesn't know I'm back, and it wouldn't be a good idea for him to find us here together."

“I’m afraid you won’t be seeing Green for the foreseeable future,” Milo said, giving her another kiss before sitting down. “Unless you happen to attend his funeral.”

“Really?” she said, sitting down across from him. “He’s dead?”

“Yeah, in fact, he died last night,” Milo said, glancing around the living room.

“What happened?”

“I shot him,” Milo said, taking another look around. “You got anything to drink?”

“I have to say, Milo, you sound pretty casual about it,” she said, shaking her head as she walked to the liquor cabinet.

“It was a long time coming,” Milo said. “But you’ll be pleased to know that, while my anticipation had begun to wane, it was no less of a satisfying moment.” He stared at her. “How do you feel about it?”

“Actually, I’m a little sad,” she said, handing him his drink and sitting down. “Ben was always good to me.”

“I’m sorry to ruin your little love nest,” Milo said, taking a sip.

“Yeah, I bet you are. Don’t worry, I’m sure I’ll get over it,” she said, grinning. “What about Jimmy? Did you manage to shoot him too?”

“Well, I had the chance, but decided to pass for the time being,” Milo said.

"Goddamn it, Milo," she snapped. "Why would you do that?"

"We're very close to putting the finishing touches on this thing," he said. "But I want to do a little more misdirection and build some loyalty at the same time before I deal with The Sleaze once and for all."

"So, I assume that Jimmy didn't take the first train to Philly to look for me?" Beulah said, grinning.

"No, I'm sorry to tell you that you aren't his first priority at the moment," Milo said, laughing.

"I'm shocked. Did he buy the letter?"

"Oh, yeah," Milo said, nodding. "By the way, how is your mama feeling?"

"Mom's great," she said, laughing. "We had a great time in Florida. Actually, she's still down there. I bought her a house."

"What a good daughter you are."

"I'm good in other ways, Milo," she said with a coy smile. "You haven't forgotten, have you?"

"Not at all," he said, taking a sip. "But my memory isn't what it used to be. It could probably use a refresher."

"Then let's go," she said, getting up from her chair.

"In a few minutes, I will definitely be taking you up on that offer," he said, also getting to his feet. "But I need to ask you something first."

"Sure. Go ahead."

"Did Green keep all his money here? Bobby said he didn't trust his workers enough to feel comfortable leaving it over there."

"Yeah, I'm pretty sure he did. But Ben was very secretive and refused to talk about it," Beulah said. "But he did mention a few times that he was going to have to find a new spot to put it since he was running out of room. Why do you ask?"

"You know the answer as well as I do, Beulah. The Sleaze loves to get his hands on easy money. It's one of the few personality traits he and I actually share," Milo said, then beamed at her. "Apart from our taste in women."

"Fortunately, you know how to treat them a lot better, Milo," she said, grinning back.

"Yeah, well, The Sleaze sets a pretty low bar," Milo said, "And as soon as he figures out that Green's money isn't at the produce center, he's gonna come here looking for it," Milo said.

"When?"

"Soon," he said. "Probably a couple of days at most. And that's why we need to get you out of here."

"Where to?"

"I got you a suite at our favorite downtown hotel," Milo said. "But you'll need to order room service and stay out of sight until I come get you."

"Okay," she said, nodding. "So, how's business?"

"It's booming, and about to get a whole lot better," Milo said.

"We're still on track, right, Milo?" she said, giving him an odd look.

"Are you referring to the business or us?"

"Why, both, of course," Beulah said.

"Everything is just fine, Miss Peppin," Milo said, giving her hand a gentle squeeze.

"Prove it to me, Milo," she said, pulling him by the arm. "And I have the perfect spot in mind. Come on, I want to show you something."

Milo followed her down a hallway, then she led him into a massive sunroom dominated by windows and plants.

"It's nice, huh?" she said, glancing around. "Ben must have had it built during the winter while I was away. It stays nice and warm, and that is a very comfortable couch I know you're going to like."

"It's great," Milo said, taking the room in and basking in the warmth of the midday sun that was streaming in. "Green did a good job with it."

Then Milo glanced down at the stone floor, and a big grin slowly emerged.

"Well, what do you know?" Milo said.

"What is it?"

"The stone floor," Milo said, pointing down. "You see how all the tilework is laid out?"

"Yeah, I do," she said, glancing around the floor. "What about it?"

"It's identical to the floor in the cooking room at the island," Milo said, kneeling down.

"That was where you found the money the previous owner had hidden, right?" she said, kneeling next to him.

"Yeah," Milo said as he started to work his way across the tiles tugging at their edges. "This has to be the place. Green must have heard Senator Miller talking about it and decided it was an idea worth repeating."

Halfway across the sunroom, one of the tiles came loose, as did the two adjacent ones. Milo sat down on the floor with his legs splayed and stared at the enormous metal box that was sitting beneath the floor.

"That's a big box," Beulah said.

"You read my mind, Miss Peppin," Milo said, slowly opening the top of the metal container. "Wow."

"Geez, Milo," she said, awestruck. "Look at that."

"It's almost as beautiful as you," Milo whispered, unable to take his eyes off the bundles of cash.

"Aren't you sweet," she said, nuzzling his neck. "How much do you think is here?"

"There's only one way to find out," Milo said, starting to remove the bundles and tossing them on the floor next to them.

"This one is twenty grand," she said, flipping through one of the bundles.

"It looks like most of them are," Milo said, tossing them on the floor two at a time.

It took them almost ten minutes to remove all the cash, and by the time they were done, they were surrounded by a three-sided border fence of dead presidents.

"Go grab a couple of suitcases," Milo said. "And don't forget to pack one for yourself."

"What are you going to do?"

"What do you think I'm going to do? I'm gonna count it," he said, still staring in disbelief at the wrapped bundles.

Beulah headed upstairs, and Milo spent several minutes counting then recounting the stacks of cash. When she returned, she sat back down next to him and opened two empty suitcases. They began neatly stacking the money inside the suitcases.

"How much is it?" she said, glancing over at him.

"A little over three million," Milo whispered. "I can't believe it."

"Well, we both knew Green was doing very well," Beulah said.

"No, it's not that," Milo said. "I can't believe the son of a bitch had the balls to ask me for a campaign contribution."

Converging Interests

Roland Doyle fought the urge to throw up as he headed across the living room to answer the phone that simply refused to quit ringing. He was tempted to rip it out of the wall but took a few deep breaths and gingerly held the receiver against the side of his throbbing head.

"Roland Doyle."

"Roland. It's Vernon."

"Vernon?" Roland said, then made the connection. "Oh, hi, Mr. Adams."

"Did I catch you at a bad time?"

"What?" Roland said, reaching for a bottle of Canadian that was sitting nearby.

"It's just that it took you a long time to answer the phone," Vernon Adams said with a snippy tone Roland didn't appreciate."

"Yeah, sorry about that," Roland said. "I was out back…working in the garden."

"I see. So, what are you planting this year?"

"Oh, you know. Stuff," Roland said, drawing a blank.

"Stuff? Good for you. Always one of my personal favorites," he said, laughing derisively and directing it at Roland. "I was calling to see if you got my letter."

"Yeah, I did," Roland said, thinking hard, then remembering what was in it. "You're talking about-"

"Oh, let's not get into it over the phone," Vernon Adams said. "I believe the letter speaks for itself."

"Okay. You're the boss."

"You should know that I sent an identical letter to our friends in Sackets Harbor and Ogdensburg," Vernon Adams said.

"Our friends? Geez, Mr. Adams, I'm not sure I have any friends in those spots," Roland said, frowning.

"Yeah, you're probably right about that. I'm talking about the people who have the same interests as us when it comes to our work."

Roland thought hard and took a long swallow, then nodded to himself.

"Okay, sure. I get it," he said. "Our friends up and down the River."

"There you go," Vernon Adams said. "Look, I was hoping to join you on your next adventure, but I'm afraid that I won't be able to make it."

"I'm sorry to hear that," Roland said with a big grin.

"As such, I'm going to need you to coordinate the event. You know, reach out to the interested parties and handle all the logistics."

"You sure about that, Mr. Adams?" Roland said, scratching his stubble. "After our last *adventure* went south, they all made it pretty clear they weren't much interested in my ideas or about anything I had to say."

"Well, this time is different, Roland," Vernon Adams said. "Because this is my idea and my orders. You will be merely *conveying* them to the other parties. Are we clear about that?"

"Sure, I get it," Roland said, grabbing a handful of aspirin and washing them down with a big slug of whiskey. "Can I ask you where you got your information?"

"No, you can't," Vernon Adams said. "Just keep me posted and remember to smile for the camera."

"Camera?"

"Yes, I'm sure the local press will want to speak with you at some point," Vernon Adams said. "And make sure they spell my name right."

"Will do, Mr. Adams," Roland said, then had an idea. "If this goes well, does that mean you'll give my transfer request another thought?"

"I'll be more than happy to think about it again, Roland. Happy hunting."

Roland heard the phone click on the other end, and he stared at the wall taking small sips as he wondered if thinking about it meant the guy was actually gonna do something. When no clear answer emerged, Roland polished off the rest of the bottle and went back to bed.

Milo took a sip and nodded. Tom handed him another glass, and Milo sipped again. He beamed and smiled at his cooker.

"They're both delicious, Tom. What are they?"

"You remember when you mentioned that I should play around with some different kinds of booze that women might like a bit better than the Red Deer?"

"I do," Milo said.

"Well, once I figured out how Billy was making his potato vodka, I cooked up a big batch, and I've been playing around with different flavors. The first one has got a touch of licorice and blackberry. The other one is flavored with citrus. You know, lemons and limes and a splash of orange."

"Fantastic," Milo said. "How's the vodka by itself?"

"Just as good as Billy's if I say so myself," Tom said with a touch of pride.

"How big a batch did you make?" Milo said.

"Two thousand gallons," Tom said with a grin. "I thought we might start adding it to our deliveries of Red Deer."

"Perfect," Milo said. "I'll get to work making a new label for it. What do you want to call it?"

"I thought we'd go with White Deer," Tom said. "You know, just for brand consistency."

"I like the way you think," Milo said. "Are you clear about what I need from you?"

"Yeah, I'll be there," Tom said. "But you promise I won't have to do the dirty work, right, Milo?"

"You have my word," Milo said. "Is Ruby up at the house?"

"I think she said she was gonna grab a blanket and lay out in the sun," Tom said. "She says spending the winter over here has turned her paler than a ghost."

"Well, she can be downright spooky at times," Milo said, laughing. "Do you need anything over here?"

"No, Birdie's doing a run to town for us at the moment. We're all set."

"Okay, I'll catch you later."

Milo headed back outside and walked around to the side of the house. He left the stone path and stepped onto the manicured lawn and removed his shoes. He enjoyed the feel of the grass on his bare feet and walked until he spotted Ruby facedown and stretched out on a large blanket.

"Going for the all over tan I see," Milo said.

She propped herself up on her elbows and yawned at him.

"Oh, hi, Milo. I must have dozed off."

"You're gonna get sunburned," he said, sitting down on the blanket.

"It's April, Milo," she said, laughing. "I'll take my chances. What brings you by?"

"I'm going to need you to be ready to go in a few days," he said, then flinched when she rolled over and sat up.

"Finally," she said. "Are you ready to tell me exactly what you have in mind for me?"

"Almost," he said, then reached into his pocket and tossed one of the bundles of cash he'd found at Green's house on the blanket. "You're gonna like it, Ruby. You're gonna like it a lot."

"This is twenty thousand dollars, Milo," she said after flipping through the stack.

"I know. I already counted it," he said, grinning.

"Why are you giving it to me?" she said, giving him a puzzled look.

"Three reasons," he said as a simple statement of fact.

"I see," she said, holding up a hand to block the glare. "I suppose one of them is to convince me to take a meeting with you?"

"I would never do that to you, Ruby," Milo said, offended. "And you know it."

"Yeah, I know that. I'm sorry, Milo," she said, flipping through the bundle again before making eye contact. "So, what are your reasons?"

"The first is to reward you for your patience," he said. "I know it was asking a lot of you to spend all winter over here."

"Oh, I managed to get by," she said, turning coy.

"Yes, I noticed," he said, laughing. "Second, I wanted to give you an idea of what's in store if you simply stick to the plan and don't lose your head. You need to remember that whenever there is this much money at stake, vigilant focus and attention to detail are essential."

"Have I lost my focus yet, Milo?" she said, stretching back out on her stomach.

"No, but I'm not sure I can say the same thing at the moment," Milo said, shaking his head at the sight of her.

"Aren't you sweet," she said, looking up at him. "What's the third reason?"

"I need you to head down to New York for a few days and get yourself the best wardrobe you can find."

"You want me to spend twenty thousand dollars on clothes?" she said, frowning.

"Well, maybe not all of it," Milo said, shrugging. "You'll probably need some for shoes and makeup."

Melvin opened the envelope and read it. He blinked several times, then reread it before sliding it across the desk. The Sleaze scanned the note then slammed his hand down on the desk in triumph.

"A thousand cases," Sleaze said, hopping out of his chair to do a little dance. "Yes, I knew he wasn't joking."

"Who wasn't joking?" Melvin said, giving him a hard stare.

"Oh, nothing," Sleaze said, shaking his head. "Just a figure of speech. A thousand cases. That's incredible."

"A couple of issues do come to mind, Jimmy," Melvin said.

"Like what?"

"Well, we just laid out a bunch for a hundred cases," Melvin said, then caught the glare Sleaze was giving him. "I mean, you just laid it out, Jimmy. And a thousand cases is gonna cost us forty grand. Can you cover that?"

"It'll be tight, but think I can swing it," Sleaze said. "But don't worry, Melvin. I have a good idea about where I can get my hands on a whole bunch of cash."

"Would you mind telling me how you're going to do that?" Melvin said, already knowing the answer.

"Actually, I would, Melvin," Sleaze said with a grin.

"Of course. My second question is how the hell are you going to unload that much product?"

"Don't worry, I've already got that covered," The Sleaze said, staring him down. "Can you imagine how much we can make unloading a thousand cases a week? At retail prices, no less."

"Retail prices?" Melvin said. "Why do I have the feeling there's something you're not telling me, Jimmy?"

"Relax, Melvin," Sleaze said. "It'll be clear as day very soon. How long have we got before the delivery date?"

"A week from today."

"Perfect," he said, getting to his feet. "I'll see you soon, Melvin."

"Where are you going?"

"Road trip."

Melvin watched him depart without even bothering to close the door behind him then shook his head slowly back and forth.

"Sonofabitch. I am so screwed."

Jimmy Sleaze climbed the front steps and knocked on the front door. As expected, no one answered, and he glanced around to make sure no one was watching him as he jimmied the lock and let himself in.

The guy at the produce center had been pretty helpful, even sounding a bit excited about having someone other than Green running the place, and Sleaze had decided this guy Bobby might be worth keeping around for a while. At least, until he had time to get up to speed about the ins and out of how things worked. Maybe, Jimmy said to himself with a grin, he'd even learn a few useful things about vegetables in the process.

He slowly made his way through the house then was stunned when he entered the sunroom and saw the gaping hole in the stone floor. Three tiles had been removed and slid to one side, and a large metal box with the lid open was in plain sight. Fearing the worst, Sleaze slowly approached and knelt down. The inside of the box was empty except for a single piece of paper folded in half. He reached inside to grab it then sat down on the cool tiles and opened it. What he read on the paper stunned him at first, then his shock turned into rage, and he roared like a wounded bear until his throat and lungs burned. He took several deep breaths to calm himself down then read the note again that was simply titled; IOU.

Sorry that anonymous isn't your thing.
You can only hope what the thousand might bring.
And if Mr. Sleaze doesn't come completely undone,
He just might collect his three million, one.

Episode 14

Taking Out The Trash

People like to say that one man's trash is another man's treasure. All I know is that the people who say that never met Jimmy Sleaze.

Milo Razner

Senatorial Surprises

Milo poured two glasses of bourbon and passed one to the Senator who was on the phone begging for money from a potential donor. The Senator paused long enough to nod his thanks to Milo and took a sip. A few minutes later, he ended the call and sat down across from Milo and lit a cigar.

"How much did they agree to give you?" Milo said, puffing his own cigar.

"Ten thousand," Senator Miller said with a shrug.

"You got more money than you know what to do with," Milo said. "Why do you keep taking it?"

"Dumb question, Milo," he said, laughing.

"Yeah, I suppose it is."

"Besides, if I didn't take every nickel people wanted to give me, that would just make folks suspicious."

"And that's the last thing we want, Senator," Milo said, raising his glass in salute. "This is good bourbon."

"Yes, it is. I get it from one of the senators from Kentucky," he said. "But don't worry, Milo. He's not in the business and doesn't know a thing about our operation." The Senator draped a leg over his knee and puffed his Cuban. "Thanks again for taking care of that little problem we had with our friend."

"I was happy to do it," Milo said.

"It was a very interesting article in the paper," Senator Miller said, raising an eyebrow. "A robbery right in the middle of a roadside picnic Ben was having all by himself."

"Well, Green always was a bit of a loner," Milo deadpanned. "But I have to say, I do like the new addition he put on his house before his tragic demise."

"Really?" Senator Miller said with a big grin. "Are you talking about a new sunroom he was thinking about adding?"

"I am. And I love what he did with the stonework," Milo said, blowing smoke up at the ceiling. "I want to thank you for giving him that design tip."

"I thought it might come in handy at some point. How much did you find?"

"All of it," Milo said.

"Don't be coy, Milo," the Senator said. "How much?"

"A little over three million," Milo said, shrugging.

The Senator thought for several seconds then frowned.

"That bastard. I think he was shorting me."

"Don't worry, Senator. Your increase to forty percent will more than cover it," Milo said.

"Yes, I'm sure it will. So, where do we stand?"

"I just need to deal with an interloper, and then it'll be full speed ahead," Milo said, sipping his drink.

"An interloper? That sounds like something that could be a problem," the Senator said, studying him closely.

"Don't worry, it's not," Milo said. "It's going to be fine, Senator. I just need a few more days to take the trash out. And I'm also making sure we have more than enough breathing room."

"Milo, given the way you talk at times, I sometimes wonder just what makes you tick," he said, laughing.

"Money, women, and booze," Milo said with a shrug. "I'm really not that hard to figure out, Senator."

"Well, then. To money, women, and booze," the Senator said, raising his glass. "And political power."

"Whatever floats your boat, Senator," Milo said, taking a long swallow.

"Indeed. Oh, I've been meaning to ask you about something," he said, leaning forward. "I ran your suggestion past some of my advisers, and they all like the idea. In fact, most of them have become quite insistent that I find myself a First Lady. They think it could send the wrong message to the voters if I don't come across as a dedicated family man once I take office."

Milo kept the smile to himself and decided to stay casual.

"That's never been a problem for you, Senator," Milo said. "Why are they making such a big deal about it now?"

"I was quite younger when I was elected to the Senate," he said, shrugging. "And people never seemed to mind that I had a reputation as a man about town. And there are dozens of politicians in Washington doing all sorts of things much worse than just being a bachelor. My lifestyle simply doesn't generate many questions down there. But when I get to Albany, I'm going to be the focal point, and my advisers make a good point. And neither one of us wants any more attention than necessary, right? Especially from a bunch of nosy reporters."

"Yes, that is a good point," Milo said, nodding. "So, you're saying you're ready to settle down?"

"God, no," Senator Miller said with a scowl. "That's the last thing I want to do. But I am looking for someone who might be willing to play the role of the devoted First Lady. As well as being capable of having some fun while she's doing it."

"So, you want to find a woman with a bit of style who's willing to sleep with you but not mind it when you, let's say, find your affections drifting elsewhere?"

"I knew you'd understand, Milo," Senator Miller said, exhaling cigar smoke.

"It could be dangerous bringing someone in that close to our operation," Milo said, letting the Senator take the lead before offering his thoughts on the matter he'd spent weeks pondering.

"Yes, my sentiments exactly."

"No one comes to mind right away," Milo said.

"As a matter of fact, I have someone very specific in mind," he said, staring at him.

"You do?" Milo said, surprised.

"Yes," the Senator said with a grin.

Milo sat quietly, then the penny dropped.

"Beulah. You're talking about Beulah, aren't you?"

"She'd be perfect, Milo," the Senator said, leaning forward. "She's smart and beautiful, she can work a room better than most women I've ever met, and she's already part of the operation. And now that our friend, Mr. Green, is no longer keeping company with her, I was wondering if you thought she might be interested in the job. Ben always said she was the best he ever had."

"She'd have to move to Albany?" Milo said, frowning and rubbing his chin.

"Eventually, yes," the Senator said. "Probably sometime soon after I take office."

"I don't know, Senator," Milo said. "Beulah plays a big role in the operation, and it would take me some time to figure out a replacement."

"Of course, we don't want to do anything stupid that would damage the business," Senator Miller said. "But a smart guy like you will be able to figure it out."

"Well, I suppose it couldn't hurt to ask her," Milo said. "Maybe you could announce your intentions and then go for a long engagement period."

"How long?"

"How the hell do I know? You just dropped it on me. I'm spitballing at this point," Milo said. "Maybe you could stretch it out for a year. But it's her call, Senator."

"Yes, I know that," he said, puffing on his cigar. "But maybe you could *encourage* her. After all, you two are good friends, right?"

"Yeah, Beulah and I are very close," Milo said.

"But you two aren't…you know?"

"Sleeping together?" Milo said, surprised. "No, we just work together. No worries there, Senator."

"That's good to hear," he said. "Because I'd hate to do anything to upset your apple cart, Milo."

"Yes," Milo said, beaming at him. "I'm sure you would, Senator." Milo chuckled and shook his head. "Beulah as First Lady. That would be something to see."

Beulah Peppin rolled off Milo onto her back then sat up in bed staring in disbelief at him. She shook her head as she lit a cigarette and blew a cloud of smoke in his direction.

"Are you out of your frigging mind, Milo?"

"It's not the craziest thing I've ever heard," he said, sitting up and lighting a cigarette of his own.

"How long have you two been talking about it?" she snapped.

"I haven't been talking about it," Milo said, now playing defense. "It was his idea. Honest, Beulah, the thought never crossed my mind."

"And you thought that now was the perfect time to tell me?" she said, glaring at him.

"Yeah, I wanted to wait until we had…a chance to catch up," Milo said, giving her a grin.

"You son of a bitch," Beulah said, punching him on the arm. "Milo, if I ever find out this was your idea, I swear you'll be singing soprano for the rest of your life."

"I'd expect nothing less, Miss Peppin," he said, draping an arm over her shoulder. "On my mama's grave, I swear he came up with it all by himself."

"Me, as First Lady," she said, shaking her head. "Can you imagine that?"

"Actually, I can," Milo said, nodding.

"Well, forget it, Milo. It ain't gonna happen."

"Of course, it's not going to happen," Milo said. "But there's no reason why the Senator needs to know that."

"Take the marbles out of your mouth, Milo."

"Think it through, Beulah," Milo said, rolling onto his side to look at her. "What could possibly be better for us than having you in close contact with the Governor and his circle of friends? Even on an infrequent basis."

"I can think of a whole lot of things," she said. "Senator Miller's a nice enough guy. But sleeping with a politician? It kinda makes my flesh crawl. Geez, I don't know, Milo. That's asking a lot."

"It's not like I'm expecting you to actually marry the guy, Beulah," Milo said. "All I'm asking you to do is to spend some time down in the Capital with him. Encourage him to get out a bit and mingle with the voters. You know, get to know your way around town. Learn how certain things work. Make some new friends."

Beulah stared off into the distance, then she slowly turned her head and beamed at him. Milo was already grinning back at her.

"Milo Razner?"

"Yes, Miss Peppin?"

"You, sir, are a goddamn genius."

"Thanks. It's nice when people notice."

"So, if I agree to start spending time down there with our new governor, I'll still be getting my full cut, right?"

"Of course," Milo said, then shrugged. "But a good-sized chunk of it is definitely gonna be coming out of his end."

Melvin Drops By

Milo put his knife and fork down then headed for the door. He opened it and frowned when he saw Melvin standing there with a forlorn look on his face.

"Sorry to drop by unannounced, Milo," Melvin said, squeezing the life out of his hat. "But I think I might have a problem."

"Well, come on in, Melvin," Milo said, standing back to give him room. "You hungry?"

"No, I already ate," the mayor said, sitting down on the couch and helping himself to one of Milo's cigarettes. "But I will be smoking several of your cigarettes."

"Knock yourself out," Milo said as he sat back down to finish his steak. "So, what sort of problem are you dealing with, Melvin?"

"The Sleaze," Melvin said, exhaling a cloud of smoke.

"Pour yourself a whiskey and tell me all about it, Melvin," Milo said, sipping wine.

"Thanks. I'll do that," he said, knocking the first one back and pouring another. "Don't let me have more than ten of these."

"Did The Sleaze threaten you?"

"Not yet," Melvin said. "What was that you said about him?"

"You mean the part about you being safe as long as he needed your help?" Milo said, slowly chewing his food.

"Yeah, that part."

"And you think you've reached the point where he no longer values your services?"

"I think we're getting close," Melvin said, lighting another cigarette. "Can I trust you, Milo? I mean, really trust you?"

"Geez, Melvin. I'm a little hurt you even need to ask," Milo said, taking a final bite before topping off his wine glass and sitting down across from him. He set his glass down on the coffee table then lit a cigarette. "Talk to me, Melvin."

"The booze business I've been doing with The Sleaze is really starting to take off."

"I see," Milo said, nodding. "Well, that's good news, right?"

"Normally, it would be," Melvin said, topping off his glass. "But I think The Sleaze has been cutting deals behind my back. And I also think he's getting close to cutting the cord if you catch my drift."

"I do," Milo said. "And I can't say that I'm surprised to hear that The Sleaze is doing it. So, where are you at?"

"Our anonymous supplier has just increased our weekly supply."

"Anonymous?"

"Yeah, whoever the guy is has been doing this cloak and dagger shit all winter. But I think that The Sleaze has managed to figure out who he is and is now in direct contact with him."

"Which means so long Melvin, right?" Milo said, casually.

"Exactly."

"How much product are you talking about?"

"A thousand cases a week," Melvin said, staring across the table.

"Sonofabitch," Milo said, stunned. "That sounds like an awful lot of booze. How the hell are going to get a thousand cases of illegal hooch across the River?"

"It's coming in by barge."

"By barge?" Milo said, frowning. "Yeah, I suppose that would work. As long as you don't get caught. I can't imagine you'd want to spend that much time in prison with The Sleaze as your roommate."

"You got that right. And that's my problem. How good a shot is The Sleaze?"

"Not as good as he is with his hands," Milo said. "But he's pretty good. It doesn't matter, Melvin. There is no way you're going out in the middle of the River with The Sleaze."

"But I have to go, Milo," Melvin said. "If I don't make the trip, The Sleaze is going to cut me out of my share. But if I do go, what do you think the odds are that he'll try to *remove me from the partnership*?"

"Who else is going to be there to meet the barge?" Milo said, finishing the last of his wine.

"Just me and The Sleaze," Melvin said. "Oscar's going to be busy that night doing something with Roland Doyle."

"Roland Doyle?" Milo said, frowning.

"Yeah, The Sleaze and I came up with a plan to have Oscar keep an eye on Doyle the nights we're making our buys."

"Good plan, Melvin. Null and Void on the prowl," Milo said, laughing and shaking his head. "What the hell have you gotten yourself into?"

"Yeah, it's a mess," Melvin said. "And it's kinda your fault, Milo."

"Is it now?"

"Yeah, you were the one who gave my name to The Sleaze in the first place."

"To keep you alive, Melvin," Milo said, fixing a stare on him.

"Yeah, but still," he said, downing his drink. "So, what do you think I should do?"

"What you shouldn't do is get on that boat. Just let The Sleaze do his thing and stay out of his way. And then you can call a town meeting and have everyone say a collective prayer that the guy packs his bags and leaves."

"Do you have any idea how much money that would cost me, Milo?"

"Unless we're talking about the price of milk, I can't help you with that, Melvin," Milo said, crushing his cigarette out.

"Well, let me tell you. It's a lot, Milo."

"Is it worth getting shot over?"

"No. Hence my problem. Unless I shoot him first."

"Are you any good with a gun?"

"Nope," Melvin said, pouring another drink. "But maybe I can shoot him in the back."

"You want to borrow my shotgun?"

"What?"

"Nothing. Just kidding, Melvin," Milo said, smiling at him. "Just call in sick. Tell The Sleaze you've got the flu. Or better yet, a stomach virus that's keeping you on the toilet nonstop."

"Yeah, that might work," Melvin said.

"And then I suggest, if you plan on staying in the booze business, you might start looking for a new partner."

"I already thought about that," Melvin said. "But the guy I had in mind just told me he's getting out of the business altogether."

"Really?" Milo said, raising an eyebrow.

"Yeah, he says it's time to do something else before the place is crawling with Feds," Melvin said, getting to his feet.

"What's he going to be doing?"

"Selling ice."

Wheels and Deals

Roland Doyle stared at the shot of whiskey Oscar had poured for him and swallowed hard. Oscar tossed his drink back, poured another, then frowned across the desk.

"What's the matter with you?" Oscar said, nodding at Doyle's untouched shot. "If you aren't here to drink, why the hell did you stop by?"

"I'm trying to cut back on my drinking before noon," Doyle said, giving the shot glass a loving stare.

"It's already noon," Oscar said, tossing back his second. "Somewhere."

"I suppose you're right," Roland said, reaching for his drink and tossing it back. "It's good. Is this from the cases we confiscated?"

"Yeah. How's your case holding up?"

"I'm running low," Roland said.

"Me too," Oscar said. "It's about time for us to do some more patrolling."

"Oh, yeah," Roland said, leaning forward to grab the new shot Oscar had poured. "I knew there was a reason I stopped by. I'm going to need your help on the 13th."

“My help?” Oscar said, belching loudly. “Doing what?”

“I’m participating in a raid. And it’s out on the water, so I’ll need you to drive the boat.”

“What sort of raid are we talking about?”

“A thousand cases are coming in by barge about three miles upriver,” Roland said, downing his drink.

“A thousand cases?” Oscar said, scowling at the Fed. “Yeah, good one, Doyle. You trying to set me up again?”

“No, this is no setup, Oscar,” Roland said. “We’ll be joining a group of Prohibition agents stationed out of Ogdensburg and the Coast Guard from Sackets Harbor. This is a big one.”

“Pretty ballsy to try and move a thousand cases in one shot,” Oscar said, pouring two more shots. “Especially on a barge. There’s no way they’ll be outrunning anybody chasing them, that’s for sure.”

“I’m sure the bootleggers are relying on the element of surprise,” Doyle said.

They both looked at the door when they heard it open and were surprised to see Milo Razner enter.

“Mr. Razner,” Roland growled.

“Hello, Roland,” Milo said, smiling as he headed to the desk and sat down. “Hi, Oscar.”

“Hey, Milo,” Oscar said, nodding. “You want a drink?”

“It’s a bit early, but what the hell,” Milo said, removing his fedora. “When in Rome, right?”

Oscar poured a shot, and Milo tossed it back. He waved off Oscar's offer of another and pointed at the bottle.

"That's good stuff," Milo said, examining the label. "Any idea where I can get my hands on some of that?"

"Canada," Roland said, staring at Milo.

"Gee, thanks, Roland," Milo said, laughing. "I need to remember that."

"So, what brings you by, Milo?" Oscar said, putting his feet up on the desk.

"I just wanted to touch base and see if you've had any luck removing that nasty piece of garbage we discussed."

"You mean Jimmy Sleaze?" Oscar said.

"Do you know of any other garbage we need to get rid of around here?" Milo said.

"Nothing that nasty, no," Oscar said. "I'm sorry, Milo. But I can't come up with a reason to run the guy out of town."

"There must be something," Milo said.

"I take it you and Sleaze had some sort of falling out," Roland said, helping himself to another drink.

"You're a quick study, Roland," Milo said. "Yeah, a falling out. Let's call it that. That son of a bitch almost ruined my life when we were all living down in Philly. I'd like to make sure it doesn't happen again."

"I understand, Milo," Oscar said, going for sympathetic. "I can't stand the guy either. And I wish I could help you out, but my hands are kinda tied at the moment."

“He’s been here five months,” Milo said. “And The Sleaze has never worked a day in his life. What’s he doing for money?”

“Probably living off his ill-gotten gains,” Roland said. “Or he’s running booze.”

“You think he might be bootlegging?” Milo said, looking at the Fed.

“Well, it is the growth industry around here. But if he is, he’s staying way below the radar,” Roland said. “If he wasn’t, I would have nabbed him by now.”

Oscar glanced over at Milo and rolled his eyes.

“Yes, I’m sure you would have, Roland,” Milo said, glancing at the Fed. “But The Sleaze has always been good at covering his tracks.”

“Not as good as he thinks,” Roland said.

“Well, I hope you’re right,” Milo said, shaking his head. “Now that the weather has turned, I’m sure The Sleaze is looking to expand whatever operation he’s gotten into. And if that creature manages to get a toehold around here, we’ll never get rid of him.”

“Don’t worry, Milo,” Oscar said, the comment about expansion nagging at him. “I’ll stay on him. And if you happen to get any tips about what The Sleaze is up to, just let me know.”

“Of course,” Milo said, getting to his feet.

“And thanks again for the new police car,” Oscar said. “It’s a beauty.”

"You're very welcome, Oscar. The only thing you could catch in that old one was a cold. Gentlemen, enjoy the rest of your day. And thanks for the booze."

They both watched Milo Razner head out the door then looked at each other.

"Man, that guy is making a fortune," Oscar said, pouring two more shots. "I should have gone into the milk business."

"It is nice to see that it's possible for a criminal to go straight," Roland said, knocking back his shot. "He bought you a new car?"

"Yeah," Oscar said, downing his drink. "Actually, it belongs to the town, but I'm the only one who's allowed to drive it."

Beulah leaned forward to make it easier for Senator Miller to light her cigarette, then she sat back in her chair maintaining solid eye contact the entire time. She exhaled smoke and cocked her head when she saw the grin on his face.

"You look like the cat that swallowed the canary, Senator."

"I'm just delighted you decided to meet with me," he said, draping a leg over his knee.

"Well, it is a remarkable offer," Beulah said. "But are you sure I can handle the job?"

"Oh, I'm positive," the Senator said with a goofy grin.

"I'm not talking about that part of the job, Senator," she said, turning coy. "I'm pretty sure I can handle the horizontal component."

"Music to my ears, Beulah," he said, raising his glass to her. "And don't worry about the rest of it. You'll have a full staff who will coordinate all your appearances. All you'll need to do is show up looking beautiful and mingle. And you'll be getting to know all the movers and shakers. Have you been to Albany before?"

"Actually, this is my first visit," she said, glancing around the living room. "Is this your house? It's gorgeous."

"No, I'm just renting it until the election," Senator Miller said. "When I take office, I'll be moving into the governor's mansion. Hopefully, with you."

"I do have some questions."

"I'm sure you do," the Senator said. "As well as some demands, right?"

"Well, demand is such a strong word," Beulah said, grinning. She took a sip of wine then gently set the glass down. "Let's call them requests."

"Of course," he said, putting his feet up on the coffee table. "I'd love to hear them."

"First off, I'll be joining you over the summer at as many campaign stops as I can manage. Preferably one's up north around Syracuse and Watertown. And maybe we can work in Rochester and Buffalo."

"That won't be a problem," he said. "I'm already starting to cut back on my campaign. I was up in the last poll by thirty percent. But I will need you at some events just so people can start noticing your presence."

"That's what I figured," Beulah said. "We need to be known as a couple before we can announce our engagement, right?"

"Exactly."

"I thought we could announce it just before the election," Beulah said. "You should get a nice bump in the polls from that bit of news. I think the voters will like me."

"I have no doubt about that," he said, topping off her wine.

"And I think we should have the wedding the following June," she said, taking a sip. "I've always wanted to be a June bride."

"Eight months?" the Senator said, giving it some thought. "Yeah, that should work. But you'll be visiting often, right?"

"Of course," Beulah said. "I need to get a head start on understanding how things work around here."

"Wonderful," he said, beaming at her. "It will take you some time to come up to speed. Government affairs can be confusing. And quite complicated."

"Yes, I imagine they are. And I'll need to find a place to stay," she said. "It wouldn't look right if I started sleeping over at the governor's mansion before we were married."

"No, it wouldn't," he said, shaking his head. "Hey, I've got an idea. Why don't I just extend the lease on this place?"

"Sure," she said, glancing around. "It's a great house."

"Five bedrooms," he said with a grin.

"Don't worry, Senator. I'm sure we'll become very familiar with all of them."

"I knew you were the perfect woman for the job," he said, again raising his glass to her.

"Okay, let's talk finance," Beulah said, lighting a cigarette.

"Finance?" Senator Miller said, raising an eyebrow.

"Yeah, money," she said, exhaling smoke. "Spending all this time with you is going to put a serious crimp in my earnings. And I've worked way too hard to let all my hard-earned money vanish into thin air."

"Oh, I see. Yes, of course," Senator Miller said with a small frown. "How much were you thinking about?"

"Twenty thousand a month," Beulah said, casually. "Starting next month."

"Twenty thousand? Jesus, Beulah. Just how much are you making working for Milo?"

"More than that," she said, taking a drag on her cigarette.

"Really?"

"What can I say, Senator? Business is good," she said, turning coy. "But you already know that, don't you?"

"Yeah, I already know that," he said, nodding. "Okay, we got a deal, Beulah. But for that kind of money, I'm going to be expecting a whole of affection."

"I'd be surprised if you weren't, Senator."

Oscar Turns Edgy

Oscar Hyde knocked and walked into the office without waiting to be invited in and saw Melvin and The Sleaze huddled at the desk studying a map. They both jumped when he interrupted them, and Melvin tried to casually fold the map up then slip it into a desk drawer. Oscar glanced back and forth at them, then headed for the liquor cabinet and helped himself.

"That was rude, Oscar," Melvin snapped as he sat down behind the desk and checked to make sure the drawer was shut tight. "Next time, how about you wait to be invited in?"

"Yeah, I'll do that, Mayor Melvin," Oscar said, glaring at them. "What was that you two were looking at?"

"That?" Melvin said. "It was nothing, Oscar."

"And it's none of your goddamn business," Sleaze growled.

"It looked like a map," Oscar said, topping off his glass.

"A map?" Melvin said, glancing at Sleaze. "Actually, it was a map, Oscar. Jimmy's thinking about buying an island, and I was just showing him the location of a couple that might be coming onto the market soon."

"Which ones?" Oscar said.

"Oh, I doubt if you would know the names of them," Melvin said. "Are you familiar with…Vulture Island?"

"No, but it sounds perfect for you, Sleaze," Oscar said, laughing. Then he cut it short when he caught the look the guy was giving him. "Where is the island?"

"Oh, it's not far from town," Melvin said, doing his best to stay casual. "Actually, I'm glad you stopped by. We're going to need you to babysit Doyle."

"Yeah, I'm all set," Oscar said. "We'll be doing our usual Wednesday night patrol while you guys are making the pickup."

"Uh, actually, Oscar, we need you to keep an eye on Doyle Thursday night," Melvin said.

"On the 14th? I wish the guy would make up his mind. Why did he change the delivery day again?"

"Our supplier must be changing things up just so nobody gets too predictable," Sleaze said.

"Smart," Oscar said, nodding. "Nobody wants to be predictable."

"No, we certainly don't want that," Melvin said.

"Hey, I meant to ask you guys," Oscar said, glancing back and forth at them. "Has the supplier talked about increasing the number of cases now that the weather has turned?"

"No, not yet," Melvin said, twitching in his chair. "Nothing's changed. It's still…fifty cases."

"That's odd," Oscar said, glancing at Sleaze. "I would have thought he'd be interested in expanding."

"If he is," Sleaze said, shaking his head. "He ain't shared the news with us."

"Okay," Oscar said. "I'll make sure to keep Doyle occupied. I've got a new spot a few miles upriver I thought I'd take him to."

"Upriver?" Melvin said, frowning as he started talking fast. "Tell you what, Oscar. Why don't you take him over by Rockport? You know, show him that route that runs behind Boldt Castle. You could even stop by the place and let Doyle take a look around. I've heard the castle is used by some bootleggers. Maybe you'll get lucky and actually catch somebody."

"That's not a bad idea, Melvin. I just might do that."

Milo set his menu aside and watched Birdie roll a cigarette. He studied his movements closely and shook his head in amazement and was more than a little pissed off that he still hadn't been able to master the one-hand roll.

"Roll me one of those, will you?"

Birdie handed him the one he'd just finished then rolled another. Milo lit both, and they sat back in the booth relaxed and smoking. Milo glanced around the empty diner then leaned forward.

"I need you to meet me at Frank's place in the morning around eight," Milo said. "That barge is slow, and it's gonna take some time to get it loaded. We want to make sure we're in place by sunset."

"You think Frank will let me drive?" Birdie said, exhaling smoke.

"He'd be a fool not to, right?" Milo said, laughing.

"It's not like you can really *drive* that thing," he said with a cackle. "You basically point it where you want to go then sit back and enjoy the view. I love that stretch of River."

"The view? It's gonna be dark out there, Birdie."

"Yeah, but I'll know where I am."

"Fair point," Milo said, shrugging. Then he glanced at the door. "Here we go. I think we should ask him to join us for lunch."

Birdie glanced over his shoulder and grinned.

"Sure, why not?"

"Hey, Oscar," Milo said. "You all by yourself?"

"Hey, Milo. Birdie. Yeah, I am."

"Have a seat and join us," Milo said. "I'll even buy you lunch."

"That's mighty kind of you, Milo," Oscar said, sliding into the booth next to Birdie. "What looks good today?"

"The special," Birdie said.

"That's fine," Oscar said, his voice barely above a whisper.

"Geez, Oscar," Milo said. "You look troubled. What's the matter?"

Oscar stared at Milo for a long time, then decided to get it off his chest.

"Have you ever been screwed by someone you thought was your friend?"

"I'm going to need you to be a bit more specific, Oscar," Milo said, laughing.

Birdie cackled and exhaled a cloud of cigarette smoke.

"No, I ain't talking about that," Oscar said. "You know, screwed over on a business deal."

"Yes, as a matter of fact, I have," Milo said. "And I hate when that happens. Who's trying to screw you?"

"I really can't talk about it," he said, reaching for his pack of smokes.

"I see," Milo said, nodding. "Well, Oscar, the only piece of advice I can give you is, if it does happen, you need to do everything in your power to make sure it doesn't happen again."

"That's really good advice, Milo," Oscar said, slowly nodding as he mulled it over.

"Words to live by," Birdie said, glancing over at the police chief. "That's what they are."

A Night Delivery

Milo paid close attention as the tarp was put in place then secured tight over the load. He looked toward the stern where Frank Slack and Birdie were chatting with a couple of the guys that had loaded the barge. He watched Birdie take one final drag on his cigarette, and Milo cleared his throat loudly. Birdie glanced at Milo then crushed out the flame with two fingers and slid the butt into his shirt pocket.

"Sorry, Milo," Birdie said. "I almost forgot."

"How many times do I have to tell you not to throw shit in the River?"

"Geez, I said I was sorry, Milo," Birdie said, his feelings hurt as he limped his way down the dock and onto the barge.

Frank laughed and shook his head as he followed Milo onto the barge. Birdie, still pouting, sat down in the captain's chair and started the engine. Milo approached and placed a hand on his friend's shoulder.

"Sorry I snapped at you, Birdie."

"Forget it, Milo," Birdie said. "My mistake."

"Okay, now that we've got that resolved," Milo said, clapping his hands once. "Let's make a delivery."

Roland Doyle tentatively got to his feet and scanned the water with a pair of binoculars.

"I can't see shit through these things," he said, glancing over at Oscar who was driving Roland's boat.

"Well, it is dark," Oscar said, focused on the water in front of him.

"Hang on," Roland said, then pointed. "Over there. See the lights?"

"I do," Oscar said, accelerating toward the two white lights he saw a few hundred yards away on their port side.

A couple of minutes later, Oscar eased the throttle back, and they coasted until they came to a stop between the two boats. Soon, all three boats were nestled next to each other, and they killed the lights.

"Hello, Mr. Doyle. It's been a long time."

Roland glanced over at the boat on his right and recognized the man's face from their first encounter when they had unsuccessfully tried to track down a thousand cases of whiskey supposedly being brought across the border. The only smuggled booze found that night were five cases in Oscar's boat that had landed the police chief in jail.

"Stanley, right?" Roland said, staring at the man.

"Yeah, John Stanley," he said, staring at Oscar with a deep frown.

"How are things with the Coast Guard?" Roland said.

"Cold and wet," he said, unable to take his eyes off Oscar. "Do I know you?"

"I don't think we've met," Oscar said, returning the man's stare.

"Hang on," Stanley said, laughing. "You're the cop Roland busted for the five cases."

"What about it?" Oscar snapped.

"Hey, Johnny," Stanley said, yelling to someone in the other boat. "Take a look at who's in the boat with Doyle."

Johnny Matters, head of the Ogdensburg Prohibition Unit stared down at Roland's boat, then laughed.

"What the hell are you doing here?" Johnny Matters said to Oscar.

"I'm working," Oscar said. "What does it look like I'm doing?"

"Not much, actually," Matters said, laughing again. Then he glanced at Roland. "What's he doing here, Doyle?"

"I needed a driver," Roland said with a shrug. "And he's the police chief in Alex Bay."

"No shit?" John Stanley from the Coast Guard said. "They gave you your old job back?"

"You got a problem with that?" Oscar growled.

"Okay, Chief," Stanley said, laughing. "Knock yourself out. Just try to stay out of the way."

"Unless they start shooting," Johnny Matters said. "Then you can feel free to provide all the cover you want."

They both laughed, and Roland and Oscar had no choice but to wait it out.

"What do you know about this thing tonight?" Stanley said to Roland.

"Just what Adams put in the letter," Roland said. "He wouldn't talk about it over the phone."

"Yeah, he's playing his cards close on this one," Johnny Matters said. "He must have somebody working undercover up here. I tried to get him to talk about it, but he wouldn't budge."

"So, how do you want to play it?" John Stanley said to Matters.

"I thought we might try to triangulate them," Johnny Matters said. We'll space two of the boats a couple of hundred yards apart on this side and put the other boat on the other side in the middle."

"Yeah, that'll work," Stanley said. "And when we see the barge, we'll hit them with the spotlights and move in together from three sides. Hopefully, that'll be enough for them to give it up. I really don't feel like getting into a shooting match tonight."

"Yeah, me either," Matters said. "Okay, why don't you take the other side, and I'll stay here with Doyle and the bootlegger cop."

They both laughed again.

"Don't worry about those assholes, Oscar," Roland said. "I have the same problem with them."

Frank passed Milo a flask, and he took a sip then handed it to Birdie. The flask took another lap before ending up back in the boatbuilder's pocket.

"It's a beautiful night for a boat ride," Birdie said.

"Turn on the light in the stern, Birdie," Milo said. "I'd hate for them to miss us."

"It'd be pretty hard to miss this thing, Milo," Frank said.

"Remember who we're dealing with."

The lights from the barge reflected off the water, and Roland felt a surge of excitement when he realized just how close he might be to getting out of this wasteland once and for all. The spotlights from the other two boats appeared then landed on the barge that was slowly making its way downriver. A siren from the Coast Guard boat screamed, then faded with a soft echo. Oscar followed suit and the vessel was bathed in light as all three boats sped across the water. The barge came to a stop when all three got close, and Roland stood up to get a better look.

"I can't wait to see the look on their faces," Oscar said with a grin. "The lying sacks of shit."

"What are you talking about?" Roland said, frowning at him.

"Nothing," Oscar said, inching the boat closer to the barge.

Roland glanced around the large barge, then his mouthed dropped open. He glanced over at Oscar who was also having a hard time believing what he was seeing.

"Drop anchor and put your hands in the air," Johnny Matters yelled through a bullhorn.

All three boats nudged up against the barge, and Roland tied his boat to it.

"What the hell is going on?"

"Frank?" Oscar said.

"Oscar, what the hell are you doing out here in the middle of the night?" Frank said.

"Hands in the air," Johnny Matters repeated, then glanced over at one of his crew. "Rack a shell just to let them know we mean business." Then he focused on the other two men who were standing in the shadows. "You two come out where I can see you with your hands up. Yeah, that's the way. Nice and easy. Just like that."

"Milo?" Roland said.

"Hello, Roland," Milo said, glancing around. "It's nice to see you. But would you mind explaining what the hell is going on?"

"Hey, Birdie," Oscar said.

"Hey, Oscar. Beautiful night for a boat ride, huh?"

"You know these guys?" Johnny Matters said, glancing at Roland.

"Sure. They all live in Alex Bay," Roland said. "I can't believe it."

"Yeah, I'm having a little trouble processing it too," Oscar said.

"Prepare to be boarded," Johnny Matters said, climbing onto the barge.

"Knock yourself out," Frank said with a shrug. "There's plenty of room."

"Remove that tarp," Matters said, motioning to two of his crew.

"I assume you have some sort of warrant to search my boat," Frank said, staying casual.

"I'm afraid we don't need a warrant, sir," John Stanley said, climbing aboard the barge.

"Whatever happened to unlawful search and seizure?" Milo said, glancing back and forth at the two men.

"Probable cause, sir," Johnny Matters said. "Probable cause."

"Okay," Frank said with a shrug then glanced over at Milo. "My lawyer is gonna have a field day with this."

"I'd be disappointed if he didn't, Frank," Milo said, laughing.

"Yeah, I'm glad you find it funny," Johnny Matters said. "You won't be laughing for long."

"I'll take my chances," Milo said.

"Sonofabitch," one of the men said, glancing around at what was underneath the tarp.

"What's the matter?" Johnny Matters said.

"There's no booze on this barge," the man said, frantically looking around the deck.

"What? Then what the hell are they hauling?"

"Rock," the man said.

"Rock?" Johnny Matters said, stunned.

"Actually, it's granite," Milo said. "Canadian granite. I just love the color."

"Goddamn it!" Johnny Matters said, stuffing his gun back in its holster. "Goddamn, I hate this stretch of River."

"Can I ask why you're hauling granite?" John Stanley said.

"We're using it to build a new school in Alex Bay," Frank said.

"And you're making your run in the middle of the night?" Johnny Matters said with a scowl.

"We had engine trouble," Frank said. "And it took me all afternoon to get it fixed.

"Sonofabitch," Johnny Matters said, chagrined. "I don't suppose an apology would be enough to make this unfortunate incident go away."

"Not even close," Frank said, glaring back and forth at both men.

"Well, I guess we should get going," John Stanley said, glancing at Matters who nodded back. "On behalf of the U.S. Coast Guard, I'd like to sincerely apologize."

"As would the Prohibition Unit," Johnny Matters said, climbing back on board his boat and motioning for his crew to do the same. "Enjoy the rest of your evening."

Moments later, both boats departed heading in opposite directions. Frank glared at Oscar.

"Him I understand, Oscar," he said, nodding at Roland. "He's was probably just following orders. But what the hell are you doing out here?"

"Helping out?" Oscar mumbled. "Sorry, Frank. You too, Milo."

"Why don't you just stick to your own business, Oscar?" Frank said.

"Yeah, that's probably a good idea," Oscar said as if he were a kid caught smoking behind the barn. "You gonna tell Melvin?"

"What would we tell him, Oscar?" Milo said. "Other than you were out fighting crime and trying to protect the good people of Alex Bay."

"Thanks, Milo."

"Don't mention it," Milo said, then turned to Roland. "What's the name of your boss in Washington, Roland?"

"Vernon Adams," Roland said with a grin.

"Vernon Adams," Milo said, nodding. "Do you spell that with one D or two?"

News Delivery

Vernon Adams woke to the sound of a ringing phone, and he raced to the living room. Expecting good news, he grinned and took a few deep breaths before answering.

"Vernon Adams," he chirped.

"Vernon Adams. Just the man I need to speak with."

"Who is this?" Vernon said, suddenly on edge.

"It's Senator Miller."

"Senator Miller?" Vernon said, puffing back up with pride. Last night's sting operation must have been an incredible success for the Senator to be calling him at home. "It's nice to hear your voice."

"Yeah, you might want to give it a minute before you say that," Senator Miller said in a tone that wasn't used to deliver good news.

"What can I do for you, Senator?" Vernon said, frantically waving a yawning woman entering the living room back to bed.

"I just got a call from a gentleman in Alex Bay," the Senator said.

"Was it about something that happened last night?" Vernon said, still holding out hope for good news.

"You bet your ass that's what it was about," he said. "And I have several things to discuss with you. But we're going to have this conversation face to face."

"Of course, Senator," Vernon said, nervously running a hand through his hair. "Should I stop by your office?"

"No, I'm in the middle of a campaign at the moment," the Senator snapped. "And I really don't have time to deal with your stupid shit. But since I don't have a choice, you're going to meet me in Syracuse next Monday. Call my staff and get it on my calendar."

"With all due respect, Senator, I should probably get the trip cleared with my boss first," Vernon said with a high-pitched stammer.

"That's already been done," the Senator snapped. "Syracuse. Next Monday. Get your ass on a train and come prepared to explain why you tried to arrest a man who was delivering a boatload of granite being used to build a new school for needy children. A school that's being built mind you, by one of my good friends and biggest contributor."

"Granite? Did you say granite?" Vernon said, stunned.

"Yeah, a bunch of rocks," the Senator said. "Just like the ones rolling around your goddamn head."

Vernon heard the loud click on the other end of the line and finally managed to get his hands to stop shaking long enough to get a cigarette lit. He stood still in the middle of the room and stared out the window at nothing. A few minutes later, the woman poked her head into the room.

"Verny, are you coming back to bed or not?"

"Yeah," Vernon Adams whispered through a cloud of smoke. "But I'm probably gonna need a minute."

Milo found Ruby in her bedroom packing. Two large suitcases were sitting on the bed, and she was quickly filling them.

"Don't be stealing the towels," Milo said with a grin as he sat down in a chair to watch her.

"Hey, Milo," she said, pausing briefly to glance over her shoulder to greet him before getting back to work. "You're early."

"Well, it's a beautiful day for a boat ride, so we thought we'd get an early start."

"You know something, Milo," she said, pausing to put her hands on her hips and look around the bedroom. "Strange as it sounds, I think I'm going to miss this place."

"There's always next winter, Ruby," Milo said. "But by then, I'm pretty sure this island will be a distant memory. Let me help you get those closed."

Milo eventually managed to get both suitcases shut and locked, then he set them on the floor.

"Have a seat, Ruby," he said, sitting back down.

She shrugged and hopped up on the bed and tucked her legs underneath her. She waved off his offer of a cigarette and waited patiently for him to speak.

"I thought this would be a good time to explain what I have in mind for you," Milo said.

"That's great, Milo," she said, leaning forward. "I've been thinking through all sorts of possibilities."

"I'd be disappointed if you hadn't, Ruby," he said, lighting his cigarette.

"Well, what am I going to be doing?"

"You're moving to Watertown," Milo said.

"Okay," she said, frowning. "To do what?"

"To manage a hundred speakeasies I'm about to take possession of," Milo said with a grin.

She sat dead still on the bed deep in thought. Then she cocked her head and gave him a puzzled look.

"You made a move on Ben Green's operation?"

"Actually, The Sleaze got the ball rolling on that front," Milo said, shrugging. "I'm merely coming in behind him to tie up some loose ends."

"Like The Sleaze?" she said, grinning.

"Remarkable," Milo said, grinning back. "I love the way your brain works. As soon as you get back from your shopping spree in New York, you'll be getting started. In fact, don't even worry about coming back to town. Just get off the train in Watertown and stay right there."

"Okay," she said, frowning. "But I'm gonna need to find a place to live."

"I've already taken care of that for you, Ruby," Milo said. "I found you a great house. And it's got a beautiful sunroom you're gonna love."

"Thanks, Milo," she said, puzzled. "What happened to Green?"

"I'm afraid Mr. Green had an unfortunate roadside accident," Milo said, staying casual.

"Car crash?"

"Well, there were some vehicles in the vicinity, but that's probably not an accurate description of events," Milo said, frowning. "But he did get hit from behind."

"The Sleaze shot Green in the back?" she said.

"That's the story making the rounds."

"I'm glad to hear that, Milo," she said, exhaling up at the ceiling. "When you gave me all that money to buy a new wardrobe, I was afraid you were going to ask me to get close to Green the way Beulah had to. And based on what you told me about the guy, I wasn't looking forward to that."

"No, I wouldn't waste your affections on a despicable creature like Ben Green," Milo said, grinning at her.

"What is it, Milo?" Ruby said, leaning forward. "That's the look you get every time you're being too clever by half."

"I'm sure you're right," he said, laughing. "While I'd never waste your talents on someone as pedestrian as Ben Green, I do have someone else in mind who is going to be…mesmerized by you."

"Mesmerized?"

"Yes, it means-"

"I know what it means, Milo," she said, suddenly testy. "Take the marbles out of your mouth."

"How would you feel about becoming the First Lady of the great state of New York?"

Milo glanced around the cooking room at the long line of milk cans stacked five deep and grinned after doing the math in his head. He hopped up on one of the workbenches and kicked his legs back and forth as he waited for Tom Collins to finish what he was doing with one of the vats of mash. Eventually, he closed the lid then grabbed a folding chair and sat down in front of Milo.

"I'm gonna need some help over here soon, Milo," Tom said, pouring a cup of coffee. "I'm getting flat worn out."

"I've been talking to a couple of my drivers at the farm," Milo said. "They said they were tired of driving the same stretch of highway and were wondering if I had something else for them. What do you need to be done over here?"

"Basically, just some muscle work. Lugging supplies and product up and down that damn incline, keeping the house and cooking room clean, taking care of the lawn, stuff like that."

"They'll be able to handle that," Milo said. "I'll have Birdie bring them over so you can have a chat with them. If you think they'll work out, just let me know."

"Thanks, Milo," Tom said. "Look, I hope you don't mind, but I started stashing my money in the storage area under the floor in here."

"Perfect," Milo said. "A lot safer than a bank."

"You sure you aren't gonna need it for yours?"

"No, I've got a new hiding spot for mine," Milo said, hopping down off the bench. "Try to get your rest, Tom. I need you bright-eyed and bushy-tailed."

"What for?" Tom said, puzzled.

"Why, expansion, of course," Milo said, beaming.

"Where are we expanding, Milo?"

"Albany."

"Can I ask you why the hell you want to set up shop way down there?"

"Because when you have friends in high places, it's always a good idea to keep a close eye on them," Milo said.

"And make a whole lot of money while you're doing it, right?"

"I do like the way you think, Tom Collins," Milo said, tipping his hat to his cooker. "I'll see you at seven. Don't be late. And make sure you take good care of your voice today."

Melvin clutched his stomach and groaned. Jimmy Sleaze grimaced and shook his head.

"Again?" Sleaze said, bewildered as he watched Melvin get up from his chair and race for the bathroom. "What the hell have you been eating?"

"Diner food," Melvin called out from the bathroom. "I knew I should have just stuck with the special."

A few minutes later, Melvin came back into his office and sat down. He wiped his mouth with a hand towel then burped loudly.

"I'm sorry, Jimmy," Melvin said, clutching his stomach. "But I don't think I'm going to be able to make it tonight."

"I see," Sleaze said, sounding way too happy about the news. "That's gonna put a serious dent in your cut, Melvin."

"I'd be surprised if it didn't," Melvin said. "But how are we going to handle tonight? I suppose we could have Oscar cancel with Doyle and go with you."

"No, that won't be necessary," Sleaze said. "I'm sure I'll be able to handle it by myself. All I need to do is show the guys on the barge where we want the booze delivered and wait until they get it unloaded."

"Okay," Melvin said, then groaned loudly as he clutched his stomach.

"Are you sure that island is safe?"

"Yeah, don't worry. I own it, and it's just an empty piece of rock and a bunch of pine trees. Just put the booze among the trees and cover it up. We'll get it to shore before anybody even knows it's there."

"The guys on the barge are gonna know," Sleaze said.

"I doubt if they're going to steal from the people who just bought it from them, Jimmy. That's a little paranoid, wouldn't you say?"

"You can't be too careful, Melvin," Sleaze said, lighting a cigar. "Especially since I'll be carrying around forty grand of my hard-earned money."

"Hold that thought," Melvin said, scrambling out of his chair and racing to the bathroom.

Milo finished the last of his beef stew then sopped up what was left of the gravy with a piece of bread. He wiped his mouth then sat back in his chair and patted his stomach. He grinned across the table at Annabelle.

"So, dear, how was your day?"

"Don't start that shit again, Milo," she said, laughing. "But for the record, my day was fine. And yours?"

"Eventful," he said. "I had a long talk with Birdie, then I went to the island and met with Ruby, then Tom."

"You had a *meeting* with Ruby?" she said, cocking her head at him.

"No," he said, shaking his head. "Nothing like that. But if there ever was a time for it, today was it. By the time I left, Ruby was walking about a foot off the ground."

"You told her about her new job?" Annabelle said, sipping her wine.

"Oh, I did more than that," Milo said. "I gave Ruby a glimpse into her long-range future."

"I see," Annabelle said, placing her elbows on the table and leaning forward. "And just what do you see in her future?"

"You know how I've been hinting about expanding our operation?" he said, giving her hands a loving squeeze.

"Yes, I have been wondering what you're up to. But I figured you'd tell me when you were ready," she said, getting up from the table and leading him by the hand into the living room. Milo sat down on the couch, and Annabelle stretched out with her head in his lap. "That's better. I assume you're finally ready to tell me, Mr. Razner."

"I am, Miss Caffey," he said, stroking her hair. "I thought we were going to have to wait out another term of our current governor, but now that Senator Miller will be taking office early next year, I decided to move my plan for expansion up. You know, since there's no reason to wait."

"Okay," she said, frowning up at him. "You want to expand into Albany?"

"Very much so," Milo said. "Our lovely state capital is about four times the size of Watertown. And that means a whole lot of booze and a whole lot more people drinking it." He glanced down at her. "I'm sure you can do the math."

"Yes, I'm sure I can," she said, laughing. "How do you see it working?"

"Well, my original plan was to put Ruby down there to get friendly with our soon to be governor. But I had to make an adjustment on the fly when Senator Miller threw me a curve."

"What did he do?"

"He already had his sights set on someone else," Milo said.

"Who?"

"Beulah."

"Interesting," Annabelle said, sitting up. "That should make it easier to tell her the bad news about us."

"It's not that simple," Milo said, shaking his head.

"It never is," she said, stretching back out with her head in his lap.

"But it's the perfect cover for now," he said. "Beulah starts spending time down there, they announce their engagement, and things are fine until she starts to get cold feet. Then Ruby works her magic on the Senator thereby freeing up Beulah to do the more important work."

"Such as?"

"Learning everything there is to know about how the booze business works down there, and who all the important players are. And when she's got it figured out, we'll sit down and come up with a plan about how we're gonna take it over."

"Just like that?" she said, frowning.

"Pretty much," Milo said. "We'll be following the basic script we used to set up shop here. A lot of the initial ideas came from Beulah. Over the years, she paid close attention to what me and The Sleaze were up to, and she learned a lot. And it was her idea to pose as the head of the local Temperance Society while she was doing her initial research up here. That was brilliant. I think the two of you are gonna get along great."

"What on earth are you talking about, Milo?" she said, again sitting up on the couch. "You want us to meet?"

"Of course, why not?"

"Well, since you're sleeping with both of us, do you really think that's a good idea?" Annabelle said, frowning at him.

"Both of you already know that," Milo said. "I really don't see the problem."

"How can you be so brilliant in business and so goddamn dumb about women?" she said, shaking her head.

"Years of practice, I suppose," he said, shrugging. "Look, it's only gonna be a problem if the two of you make it one."

Annabelle gave it some serious thought, then glanced up at him.

"Well, it's not like I'm going to be seeing her very often," Annabelle said, pursing her lips.

"What makes you think that?" Milo said, staring down at her.

"Because she'll be down in Albany, and I'll be here," she said, then frowned when she caught the grin he was giving her. "You've got that look. What is it now, Milo?"

"I think it might be time for you to ask Vernon for a transfer," Milo said, his eyes dancing.

"Why would I want to do that?"

"Two reasons. One is to help Vernon repair his relationship with Senator Miller which has taken a serious hit. And the second is for you to do that by giving him all sorts of information about the illegal booze business operating in our capital city."

"Information that Beulah uncovers, I presume?" Annabelle said, shaking her head in disbelief.

"I knew it wouldn't take long for you to catch up."

"Beulah tells me what she knows, I tell Vernon, and he locks up the bootleggers and throws away the key."

"And we move in to fill the void left by the departure of the previous tenants," Milo said, nodding.

"Just how much more is there, Milo?"

"What?" he said, puzzled.

"How far down the road have you got this thing figured out?"

"Oh, I'm working way down the road, Miss Caffey. You want to hear all about it?"

"No, I don't think my brain can handle anything else at the moment," she said, squeezing his thigh. "How long have you got before you need to leave?"

"I need to get going soon," Milo said, glancing at his watch.

"Do we have time to head upstairs?"

"No, I wish I did. But I need to get to the train station."

Night Delivery Redux

Jimmy Sleaze started Melvin's boat and did his best to remember what Melvin had told him about how to drive the damn thing. Growing up dirt-poor in the slums of Philadelphia hadn't offered him much of a chance to be around boats. Or even water for that matter. And his swimming skills were pretty much confined to jumping in the water then sinking right to the bottom. But the boat seemed stable enough, and he headed upriver gripping the steering wheel tight with both hands.

He drove slowly, scanning the water for signs of the barge as darkness descended and the sunset began to fade. A few minutes later, he spotted a dark shape that seemed to be anchored near a rocky outcrop. Sleaze slowed and came to a stop about a hundred feet away from the barge and grabbed the revolver he'd borrowed from Milo off the seat.

Milo, he said to himself with a sad shake of his head. Why the dumb bastard had decided to go straight just as the biggest opportunity to get rich in a hurry had opened up continued to be a mystery. But the Sleaze shook it off and grinned at the barge.

"More for me," Sleaze whispered, then chuckled softly.

As instructed, he flashed three quick beams from a flashlight then waited for the signal to be returned. Then he accelerated and came to a stop next to the barge. He couldn't help but notice the bulge in the middle of it covered by an enormous tarp. In the dim light, a figure emerged from the shadows and stood near the edge of the barge.

"Mr. Sleaze, I presume," the familiar voice said.

"Yeah, it's me," Sleaze said, sliding the revolver into his jacket pocket. "Are you ready to tell me your name, or are you gonna stick with this anonymous shit?"

"My name is Tom. Tom Collins."

"Like the cocktail?" Sleaze said, laughing.

"That's the one. Toss me that line then climb aboard. And bring the money with you."

Sleaze did as he was told and was soon standing next to the man who seemed to be studying him closely.

"You come by yourself?" Sleaze said, glancing around.

"Yes, I like to handle as many details as I can by myself," Tom said. "But I am surprised you came alone. It's going to take you a long time to unload a thousand cases."

"Shit, I thought you'd have a crew with you to handle that," Sleaze snapped. "You're gonna help me, right?"

"No, I'm afraid that is one of the details I leave to others," Tom said, chuckling. "The money, if you would be so kind."

Sleaze handed him a satchel, and the guy opened it and flipped through the stack of cash.

"It seems to be all here," Tom said, closing the satchel and tossing it on the deck.

"Of course, it's all there," Sleaze said, glaring at him. "Unlike the three million you ripped off from Green."

"Three million? I'm afraid you lost me, Mr. Sleaze."

"Yeah, I bet. So, can I count on this much product on a regular basis?"

"That might be a bit hard to guarantee, Mr. Sleaze. But I'm sure we'll figure something out," Tom said. "Would you like to take a look at the product?"

"You read my mind, Mr. Collins," Sleaze said. "How about you remove that tarp so I can get a good look?"

"Certainly," Tom Collins said, untying one corner of the tarp and pulling it back.

Sleaze grinned as he started to take a step forward but froze in his tracks when a man jumped up from underneath the tarp and racked a shell into the shotgun he was holding. The sound reverberated over the calm water, and Sleaze glanced back and forth at both men.

"Hey, what the hell?" Sleaze said. "I ain't looking for any trouble."

"No, it just seems to follow you, Jimmy."

Sleaze's eyes darted around the barge then landed on a figure partially hidden by the cargo and dim light.

"Milo?" Sleaze said, stunned.

"How are you doing, Jimmy?" Milo said, stepping out of the shadows. "Great job, Birdie. Tom, if you would be so kind to search our friend, The Sleaze."

"I'll be happy to do that," Tom Collins said.

"Nobody calls me that name and lives, Milo," Sleaze said, glaring at him.

"Sorry, Jimmy. Old habits die hard," Milo said, casually lighting a cigarette as he stared at Sleaze. "Questions?"

"You son of a bitch," Sleaze said. "I should have known you were lying the whole time. Dairy farmer. You always were full of shit."

"It does come in handy," Milo said, grinning. "Tom, if you would keep that pistol pointed at The Sleaze's head for a moment, I'd appreciate it."

"You got it, Milo," Tom said. "Should I shoot him if he moves?"

"Oh, I doubt if he's going to move, Tom," Milo said. "Jimmy's is going to want to stick around and see the surprise. But if necessary, sure, go right ahead."

"What surprise?" Sleaze said.

"Hold your horses, Jimmy," Milo said. "That's always been the problem. You've never been able to take the long view. You have what doctors call a need for immediate gratification."

"Do I now?" Sleaze said, his voice low and threatening.

"Birdie, if you would hand me the shotgun and then untie Melvin's boat, I'd appreciate it."

"You got it, Milo," Birdie said, holding the shotgun out. "I've already got a shell racked."

"Yes, I heard," Milo said, watching Birdie untie the boat then step back out of the way.

Milo pointed the shotgun at the boat and blew a hole in the side right above the waterline. The blast echoed for a long time then gradually faded. The boat immediately began to take on water.

"Melvin's gonna need a new boat," Birdie said.

"Yes, I noticed," Milo said, nodding. "But I'll get him a new one. It's the least I can do. By the way, Jimmy, how is Melvin doing with his tummy troubles?"

"Sonofabitch," Sleaze whispered as he shook his head. "This whole thing was a setup right from the start, wasn't it?"

"Yeah. Good one, huh, Jimmy?"

"Damn you, Milo," he said, shaking his head. "But why would you do that? Especially after all we've been through."

"Primarily, because you're a worthless human being," Milo said, shrugging. "And you're also in the way."

"C'mon, Milo," Sleaze said, pleading. "There's plenty of money to go around."

"Yes, there is," Milo said, glancing at Birdie and Tom. "Wouldn't you agree, gentlemen?"

"Oh, yeah," Tom said.

"No argument from me," Birdie said. "I can even come close to spending it all."

"C'mon, Milo, be reasonable," Sleaze said. "Look, I'm sorry if I stepped on your toes. What can I do to make it up to you?"

"No, that's not it, Jimmy," Milo said. "You haven't done anything out of the ordinary since you got here. You just started doing the same stupid shit you always do. My problem with you is more…historical."

"I'm not following you, Milo," Sleaze said, shaking his head again.

"Then let me make it easier for you," he said, handing the shotgun back to Birdie. "Rack another round and point it at his chest." Milo did a half-turn and raised his voice. "C'mon out."

Sleaze focused on the figure emerging from the shadows near the back of the barge, then his eyes went wide.

"Beulah?" Sleaze whispered in disbelief.

"Hello, Jimmy," she said, glaring at him before draping an arm over Milo's shoulder. She gave him a kiss on the cheek then nuzzled his neck. She stood close to Milo and gave Sleaze a big grin. "Surprise," she whispered into the night air.

"What?" Sleaze said, glancing back and forth at them. "You two? How long has this been going on?"

"Well, let's see," Milo said, glancing at Beulah. "We started talking about it right after he got arrested."

"Yeah. But at first, I was mostly listening," Beulah said, then glared at her ex-husband. "We had to wait a few days until I was able to start talking again. You know, since my mouth was swelled shut after you beat the shit out of me."

"I'm so sorry I did that to you, Beulah," Sleaze said, staring at her. "I tried to apologize from jail, but I couldn't ever get in touch with you."

"No, you couldn't. Milo made sure of that," she said, squeezing Milo's arm.

"And since it was the fifth time you'd done it," Milo said. "Beulah finally decided she'd had enough."

"Sixth," Beulah said, glancing at Milo.

"That's right. I'm sorry. It was the sixth," Milo said, giving her a kiss. "And after I got a look at what you'd done to her, I made a decision that has truly changed my life."

"Yeah? What was that, Milo?" Sleaze said, glaring at him.

"That was the night I decided to give you up, Jimmy."

"You did what?" Sleaze said, about to take a step toward Milo but quickly changing his mind.

"If I hadn't gone to the cops and let them know about all the things you were doing to the *financial institutions* around the city, you would have eventually beaten Beulah to death. And I wasn't about to let that happen."

"I can't believe you sold me out," Sleaze growled. "You better make sure you kill me, Milo. Because if you don't, you're a dead man."

"I suppose I would be," Milo said, shrugging. "But I kinda like my chances tonight, Jimmy. Anyway, I spent almost three months taking care of Beulah until she recovered." He glanced over at her. "It was pretty touch and go for a while there, huh?"

"Yeah, it was," she said, grinning at him. "But you saved me, Milo."

"Nah, you did most of the work," Milo said, squeezing her hand. "At first, the plan was for me to help Beulah get away from you forever. But after we started talking and coming up with some ideas, we decided to take off together. And things just sort of developed from there."

"This is very touching," Sleaze said. "You prick. Go right ahead, Milo. Let's see you try to keep that bitch happy."

"Harsh," Milo said, laughing. "What do you have to say about that, Beulah? Are you happy?"

"I'm goddamn delighted, Milo," she said, again glaring at her ex-husband. "But not as happy as I'm going to be in a few minutes."

"Yeah, let's get this over with. I'm starting to get a chill," Milo said, taking the shotgun back from Birdie. "You know, Jimmy, you should feel good about one thing."

"What's that?"

"You're actually causing me to break one of my cardinal rules," Milo said. "And it takes a very special person to do that."

"Cardinal rule, huh?" Sleaze said, clenching his fists. "Which one is that, Milo?"

"The one about not throwing shit in the River."

Birdie let loose with a cackle that echoed across the water.

"So, what's it gonna be, Jimmy? Shotgun blast in the face, or would you like to try and swim for it? Your choice."

"You know I can't swim," Sleaze said, glancing out at the water just as the last of Melvin's boat slowly sank beneath the surface.

"Okay," Milo said, raising the shotgun until it was pointed at Sleaze's eyes. "This is gonna make one hell of a mess on the barge, but if that's your call, so be it."

Jimmy Sleaze bolted to his right and made it to the edge of the barge with three giant steps. He launched himself off the side, landed with a loud splash and disappeared briefly from sight. Then he popped to the surface, slapping at the water with both arms flailing and gasping for breath. His head dipped below the water, then popped back up.

"Milo," he managed to sputter. "Don't do this. Please, Milo."

"Sorry, Jimmy," Milo said without emotion. "But hang in there. Maybe you'll get lucky and end up on a shoal."

"Do you really want to take that chance, Milo?" Tom Collins said, staring down at the frantic man in the water right next to the barge.

"Maybe you're right, Tom."

Milo casually walked to the side of the barge and pointed the shotgun down at the water. The blast echoed until it was eventually replaced by the sound of a cool breeze starting to kick up out of the north.

"Thank you, Milo," Beulah said, pulling him in for a long kiss.

"My pleasure, Miss Peppin."

They broke their embrace, and Milo glanced at Birdie.

"Okay, let's get this booze back to Rockport. Daisy's still at the furniture store, and I'm sure she would like to get home before midnight."

"You got it, Milo," Birdie said.

"Tom, why don't you break out a nice bottle of something for the ride home?"

"Good idea," Tom said, opening one of the cases. "Hey, what was The Sleaze's comment about three million bucks all about?"

"I believe he was referring to a recent windfall Beulah and I had."

Kicking Ass And Taking Names

Vernon Adams knocked tentatively on the door and removed his hat. Moments later, a woman opened the door and greeted him with a smile. She waved him in and took his hat and coat.

"Mr. Adams, I presume," she said, gesturing him into the living room of the suite and pointing at a couch.

"Yes. And please call me Vernon," he said, unable to take his eyes off her. "And you are?"

"Beulah Peppin," she said, pouring three drinks.

"Peppin?" he said, surprised. "Your mother wouldn't happen to be the national head of the Temperance Society, would she?"

"That's my mama," Beulah said, handing him his drink. "But since the law was passed, she's retired. She just moved to Florida to spend her days walking the beach."

"I take it you don't share her opinions when it comes to the *deadly scourge of alcohol*," Vernon said, chuckling as he tried to turn on the charm.

"Uh, no," Beulah said, taking a long sip of whiskey. "Oh, there he is."

Senator Miller entered from the bedroom and glared at Vernon as he walked across the room. He accepted the glass Beulah was holding out and gave her a kiss on the cheek. He sat down across from the Fed, draped a leg over his knee, and lit a Cuban cigar without offering Vernon one. The Senator puffed several times until the end was glowing then exhaled a cloud of smoke.

"Senator Miller, I'd like to start by apologizing right up front," Vernon said. "I got some bad information."

"Did you now? From whom?"

"From one of my former undercover agents I had working in that neck of the woods," Vernon said.

"Former? You fired him?"

"Actually, it was a woman," Vernon said, his eyes darting away for a second. "But yes, I did. Right on the spot. As soon as I learned what had transpired, I told her to hit the road and not look back," Vernon said, nodding vigorously.

"I see," the Senator said, twirling the cigar in his hand. "Do you have any idea how much trouble you've caused me, Mr. Adams?"

"I can only imagine, Senator. Again, I am deeply apologetic for that unfortunate incident."

"That man is a pillar of his community," the Senator said. "Milo Razner is a respected businessman, and widely regarded as one of the kindest and most generous men you will ever meet. In addition to the new school he's building with his own money, he also provides free breakfast and lunch to every child in school. Does that sound like someone who would be smuggling booze across the River?"

"Uh, no, sir, it doesn't," Vernon said, taking a sip of whiskey to calm his nerves.

"Consider yourself fortunate that Mr. Razner has decided to let the situation pass without further comment," Senator Miller said. "If he hadn't, you would have an even bigger problem than you do at the moment."

"Yes, Senator. I understand completely," Vernon said, lighting a cigarette with some difficulty. "Thank you. And please apologize on my behalf to Mr. Razner the next time you see him."

"Let me ask you a question, Mr. Adams."

"Of course, Senator. Anything."

"Do you have other undercover agents working in that area?" the Senator said.

"Uh, just one," Vernon said.

"Well, let me make you a suggestion, Mr. Adams," Senator Miller said, again giving him a hard stare. "I would highly recommend that you consider reassigning that individual."

"Reassign?"

"Yes, I would imagine there are other geographic locations more in need of that sort of help. And I can only imagine the sorts of shenanigans your undercover agents are getting up to."

"I can assure you they're a dedicated group of professionals, Senator," Vernon said, taking a quick puff from his cigarette.

"You mean, dedicated professionals like the one who gave you that last tip?"

"Yeah," Vernon said, deflated. "I'm really sorry about that, Senator."

"Again, I strongly suggest that you consider reassignment, Mr. Adams," Senator Miller said, lowering his leg to the floor and leaning in close. "Because if I hear about so much as a phone call to Mr. Razner wishing him a happy birthday, you will be on permanent stakeout looking for Russian vodka being smuggled across the Aleutian Islands. Am I making myself clear, Mr. Adams?"

"Absolutely, Senator."

"Good. Now get the hell out of here."

"Can I finish my drink first?"

"Take it with you."

Roland Doyle glanced around the living room and frowned as he sniffed the air. He drained half of his drink then spotted Oscar coming back into the room carrying a tray of cheese and crackers. Oscar set the tray down on the wobbly dining room table then sat back down and topped off both their drinks.

"This is all I got to eat in the house," Oscar said, slicing a piece of cheese off the block of cheddar. "I ain't had time to get to the store yet."

"It must be nice being back in your house," Roland said, taking another look around and deciding that the best word to describe the décor was shitty.

"Yeah, it is," Oscar said, wolfing down the cheese and cutting another piece. "Help yourself."

"Where the hell did the guy go?" Roland said. "It's like he vanished into thin air."

"If we're lucky, he's at the bottom of the River," Oscar said. "Maybe he just got scared and took off."

"Jimmy Sleaze scared?" Roland said, shaking his head. "If he did, it would be the first time."

"Maybe he'll surface at some point," Oscar said, tossing back his drink. "But for now, I ain't gonna spend a second worrying about The Sleaze. So, what did you want to talk about?"

Roland swirled the whiskey in his glass then took a sip and set the glass down.

"I've been thinking Oscar."

"About what?"

"I think it's time we combined forces," Roland said.

"I thought we already did that," Oscar said, frowning.

"I'm not talking about working together on law enforcement," Roland said, shaking his head. "After the other night on the water, I started thinking about just how incompetent the people responsible for catching bootleggers are. Present company excluded, of course."

"Of course," Oscar said. "Where are you going with this, Roland?"

"On our measly salaries, after we pay for rent and food and have a little fun, we aren't left with two nickels to rub together. Then I got to thinking. Why should all those other bastards be getting rich while we spend all our time busting our asses trying to catch them?"

"Can't argue with that," Oscar said, studying the Fed closely. "So?"

"So, I thought it was time for you and me to get into the booze business."

"You know what, Roland?" Oscar said with a grin.

"What?"

"I'm beginning to think that I may have misjudged you."

Senator Miller and Beulah walked arm in arm down the hall and knocked on the door. Milo opened it and beamed at them.

"There they are," Milo said, ushering them in. "Come on in."

They sat down next to each other on the couch, snuggled close. Milo poured drinks and was delighted to see how friendly the two of them were with each other. Milo passed out the drinks then raised his glass.

"To the happy couple," he said, clinking glasses. "How did your chat go with Vernon Adams?"

"I thought he was going to shit himself," Senator Miller said, laughing. "Oh, he asked me to apologize to you for his behavior."

"It's the least he can do, right?" Milo said, laughing along.

"Don't worry, he won't be bothering you in the future."

"Good. The prick," Milo said, taking one of the cigars the Senator was offering.

"But he did mention that he had another undercover agent working up there. I suggested a transfer, but who knows what he'll end up doing. Is that going to be a problem, Milo?"

"No, I'm all over that one, Senator," Milo said, firing up his cigar. "Don't give it a second thought. And my guess is that Adams will definitely be taking your advice."

"If you say so, Milo," he said, glancing at Beulah then back at Milo. "Doesn't she look beautiful tonight?"

"Oh, stop," Beulah said, squeezing the Senator's arm.

"I couldn't agree more, Senator," Milo said, beaming at Beulah.

"So, Milo, did you come to town by yourself?" the Senator said.

"No, actually, I have company," Milo said, smiling. "She's just finishing up getting dressed for dinner. She'll be right out."

On cue, the bedroom door opened, and she strolled into the living room and glanced around with a big smile on her face.

"I believe you two ladies know each other," Milo said.

"We do," Beulah said. "It's so nice to see you."

"It's been too long. How are you, Beulah?"

"I'm wonderful, thanks."

"Senator Miller, I'd like you to meet Ruby Crankovitch."

Ruby approached the Senator and beamed at him as she extended a hand for him to kiss. Milo couldn't miss the look of pure lust on the Senator's face as he bowed slightly and slowly raised her hand to his lips. Milo glanced at Beulah who smiled back and gave him a small nod.

"It's so nice to meet you, Ruby. And I must say, that is a beautiful dress you're wearing," the Senator said, unable to take his eyes off the woman whose hand he was still gently holding. He pulled her hand close and kissed it again.

"Tell me, Ruby," the Senator said, cocking his head at her. "Where on earth has Milo been hiding you?"

"On an island."

"Really?" the Senator said, glancing at Milo. He looked back at Ruby and again stared deeply into her eyes. "That's fascinating."

"Yes, I had a memorable stay there," Ruby said, then displayed her pearly whites as she rolled her tongue along her bottom lip.

"An island," Senator Miller said, nodding. "Whisperer?"

"Occasionally," Ruby purred. "But most nights, I tend to get loud."

www.ingramcontent.com/pod-product-compliance
Lightning Source LLC
Chambersburg PA
CBHW061507020726
47502CB00006B/1964
* 9 7 8 1 9 4 2 6 9 1 4 9 5 *